DIRECTOR'S CUT

BOOK II OF
THE BOX OFFICE OF TERROR TRILOGY

RUSSELL C. CONNOR

Visit us online at
DarkFilament.com

Contact the author at
facebook.com/russellcconnor
Or follow on Twitter @russellcconnor

Cover Art by SaberCore23 Artwork Studio
For commissions, visit sabercore23art.com

ISBN:
978-1-952968-03-7

Third Edition: 2021

Also by Russell C. Connor

Novels
Race the Night*
The Jackal Man
Whitney
Finding Misery*
Sargasso*
Good Neighbors
Between
Predator

Collections
Howling Days*
Killing Time*

The Box Office of Terror Trilogy
Second Unit*
Director's Cut

The Dark Filament Ephemeris
Volume I: Through the Deep Forest
Volume II: On the Shores of Tay-ho
Volume III: Sands of the Prophet
Volume IV: The Halls of Moambati

eBook Format Novellas and Shorts
Outside the Lines*
Dark World
Talent Scout
Endless
Mr. Buggins
The Playground
Some Say In Fire: Decay
Some Say In Fire: Prisms
Some Say In Fire: Return

*Indicates Dark Filament Ephemeris supplementary connection

For Smith, Nolan, Tarantino, Jonze, Scorsese,
Jackson, Roth, Spielberg, Lucas, Hitchcock,
Coen, Coen, Boyle, Soderbergh, Cameron,
Scott, Fincher, Burton, Apatow, Gilliam,
Howard, Cuarón, Lee, Lee, Hughes, Bay,
Anderson, Anderson, Luhrmann, Wright, Bird,
Whedon, Zombie, Brooks, Raimi, Mendes,
Wachowski, Wachowski, Favreau, Affleck,
Ritchie, Craven, Russell, and Carpenter…

to name a few.

And yes, even Shyamalan.

pre-production

The set of *Island Breeze* was closed and abandoned, stage lights out, air-conditioning off, the fake palm trees looking like the drooping, twisted fingers of skeletal hands in the dark. The last of the reshoots had finished up a week ago, and the whole place was scheduled to be dismantled on Monday to make room for a new production.

Which was why Tonya Werdner had to act now.

"Goddamn Nealy," she muttered. "You're a hack director now, and you're always gonna be a hack." Her words sounded small and lonely as she tip-toed across the huge soundstage in a pair of four-inch high heels, and the skirt and sleeveless top she'd worn out to the clubs earlier. This little side trip had been very spur-of-the-moment, an idea that sounded so much better with five or six bellinis in her bloodstream and an entourage of desperate wanna-be's egging her on. Of course, those little collagen-inflated bitches had all bailed the moment they saw how serious she was.

Even with a lightened step, her footfalls still made sharp clacks against the concrete floor. They rang off the rafters until she reached the portion of the room covered with grass sod. Then her heel spikes sank into the faux lawn, dampening the sound but making each step a chore.

The only illumination came from emergency tract bulbs

along the periphery of the high ceiling, enough to cast a ghostly soft pallor across the stage. Tonya stopped to admire the forest of palm trees stretching away to a painted canvas backdrop of blue sky and clouds on the wall, barely visible in the dim light. The fabricated Hawaiian landscape had saved the cost of shooting on location, but it looked about as authentic as double D's on a 90 pound model.

She'd worked on this set. For a whopping two days, when production first started back in January. She remembered because the temperature had gotten down to the low 40's, and she'd been coming to work in an ankle length fur coat with nothing underneath but a bikini, and Nealy, that asshole, had kept the studio hangar door open and then gotten pissed off at her when she couldn't stop her breath from pluming on camera and her goddamn nipples from jutting through her top. Tonya had taken 20-percent-over-scale pay for what amounted to a glorified cameo and gone on to a basic cable role her agent had lined up.

But that had been *before*. When she'd thought Nealy was just making a forgettable little teen sex romp. Now, insiders who'd seen early cuts of the film were talking Christing *Oscar*, if you could believe it. Sure, it was just for Sound Editing, the most pointless of all Academy Awards, but still, the buzz being generated just about guaranteed the film would be a money-printing machine when it released in the fall.

Just another win for Apex Pictures, the studio that could do no wrong.

Tonya had gone to Baxter Devlin and tried to renegotiate her pay. Everyone loved that ancient old goat, all you heard was generosity-this, charity-that, saving-little-starving-children-in-Botswana-or-somewhere, but he hadn't done jack shit for her. The geriatric bastard had told her, in kindly, patient tones while he tried not to drool on himself, that a deal was a deal, she'd been paid what she agreed to in her contract, and back in his day blah blah blah, and then Cordero—the shark prince biding his time for a chance at the throne—had shown her the door. She'd had her lawyer file an injunction to get her scenes removed (a petty, vindictive ploy, especially with her agent insisting she needed the exposure), but that had been a bust.

So now, here she was, sneaking across the old set after charming her way on to the lot, intent upon restitution or, failing that, revenge.

Because no one fucked with Tonya Werdner. She'd beaten a lot worse than these gimps by being tougher, faster, and stronger than the competition. The great Susan Campbell might've gotten all the recognition for surviving Torsten Gross's 'rampage' a few years ago, but the world had better not forget Tonya was there too, goddamn it.

She hurried past the palm tree forest and crossed the last of the dark set, heading toward the metal staircase that led up to the soundstage office suspended three floors above. Nealy had practically lived in there during the shoot. When she reached the top, she found her gamble had paid off: the director had never thought to have the lock changed after giving her a key. Tonya slipped inside and closed the door behind her, praying that he hadn't moved his personal effects off the premises yet.

Accommodations in the bare-walled rectangular room were sparse. A couch, file cabinet, table and chairs, soundboard and editing equipment at the long window that overlooked the set below.

And the cameras he'd installed in the corners.

If there was one thing Ron Nealy loved, it was making amateur porn videos of himself fucking anything with a hole between its legs. Including Tonya herself.

She made her way across the room, banging her hip on the table in the dark. The file cabinet in the corner was unlocked, and she pulled open the bottom drawer. It contained a collection of neatly labeled discs; the entirety of his sexual conquest library. In what the director probably thought was an inspired bit of meta-filmmaking, he'd convinced Tonya to let him play a couple of them while he bent her over the arm of the couch and fucked her in the ass, thereby making a video of himself *having* sex while *watching* himself have sex. She'd only agreed because he'd hinted there might be a bigger role for her somewhere down the line, but that didn't look likely anymore. Since it was too dark to read the labels, she dropped all the discs into the extra large purse she'd brought for the heist.

By tomorrow morning, all of Nealy's home movies would be internet tabloid fodder (hers excluded, of course; *that* one would disappear as mysteriously as Nixon's long lost 18 minutes). She ran the risk of turning the other little whores into the next crop of Kardashians, but the embarrassment to Nealy and the studio would be worth it. And if she could make some money selling them somewhere, maybe to that slob Marion Brown's website, then all the better.

Tonya turned to leave, walking past the huge glass wall, but something caught her eye. She turned and leaned closer to the window, until her forehead almost touched the glass, and peered down onto the set.

From this high vantage point, Nealy's Hawaiian stage—taking up the entire right side of the warehouse soundstage—looked more like a nighttime jungle, the synthetic trees creating a tangled web of overlapping shadows. The left side of the space was a jumble of towering old set pieces, costume racks, and other paraphernalia from past productions.

She could've sworn something moved down there, just a quick flicker of motion. She strained her eyes, looking for a janitor or maybe even security, but the movement wasn't repeated. Tonya left the office, not even bothering to lock the door behind her, and lugged her full purse down the stairs.

As she reached the last step, something screeched out in the darkness.

Her body tensed. That sound…it had been like carpentry nails dragged down sheet metal. She searched the warehouse again for movement.

"Hey!" she called out. Her voice echoed off the high rafters. The unease creeping up her back was only serving to piss her off. "Somebody there or what?"

There was no answer, but this was all beginning to feel too familiar, a little too much like the only horror film she'd ever worked on.

The one that had turned out to be more than just a movie.

Tonya started walking, much faster than on her way in. The unease was quickly becoming cold fear. When she reached the grass, her left heel got stuck in a muddy piece of sod, snapping the stem and sending her toppling forward on hands and knees. The discs flew from her purse.

"Fuck, fuck, *fuck!*" She pulled off her uneven shoes and crawled forward, scooping her loot back into the bag.

From her left came a furtive noise. She turned to look.

With her head almost on the ground, she could see through the jumbled junkyard on the left side of the warehouse. There was a figure hiding in there, a hunched shadow that seemed to peel away from one pool of darkness and blend in with another, scrambling between the cardboard cutouts and set pieces as it moved toward her.

"All right shithead, I s-saw you!" The fear in her voice was sickening; she got a grip on it before continuing. "You better get the fuck outta here and leave me alone! The last pervert who tried to stalk me got his dick shoved in a blender!"

Another screech answered her, this one louder and meaner.

Tonya began to hurry, grabbing blindly at the discs and cramming them back in her purse, but now she could hear scrabbling footsteps approaching. Sudden, irrational terror swept her like a flash flood. Or maybe *not* so irrational; after all, no one knew better than her that there were monsters in this world. She abandoned the purse and crawled on hands and knees into the midst of the palm trees to hide.

In here, the canopy of plastic leaves overhead created a murky darkness. Tonya had to crawl with one hand out to make sure she didn't bang her head against the rough tree trunks. After she'd clambered several yards into the forest, she turned around, crouched behind one of the palms, held her breath, and peeked around the side.

Quiet returned to the warehouse, long enough for her heartbeat to slow. Long enough for her to think she'd imagined it. Her fear was replaced with anger over the grass stains on her hands and knees. Tonya Werdner did not crawl, Tonya Werdner was a goddamn movie star, and—

The palm tree to her right shook hard enough to rattle the leaves with a whispery *shush-shush-shush* sound. Tonya screamed and lurched away from it, scooting backward across the lawn on her ass. She thought she could see a figure on the other side, but it was too much of a shadow for her to be sure.

Another tree behind her gave a shiver. The coconuts knocked against one another like snare drums. From her left, something gave a high-pitched squeal, as though taunting.

She changed directions again, thinking of those high school hijinks where the strong would form an airtight ring around the weak to more effectively bully (she had no knowledge of what it was like to be in the middle of that ring, as she was usually the one helping to form it), but before she could get very far, *all* the trees began to quake around her, the entire forest jittering until the noise was overwhelming. Tonya spun in a terrified circle, straining her eyes to find the source, but all she could see were leaping, slashing shadows.

Then, as the trees fell silent and the darkness crowded in around her, she understood.

The shadows *themselves* were the culprits.

She got to her feet and fled now, without looking back. The palm trees got denser as she went, forcing her to slow down as she dodged between them, but then they cleared out ahead, and she could see sky and clouds and…

And *ocean?*

Tonya hit the backdrop at the rear of the set like Wile E. Coyote smacking into one of his own painted traps, her nose impacting hard enough to cause a burst of stars across her vision. She rebounded and fell back to the ground.

Behind her came an almost gleeful yip, followed by a whisper of motion across the back of her neck.

As dark figures closed in on her, Tonya Werdner began to shriek.

SCENE I

(quiet on the set)

TAKE 1

Diedrich Müller pressed the knife harder against Carol Harper's throat, releasing a pencil-thin dribble of blood down her creamy skin. The man—trained by the best the KGB and CIA had to offer—was an expert with these blades. She whimpered and tried to twist away, but there was no escape; the chair she was tied to prohibited all movement.

He leaned over her shoulder from behind, smelling of musky sweat. Deep within the bowels of his jungle fortress, the air was stiflingly hot. With his bushy white mustache just inches from her ear, Müller growled, "Time's almost up, Mrs. Harper. Your husband has failed my little test. But don't worry. He'll soon be joining you."

Across the room, the door of the windowless cell crashed open. A figure leapt into the room.

"John!" Carol shouted. "I knew you'd come!"

John Harper—former Marine turned private detective—stood just inside the door, panting, white t-shirt ripped down the front to reveal a slab of rippling muscle, bleeding from a dozen small wounds inflicted by the henchmen he'd neutralized during his assault on the base. He took in the situation and leveled a finger at Müller. "This is between you and me, Diedrich. Let her go and we'll settle this like men."

The madman grabbed a handful of Carol's red hair and

wrenched her head back, eliciting another murmur of pain. Harper started forward, but Müller waved him off with the knife. "I'm not interested in a pissing contest, John. I only care about making you pay for what you did."

Harper swallowed, his eyes rooted on his wife's as he searched for words. "Diedrich…I'm sorry about your father. What happened…it haunts me every night. But *I'm* the one you want. Take me."

Müller glared holes in him, his eyes full of hate as he straightened, clenched his fists around the handle of the knife and said, in a sudden British accent, "You…buffoon. Do you actually read these scripts, or just use them to wipe the snot from your Neanderthalic nose?"

TAKE 2

"Cut," Davis Lowe called miserably from his director's chair. He dropped his head into his hands.

"What?" Derek Mahoney asked from the set, his chiseled face all innocence. "What did I do?"

Davis raised his head to answer the musclebound star of the *Killing Blow* series, but Isaac Crosby—or rather, *Sir* Isaac Crosby, as he'd reminded the entire crew several times—did it for him.

"Harper killed Müller's *brother*, not his damn father, you bloody idiot." Crosby tossed the blood-oozing knife to one of the prop guys and gave a full body shiver, completely shedding himself of the villain persona. As an accomplished thespian of both stage and film, the 62-year-old actor took the process of slipping in and out of character very seriously.

He pulled the zipper on the front of the camouflage jumpsuit provided to him by wardrobe for the climax of the film and fanned his narrow chest, where a sweat stain was spreading. "Even if you hadn't done it yourself in the first film of this dreadful franchise, you'd think you could at least be bothered to peruse your lines before coming to work."

Still tied to the chair in front of him, Heady Tillman turned her head away to hide a snicker.

"I'm sorry!" Mahoney clasped his hands together in a gesture of frustrated pleading. His biceps bulged. Davis had come to realize these muscles were much more reliable than the one in his head. "This movie has more dialogue than the others! I'm bad at memorizing!"

Davis said, "Let's set it up and go again from where Harper busts into the room."

Crosby turned to him and struck a dramatic pose to show his exasperation: ramrod straight, arms held out at an angle, palms up, turning his body into a perfectly symmetrical arrow. He was still in good shape for a guy his age, sinewy muscle and the sort of flawless, wrinkle-free skin that only came from a combination of surgery and spas. "Lowe...I told you before, I cannot work like this."

"Calm down, Isaac. He flubbed a line. It happens."

"No, he flubs *every* line. It is unprofessional, and I shouldn't be expected to put up with it."

Davis gritted his teeth. The entire crew had stopped to watch this exchange with wide eyes, life on the set grinding to a halt. "What do you want me to do then? What would be an appropriate punishment? You want me to castrate the guy?"

"You can *do* that?" Mahoney asked in amazement.

"What I want," Crosby continued, "is a director who allows the acting process to flow." His careful enunciation of the last word seemed to make each letter its own syllable, turning it into something exotic. And it might as well be, since Davis had no idea what he was jabbering about. His drama queen theatrics reminded Davis of a 13-year-old girl.

Davis tried to figure out what to say to that, but Crosby wasn't looking for a response. He about-faced and marched off the grimy cinderblock stage that served as Diedrich Müller's underground lair.

"Where are you going?" Davis called after him.

The actor flung a hand over his shoulder like he was about to dance the flamenco. "To my trailer, where I shall remain until I am satisfied that everyone involved in this production respects the craft as much as myself."

With that, he strolled into the narrow shaft of sunlight created by the floor-to-ceiling hangar doors that took up one wall of the warehouse.

TAKE 3

"So much for 'the show must go on,'" Davis muttered. The rest of the cast and crew were waiting on him to give direction. "Everybody, just...take five until we can get this sorted out."

Heady squirmed in her chair. "Not that I don't love some bondage now and then, but does somebody wanna untie me?" A platoon of male crewmembers rushed to her aid. After a decade of second unit work and then directing some low-budget studio fare, it was still hard for Davis to get used to all these people on his set. He didn't know what half their job titles were, or, hell, even who hired them. And, until now, things had been going so smoothly on the biggest film of his short professional career, he'd been too afraid to ask questions that might upset the unseen balance of things.

He moved to the edge of his chair to stand, but then someone appeared at his side, leaning an elbow on his shoulder.

"You see the way he swished his hand around when he left?" Jared Mane asked. "I'm beginning to think ol' Sir Isaac might be a bit of a rainbow romper."

Davis rolled his eyes. "That's ridiculous."

"Oh c'mon, Davis. *Ridiculous?* All those Broadway adaptations he does? I mean, his IMDB page reads like the float order in a gay pride parade."

"Jared…he played James Bond."

"Yeah, and do you have any idea how many homosexual men masturbate to that character?"

Davis threw an elbow out to shove him away. "Shut up before somebody hears you and we all get dragged before a GLAAD inquisition."

The crew was milling now, talking and hitting the craft services tables. Mahoney cut through the crowd to get to Davis. He was an imposing figure—six-two, built like a side of beef, square-jawed with bristles of jet-black hair—but his disposition was pure cornfed, aw-shucks Midwesterner. "Mr. Lowe, I'm really sorry. I'll do better next time. Please tell Mr. Crosby that too."

Davis flashed what he hoped was an understanding grin. He had to keep in mind, the guy was only 28, seven years younger than Davis himself. And, for someone that had shot to the A List as fast as Mahoney did, he was refreshingly down-to-earth. He'd won the John Harper role in an international talent search six years ago, made the first two

Killing Blow movies, a few romcoms, and an animated kid's movie for which he provided the main character's voice, and was now one of the biggest heartthrobs in the world.

"It's okay," Davis told him. "This is Crosby's last scene, then he's finished on location."

"Which is why we shot all his stuff first," Jared added. "Get the buzzkill outta here so the rest of us can enjoy ourselves."

Davis bumped the side of his fist against the actor's thick arm, next to one of his fake wounds. "Don't worry about any of this. You're doing fine, and you look great out there. The only thing I want you to worry about is getting some sleep for tomorrow. Those stunt cars aren't gonna drive themselves."

Mahoney brightened at that. "Okay, thanks, Mr. Lowe." He started to walk away, then turned back and said, "Just so you know, you're my favorite *Killing Blow* director. Well, so far."

Considering that list included John McTiernan and Luc Besson, Davis would take that as a compliment. "Thanks, Big D. Go grab some food. We'll start up again when I can coax Crosby out."

Mahoney left—his gait and the swing of his thick arms reminding Davis of a gorilla—and Heady Tillman, freed from her bondage, breezed by in a cloud of glossy red hair and Ralph Lauren's *Romance*. "How was I, Davis? Too melodramatic?"

"Perfect, don't change a thing."

The actress slipped an arm around Jared's waist and asked in a voice several octaves lower than normal, "Wanna see if we can borrow the rope for tonight, big boy?"

"Only if we grab some more lube on the way to your place. I think you're almost out from the last time we played Little Orphan Heady."

"Charming, you two." Davis looked away before the public make-out session started and had a coffee shoved in his face.

"Two creams, one sugar." Scott Meyer, his acne-ridden, 18-year-old production assistant, held out the Styrofoam cup until Davis accepted, then checked a clipboard in his other hand as he proclaimed, "We're behind schedule, sir."

"I know. Start reworking the shoot list for next week to make up time. My sole focus today is on getting Crosby finished up."

"Already in progress, sir. I also took the liberty of ordering a bottle of *pinot noir* and a collection of world cheeses to be sent ASAP to Mr. Crosby's trailer, with an apology card from you. I paid extra to make sure it arrives in the next twenty minutes."

Davis sighed contentedly and sipped at his perfect coffee. "What would I do without you, Scott?"

"Probably crash and burn, sir." The kid paused, fiddled with the top of the clipboard, and gave a nervous cough. "However, if you're looking for a way to repay my exemplary minimum wage service, I *am* working on a script..."

The words were lost on Davis, not just because every waiter, valet, and receptionist had a script for him to read these days, but because his attention had been grabbed by the two figures that just walked into the warehouse. Not necessarily the first—that was just Ralph from security, looking dumpy and not the least intimidating in his ill-fitting uniform—but the second person caused a tumble of memories and a creeping dread that spread down his spine like molasses.

From the far side of the room, Sidney Spitzen raised a hand and gave them a short wave.

TAKE 4

"Sorry to interrupt, Mr. Lowe," Ralph said, as Davis walked over with Scott on his heels, Jared limping along behind them on his bum left leg, and Heady slowing herself to match his pace. "I told this guy there wadn't no media visitation scheduled for today, but he kept insistin he knew ya, and that it was urgent. I couldn't get you on your cell, so I figured I better check. If you want, I can haul him right back outta here."

"No, Ralph, it's fine," Davis told him, although, for the barest of heartbeats, he wanted nothing less than to have the newcomer removed from his presence as efficiently as one would excise a tumor. Not because he disliked the freelance reporter, but just because of the associations that came along with him, associations that Davis had done his best to bury and forget.

As he told so many of the actors working under him, it's not the *dialogue*, but the *subtext*.

Ralph touched his brow with two fingers and waddled back through the door. Davis stuck out a hand, trying not to seem too stiff, and watched as Spitzen gave it a hearty pump. "What's it been? Three years?"

"At least." Spitzen used a finger to push his narrow glasses up on his nose. Davis was a little shocked to see the frames were bent out of form, with a little piece of tape holding one of the earpieces together. The last time he'd seen Spitzen, the reporter meticulously dressed and groomed like an early pioneer in the hipster movement that had all but taken over L.A. Now he had more in common with the homeless than the ironic elite. His choppy blond hair had grown out into limp wings almost as long as Jared's ponytail but not nearly as clean, and his clothes—a pair of vintage blue suede pants and black t-shirt—were shabby and stained, and not by design. His nose was the worst though. It'd never quite healed right after being broken, and time had turned it into a bulbous, crooked lump in the middle of his face. All told, the man looked like a shell of his former self.

Then again, what did Davis expect? After they'd parted ways, the man's career went from news mag to entertainment rag to tabloid, rolling down the journalistic integrity ladder as employers and readers grew tired of his conspiracy theories and stories about monsters. As far as Davis knew, the guy hadn't written professionally in at least a year.

Spitzen turned to Jared next. "How's it hanging, cameraman?"

"Almost to my knee, Spitz. And it's *cinematographer*, now. I get to boss the cameramen around." He gestured to the woman beside him. "This is Heady Tillman."

"I know, I'm a big fan," Spitzen said. "I loved you in the *Underverse* movies."

Heady smiled graciously. "It's that skintight leather outfit they make me wear. So you're a friend of Jared and Davis, huh?"

"Well…we helped each other out one time."

"And this is my PA, Scott," Davis rushed to introduce the boy. "Scott, this is—"

"Sidney Spitzen, the reporter involved in the Torsten Gross incident," Scott finished the sentence like a textbook recitation, the same way he'd probably given answers in school before he'd graduated just a month ago.

A moment of uncomfortable silence followed this declaration, in which Davis's and Jared's gaze met. No one had said that name to him in some time. For a while, it had been the only topic of conversation on every set, one he'd found himself steered into over and over again with every actor, crewman, fellow director, and studio suit, all of them nodding conspiratorially and assuring him they would never say a word to anyone if he wanted to confide the *real* story to them. But Hollywood has a short memory, and as soon as enough scandals about drugs, tranny hookers and racist rants had passed, the world forgot all about the rumors surrounding the disappearance of the German horror director.

Or maybe not.

All about the subtext, he thought.

"Wait a minute, you're *that* guy?" Heady asked. She hooked a thumb at Jared. "Well, Mr. Spitzen, maybe you'll fill me in on what all that was about, since I haven't been able to get anything out of this chickenshit." Jared tugged a lock of her red hair, and she punched him in the arm hard enough to make him stagger

"There's nothing to tell," Davis said. "It's all just…stories."

"Not according to Mr. Spitzen," Scott added quietly.

"Can't believe everything you read in the *National Enquirer* kid." Jared gave the reporter a pointed glance. "Or anything, for that matter."

"So what was so urgent, Spitzen?" Davis asked. "I'm assuming you didn't drop by just to catch up."

"Actually, I really need to talk to you both." A dark cloud crept into the reporter's eyes behind his crooked glasses just before he tilted his head at the door. "And it might be better to do it alone."

"Uh, sure." Davis's breakfast suddenly felt heavy in his stomach.

"Okay boys, I know when I'm not wanted." Heady leaned forward as though to give Jared a kiss on the cheek, and bit his ear instead. He squealed in pain, but she sauntered away before he could retaliate.

Scott followed her, giving a longing glance over his shoulder. "I'll keep the crew happy until you return, sir."

"Looks like your little sidekick's upset," Jared said to Davis after the boy was out of earshot.

"I thought *you* were my sidekick, dickhead."

"C'mon guys." Spitzen beckoned to them.

Reluctantly, Davis and Jared followed him out of the soundstage.

TAKE 5

Outside, the sun was bright, the temperature a pleasant 86 degrees with no breeze. The warmth felt wonderful to Davis; it helped smooth out some of the gooseflesh that had been trailing up his arms since he'd caught sight of Spitzen. The three of them stood on one of the quaint cobblestone paths running between studio warehouses on the east side of the lot. At the next intersection, a group of actors in western garb hurried past on their way to or from a set. Other than that, they were alone.

"So what's up, Spitz?" Jared asked. "Does all this secrecy mean you got a lead on the grassy knoll gunman or what?"

"Funny," the reporter said acidly. He waved his hands above his head like a carnival barker. "C'mon, look at the big conspiracy theory nutjob, everybody! I would remind you I was a respected journalist until you came knocking at my door, Mane."

"Hey, you were investigating the case way before I got to you." Jared's typical smirk fell away. "Besides, what did you think was gonna happen if you went around trying to get everyone to believe a story like that? You got your tabloid journalist of the year award and picked up some pretty good gigs from the residual fame. So why couldn't you just keep your mouth shut like Davis and me?"

"Because the world needs to know," Spitzen said through clenched teeth. "If what we think is happening is really happening, it's our responsibility—nay, our *duty*—to warn people."

"*Nothing's happening*," Davis said firmly. Now his breakfast wasn't just heavy, it was roiling like a witch's cauldron. "And the last thing I want is this mess stirred up again. If that's what you came here for, Spitzen, then maybe I should have you escorted off the premises after all."

"I guess you haven't heard then."

"Heard what?"

Spitzen's voice softened as he jammed his hands in the pockets of his pants and looked down at the cobblestones between his feet. His hair dropped into his face. "Tonya Werdner was murdered last night."

"Werdner?" It actually took Davis a moment to place the name. "As in…?"

"The woman who saved our lives? Yeah, her." Spitzen didn't look up as he added, "Somebody slit her throat last night. Actually, that's putting it lightly. Her head was just about torn off, from what I understand."

"Jesus," Davis whispered. Images flashed through his head. A nameless woman butchered by a huge maniac on grainy black-and-white footage. Jared in a hospital bed, hooked up to a hundred machines as he slumbered. Otter—

poor, sweet Otter, who made Davis flush his dead goldfish down the toilet when they were in ninth grade because he couldn't bear to—covered in blood, with a blank, empty look in his eyes.

"Okay, that's horrible," Jared agreed, bringing Davis out of his head. "Thanks for bringing us the news Spitz, but it's not like we were close to the woman. She made sure to put as much distance between us and her as she could after…you know. And besides all that, she was just generally an awful person. So why should we cry ourselves to sleep if that bitch finally got what she deserved?"

Spitzen looked up, his crooked nose as red as a chronic drunk's beneath the curtains of his hair. "Because it happened right here, on the Apex studio grounds. They found her body this morning over on the set of Ronald Nealy's movie."

"*Island Breeze*." The day's warmth was gone, leaving Davis close to shivering.

"That's the one. The cops are still over there right now, but the studio is keeping a tight lid on it. The story hasn't even broken to any of the major presses yet."

Jared asked, "Then how'd you hear about it?"

"Just because I'm a laughingstock doesn't mean I don't still have some connections. An old contact on the force called. He thought I'd wanna know since Tonya and I were sorta…" He trailed off, his voice getting thick.

"Aw god, man, I'm sorry," Davis said. "I totally forgot you two dated for a while."

"Don't know if I'd call it 'dating.' She'd text when she was horny, make me drive across town to fuck her, then verbally abuse me till I left in tears." Spitzen took a deep, wistful breath. "I haven't found a hooker yet that can do it as good as she did."

"They have any leads?"

"Nothing yet. Still too early. But that brings me to the other thing I was able to find out, and the real reason for me being here." He removed his hands from his pockets, the left bringing with it a sheet of paper which he unfolded and held out to them. On it was a quick pencil sketch of a diamond with curved protrusions growing out of either side, beneath two offset, interlocking triangles. "Whoever killed Tonya burned this symbol into her forehead. This mean anything to either of you?"

Davis studied the drawing, especially the rudimentary horns. "Not really," he said, but something twinged far back in his mind as he did.

Jared squinted. "Should it?"

"I don't know, that's why I'm asking."

"Well, it doesn't. It's probably the call sign of L.A.'s newest serial killer. Which leaves me still wondering why you would've come all the way out here to see if we knew anything about it."

Spitzen refolded the paper and slipped it back in his pocket. "I just thought...maybe this could have something to do with Gross."

"Why in hell would you think that?" Davis blurted. "Wait a minute, Lars Krieg, is he—?"

"Still in Conway Sanitarium, practically lobotomized. I checked this morning." Spitzen shifted his weight uneasily. "It just seems kinda coincidental, don't you think? Five of us had a hand in taking him down, now one of us turns up dead?"

"Yeah, almost four years later." Davis snorted. "I hate to break it to you Spitzen, but we're all gonna die eventually. If I get hit by a car crossing the street, it doesn't mean Gross had anything to do with it."

"But this wasn't an accident, she was murdered! On the same lot where you guys work! And in a very violent, very strange way that just screams revenge to me."

"Then get your ears checked, because Torsten Gross is *dead*. Whatever he was, wherever he came from, he's dead. You killed him yourself, so you should know."

"Fine." Spitzen gave a slow nod. "Just thought you'd wanna know. I'll let you pass the word on to Susan if you want. I heard she was on set here also, but..."

He trailed when he saw Davis wince at the mention of the name. Boy, today was just a stroll down memory lane that wouldn't quit.

The reporter pushed hair out of his eyes and mumbled, "Anyway, I'll be in touch if I hear anything else."

"See you, Spitz," Jared said.

He went past them down the avenue, turning right at the first cross street and disappearing between huge studio warehouses, but he didn't take the sense of doom he'd brought with him. That stayed behind, hanging over Davis like a personalized storm cloud. He and Jared looked at one another.

"I never would've said anything to stoke his fires," Jared said, "But you don't think maybe...just *maybe*...he had a point?"

"No, I do not. I think he's so hungry for another story he would connect the dots to form whatever picture he wants."

"Seemed pretty sincere to me. And broken up about ol' Werdner, God rest her slutty soul."

Davis couldn't argue that. He didn't believe Spitzen's assertions, but there was still this uneasy dread gnawing at him. And, if there was even the slightest possibility that Tonya Werdner's death meant danger for them...

Well then, they really shouldn't take any chances.

Davis turned and started jogging away from the sound-stage, toward one of the lot's main streets. "Tell everybody I said break an hour for lunch!" he called over his shoulder.

"Where are you…? Oh man, you're not!" Jared shouted after him. "She stopped taking your calls two years ago, Davis! Don't do this to yourself!"

But he had to. He told himself that she deserved a warning, the same way they did.

And that this wasn't just a convenient excuse to see her.

TAKE 6

You had to suffer for your art.

Susan Campbell knew this, believed it to be inherently true.

But if her agent ever pitched her another script that required her to wear a corset, she would seek representation elsewhere.

Now though, she stood still on the little tailoring platform with arms above her head, trying to take the tiniest sips of air and then expel them again immediately to keep her lungs from expanding, while the costume designer for Apex Films' production of *Persuasion* all but used a crowbar to tighten the laces on the 17th century torture device.

"*Tighter*," Dwight Killam insisted as he hung over the woman's shoulder, inspecting her work. "I want her to have a perfect hourglass figure. It has to be completely authentic."

"Any tighter and her guts will squeeze out like toothpaste," the designer, a young, black guy with dreadlocks, grumbled. "Then again, maybe that's the kind of 'authentic' you're looking for."

"Many women of the era lost consciousness or even died for their concept of beauty. The pursuit of truth is all that matters."

"But…isn't your version gonna have vampires in it?"

The director waved a hand. "Irrelevant."

"Dwight," Susan gasped. Her vision was dotted with little black circles; she knew from experience what that meant. "Dwight, I can't breathe…"

Killam sighed wearily. "Let's stop for a moment."

The costume designer relented, releasing his hold on the lacing up the corset's spine. Susan collapsed into the chair behind her and sucked at the air.

Not that she was ungrateful. If offered the lead role in this twisted Jane Austen adaptation all over again, she would take it. A chance to not only work with Killam—visionary director and auteur—but also Apex, the studio that was garnering Oscar noms faster than the Academy could think up categories, and whose total box office for the year had more zeroes in it than the national debt. And it didn't hurt that they thought she could still play a convincing 27-year-old when she was closing in on 34. Pretty good for someone whose seventh movie had just been released the month before.

Seven movies. She was always amazed at the number. Three of those seven had 'performed,' as her agent put it, a term whose clinical coldness seemed to reduce the art of filmmaking to the droning machinery the studios wanted it to be. The other four, including the one in theaters now, were bonafide hits. She actually got asked for her autograph on the street now. Two or three times a week she would walk out of a restaurant or store and find the paparazzi waiting to snap those candid pics that websites like *TMZ* and Marion Brown's *Naked Hollywood* just loved. She even had her very own celebrity stalker. Those were the perks for which one suffered in this business.

And, as the costume designer was escorted from the closet-sized sound booth by Killam—a room with baffled walls and a glass window to her left for observers—Susan wondered if she was about to suffer again.

Killam closed the door. Turned the lock. A tingle went through Susan's stomach. The director spun on his heel and put one curled fist to his mouth like Rodin's Thinker. She noticed, for the first time, that his green, loose-fitting shirt was almost strategically buttoned to reveal a swatch of waxed and bronzed chest in the open V at the top.

"Susan," he began. "I need to be sure this project is something you're committed to."

"I am. Totally."

"Are you sure? Rehearsals don't start until next week. Until the cameras roll, it's never too late to back out." He tipped his head as though listening to a voice only he could hear. "Or be replaced."

"No, this role is very important to me, Dwight. You have me completely." She regretted the phrasing as soon as it was out.

"Good." Killam crossed the small space, coming around behind her chair and laying his hands on her bare shoulders above the corset top. He began to knead the flesh there. It felt good, but she couldn't help thinking of the strange audition for her first film. Her *actual* first film, not one of those seven that her agent loved so much. No, this one remained unreleased, and probably sitting on a shelf somewhere in the bowels of Trimax Studios.

And an LAPD evidence locker, no doubt.

"As you may know, I like to work with all of my performers on a one-on-one basis," Killam said as he massaged her.

Oh yes, I've heard that, Susan thought. *Especially the actresses.*

"We're going to be spending a lot of time together, so I want to make sure we're comfortable with one another." He came around in front of her, knelt down like a prince with a glass slipper, and put his hands on her knees. A crop of goosebumps rose along her smooth legs as his palms slid upward at a snail's pace, his thumbs working their way beneath the hem of her skirt. He gently forced her legs apart and maneuvered his chest into the gap between them.

Susan gave him what she hoped was an encouraging smile. She was far past the point in her career where the prospect of sex for roles was still entertained, but that's not what this was. Killam had been not-so-subtly hitting on her for a while, and she had wondered a) when he would make his move, and b) what her reaction would be when he did. He was a ladies' man, sure, but he was only a few years older than her, a commanding presence, good looking with a mess of baby-fine brown hair, perpetual stubble on his narrow face, and piercing green eyes the color of seafoam.

And it *had* been a while since she'd gotten laid. As long as he could be discreet, Killam might be just the kind of no-strings-attached fun she needed to get back in the game. The last thing she wanted was for anybody to find out about this and get the rumor mill started.

"I'd like that," she told him.

"Excellent." He moved toward her lips. She leaned down to meet him, eager to go with the flow for once in her life.

Until an amplified voice boomed through the soundbooth's speakers, "Hey, Suze. Hope I'm not interrupting anything too important."

TAKE 7

Susan and Killam both turned their heads to look at Davis in the sound booth's control room, her face reddening in embarrassment, his in anger. To Davis, the director looked like a middle-aged pretty-boy trying way too hard to be brooding by highlighting his cheekbones and making sure his hair had just the right amount of bounce. Then again, it obviously worked for him. Davis hid the fireball of jealousy that welled up in his throat by grinning widely and waggling his fingers.

Killam jumped up from his kneeling position between Susan's legs, flew to the door separating the rooms, and yanked it open. Behind him, Susan smoothed down her skirt and jumped to her feet. "Who the hell are you?"

"Relax Dwight." Davis put down the booth's microphone and held out his hand. "Davis Lowe. I'm a big fan." *At least I was before seeing you with both hands far enough up my ex-girlfriend's skirt to deliver a baby.*

"Lowe?" Killam's brow wrinkled as he glanced at Davis' hand. "Am I supposed to know that name?"

"I directed *The Peretti Agenda* last year. You see it? No? Well, it got a pretty small release. How about *Switchblade? Cripple Creek?*"

The other man flared his nostrils. "I only create modern cinema, I don't watch it."

Davis reeled in his hand. "Gotcha. Anyway, I'm on set here at Apex too. Directing the next *Killing Blow* sequel—" Killam's sneer at this point was almost enough to make Davis feel embarrassed. "—and I thought I'd mosey over and say hello to a dear old friend." He looked at Susan and cocked an eyebrow. "Hello, dear old friend."

"Jesus, Davis," she groaned.

"Look, I don't care who you are, no one barges on to my set without an invitation." Killam made a karate chop motion past Davis's shoulder. "Please leave."

"I promise, I'll be outta your way ASAP so you two can get back to...*rehearsals*...but first, I have to steal Miss Campbell for just a second."

"Perhaps you didn't hear me." Killam put a hand on his chest and shoved. "Get out!"

Davis stood his ground. "Don't get pushy, Dwight. You might break your coke nail."

The other man's face blazed with rage, but he paused when Susan said, "Dwight, please, give us just a minute."

Killam glared, considering, then stormed past, making sure to bang against Davis with his shoulder.

Susan moved to the other side of the room's only chair, as though positioning it between them. Corsets and 19th century garb weren't exactly Davis's thing, but the skirt she'd worn underneath for the fitting showed off a mile of smooth leg. Even though it sent poisonous arrows through his heart, he couldn't help wondering if she'd shaved and lotioned specifically for Killam.

He moved his gaze up quickly and met Susan's eyes in real life for the first time in over two years. Davis had been to see every one of her movies on opening night, but staring into those clear baby blues just wasn't the same when they were five feet wide.

"*Him?*" he asked.

"Shut up, Davis."

"You do know the credits at the end of his movies are just lists of the women he's slept with, right?"

"It's not like that."

"So you were just having your very own MeToo moment then?"

She stuck out her jaw, her hands tightening on the back of the chair. "When I heard you were working at Apex, I was afraid you wouldn't be able to stay away—"

"Oh, don't flatter yourself!"

"—but I thought," she continued, "that you could at least be an adult about this."

"I *am* being an adult. I'm looking out for you."

"No, you're looking to get me fired."

"Probably for the best. I hear the great visionary's screenplay for this thing is like Stephanie Meyer on acid. Couldn't be good for your career."

She sighed. "What do you want?"

"I'm sorry. I didn't come here to fight." Davis took a deep breath. This had really not gone the way he planned in his head. In his version, *he* was the one between her legs, after she wrapped them around him as thanks for his concern. "Spitzen just came to see Jared and me. Tonya Werdner was murdered last night, right here at Apex. Over in studio 14, I think."

"Wow." The red hue of anger faded from her cheeks. "I...I hadn't talked to her in so long. Do they know who did it?"

"Not yet." He recounted the bare facts provided by the reporter, skipping over the weird symbol for the sake of brevity. "Anyway, Spitzen—you know how he is—well, he has this insane idea that it has something to do with...Gross."

He whispered the last word to soften the blow, but she still recoiled from it as violently as he had. "Oh my God. Oh my God, what if it does?"

"It doesn't."

"How do you know?"

"Because we saw him die."

"No, we saw him melt like the Wicked Witch of the West! We have no idea what he even was! What if he *can't* be killed? What if it took him four years, but he finally pulled himself back together and now he's coming after us?"

"If he is, then we'll kill the son of a bitch all over again."

"Okay, but what about Krieg?" She said the hulking German actor's name with a grimace, like an old copper penny in her mouth.

"He's still in the loony bin with his brain fried. But really, I don't believe this has anything to do with us."

She frowned. "Then why'd you even tell me?"

"I just wanted to…give you a heads-up. So you could keep an eye open for anything strange. Just in case."

Susan studied him for a moment and he knew, beyond a doubt, that she could see right through him. She always could. Her voice softened just a bit as she finally came out from behind the chair. "All right. Thanks. I'll watch out."

Davis thought about saying more, but decided he could only screw up from here. Might as well leave things on a high note. He left her there and passed by Killam in the hallway outside.

"She has herpes," Davis whispered from the side of his mouth.

Killam gave him a smug sneer. "So do I."

SCENE II

(roll tape)

TAKE 1

The rest of the day was a wash. Crosby couldn't be lured out of his trailer even with the wine and cheese basket (the $235 apology sat on the steps of his trailer in the sun all afternoon), and Davis finally released the rest of the cast. The old British bastard was only delaying himself, since Mahoney would be tied up with stunt shots the next day, unable to finish their final fight scene. Davis and Jared stayed late to review the dailies, then Davis went out for a drink with some of the crew. He tried to get Jared to come, really needed the company, but his best friend insisted he had to get some sleep, which was usually the excuse he used to get women out of his bed.

At first, the alcohol helped drown all the emotions dredged up by seeing Susan, but by the end of the night, the old regrets had bubbled up in Davis, and all he could think about was the jewelry box sitting in the bottom of his sock drawer for the past few years. It was close to two in the morning when he got to his place in Van Nuys, but the shoot out at Irwindale didn't start until ten, so he figured he would be all right.

Which was why he wanted to smash his cell when it went off at 6:30.

"'Lo?"

"It's Scott, sir."

"Scott, I forward my phone to you so I don't get early morning calls. That's how this whole PA thing works: you get the shit I don't wanna do."

"I know, but Mr. Cordero called. Mr. Devlin wants to see you in his office at 8."

"On a Sunday?" Davis sat up and swung his legs out of bed. He knew people said that Baxter Devlin rarely left the office, but this was ridiculous. "He say what it was about?"

"No sir."

"All right, fine. Maybe he just wants an update. I'm up and on my way. When Jared gets there, have him wait for me at the studio so we can go over the shot list before we head over to Irwindale."

"Um, sir? I can leave him a message, but I'm coming in late today, remember?"

"What? Why?" Davis felt a moment of panic at the prospect of facing this long, complicated day without his right hand.

"I...I have to take my father to chemotherapy this morning."

"Oh." He grimaced. "Damn Scott, I completely forgot. Um, how...how's he doing?"

Scott hesitated. "Honestly, he has more bad days than good. And his insurance isn't covering a whole lot."

"Okay, just hang in there. Things'll get better. Take all the time you need."

"Thank you, sir."

Davis took his phone off forwarding and jumped in the shower. While he shaved, he turned on the small TV in his bathroom and looked for news about Tonya Werdner's murder. There was still nothing, which either meant the actress hadn't rated important enough for a mention, or Apex was still keeping a gag on the story, as Spitzen had suggested. His gut told him it was probably the latter; he knew from experience how powerful an influence the studios could have.

He had just pulled on a pair of jeans and was buttoning up a shirt when his cell went off again.

"Scott, I don't—"

"*I haven't forgotten what you did, you bastard,*" a hoarse female voice rasped.

Davis sank back down on the corner of his bed. "Hello, Mrs. Ottman."

"The Lord knows what you did to my boy, Davis Lowe." He hadn't received one of these calls from Muriel Ottman in more than a year, had filed them away in the same mental dustbin where he put the rest of the memories involving Gross and *Arterial Slice*, but it was like Spitzen's arrival yesterday had opened a floodgate. Davis could picture the woman on the other end of the line, all three hundred pounds of her, beehive hairdo, thick silver cross around her neck like an albatross. "He saw it all, and He will punish you for your sins."

"Mrs. Ottman…you read the police reports. You heard what your own lawyer said when you tried to sue us for wrongful death. For the last time, I didn't have anything to do with Otter's—"

"*THAT WAS NOT HIS NAME!*" she roared, loud enough to rattle Davis's eardrums. "*His name was Terrence Ottman the Third, and he was a* good *boy until you dragged him out there to that vile city of sin with you! I don't care if that Cox woman was the one driving the car, I hold* you *responsible! Now he's in his grave while you strut around filming those horrid movies, no doubt taking drugs and… and…and having depraved sex with all manner of harlots!*"

Davis's eyes burned. He swiped at them and swallowed a wad of thick spit before answering. "I was his friend. Just about his only friend."

When she spoke again, her voice was back to its gravelly snarl. "Then I hope for your sake that's enough to clear your name when you and your other long-haired friend stand judgment before the throne. Because that time is coming soon. I *promise* you that."

Then she was gone, leaving Davis alone in his empty house.

TAKE 2

Everyone in L.A. wanted to work for Apex Studios.

Eight years ago, they'd been a low-level player on the edge of the city, snapping up the indie scripts that fell through the cracks of the bigger studios and producing them straight to the various streaming services that had replaced the DVD market. Then Derek Mahoney and the first *Killing Blow* movie had come their way, and a mediocre action movie had become a worldwide blockbuster.

But it hadn't ended there. They'd spun shit into gold so many times since then, the industry was calling them the fastest growing studio in history. Audiences and critics both loved their productions. Seventeen Oscar nominations over the last three years, one win for Best Picture last year with *French Calling* (a film that Davis found too pretentious to really enjoy, but whatever got those old farts' rocks off), and a score of other awards. They'd bought up a 200 acre lot just north of Culver City and Rosa Parks, not far from 20th

Century Fox, and were now considered a serious competitor for the so-called Little 3 studios, if not the Big 5.

All credited to the business savvy of its founder and owner, 68-year-old Baxter Devlin, the man who had become known as the Steve Jobs of Tinseltown. He took as much of a personal hand in the running of each of the studio's projects as their various producers did.

And, for some reason, he'd entrusted the next installment in their flagship franchise to Davis Lowe, whose previous directing credits had all been for films with budgets under $2 mill, and had a combined theatrical run of less than three months.

But *Killing Blow 3* would change all that. It was a guaranteed moneymaker, so if he did even a halfway competent job, his name would be attached to a successful blockbuster. His agent assured him he should have his pick of projects after the new John Harper thriller opened.

Of course, Davis had to do even a halfway competent job first.

TAKE 3

The gates of the Apex lot were presided over by a monolithic arch, black granite emblazoned with the studio logo—a lushly illustrated mountain range with two towering, snow-dusted peaks in the middle—and its motto: *Ever onward, ever upward.* It had already become nearly as iconic as Universal's turning globe or MGM's lion, a stop on every city tour.

As Davis checked in at the guardhouse beneath, the call with Otter's mother still weighed heavy on him. That, and

Werdner, and all that damn doom and gloom Spitzen had spread. He tried to get them all out of his head as he drove to the headquarters building in the middle of the lot, a sleekly modern structure and one of the few with adequate parking. His destination was at the top, at the end of a long, glass hallway that gave access to the offices of all the studio heads and vice-presidents. He was announced by Devlin's personal receptionist and breezed into the office.

The studio owner waited for him just inside the door. Baxter Devlin was a tiny, stoop-shouldered man with wavy white hair and cheerful eyes, dressed today in black slacks and a dress shirt with no tie. He came forward and shook Davis's hand warmly in both of his. His fingers were gaunt, the bones all but swimming in the loose, liver-spotted skin. A perpetual tremor ran through them, a palsy that caused him to all but vibrate.

"Davis, my boy, it's so good to see you!"

"You too, Mr. Devlin." He meant it, too. This man was the best boss he'd ever worked for.

"I told you to call me Baxter, son! You're part of the Apex family now!"

"I'll try."

"Come in and have a seat," Devlin invited. "You'll have to excuse the mess, I'm remodeling."

Davis looked around the office. It was such a long, wide rectangle, you could've parked city buses in it, several side by side. The entire left wall was glass, letting in a stream of beautiful early morning sunlight and a rolling view of down-town. The rest of the room was clean and modern, all steel and smooth lines, with a desk made of smooth, glossed ob-sidian at the far end from the door. At first, Davis couldn't see what mess the man meant, but then he spotted the wall behind him, which he'd passed on his way in. Usually, it was full of shelves that held various honorarium bestowed upon Devlin: the studio's Oscars, awards for his charity work, pictures with stars and the president, even his family crest and college degrees from Minnesota State. Now though, an opaque tarp hung down over the entire wall. Davis could see that all of the memorabilia had been removed, but not what kind of remodeling was underway.

He followed Devlin to that beautiful black glass desk and sat in one of the plush padded chairs in front. The president went around and lowered himself into the leather chair on the far side with an elderly wheeze.

Another man perched on the edge of the wet bar just behind him. He was the polar opposite of Devlin in every way: tall, broad and power-suited.

"Good morning, Mr. Cordero," Davis greeted him.

Samuel 'Buddy' Cordero (Davis has never heard anyone other than Devlin use the nickname) lifted one corner of his mouth in response, then crossed his thick arms and glared.

Davis turned back to Devlin. "So what can I do for you?"

The old man leaned forward and clasped his bony hands on top of his desk. Even at rest, the slight jitter in them was apparent. "First, I wanted to check in with you and see how things were proceeding with *Killing Blow 3*. This film is a top priority for us. You know that, don't you Davis?"

"Of course. And things are going fantastic. I don't see any reason we shouldn't finish on time and under budget."

Devlin drummed those thin fingers nervously against the shiny desktop. "You're sure there's nothing at all you need assistance with? I want all my people to feel like they can come to me with anything. Your problems are my problems, so to speak."

"Okaaaay." This time Davis hesitated as he answered the question. "I've got everything under control. Why?"

Devlin fidgeted again. "The, ah, problem with Isaac Crosby has come to my attention."

"Oh, for Christ's sake! Did that uptight prick actually come whining to you about what happened yesterday?"

"No, his agent did. It seems Mr. Crosby has changed his mind about appearing in the film. He wants to be released from contract immediately and have the scenes he's filmed so far excised."

"*On what grounds?*"

"He's citing…" Devlin turned around and looked to Cordero. "What was it again, Buddy?"

"Unprofessional working conditions and director incompetence," Cordero said, without taking his eyes from Davis.

"This is ri-goddamn-diculous," Davis groaned. He was embarrassed, not so much because the accusations were baseless, but because this had to be happening now, in front of Devlin. He hadn't wanted to please anyone this much since his father, and that had gone right out the window when he went to film school. This was his one test, his one hurdle to jump on the way to a tiny measure of creative freedom, and he couldn't even keep his actors in check.

"Now, now, don't fret about this." Devlin patted the air as if he were soothing a mad bull. "I told his agent I thought that would be bad for all of us, and he agreed. He's convinced Crosby to come to the arbitration table this morning at eleven to get this all talked out. Leo will meet you at the agency."

"This morn—? Mr. Devlin—Baxter—I'm filming a car chase with Derek this morning out at Irwindale. I have the whole place shut down for the morning, and a full stunt team and NASCAR consultant will be on location in an hour and a half. This will be a real delay." *And that British fuckhead knows it.*

"If we lose Crosby, that'll be even more of a delay, won't it? All those reshoots, and the negative publicity...ugh, it makes my head hurt. I usually don't condone renegotiations after the ink is on the contract—I'm a firm believer in a deal-is-a-deal—but in this case, I think it's necessary." He reached out and patted Davis's hands. "I trust you to handle this, my boy. Talk Crosby down off the ledge. Offer him a ten percent increase, if you have to. Preferably eight."

Davis sighed and nodded. "I'll take care of it."

He started to stand, thinking the meeting was over, but Devlin waved him back down with that shaking hand. "There is one other matter that needs to be discussed and, unfortunately...it's a bit more unpleasant."

With that, Devlin swiveled his chair to face the window, looking out over the Apex lot. At the same time, Cordero stood up and stalked toward the desk, taking control of the meeting, like a tag team wrestling match. It was well known that good-natured ol' Devlin hated confrontations, and had hired Cordero for the same reason that Davis employed Scott: to deal with the shit he didn't want to. Out of all the current executives, he'd been with the studio the longest, taking a Vice President of Operations appointment just before the Apex rocket took off. Rumor had it he was set to take over when Devlin retired.

"Goddamn it, Lowe," the man snarled. Davis had known plenty of corporate shills—Phillip Reilly over at Trimax always came to mind—but Cordero seemed to draw blood for pleasure, rather than business. "Have you seen *Naked Hollywood*'s homepage this morning?"

"What? No, I don't read that fanboy web rag."

Cordero reached the desk, grabbed Devlin's monitor, and turned it around to face Davis. On the screen was the familiar gold and red logo of Marion Brown's one-stop gossip shop, nothing but movie rumors, news, celebrity photos, and hundreds of thousands of angry geek commentators ready to laud anything they still considered cool and trash anything that fell below the threshold. And where that threshold lay depended on the day of the week and the hour of the day.

The top headline, splashed below the banner, read, "SPY PHOTOS FROM *KB3* SET!"

And below that, a series of grainy pictures of his set, his actors, his crew. There was one from just yesterday, before Crosby threw his hissy fit. Davis himself was even in a few of them.

"H-how?" Davis stammered. "H-how did...?"

"Figure it out. You have a traitor in your midst, one selling cheap cell phone pics to Marion Brown. Not only that, but Brown is promising a full script up on the site by Friday." Cordero jabbed a finger at the screen, face turning the purple-reddish shade of an onion. From this hand, a silver pinkie ring threw out a chip of light. "If he does, we'll sue his ass and have it taken down within the hour, but by then it'll be too late. It'll spread all over the internet. A leak like that could cost this studio millions on the release."

"Jesus. I don't know what to say."

"If it happens, it's as much your fault as anybody's, Lowe. Get your goddamn set in order or I'll do it for you. Find the leak and plug it up."

Davis sat there with a hundred half-formed questions, the most prevalent being, how in hell was he supposed to do that? Fifty people traipsed through his set every day, brought in by some crew or sub-contractor, and he didn't even know half their names, let alone who would have the impropriety to do something like this.

Devlin spun his chair back around, tired of bird-watching or napping or whatever he'd been doing while Cordero reamed Davis out. "We put this film in your hands because we knew how capable you were. Your body of work speaks for itself. I know you won't let us down."

The intercom on his desk buzzed. The receptionist outside said, "Mr. Devlin, the police are here again to see you."

Speaking of the police, the good cop/bad cop routine was over, it looked like. Devlin walked Davis to the door. Just before the old man opened it, Davis couldn't resist asking, "Are the police here about Tonya Werdner?"

Devlin's mouth fell open as he looked up at Davis, his jowls jittering. "How did you know that, son?"

"She was a friend. Sort of."

The other man clucked his tongue. "Terrible business about Miss Werdner. Who would want to do such a thing to another human being? And the fact that it happened here, on studio property, just makes me livid."

"I'm surprised it hasn't been reported yet."

"The police want to keep it quiet until they decide how much information to release, and I agreed. Even though she was trespassing at the time, we still wouldn't want any negative associations with the studio."

Davis nodded. *Negative associations.* Sometimes it seemed that was the only thing motivating this town. And he couldn't help wondering if it was the police that convinced the old man to keep the details under wraps, or the other way around.

As he walked out, Devlin clapped him on the shoulder, then stood aside to let through two uniformed officers and a lean, Hispanic, plainclothes detective-type. This last man met Davis's gaze as he went past. Just before the door closed, Davis heard Devlin say, "Excuse the mess gentlemen, I'm remodeling."

TAKE 4

Davis tried calling Scott three times as he walked across the lot to the set, before remembering the kid was gone this morning. He needed numbers for everyone due on location today so he could cancel. God, he'd become way too dependent on his PA. By the time he reached the set, his stomach felt like the bottom of an active volcano.

He had no idea what to do about Crosby, Brown, the schedule changes, any of it. Leo Botstein, the executive producer for the *KB* series, should probably be handling some of this bullshit, but Davis had found out several weeks into production how useless the man was.

And the idea of asking his partner for help was, sadly, laughable.

Partner; even after all this time, he couldn't drop the habit of thinking of Jared in those terms. The Lowe-Mane Production Company had pretty much dissolved without Otter to hold it together, but by that point, Davis was picking up real directing gigs for minor studios, and it just seemed an unspoken agreement that his best friend would come along as cinematographer. They were a package deal, but that didn't mean the package was equally weighted.

The soundstage warehouse had a tiny office and film room just off the main floor. Jared was stretched out on the couch in the office, where they'd agreed to meet before heading out to Irwindale. Davis gave him the rundown.

"That tubby, J.J.-Abrams-rim-jobbing son of a bitch." Jared balanced his laptop on his chest and scrolled through the *Naked Hollywood* website. "Marion Brown's not a journalist, he's pop culture cancer."

"Be that as it may, if he doesn't already have a copy of the script, he's claiming he will on Friday. And somebody in our own camp is gonna give it to him."

"That should be easy to figure out. Who has access to the scripts?"

"Uhhhh…"

"You didn't lock those things down? Watermark them? Anything?"

"I have enough to worry about without hiring 24-hour security for the damn scripts, okay? Stupid me, I trusted my people." Davis snorted in disgust, but it was mainly aimed at himself. "Just do me a favor and watch for anybody suspicious, but don't tell your guys. For all we know, it may be one of them."

"*My* cameramen, taking pictures of this shitty quality? Surely you jest."

"Whatever, I'll deal with Brown later. Right now, I have to go to this arbitration with Crosby and kiss his limey ass to get him back to work. Which means we have to cancel the car chase shoot."

"No, no, no!" Jared tossed the laptop aside and sat up on the edge of the couch. "No way, Davis, that's exactly what Crosby wants and you know it!"

"What am I supposed to do? I don't trust the second unit guy with a scene this big, he's more green than we ever were."

"So let me do it!"

Davis frowned at him.

"C'mon man, there's no acting in this scene, Mahoney doesn't even have any lines! It's all stuntwork and cinematography!"

"Jared, I don't know..."

The other man stood up from the couch. There was a gleam in his eye that Davis couldn't remember ever having seen before. "Man, I'm your partner, right? We're a team. So trust me to do this, if for no other reason than to keep Crosby from getting his way."

Davis studied him in amazement. "What's up with you? You never want any responsibility, and last night you bail on me to go home and..." He trailed as he looked his friend up and down. "Hey, you're wearing the same clothes from yesterday! You...you spent the night at Heady's! As in, the *entire* night!"

Jared smirked and rolled his eyes. "I'll have you know, I banged the bottom out of that. Her orgasm is probably still going on as we speak."

"And then what, you couldn't find a way to sneak out after the deed was done? Or—God forbid—am I actually witnessing the taming of the great Jared Mane?"

"Davis...she's different. Smokin hot, funny as hell, more perverted than even I am..." A look of surprise dawned on his stubbled face. "I think I'm in love with her."

Hearing Jared actually admit it sent a tiny needle of pain jabbing into Davis's heart. He could remember how love changed you like this, made you want to be a better person. But sometimes, that feeling just slipped away. Close to the end of things for him and Susan, when she'd finally called it quits, he'd been so ready to blame it on the sudden distance fame had brought them, both of them at opposite corners of the world on various projects for months at a time. Now though, he wondered if anything could stand in the way of that, when it was true and right.

He recalled how it felt to see her the day before, of that Killam asshole getting ready to kiss her.

"Do the shoot," he said. At least if he didn't have love in his life, he could support someone who did. "I'll get out there as soon as I can."

"You won't regret it." Jared gave him a pat on the cheek. "And don't worry, Davey. You'll always be my one true love."

TAKE 5

Susan came to the set even though she wasn't needed for any of the day's activities. It was either that, or hang around the house she was leasing outside Beverly Hills. The place was nice, but it wasn't home; nothing had felt like home since she'd given up that comparatively cramped one-bedroom apartment she and Davis used to share, but she'd been travelling so much for various shoots, it just didn't make sense to keep it. She told herself that after this movie wrapped, she would take some time to find a permanent residence, maybe something up in the hills, away from the bustle.

Based on the grin Killam gave her, he undoubtedly believed her presence on the set was for his benefit. Rather than have him think otherwise, she lounged on a sofa, drinking coffee, reading the paper, and occasionally giving him a wink.

She'd seen nothing about Tonya Werdner in the news, but word was out among the crew here today for preproduction. Someone from set design had seen the police parked outside the warehouse on the other side of the lot, and the propmaster claimed to have seen the coroner rolling out the body late last night. There was talk of serial killers, jealous boyfriends, and stalkers, the latter making Susan feel cold and nervous as she remembered the venomous notes that had been sent to her own publicist's office over the last few months.

Killam buzzed around, giving directions to the Hispanic work crew on how to turn the set into a lovely Victorian manor from which Jane Austen's heroine would slay vampires. Finally, at close to 11, the door opened, letting in a shaft of sun and a large, good-looking guy in an expensive suit.

Her director walked over and shook his hand. They exchanged words and smiles, and Killam gave the other man a friendly slap on the back. Then they headed her way together.

"And here's the star of the show," Killam said when they got within earshot. "Susan, have you met Samuel Cordero? He's a producer on the film."

Now that she'd heard the name, she realized she did recognize the studio VP of Operations. Cordero had old-world Italian features, dark and swarthy, with a facial structure that always seemed a bit too symmetrical, although that was probably more genetics than plastic surgery. "So nice to meet you, Mr. Cordero." Susan set her coffee aside and stood up to greet him.

"A pleasure," Cordero told her, taking her in with a lingering glance. His demeanor was overbearing and somehow hungry, despite the fact that he was a well-known family man. And she wasn't the only one to notice either; Killam stepped possessively close to her, like a wolf asserting dominance. "I'm a fan of your work. In fact, it was me that suggested Dwight bring you in as the lead when Hathaway had to drop out."

"Well then, I owe you big time! I have to admit though, I didn't realize you were producing on this."

"I stepped in at the last minute as a favor."

"Samuel and I were college roommates at Duke," Killam explained. He slapped Cordero on the back again. "But back then, we were Buddy and the Dingo! Remember that?"

"Good times," Cordero agreed, his deadpan tone suggesting otherwise.

Well, this explains a lot. These two must have had the same professor in domineering power management.

"It was nice meeting you Susan, but I need to speak with Dwight. Privately." Cordero threw a withering glance at Killam. "I'm sure we'll meet again." The two of them disappeared into the maze of set construction, heading toward the office in one corner of the warehouse.

Susan almost sat down and went back to the paper…but something about that look at the end of the conversation had piqued her interest. Killam was about to get a tongue-lashing from his old dorm mate, it seemed. And she suspected he was the sort of man that would take it out on every one else around him. Seeing him bitch out the crew might turn off whatever little attraction she had for him, and if she suddenly started spurning his advances, this was sure to become the longest shoot of her life.

She grabbed her purse and hurried through the backstage entrance beside her. Beyond was a hallway with cheap corrugated steel walls that wound around behind the main filming areas to give access to the dressing rooms. It should put her out close to the soundstage's exit, so she could sneak away unnoticed. But the dim passage—lit by weak hanging bulbs every ten yards or so—allowed only a handful of steps before turning a corner that put her exactly where she didn't want to be.

Next to a large window that looked straight into Killam's office.

Susan caught a quick glimpse of director and producer talking in the middle of the room before she jerked back. She retraced her steps and found the door she'd come through locked. So her only options now were to wait until they were finished, walk by and give a friendly wave, or slink under the window.

As demeaning as it sounded, she chose option three.

Her cheeks burning, she knelt and crawled back around the corner, keeping her head beneath the level of the window and dragging her purse at her side. As she neared the center, she could hear Cordero's deep timbre coming through the glass. The words were lost, but the cadences indeed suggested anger, and Killam was giving as good as he got.

She paused, trying to get the gist of the argument. Only one out of about every six words made it through. She heard 'accounts,' and 'no more,' then Killam spat something about 'the old man.' She could only assume he meant Devlin.

A budget fight. Had to be. Killam wanted more money for his twisted take on *Persuasion*, and Cordero was here to tell him the coffers were empty.

Susan started to crawl on, but Cordero's next words, as loud and clear as if she were beside him, stopped her cold.

"Just wear it, goddamn it!"

Try as she might, she couldn't make the phrase fit into the logical flow of the conversation. She kept imagining Cordero ordering Killam to put on a leather bondage suit before riding him around the room like a pony and bit down on a snicker.

Her curiosity wouldn't let this one rest. Even though it would probably be the end of her work on this film if she were seen (not to mention really, *really* embarrassing), she rose up enough to see over the window ledge.

She needn't have worried. A tangle of table and chair legs stood at this height on the other side of the glass, providing her a clear line of sight and the perfect cover.

Cordero had his hand extended to Killam, and from it dangled a round silver medallion the size of a half-dollar on a fine-link chain. Killam stared at it for a moment, shaking his head angrily, and said something about, "just putting me on the radar," to which Cordero replied, "Actually, it's taking you *off*. This is a courtesy, Dwight. For all those good ol' Duke days. But if my generosity is not appreciated…"

"No!" Killam shouted. Practically pleaded. His eyes were shiny with sudden fear as he accepted the strange offering, slipped the chain over his neck, and dropped the silver coin down the front of his shirt.

A tingly sort of alarm bell went off in the back of Susan's brain.

One that told her being fired from this film might be the least of her worries if she were caught now.

She lowered to hands and knees, planning to get out as fast as she could, but saw something that froze her in place.

Was it her imagination, or had this hallway gotten even darker? The overhead lights were still on, but they seemed dimmer, allowing inky black shadows to creep across the floor and along the wavy surface of the walls.

Susan crawled ahead, then got to her feet once she was past the window. As she walked, the darkness pressed in on her from all directions, making her feel cold and smothered. She moved faster, breaking into a run as she passed the restrooms. The door out of this hall was just ahead, clean white light visible under the crack at the bottom, but now she could see movement from the corners of both eyes, unnatural flickers of shadow that were gone as soon as she turned to look at them, and a scream was rattling around in her throat as she burst through the door and back onto the set.

The construction crew halted their work to stare at her as she panted.

On the other side of the soundstage, Cordero and Killam came out of the office. The VP made for the closest exit as Killam shouted, "Finish this all up! I want my set done by tomorrow! SUSAN!"

"Over…over here," she called, still catching her breath.

"Get your script! We're running lines!"

She sighed and nodded. It didn't look like there would be any escape for her today after all, but as long as she didn't have to go back into that hallway, she didn't care.

TAKE 6

Davis figured Leo Botstein had to be pushing 80. The Jewish man was taller than Devlin but just about as thin, completely bald on top but with more than enough hair growing from ears, nose and neck to make up for it, and a suntan at least three shades darker than mahogany. He'd made a fortune in investments throughout his life, and one of the more recent gambles that had paid off in a big way was Apex Studios and the first *Killing Blow* film. Then he'd decided he wanted to be 'more involved with the moving picture process,' so Apex had started giving him honorary producer credits to keep the money flowing. God bless him, he tried to help whenever he could, but he knew so little about modern filmmaking, Davis ended up babysitting the guy. Leo was waiting outside the Smith-Klein Agency in a red leather jacket and large sunglasses trimmed in gold, like something from a Michael Jackson music video, as Davis pulled up and surrendered his Jeep Cherokee to the valet.

"Can you believe this wonderful weather?" Leo turned his leathery face up to the sky. "I moved to L.A. twenty years ago just so I can have sun like this all year round! Better for the sinuses, you know."

"It's great, Leo," Davis agreed. "Listen, I think it would be best if you let me do the talking in here."

"Oh, but Davis, I'm a wonderful negotiator, wonderful! I can have Sir Crosby back *schticking* in front of your little lightbox before you know it!"

Davis gave him a forced grin. "I know you could, but I have a feeling Crosby's gonna be a prick just to make this difficult."

"A prick, you say? Why would he do that, he's an actor!"

"Exactly."

Leo chuckled. "Davis, you little *shagetz*, you worry too much! Trust me when I tell you, everything's going to be just fine!"

He said it with so much confidence, Davis almost believed him.

They went inside and were taken to a long boardroom table. Davis tried to stay calm. He'd already promised himself he would say whatever it took to end this, lick as much bootheel as needed to make Devlin's trust worthwhile. They were kept waiting an outrageous forty-five minutes, until Crosby came in with a middle-aged guy who introduced himself as William Klein.

"As I'm sure you know, Mr. Crosby is seeking an injunction to have himself removed from *Killing Blow 3* entirely," Klein said, settling in across from them. He was dressed as smartly as Cordero, suit and tie even on a Sunday morning, but agents of his caliber were 24/7. "I arranged this meeting because I'd like to see us all come to an agreement that'll get us back to making this movie."

Leo nodded happily. "Wonderful!"

"That's why we're here." Davis glanced over at Crosby. The man kept his eyes fixed on the wall. "Isaac, let's cut to the chase. Things were going well, you were almost finished shooting. Why go through this now?"

Crosby swung his gaze around to meet Davis. "It's the principle of the thing, Lowe. Although I'm sure you'd know nothing about that."

Across the table, Klein grimaced.

"What's that supposed to mean?" Davis asked, struggling to keep his voice from reaching a higher octave.

"It means I am someone to whom pride in one's work still means something. You, on the other hand, I have doubts about."

"Then you've severely underestimated me. All I'm asking for is the chance to prove that to you. Finish the shoot, and if you don't like my work, well then…" He shrugged. "At least you'll never have to work with me again."

"That sounds reasonable," Klein added eagerly.

But Crosby just smirked. "Let me put this plainly, since you don't seem to be taking the hint: I think you are a hack. I think this entire production is a disaster and that the film will flop, and I don't want my good bloody name associated with it."

"Now, I don't know about any of that," Leo cut in. "I don't think anyone will be doing any… 'flopping or hacking,' will they Davis?"

"Shut up, Leo," Davis told the producer. "Where do you get off with this attitude, Isaac? You read the script, you signed on for the sequel in the action movie franchise, what the hell did you expect? You wanna make art house cinema, go find Branagh. Better yet, I hear Dwight Killam's doing some bang-up Jane Austen right on the lot."

"This isn't the most productive use of our time," Klein said, but both of them ignored him.

"Don't attempt to hide your own shortcomings behind the genre." Crosby's eyes flashed jubilantly. He was actually having fun with this. "Any film can transcend its labels...*if* the man at the helm is competent."

"*Oy vey*," Leo muttered.

Davis forced a full breath into his lungs, in a last ditch effort to get himself under control. For just a second, he'd been back on the phone with Torsten Gross before their final showdown, listening to the director tell him how incapable he was of creating art because he let fear of the future control him. "This wasn't even about me. This was about you and Mahoney. I understand, the guy's not the sharpest tool in the shed, and he's probably not easy to work with. But why're you taking it out on *me*? I mean, for god's sake, what do I have to do to get us past this so we can get back to filming? I can offer you an extra ten percent, take it or leave it."

Crosby shook his head sadly and pushed back from the table, then swept one hand at Davis in a grand gesture that made him think of Jared's insinuation about the man.

"Just the fact that you think this is about money shows you are exactly what I said you were."

Sir Isaac Crosby turned and strode from the room, leaving Klein to squeeze his temples, and Davis to marvel how stupendously awful he'd been at this.

"Well." Leo turned to look at Davis. "That certainly could've gone better, yes?"

TAKE 7

The Irwindale Speedway was reserved all day for the filming of the car chase that occurred midway through *Killing Blow 3*, a scene where John Harper tried to outrun a team of Diedrich Müller's hitmen through downtown L.A. just before crashing and being taken hostage. The track was just a flat standard NASCAR oval, so some of the background would have to be inserted digitally in editing, but one end of the race strip had been hastily converted into a city street for the climactic crash at the end. The wooden and plaster building fronts appeared completely fake out here, but Jared thought they should look fine at the speed they were filming.

His team had started the morning getting footage of the two vehicles chasing one another around the track, weaving in and out of other traffic, along with a few close-up shots of Mahoney driving Harper's red Mitsubishi Eclipse, and the henchmen in a white Toyota Supra, spraying blanks from machine guns. Both cars—along with a second Eclipse to be destroyed—had been donated by their respective companies, and gleamed crisply in the morning light. The stunt guys took care of everything, setting up each drive and walking Mahoney through his actions, so all Jared had to do was sit back and let his guys roll tape.

But as noon approached, Jim Reid, the stunt team coordinator, came over to Jared's chair and said, "Crash site's all set up. We're ready to do this whenever you are."

Jared took one look around the track before answering, hoping he would see Davis strolling up to take the reins. Cigarette cravings had been hitting him all morning even though he hadn't taken so much as a puff in almost three years, a sure sign of how apprehensive he was about doing this on his own. His volunteering for this assignment had upset a long-standing distribution of work between the two of them. As in, Jared did as little as possible, and Davis pulled them both through. But lately, the ambition bug had bitten him hard. For the first time in his life, he was thinking of himself as more than just a 'cameraman.' Still, he'd felt like a tight rope walker *sans* net all morning.

As he scanned the speedway full of milling crew and stuntmen and extras, Jared didn't see Davis.

But he did see the person he suspected was behind his recent motivation boost.

Heady Tillman made her way across the track toward him carrying a brown paper sack, her red hair like a flaming torch as the sun caught it. Several male extras in the stands whooped when they recognized her. She stopped, struck a pose with a cocked hip and pursed lips, and laughed boisterously when they cheered.

"Okay," Jared told Reid, without hesitation. That yearning for a cigarette had vanished. "Get everybody into position and I'll be there in a minute."

Reid walked away. Jared climbed up out of the chair and winced as his bad leg hit the ground, sending a screaming bundle of pain up his spine. The limb had its good days and bad. The doctors told him the nerve severed during the car accident that killed Otter and Samantha Cox would most likely never heal, and that he should really just be thankful he was alive at all. As he limped out to meet Heady and slipped his arms around her waist, being thankful was easier than at any other time since the accident.

"I thought you were doing publicity interviews for the John Woo flick," he said.

"Ducked out early." She stretched on her toes to touch her lips to his, sliding her tongue playfully around the inside rim. Even though they'd had sex just a few hours ago, he wanted her again. The last female to excite him this much had worn braces and gone down on him after senior prom. "Told the costars I couldn't miss my man's directorial debut."

Their relationship hadn't gone public yet, not even in the tabloids, but she didn't seem interested in keeping it a secret.

He said, "I don't know what scares me more about that sentence, the 'my man' or the 'directorial debut.'"

She punched his arm and tossed the sack at him. "Be nice. I brought you lunch."

"Thank you. Seriously."

"Yeah, well, technically my assistant bought it, but I told her what to get you." She nodded at the track. "How's it going out here?"

"A lot better than I figured. One last stunt and we're pretty much finished."

"See? I told you it would be fine. You really will be directing before you know it."

"Yeah, but I don't know if I *want* to direct. That's Davis's bag."

Heady gave him a look that suggested she knew better, then reached out and pinched him on the ass. "Go get this last shot done, Mr. Mane, and I'll let you direct me all afternoon."

Jared grinned. "My work is never done."

He left her with his lunch and hobbled out to meet Reid and Mahoney at the end of the fake Los Angeles street set. A sidewalk had been added since the last time he came by, complete with mailboxes, electric poles, and parked cars for authenticity. The extra Eclipse to be used in the stunt wreck was parked beside the two men, windows pre-shattered and a plethora of bullet holes across its hood and side panels. The actor slapped the hood of the vehicle as Jared approached.

"I can do this, nothing to it!" Mahoney was telling Reid excitedly.

"Do what?"

Reid hawked a wad of tobacco next to the wheel of the Eclipse. "Your boy wants to drive the stunt hisself. Told 'im to talk to you."

Jared shook his head. "No way, Big D."

"Aw man, why not?" Mahoney sounded like a whiny six-year-old. "The insurance covers me for all stunts performed under professional supervision."

"Because if I get you killed, Davis'll have my balls."

"*Get me killed?* C'mon, I've been driving these cars all morning, no sweat! And this is even easier, Jim just said so!"

Reid shrugged. "He's right, it's just a straight line drive to speed, and the 'technics take care of the rest."

"I don't care if God Himself is riding shotgun, I'm not letting you do it, Derek."

"But Jared, with me behind the wheel, you can bring the cameras in closer for the final shot! What's the point in even having the stunt if it looks like shit from fifty yards away? Please, I *really* wanna do this!"

Jared hesitated. Mahoney was right, the shot would be incredible if they could get deeper. He knew plenty of other actors that had worked on their own stunts, but he just didn't think this was the play Davis would make.

But Davis isn't here. You *are.*

"Walk me through the stunt before I make a decision," he said.

Reid pointed at the far end of the track and then swept his finger along the ground back toward them and up the street set beyond. "Straight shot right up the middle where you see those lane marks. Only thing the driver has to worry about is hittin fifty or better 'fore he reaches this line." He scratched his foot along the ground, right in front of a flat, rectangular metal panel laid out on the concrete, just behind and to the right of the rear bumper of a parked car. "The pyros are primed to go off and lift the outside of this ramp, sendin the vehicle into a corkscrew, so it misses the other cars and rolls over onto its roof as gently as a momma layin her baby down for a nap. Should skid another twenty yards or so before it stops. Look like an explosion caused it to flip."

"Safety issues?"

"Whole interior is padded, with hidden reinforced crash bars and restraints. As stunts go, it's child's play." Reid shrugged and spit another phlegmy brown wad. "But just so we're clear, this is *your* call. I got guys standin by who can do this."

Mahoney watched them, waiting for Jared's verdict.

"Fine. Get set up. But this is the only wrecker we got, Big D."

Mahoney gave him a fist bump. "If I mess this up, I'll personally buy you another car to crash!"

It took another ten minutes for Jared's team to get the cameras refigured for a closer shot. During that time, he expected Davis to show up any second and put a stop to this insanity, but it didn't happen. He reached to check his cell, just to see if there was a message, and realized he'd left it at the office. He'd just gone and sat down with Heady directly across the track from the ramp, where they'd have the best view of the action, when Reid gave him the thumbs up. After radioing his guys to make sure tape was rolling, Jared returned the gesture.

The road was cleared of crew. From their vantage point, they could see Mahoney behind the wheel, strapped into his seat. With the sun overhead, the interior was catching a lot of shade, but the cameras—positioned all along the track in front of Jared to get a continuous shot of the action—would still have an awesome view of the actor in there. Davis was going to shit himself when he saw this.

Jared picked up a megaphone. *"Scene 31, take 1! Roll tape, aaaand...action!"*

The Eclipse's tires squealed and threw up reams of smoke as they spun against the asphalt. Mahoney popped the brake and left a patch of rubber as he surged forward, speeding toward the collision site directly in front of them. The sound of the engine was a building growl.

Heady grabbed Jared's hand and squeezed it, leaning forward in anticipation. He was excited himself. It wasn't every day you got to wreck a brand new $30,000 automobile with your best gal by your side.

As Mahoney approached the metal plate, he saw Reid give the signal to light the explosion and lift the ramp. The tech pushed buttons...

And nothing happened.

"Stop!" Reid yelled immediately, waving his arms at Mahoney, but he either didn't see or couldn't stop.

After that, events happened so fast, it would only be later that Jared sorted them out in his head.

Mahoney's car ran over the metal plate and the pyrotechnics finally blew, producing a plume of sparks and black, oily smoke; a showy, oddly silent explosion. All in all, Jared figured they'd only been about two seconds late, but it was a crucial two seconds. Instead of the ramp popping up to meet Mahoney's front, driver's side tire and roll the car over, it came up midways into the undercarriage hard enough to fling the entire back end into the air. The Eclipse's front bumper dragged the pavement for a few yards until it clipped the first parked car, and then the vehicle tumbled end over end in a spectacular wreck.

At the start of the accident, Jared had his eyes rooted on Mahoney, first through the tinted front windshield and then, as he pulled even with their seats, straight through the missing passenger window. He would remember that, later on.

As the Eclipse's tail went skyward, he had a perfect view of the actor, could even see his mouth opening in surprise as the vehicle tilted to give him a view of nothing but the concrete track.

A second later, there was an odd blur of dark motion that blotted him out entirely.

Jared had time to blink once and wonder if he were seeing things before the car got rolling too violently for him to follow anymore. It smashed against the ground again and again, undoubtedly far worse than any NASCAR accident that had ever happened on this same track, tumbling hundreds of yards and leaving a trail of debris. The entire back end sheared away at one point and flew into one of the empty crew pits. The noise was horrendous, like an anvil dropped repeatedly on sheet metal and magnified by a thousand.

Jared was already out of his chair and running as fast as his bum leg would carry him, screaming for medics. An EMT team was standing by; he saw them sprinting across the tarmac ahead, toward where the vehicle had finally come to rest upside down in a crumpled mess. Reid came from the opposite side of the track to fall into step beside him, and Jared demanded, *"What the fuck happened?"*

"The pyros just went late! Jesus Christ, a wreck like that, he's bound to be dead!"

"*Shit!*" Jared's stomach hit the ground beside his shoes.

He'd gotten a multi-million dollar actor killed. He and Davis would never work again.

Everyone converged on the vehicle at the same time, Jared and Reid, the EMT's and various other crewmen looking to help or watch. The car was compacted to almost half its previous size, red paint sanded off, doors and roof caved in, axles bent in four different directions. A tart, aromatic mixture of oil and gasoline hung over it in an eye-watering cloud. As they closed in, Jared prepared himself for blood, for severed limbs, but not for what he saw.

Mahoney was wriggling out of the vehicle through the bent driver's side window, his muscular upper body almost too big to fit. Everyone stood back and stared as he got to his feet, dusted himself off, and asked, "Did we get it?"

TAKE 8

Davis came through the ER entrance and spotted Jared and Heady standing in the crowded waiting room. "How is he?"

"They're almost done with him," Jared said. He looked frazzled, his eyes glassy and loose hair spilling out of his ponytail. "But the docs came out a minute ago and said he's fine. Not a scratch on him."

"Thank God." Davis leaned against the wall to catch his breath. "How did this happen?"

"Problem with the special effects."

"No, I mean, what was he doing behind the wheel in the first place?"

Jared hesitated, until Heady put a hand on his shoulder.

"It was my call. Mahoney wanted to do it, and I let him."

"For God's sake, Jared. You have any idea what would've happened if he'd died?"

"Well, *KB3* would probably have a reeeeally different ending."

Davis glared at him. "Don't start."

"It's not his fault," Heady said. "He just did what he thought was best at the time."

Before the argument could go on, a door up the hall opened, and Derek Mahoney stepped out with a big, goofy grin on his face. He raised a hand to wave. "See Mr. Mane, I told you I didn't need to come! No internal bleeding or anything!" At the sight of him, several people in the waiting room got the big, excited grins of those who just spotted a movie star. A general rustling began as people dug for their cell phones.

Davis rushed to Mahoney, seized his shoulder, and guided him back down the hall, to the nearest empty room. "Are you sure, Big D? We can put off the shoot for a few days if they need to keep you here. Better not to take any chances."

"No way, Mr. Lowe! I'm all good!"

Jared and Heady came into the room to flank Davis, and Heady asked, "Derek…do you remember anything at all? About the crash?"

"Pretty much. But it happened so fast, none of it really makes sense."

"Give it a shot," Jared invited.

Davis turned and frowned at him. "What are you doing, he doesn't wanna relive that!"

"No, it's okay," Mahoney told them. "Really. It was kinda weird anyway."

Jared moved closer to the actor, almost pushing Davis aside. All three men were just about within kissing distance now. "How so?"

"Well, when the car flipped up and then started to roll, it was like…" Mahoney squinted and prodded at his temple with his fingertips. "Like suddenly, I blacked out or something, but I could still hear and feel everything. It was more like being in a really dark room. Does that make sense?"

"Yeah." Jared's nod was so assertive, it could only mean he knew something. Or *thought* he knew something. Based on history, Davis figured the all-important subtext pointed to the latter. "I think I understand."

"And another thing," Mahoney continued. "Even though I was strapped into my seat by that harness, you'd think I would still get slammed around a lot in an accident like that, right? Except…"

"Except what?" Heady prompted, sounding as eager as Jared.

Mahoney pursed his lips and moved them around against his teeth. "This is gonna sound crazy."

"Nothing will sound crazy to us, believe me," Jared said. Davis elbowed him.

"I…I felt like there were these hands all around me, but I couldn't see them. They were pressing me back into the seat. Sorta…cradling me. Now, I know if I called my momma back home and told her all that, she'd say it was God protecting me, but…this didn't make me feel too heavenly, if you get me. It was creepy as hell."

Jared looked at Davis, whose tongue had suddenly grown thick and heavy in his mouth. When it finally worked again, he said, "Maybe you better stay here overnight. Just in case."

TAKE 9

Sir Isaac Crosby spent the rest of the day after his meeting with Davis shopping, drinking, and avoiding calls from his agent. William Klein had made it clear he believed pushing through with the injunction was a bad idea, and Crosby grew tired of hearing his money-grubbing arguments. He'd long ago risen to the level of fame where he didn't have to worry about acquiring roles, or how box office receipts would affect his next paycheck.

In theory though, he agreed with the man. This whole protest started out as a lark for Crosby, a way to teach those green newcomers Lowe and Mahoney a much-needed lesson about this business, but as he sat at the arbitration table this morning, goading the director into losing his temper, he realized the things he was saying were true. *Killing Blow 3* wasn't a movie fit for someone who'd been knighted by the bloody Queen of England. He'd only signed on for the thing because Klein told him it would probably be his last shot at an action flick. 'Due to his age,' as he delicately put it. But it was because Crosby was getting on in years—the big 7-0 just around the corner—that he needed to start thinking about his legacy. God forbid he should get hit by a bus or suffer a heart attack after wrapping this piece of lowest-common-denominator trash.

So, as he made his way up to his room at the Beverly Wilshire with a handful of shopping bags and a gut full of whiskey, Crosby made the decision to call the agency in the morning and tell Klein to start looking at more Broadway roles for him.

The sooner he saw Davis Lowe in the rearview, the better.

The hallway down to his room was empty as he stepped off the elevator, pressing a crisp 20 dollar bill into the operator's hand. He staggered down to his door, putting the bags on the floor as he dug out his keycard and tried three times to swipe it. He was still trying to calm his shaking hand when the light over his shoulder dimmed.

Crosby turned bleary eyes up to the closest hallway ceiling bulb. The damn thing flickered inside its fancy glass shell. As he watched, the light went out for good.

"Luxury, my ass," he muttered. "With as much as these rooms cost, you'd think they could keep up the bloody maintenance."

Further up the hall, another light blinked out, plunging the area in front of the elevator into darkness. The row of wall sconces—made to look like candles but with electric flame bulbs—began to go out one at a time, marching in a line toward him. A well of shadows crept down the hall.

Crosby, seized by a sudden strange panic, redoubled his efforts to get into his room. He'd just gotten the card through the electronic reader when there was a burst of noise to his left. He yelped and fell against the wall.

The door to the room next to his had opened, letting out a stream of thumping rock music. His neighbor, the singer for some atrocious old metal band called Ironhorse, stepped out with ladies half his age on each leather-clad arm.

"'Ow they 'angin, Sir Crosby?" the man—Crosby thought his name was Marchance—asked in his guttersnipe British diction as he and the two ladies walked past. Crosby straightened and watched until they reached the elevator, where the lights were all working again. He pushed open the door to his room and stepped inside.

And spotted an envelope with his name on it waiting on the tile entry.

Crosby got his bags inside the door, turned on every light in the suite, then snatched up the envelope. He crossed the room to the desk while he tore it open. Inside was a piece of paper folded around a small stack of 4 x 6 photographs. He thumbed through a few and then tossed them away so fast they might've burned him. They scattered across the carpet in a fluttery rain.

His hands shook even harder as he went to the wet bar and poured himself another drink. He had to get the whole thing down his throat before he could work up the courage to go back and look at the photos again, to confirm he'd seen what he thought he'd seen in those slick, glossy prints.

The pictures were of him. Him, and the 19-year-old twink in the cabana boy outfit he'd ordered last night. Every last filthy position they'd undertaken in this very room, all the indignities Crosby had made the kid inflict upon him, all captured in high-definition black and white. Looking at them now, still strewn across the floor, made him feel nauseated.

He'd tried so hard, been so careful over the last forty years to not let anyone catch on. No one knew, not for *sure*, not even his mother, before she died. His relationships were discreet and short term, ending when the other party started talking about public commitment. Even when he ordered boys like the one in those photos, it was all handled anonymously through an agency, and the boys themselves knew better than to talk. Sure, there were a few rumors here and there, but he'd been quick to squash those by going on splashy pussy benders.

Because, if Crosby had learned one thing in all his years of acting, it was that you might be able to get above ass-kissing and box office receipts, but you couldn't escape public opinion; just ask Kevin Spacey. And even though Hollywood was infinitely more understanding in the gay arena these days, that was one ring he'd never wanted to fight in.

Now, here sat irrefutable proof of his sexual orientation, and a pretty extreme sampling, at that.

Two questions came to mind: *how* and *why*? The twink hadn't brought a camera or even a bag, but, judging by the angles, these photos had to've been taken from inside the suite. Perhaps the place was bugged.

As for the why…

The sheet of paper that came with the pictures had fallen beneath the table. Crosby picked it up—his drunken equilibrium threatening to spill him into the floor—and unfolded it.

Only one line was typed within.

Finish the movie.

Crosby blanched, both horrified and enraged. This was actually about that goddamned film. But who had done it? He couldn't imagine Lowe capable of something like this.

Which meant the ugly truth he'd hardly been able to face his entire life was now in the hands of a stranger.

A stranger who could hold it over him forever, just to watch Sir Isaac Crosby squirm.

The great British thespian sank into the chair at the desk and began to sob.

TAKE 10

Davis spent the rest of the afternoon at the warehouse studio, looking over footage the special effects programmers put together, and dreading a phone call from Devlin or Cordero. By now, word might've reached them about the failed negotiations with Crosby, and maybe even the disaster with Mahoney. Two strikes in one day. If a copy of the *KB3* script showed up on *Naked Hollywood*'s homepage tomorrow instead of Friday, he would've failed at everything he'd been tasked with.

It made Davis furious to think the Müller role would have to be recast, all the scenes reshot. Not to sound as old-fashioned as Devlin, but did a contract not mean anything these days? This would be an utter disaster for Apex Studios, the break in their golden win streak.

And, on top of all that, he couldn't get Crosby's last words out of his head, when he'd essentially accused Davis of being a sellout.

Ha, I should be so lucky, he thought. *Sellouts get rich.*

But at least they'd gotten what they needed today, accident or not. After leaving Mahoney at the hospital, Davis tried to pry information out of Jared about what had happened at the stunt shoot, but his partner remained uncharacteristically aloof. Mahoney's crazy description of the accident obviously rattled him. He guaranteed Davis he could make the footage they shot work and disappeared into the film room at the soundstage. Scott came by to help out after his father's appointment was finished, but Davis sent him home after a few hours.

The news about Tonya Werdner broke also, but it rated little more than a mention at the end of the local segment. The newscaster made it sound like a botched mugging attempt. There was no mention of the strange symbol Spitzen showed them.

Finally, as the sun started to go down, Davis dialed directory assistance and asked to be put through to the offices of *Naked Hollywood*. On a Sunday night he expected to leave a message somewhere, but actually got a live female receptionist. He told the girl who he was, asked to speak with Marion Brown. The man got on the line so fast, Davis didn't think the call had even been transferred.

"*The* Davis Lowe, I can't believe it," Brown declared proudly, snorting with excitement. Davis had seen the rotund, disgusting bastard once on some talk show. He sounded just as sleazy over the phone as he did on TV. "This is more exciting than the time George Lucas slapped me. To what do I owe the pleasure?"

"I think you know," Davis told him. "Where'd you get the pictures?"

"I'm afraid that's a confidential source. Can't betray their trust."

"Are you really gonna have a copy of the script on Friday, or is that bullshit?"

"Oh no, I've *already* got it. Right here on my desk, as a matter of fact. Paid two grand for it. Page 76, with the reunion scene, is especially touching."

"Goddamn it," Davis groaned. He knew the amount of hits the *Naked Hollywood* website would get—and the resulting ad revenue—would turn a profit over what the man paid, but money wasn't what motivated guys like Marion Brown; that was just the attention and popularity they'd been denied in high school. "You know Apex will come after you if you distribute, right?"

"We'll see."

"I don't get it though. If you already have the script, why wait till Friday to put it up? You trying to make all those pathetic geek fanboys drool?"

"Pathetic geek fanboys are the core audience for your movie, Mr. Lowe. Don't forget, us nerds have saved Hollywood time and time again." Brown chortled. "But the reason I haven't posted the script is because I was hoping you might get in touch. And, lo and behold, here you are."

"Why?"

"To offer you the chance to give me a better story, of course. Something I might want to trade for the script."

Davis frowned. "Like what?"

Brown smacked his lips hungrily over the line; it made Davis think of a giant frog. "The rest of this city may've forgotten about the incident between you and Torsten Gross, but I sure haven't."

Davis's fingers clenched around his phone. "There's no story there that wasn't already reported, Brown. Gross was a sadistic psychopath that killed some of his actors, tried to kill me and my friends, and then disappeared before the cops could close in."

"That's not what Sidney Spitzen says."

"Then go blackmail him! I couldn't talk about it even if I wanted to. Trimax Studios is involved in all that, and Phillip Reilly would love to sue the hell out of me for slandering them."

"No, no, I don't think you're understanding me," Brown said. "I don't wanna report this; I just wanna *know*. Ever since all that happened, I've been dying to find out the real story. No more of Spitzen's tabloid trash, no more urban legends, just the truth, straight from the most reliable source. And now, what with Tonya Werdner's murder..." He trailed, implying something that Davis wasn't quite getting. "Anyway, you come in, talk to me, I agree never to tell another living soul anything you say, and I'll hand over your script."

"No deal. I have no reason to trust you."

"I'll sign a non-disclosure if you want! Hell, I'll even tell you who your little Benedict Arnold is over there on the *KB3* set!"

"Confidential source, huh? Oh yeah, you're a pillar of journalistic integrity." The man disgusted Davis, but even so, this latest offer intrigued him. He would love to know who sold him out, and finding out the traitor's identity meant he could get rid of them before they did any more damage.

"Whatever," Brown huffed. "Have it your way. But just know that I'm pressing the button on this thing at nine AM on Friday. If you haven't come to see me by then, the whole world is gonna know how next summer's blockbuster tentpole ends before you've even filmed it."

The scumbag hung up, but Davis's phone rang again almost immediately.

"It's Crosby." The actor's voice was little more than a raspy whisper. "You win. Let's finish my scenes tomorrow."

Davis grinned.

Back in business.

SCENE III

(action)

TAKE 1

Production got an early start on Monday morning. Everyone was on set promptly, processed through wardrobe and makeup, and ready to go, even Crosby. Davis expected the actor not to show after all, another gambit in whatever power game he was playing, but he arrived and took direction with a meek, almost downtrodden attitude, not even meeting anyone's eye. He, Mahoney, and Heady worked their way through the final battle, coached by fight choreographers, and between takes Crosby would sit quietly by himself in a corner and stare at his knees. Even when his costar flubbed a line, he took the cuts with grace and restarted the scene without comment.

He wasn't the only one acting weird, either. Jared gave his guys instructions for the shoot and sequestered himself in the film room once more. He looked pale, but Davis didn't have time to be concerned while organizing the shoot and keeping an eye out for his spy.

They finished by eleven-thirty. Crosby's part in the movie was filmed, so he couldn't hold that over their heads anymore. Davis didn't even think an injunction would be looked upon too kindly by the courts at this point. He called lunch and walked over to the actor as he peeled off fake latex wounds.

"I'm sorry things got so heated yesterday," he said, "but I appreciate you coming in to get this done. For what it's worth, I think you're a fantastic actor." It felt good to not just say it, but to really mean it. If the man wanted to call him a sellout, that was his business, but at least Davis tried to get along with his people.

Crosby gave a dignified grunt, still not looking up, and turned to head toward the dressing rooms.

"If you don't mind me asking, what made you change your mind?" Davis called after him.

The older man mumbled over his shoulder, "I didn't have a lot of choice in the matter."

More theatrics. Davis rolled his eyes. Crosby was one of those actors he would never understand. "All right, well… nice working with you. I'll send you info on the wrap party, in case you wanna come by. Should be a gay old time."

Crosby stiffened with his hand on the door. Then, without warning, he flew back toward Davis, jamming a finger practically up his nose as he snarled, "*Was* it you, you conniving little whoreson? How dare you! *How dare you!*"

Davis raised his hands slowly in a gesture of surrender. "Isaac…I have no idea what you're talking about."

The actor stayed where he was for another long moment, searching Davis's face until he found the truth for himself. Then his forehead scrunched, and Davis saw the first teardrops leak down his cheeks as he turned away and hurried through the door out of the room.

"This town just gets weirder and weirder," Davis muttered.

"You ain't seen nothing yet."

Jared stood behind him. He still looked shaky, his jaw a little slack as he said, "Come with me. I need to show you something."

TAKE 2

Jared led him into the film room and closed the door. Places like this always reminded Davis of Otter's studio at the old office, banks of playback monitors and equipment whose purposes he couldn't even guess at.

"You ready to point out the big bad bee that flew into your bonnet?" Davis asked, sinking into a chair.

"That depends. You ready to listen?"

Davis waved two fingers in a circular, let's-get-this-over-with motion.

"Okay. You remember what Mahoney said at the hospital, right? His description of the accident?"

"I remember hearing the ranting of a man that'd just been severely traumatized."

"Doctor said he was fine."

"Yeah, but that doesn't mean his recounting of events is totally reliable."

"Thought you'd say that, Scully." Jared pressed buttons on the console, bringing up an image on the playback monitor. "This is the raw footage of the accident from yesterday. No sound, but we don't need it."

He started the recording. Davis watched as the red Eclipse raced up the track toward the camera and the stunt equipment positioned on the ground across the track. On the far side of the road, barely in frame, a figure began to wave his arms frantically just as the staged explosion erupted. The car flipped up on its front end and tumbled down the track like a flat stone skimming across water. The camera followed the vehicle all the way until it skidded to a stop on its roof, now beaten to a pulp, the image freezing as crewmen converged on it.

"Holy sheeee-it," Davis gasped. "That. Is. AWESOME! Nice work man, we'll get the CG guys to clean that up, enhance the background…hell, it'll be one of the slickest stunts in this thing."

"Davis…Mahoney should've died in that wreck."

"But he didn't. People survive stuff like this all the time, Jared. Hell, you lived through a car wreck almost as bad as that with barely a scratch!"

Jared lifted his left leg off the floor and flexed it with a wince, as though reminding Davis of just how bad that scratch had been. "Then let me enter exhibit B into evidence." He flicked switches and turned dials, running the footage back to the moment just before the accident began, as the car rolled onto the hidden ramp. Then he zoomed. With the HD quality, he could get close and tight on the front windshield without losing resolution. Inside the shadowy vehicle, Mahoney's face paused in an expression of eager expectation, like a teenager on a rollercoaster before the first big drop. "I've watched it from every angle, and this camera caught the clearest view. Keep an eye on the interior."

The tape began to roll in super slow motion, almost frame-by-frame, and, as the accident unfolded again, Davis found himself leaning forward until his nose almost touched the screen.

The car came forward, and the ramp bounced the rear half into the air. Mahoney's expression went from excitement to gradual realization that this was not the correct course of events. The vehicle began to skid on its front bumper. By then, it was close enough to the camera's position that they had a view through the passenger window rather than the front, and Davis could see something strange happening inside.

Black, paper-thin tendrils shot out from the dashboard. They seemed to come from everywhere at once, creeping out of the A/C vents, joints in the plastic, around the radio knobs, anywhere there was a crevice. The tentacles had no features, no substance. In fact, they were so gossamer and delicate as to be almost see-through, like concentrated smoke. In the frame after they first appeared, they stretched up through the now-vertical car toward the driver; in the next, they had ensnared Mahoney's arms, reached out to his face and shoulders. They coiled around his neck and biceps like miniature pythons, then began to spread, wrapping him up in black mummy bandages. The transformation happened so fast that the actor was completely enveloped within another four frames. Then they lost their view as the car catapulted onto its side and flipped out of frame.

In real time, it took no more than a split second, hardly enough for someone living through it to even register what had happened.

As if reading his mind, Jared said, "I saw it. Just barely. With the naked eye, it was just this...black blur. Like shadows within shadows."

In his head, Davis heard Mahoney saying, *I felt like there were these hands all around me...pressing me back into the seat...*

"What are they?" he asked. That foreboding gloom was back, goosepimpling his skin.

"You tell me."

"Did anybody touch this footage? Tamper with it?"

Jared shook his head. "Nobody's even seen it but me."

"So you're trying to tell me this…stuff…it came out and, what? Saved Mahoney? Protected him during the crash?"

"That's what it looks like."

Davis rubbed his eyes, which had been wide open for so long as he stared at the monitor they were beginning to dry out. "It's gotta be something Reid rigged the car with. Some kind of safety feature. Hasn't the automotive industry been trying to develop a cushioning foam?"

"Sure, but that stuff's in the developmental stages and far too expensive for us to get. Besides, if it was securefoam, where was it after the accident?"

"I don't know, Jared. I can't explain it and neither can you. Maybe nobody can. So what's the point of all this?"

"The point is, after what Spitzen told us, I thought we were keeping an eye out for anything suspicious." He nodded at the monitor. "I'd say that qualifies."

"You know…I was afraid of this," Davis said slowly.

"Afraid of what?"

"That Spitzen got inside your head."

"Nobody got inside my head. But you certainly took him seriously enough to go running off and warn Susan."

"That's different." Davis tapped the screen. "You must know this has nothing to do with what happened to Werdner."

"I'm not saying it does. All I'm saying is that this is some weird shit. And the last time you and I ran into some weird shit, people started dying."

"There's a rational explanation."

Jared crossed his arms as he sat on the edge of the desk. "Now, where have I heard that before?"

Davis slapped at the equipment in frustration, but only because the man was right. "Play it back, we'll watch it again. Give me some other angles."

Jared set the scene up on three consecutive monitors this time, all from different angles, and ran through the accident again, even slower. The first perspective was still the best, but the others all confirmed the same diagnosis: the dark tendrils spiked out of the dashboard and wrapped Mahoney in a thin cocoon. Jared froze on an up-close view of the actor's face from the front just as the smoky whips oozed over his mouth, nose, and forehead like liquid latex, leaving only tiny breathing holes around his nostrils.

"What is that?" someone asked behind them. They spun in unison.

Scott stood in the open doorway, gaping at the monitor. "Are we doing creature effects in this one?"

"Ever hear of a lock, Jared?" Davis asked.

"I didn't think I had to lock it!" Jared lunged to shut down the monitors. "Jesus kid, can't you knock?"

"Sorry sir, I didn't know this was top secret." Scott started to back out, his eyes still rooted to the image on the screen.

"No. You know what, it's fine." Davis waved him inside. "Come on in, maybe a fresh set of eyes is exactly what we need."

Jared's gaze flicked between Scott and Davis. "You think that's a good idea?"

"Why? You afraid to inject a little sanity into this situation? Just play the stupid thing."

Another viewing, this time with Scott's skinny frame seated between them and the door firmly locked. When it was over, Davis asked, "What do you think?"

Scott turned his chair around and looked up at them with his pimpled brow furrowed suspiciously. "What am I supposed to think, sir?"

"Just tell us, what does that look like to you?"

"It looks like Mr. Mahoney is being attacked by a black octopus. And if that's what you're going for, I have to say, the effect looks really fake."

Jared snickered.

Scott glanced at him, then back at Davis. "Is this a joke, sir?"

"No joke, Scott. That's completely unaltered footage of the accident yesterday. Whatever those things are, they seem to've saved Big D's life." Davis looked over the teenager's head at his partner and smirked. "And, surprise, surprise, Jared thinks there's a supernatural element to it."

"Not to sound disrespectful sir, but I think the briefest way to phrase my response would be…'Duh?'"

Davis stopped himself just short of a double-take at the kid. "What are you saying?"

"Well…what else could it be? If this is as real as you say, then those rope-things are moving with obvious purpose. They squeeze out of the dashboard and then sort of…ooze all over Mr. Mahoney. Unless you can think of any manmade substance that moves and reacts like that…" He looked over his shoulder at the monitors one more time. "The car is so dark, it's really hard to tell, but they almost look like… shadows. Shadows moving on their own somehow."

"Ha, told you!" Jared gloated.

"Oh, congratulations, you got an 18-year-old on your side! Now I'm convinced!"

"Whatever, man. I don't know why you're fighting this so hard."

"I'm not fighting! You wanna call it a miracle, fine, I'll say 'Hallelujah' with you! But I know what you're *really* implying, that this has something to do with…" He trailed and glanced at Scott, now regretting that he'd let the boy in for this.

"Torsten Gross?" Scott asked, perking up. "Is this what

happened when you worked for him?"

"No, it isn't!"

"You sure?" Jared countered. "Because I remember you telling me after I came out of that coma that he turned into some kind of black, oozy puddle at the end, after he melted."

Scott's eyes grew round and shiny. "Gross *melted?*"

Davis took a deep breath before answering. "What you have here, Scott, is just more of Jared's eagerness to jump off the deep end as a first response." He pushed up from his seat and started out of the film room, throwing over his shoulder, "And all of this just seems too goddamned familiar for me."

He'd gotten halfway across the set when Jared burst out behind him and shouted, "Why is that, Davis? Because *I* was the one who kept insisting there was something up with Gross last time?"

Davis saw heads all over the room turn to look at them, the crew, and set construction guys, and Jared's cameramen. He walked back to his partner and hissed, "Would you keep your voice down? And there's no *last* time, because there's no *this* time. Think about it: if this has anything to do with Torsten Gross' revenge from beyond the grave, he sure has a funny way of going about it, considering he just saved the star of our movie."

Davis ducked through the door leading to the dressing rooms, hoping that would end the debate. Jared stayed right on his heels like a yapping dog.

"Just look at the facts," he argued. "Werdner gets murdered and two days later, we run into some more crazy shit that's caught right on camera, which was Gross's forte. It would have to be a pretty big coincidence if it wasn't all related to him somehow, right?"

The door to the female dressing room opened as they

went past. Heady leaned out wearing a fuzzy pink robe. "Hold up. Are you guys having an actual, out-loud conversation about Gross?"

"*No!*" Davis snapped at her without stopping, but it was too late, she stepped the rest of the way out and followed them, and now Scott tried his damnedest to catch up from the opposite end of the hall, looking timid but determined. Davis felt like he was being surrounded by lunatics. Just like when they'd lived through that nightmare, the German horror director's name seemed to be on everyone's lips.

And can you blame them? Jared has a point, and you know it. The admission only served to harden his resolve.

He was *not* going through this again.

Davis stopped with his hand on the knob to the male dressing room and faced them.

"In case you forgot, Gross's *forte* was having his victims commit suicide after he sucked out their souls." Davis turned the knob and shoved open the door, meaning to back inside and lock them all out. "And I don't know about you, but I don't see anyone committing—"

Heady shrieked.

Davis was so startled, he backpedaled away from the door, fell over the legs of an overturned chair behind him, and sprawled on the floor just beneath the form of Sir Isaac Crosby, dangling from the ceiling girders by a noose made of twine.

TAKE 3

The LAPD arrived within twenty minutes, a response time you could only get north of the 105. They photographed the room before taking down Crosby's body, one cop standing on a ladder to cut the thin rope loose and three more waiting to catch the weight. The actor's face had turned blue and bloated, his tongue like a thick, dead slug as it hung from his slack jaw. Davis found it a relief when he was finally on the coroner's gurney and covered by a sheet.

The police that arrived first got some preliminary information, then the lean Hispanic detective Davis had seen in Devlin's office yesterday morning gave him a quick interview. His name turned out to be Alvarez.

"So the body was found by you, Miss Tillman, and a…" He checked a small spiral notebook. "Jared Mane and Scott Meyer?"

"That's right. My cinematographer and production assistant."

"And I understand you were the last person to talk to him?"

"Uh…yeah, I guess so."

"Was he acting strange at all, give any indication he might try something like this?"

Davis gave that question serious consideration. "He was quiet. Reserved. It wasn't much like him. But he didn't do anything to make me think…"

Alvarez nodded sympathetically. "I understand. Don't take it too hard, you couldn't have known. Sometimes people in this frame of mind decide to do it on the spur. Just wish the guy had left a note."

Davis looked away and bit his lower lip like he was about to tear up. It was either that, or look guilty.

Because what this detective didn't know is that Crosby *had* left a note, a hastily-scrawled missive on a cocktail napkin that had been left on the dressing room counter and was now shoved in Davis's back pocket. He'd spotted it just before the cops walked in, read what was on it, and grabbed it before anyone else could see.

Alvarez started to open his mouth, glanced at his little notebook, and then looked at him with renewed interest. "Davis Lowe? Why do I know that name?"

"You probably saw *Valley of Blue* last year. Lotta cops liked that one. I'd be happy to give you an autograph."

"No thanks, I thought it was overrated." Alvarez waved the offer away and then tapped his pen against where he'd written their names. "Weren't you and this Jared Mane involved with Katherine Wickersham's suicide a few years ago?"

"Yeeees, Jared was there when she...when it happened," Davis said, trying to draw out each word long enough to gather his thoughts. This was becoming a pit of quicksand, and fast. There had never been enough evidence for Wickersham's suicide to fall under the umbrella of Gross's killing spree; they were two separate incidents, as far as the cops were concerned. The connection had never even occurred to Davis, but now that it'd been made, Crosby's death might start looking awfully coincidental. And, of course, it could get exponentially worse if the cops got their hands on the actor's last testament. "He was a suspect at first, but he was never charged with anything."

Alvarez watched him for a long moment, his face as unreadable as a stone. "Can you send him over, please?"

"Um...absolutely." Davis walked across the dressing room to where Jared sat with his arm around Heady. Her tears had finally dried up, but she still looked a little shellshocked. "He wants to talk to you."

Jared frowned. "Why?"

"He connected you to Wickersham. For God's sake, just play it cool and don't say a word about the damn Mahoney footage."

"Why would I?" Jared stood, glaring at him. "After all... the whole thing's unrelated, right?"

After he left, Davis patted Heady's back and then went to sit down beside Scott. "You all right?"

"I think so. I've never seen a dead body before."

"I'd like to say it gets easier, but that'd be a lie." He thought about Scott's father, the cancer eating away at him, and regretted the words.

But Scott didn't seem fazed. "Will this affect the movie?"

"Not unless Crosby's estate tries to hold up his scenes with litigation. But really, I think that script Marion Brown claims he has will hurt us a lot more in the long run. I'd love to find whoever gave it to him."

"You don't have any idea about who did it?"

"Not a clue. There's so many people traipsing through this set every day, it could've been the Fedex guy that swiped it. Nobody's reported a copy missing, and I didn't even think to watermark the damn things. Just keep your ear to the ground and let me know if you hear anything."

The kid nodded, then leaned over until his elbows were on his knees and stared at the floor. "Sir, if I ask you a question, will you be honest with me?"

"That's a hard promise to make, but I'll try."

"What did Mr. Crosby write on that piece of paper?"

Davis snorted in surprise. So much for his espionage skills.

"You can trust me, sir. I promise."

He thought about it and decided, why not? He'd already brought the boy this far into the insanity and besides, it somehow felt more rational to discuss this with him than with Jared. "It just said, 'I won't be anyone's puppet, Lowe.'"

"What does that mean?"

"No clue." The written words had an angry air to Davis, the last declaration of a man too proud for his own good. "But I can only guess what that detective over there would make of it."

"Maybe Mr. Crosby was just upset about filming the rest of his scenes."

"If so, I don't understand why he'd blame me. He had me by the short hairs, then all of a sudden he wanted to come back. And even if he was mad, why the hell would he hang himself over it?"

Scott straightened and looked up at Davis. "I know what you told Mr. Mane, but...are you *sure* this doesn't have something to do with Torsten Gross? I've read all the news reports and Mr. Spitzen's stories and even some of the German coverage. I know about the suicides, and how people acted strange just before they killed themselves. And judging by what you said back there, I'm guessing it's all true, that Gross was some kind of..." He choked on the last word. "*Monster.*"

Something in the kid's voice reminded Davis of Marion Brown's panting eagerness. "Scott...why are you digging into all this?"

"I did it when I started working for you. Oh, but I researched everything about you, not just that!" His pimpled cheeks turned a shade of red that would've given Heady's hair a run for its money. "I just wanted to do a good job. You're...sorta...one of my heroes. Have been ever since you made *Star Gazer*."

The film was an adaptation of a little-known sci-fi novel that still hadn't been released by the tiny studio who owned the rights, and was available only in bootleg. Davis had seen a few cuts out on the merchant tables at various comic book conventions, which is where he'd met Scott while doing early publicity for *Killing Blow 3*. It was this kind of endearing honesty that had made him hire the kid as a PA.

Davis put an arm around the teenager's shoulders. "You're doing a great job."

"So do you think Gross had something to do with Mr. Crosby?"

Davis replayed that last strange conversation with the actor. Thought back to how Otter had been at the end, eyes dead and empty, acting like someone doped up on Thorazine. "No, I don't. Crosby was showing too much emotion. He got mad. Plus, there's no way he would've been able to shoot his scenes today if he'd gone through the same thing as Gross's other victims."

Scott nodded, satisfied. Davis watched the conversation between Jared and Alvarez, which was taking far too long. Then, just as he got ready to butt in, the door to the dressing room opened and Baxter Devlin rushed in, followed by Cordero.

"What's all this then?" Devlin asked. "Detective, why are you interrogating my people?"

"I'm not interrogating, Mr. Devlin, I'm questioning. Considering you've had two deaths on your lot in the past four days, I would think that's exactly what you want us to do."

Devlin flapped his trembling hands. "Surely you're not suggesting Miss Werdner's death has anything to do with this!"

Alvarez glanced at Jared. "That's what I'm trying to find out."

Cordero straightened his impeccable tie. "Unless you're detaining someone, handle it through the studio attorneys. They can take all the depositions you want."

"Right." Alvarez flipped his notebook closed and said to the cops and crime scene techs, "Finish up in here, boys. I want a full analysis." He strode out of the room.

Davis stood with Heady and Scott. They, along with Jared, converged on Devlin and Cordero.

"I got here as soon as I could. This is awful, just awful." Devlin bowed his head. "What a tragedy to lose such a fine actor."

Cordero looked at Davis. "But I understand he'd filmed the last of his scenes, so it's not a total loss. Correct?"

Davis blanched. Another echo of Torsten Gross, saying essentially the same thing about Katherine Wickersham at a press conference. "Yeah. Yeah, that's right."

"Buddy, for God's sake, must you be so mercenary?" Devlin chided. Cordero closed his mouth, but didn't look in the least bit chastised. "Davis, don't worry about this. We'll take care of the press and the police. You just concentrate on the movie. And Heady, dear, if you—or any of you—need anything at all, please don't hesitate to call. An event like this can be traumatizing."

"Thanks," Heady sniffled. Jared put an arm around her.

Devlin talked to them for another few minutes, more reassurances that he would take care of everything, but Cordero pulled Davis aside. He felt like a lamb being led to slaughter as they stepped outside the warehouse

"Devlin's too nice to say it, so I will: this one fell in our favor. But what about Marion Brown? You make any headway there?"

Davis tried not to visibly squirm. "I've...been in touch with him. I think he might be persuaded to drop the whole thing."

"What about the spy? I want that name."

"I'm sure I'll be able to get that, too."

Cordero grinned. Even his rare smiles were too perfect, with incisors as sharp as a wolf's. "That's how you stay on my good side, Lowe. And trust me, that's exactly where you want to be."

TAKE 4

Susan had been on set all day to meet the rest of the cast for their first read through, a process lorded over by Killam, who attempted to grope her every time they took a break. The rest of the talent was surprisingly low on the totem pole—a group of unknowns that clearly idolized her—leaving her to wonder if the casting budget hadn't been blown entirely on her. After that last film opened to big numbers, her agent said her price tag was hovering at the two mil mark, a fact she never would've been aware of otherwise. For God's sake, she'd actually reached the point where an accountant was necessary to keep track of her money.

It was eight o'clock before they started leaving. Killam asked if she wanted to go for a drink, but she managed to wiggle out with the promise of a raincheck. The odd meeting with Cordero the day before had been on her mind all day, but she couldn't tell if the director was still wearing the necklace he'd been given. She left him with some of the other actors worshipping at his feet and started across the lot.

A few of the soundstages had night shoots going. She stopped to watch, saying hello to acquaintances as she went. She found herself taking a roundabout path, weaving through the huge warehouses until she was standing outside number 14. It was closed up tight, but there was still yellow police line tape strung across every entrance.

Tonya Werdner died in there, she thought. Almost like visiting a grave. Susan could remember the woman from when they'd worked together. She was rough around the edges, but Susan had always believed she was decent at her core. Or maybe that had been doe-eyed optimism. In any case, she certainly hadn't deserved the end she met. They hadn't kept in touch, but Susan intended to go to the funeral, as soon as the cops were finished with the autopsy.

Is that enough? Don't you owe her something more? She did save your life, after all.

Susan wished she could talk to Davis a little more about all this. For a moment, she considered walking over to his soundstage. Instead, she continued on toward her car.

When she reached the main cobblestone avenue, a golf cart pulled up behind her, its engine a steady hum. "Evening Miss Campbell," Ralph called. The guard always seemed to be patrolling, day or night. "You need a ride to your car?"

"No thanks, I'm outside the lot today. Didn't get here early enough to grab a spot. They really didn't leave much room for parking when they built the place, huh?"

"There's a rumor Mr. Devlin is getting ready to buy out the Fox annex next door for just that reason."

Susan laughed. "Have a good night, Ralph."

"You too, Miss Campbell."

He drove on, leaving her to walk through the dark studio lot alone. At the front gate, she waved to another guard, passed beneath the huge granite arch, and started down the sidewalk beyond, toward the side streets where everyone who wasn't lucky enough to grab an inside spot parked.

Most of these streets were empty; Monday nightlife was all in the clubs to the north and east of the studio. This morning, she'd parallel parked in front of a coffeehouse that was now closed and dark. Her Mercedes M-Class sat all alone under the streetlight closest to the corner.

As she got closer, she saw a folded sheet of paper under

her windshield wiper. She slipped it out as she fumbled her keys out of her purse, meaning to toss the local band flyer or spa coupon in the SUV's passenger seat with the rest of the trash she accumulated.

Then it flopped open, and she spotted the watery, rust-colored handwriting inside.

The back of Susan's neck turned warm and tingly with fear.

She forced her arms to move, holding the paper up to the streetlight so she could see its contents.

Scrawled on the typing sheet in two lines of sloppy red dribbles that looked like dried watercolor was MAKE THE PANE STOP, I NEED YUR HART.

Ten months ago, a series of misspelled, unsigned notes like this one had started showing up at her publicist's office on a regular basis, in plain brown envelopes with no return address. They'd started out friendly, praising her acting and beauty, turned beseeching, and then began to accuse her of all manner of insanity, like creeping into the author's home and poisoning him with "LUV JUSE" and stealing his penis so that he could never be whole. The police were called after the fifth or sixth, which had promised suicide if she didn't meet the author face-to-face. They told Susan there was no way to trace their origin, but not to worry, the weirdo surely didn't know how to find her, which was why he'd sent the letters to her publicist.

Oh, and the cops had provided one other comforting little tidbit.

Those dried maroon scribbles? That was actually blood. Probably the author's, but they had no way to know that for sure.

And now, here was a new one—fresh off the press, judging from the way the paper still felt damp between her fingers—and it hadn't been sent to her publicist, it was under her damn wiper blade, proving that the police had been wrong about their one assurance.

"All I ever wanted is for you to love me," a gruff voice said behind her.

Susan spun, dropping both note and purse. Across the street was a narrow alley between stores, barely wide enough for a dumpster. A figure stood in the shadows, invisible save for the cherry-red flare of a cigarette casting a glow across the face. Narrow eyes regarded her.

"S-stay away from me," Susan said. She tried to make her body bend and retrieve her purse, but she locked up once again, her usual reaction to fear turning her into a statue.

"But I love you," the figure growled as it emerged from the mouth of the alley and into the streetlight. Susan waited for the scuzzy, ratlike features she'd been imagining, and was utterly shocked to see the soft cheeks and rounded jaw of a female instead, framed by choppy locks of sandy blonde hair that formed a mullet down her neck. Even with the un-flattering haircut, she was still rather pretty in the face, but the accompanying body was entirely mannish. She was big-ger than Susan, heftier by at least fifty or sixty pounds, and wearing nothing except jeans, combat boots, and a yellow life preserver vest that revealed her tan, muscled arms all the way up to the shoulder. "I love you, but you just hurt me and hurt me and hurt me."

Susan swallowed. She wanted to run, wanted to scream, but until she worked through the fear, she couldn't even turn her head to look for help. "If…if I hurt you, I'm sorry. But we've never even met. I don't know you."

"Oh really?" the woman asked. Her voice was deep and rough. She stepped off the curb on the far side of the street, flicking the cigarette into the gutter. "Then how come you keep visiting me in my dreams? How come you stole my cock so I can't be a real man no more?"

"Look...I don't even know what the hell that means." *That's right, get mad*, she thought, *a little anger will wash that fear right away.* "The police already know about you though. You need to leave before I call them."

"The police can't keep us apart." The woman stopped in the middle of the street, just a few yards from Susan, grasped the edges of her life preserver, and ripped the vest open with the flair of a stripper. Her naked breasts—full, veiny, and sagging—were crisscrossed with a series of slashes, older scar tissue near the tops, and wounds so fresh by the nipples they were still weeping scarlet. Susan would bet the blood from those latter slices had been used to compose the note at her feet. "You see the sacrifices I make for you?"

"Fine, you lunatic, you've sacrificed. What do you expect me to do now, go to dinner? Buy a condo? Live out our lives tastefully mutilating one another?"

The woman reached to her back and pulled out a thin-bladed knife. "Now it's time for *you* to sacrifice, Susan."

The last of the paralysis broke at the sight of the knife. Susan dove for her purse, scrambled for the keys inside. The big dyke charged her with a banshee's wail, slicing out with the knife just as Susan jerked back and threw herself against the hood of the Mercedes. This time, when the attack came, she jabbed out with the keys and watched as the one that opened the door of her leased house disappeared into the stalker's exposed chest. A superficial wound, but enough to make the woman grunt and stumble back, giving Susan room to run.

She made it only a few steps when a booted foot swept her legs out from under her. Susan hit the pavement face down, hurting both wrists as she tried to catch herself and bouncing her chin off the street. Her vision blurred. Then the woman straddled her back, heavy enough to keep her from getting a good breath. She pinned Susan's arms with her knees. Fingers twined through her hair and jerked her head back painfully, but she was too dazed to struggle. The edge of the knife pressed against her throat.

Above them, the sole streetlight winked out, leaving them in the darkness of a half-moon.

The stalker seemed startled. Susan's head was released and fell back to the pavement. She found herself staring into the gap between her car's undercarriage and the street, where something moved.

A viscous black shape flowed out from between the tires beside them, seeming almost to tear away from the deeper darkness under the car. To Susan's bleary eyes, it looked like an oil puddle, but it had form as it reared up from the concrete. It gradually solidified, forming four appendages beneath a rounded blob suggestion of a head.

The other woman saw it and screamed. Her weight disappeared from Susan as she tried to scramble away. By now, the thing had the vague shape of a large dog, but was still made of only that smooth, flowing blackness, like a shadow come to life, hard to see in the dim light. It leapt over Susan's prone form; she turned her head against the street to follow it.

"*What is that?*" her attacker demanded. She brandished the knife as the dark shape circled around her.

A hole formed in the featureless head, from which an odd, piercing screech emanated. One of the creature's appendages pistoned out, stretching and blossoming to become something the size of an anvil as it rammed forward. It struck the huge woman dead center in her mutilated chest hard enough to knock her off her feet. She flew through the air for several feet before slamming into the lamppost. Susan heard a stiff crunch as the woman's neck snapped. Her stalker slid down to the sidewalk, twitched several times, and grew still.

The black creature gave another shriek and dove back beneath her car. Susan tried to get a clearer picture as it swept by, but she was so dizzy, and it moved so fast. The darkness appeared to swallow it up in an instant, as though it were really jumping into a hole in the ground instead of insubstantial shadows.

A second later, the streetlamp buzzed back on, illuminating the corpse at its base like a spotlight.

Refusing to pass out, Susan crawled to her purse and dug out her phone.

TAKE 5

The *Killing Blow* set proved to be unusable the rest of the day as the LAPD finished up their investigation. Davis and Scott hung around to watch the proceedings, mostly to make sure Detective Alvarez's men didn't get their hands on certain footage in the film room. Probably paranoia; they would surely think the film as fake as Scott had at first, movie magic, and even if they believed it to be real, it didn't have anything to do with Crosby. And now that the actor's suicide note had been destroyed (an act Davis felt completely justified in, since the damn thing was addressed specifically to him), there was no evidence at all. Still, Davis wanted to talk to Jared about the detective and their conversation, but his partner ducked out to take Heady home without a word just before Mahoney and the rest of the cast cleared out. It was close to five when the parade ended, and Davis had his soundstage back.

"You can go home too," he told Scott. "Not gonna need you for anything else tonight."

"But sir, we should really talk about what all this means." He leaned closer, lowered his voice, and, even though they were alone, spoke from the side of his mouth like a spy in an old black-and-white. "And maybe we should stick together. You know, until we figure out if the rest of us are in danger."

"We're not. I already told you that."

"Actually, you told me this didn't have anything to do with Torsten Gross. And I believe you. But that doesn't mean we shouldn't be concerned."

Davis shook his head. He'd created another Jared. "Go home, Scott."

His production assistant gave him a doubtful look and then grudgingly left.

After which Davis spent the next two hours drinking from the bottle of scotch in his desk, watching Jared's footage of the crash over and over again, and trying very hard not to think about Crosby, Otter, or Gross.

Then his thoughts landed on Susan, and that was far worse.

At some point, he dozed, then woke up at eight-thirty with a gummy mouth and headache. Davis stumbled out of the soundstage and headed out into the nighttime Apex lot, just sober enough to make it home. But he got only as far as the front gates when red and blue flashing lights up the street caught his attention. He turned and drove by a collection of police cars and emergency vehicles several blocks up, would've gone right past if his rubbernecking hadn't revealed Susan sitting in the open back door of an ambulance with an ice pack under her jaw.

Davis pulled to the curb as soon as he could find an open spot and jogged back. Along the way, he passed a sheet-covered form at the base of a nearby streetlight, but kept going until he reached the ambulance against the curb.

"Susan? Jesus, are you all right?"

She'd been looking down at the knees of her jeans blankly, but now her head came up and relief flooded her face at the sight of him. "Davis, oh god." She dropped the ice pack and held out her arms. He sank into them without hesitation, pulling her close. It felt wonderful, but more than that, it made him feel *awake*, for the first time in more than a year, as if he'd been drifting through the rest of his life since they stopped seeing each other. Susan sagged against him, but when she tried to rest her head on his shoulder, she drew in a sharp breath.

"What happened?" he asked. "Who's under that sheet?"

"I was attacked. By a woman that's been stalking me."

He broke away from her embrace, cupped her cheek gently and turned her head up so he could see the underside of her chin, where blood had crusted. "And she did this? Are you okay?"

"Yeah, I just scraped it on the street. I think the blow scrambled my brains a bit." She reached up, took his hand off her cheek...but held on to it. "I'm fine, really. Thank you. I'm...I'm actually glad you're here."

The words were heavenly. Davis started to reply, but sensed someone coming up behind him.

"Well, well. Another dead body today, and Davis Lowe is once again at the scene." Detective Alvarez watched him carefully, with eyes as preternaturally calm as the beach before a hurricane. "This is getting to be a real habit."

"I could say the same thing about you. With as much as you've been hanging around lately, you'd think you were trying to score an acting gig."

"Seeing as how Apex Studios is exporting more corpses than movies these days, my chief has pretty much reassigned me here."

"What does he mean, 'another dead body *today*'?" Susan asked.

Davis grimaced. This was the last topic he wanted to re-visit in front of Alvarez. "Isaac Crosby committed suicide on my set this morning."

She put a hand to her mouth. "Oh my god, that's terrible! I'm so sorry."

"Yeah, we're all real sorry. Aren't we, Lowe?" Alvarez was as still as a mountain. A glowering mountain. His attitude from this morning—that subtext of professionalism and sympathy—had completely evaporated. "Let's take a walk."

Davis squeezed Susan's hand and let it drop, then followed Alvarez up the sidewalk, toward that covered body against the lamppost. It seemed strange that they'd already draped it if this was a potential crime scene, but he wasn't about to look a gift horse in the mouth. Davis didn't think he could take inspecting another corpse today. "What happened here?" he asked, trying to take charge of the conversation.

"Your girlfriend packed quite a punch, that's what happened."

"She's not my girlfriend." *Not anymore.*

Alvarez shrugged and pointed a toe at the sheeted body. "She got attacked by this big gal, who's apparently been sending her love letters for the past year. Woman came at her with a knife, Miss Campbell stabbed her with her keys and, according to her, the woman tripped on the curb, fell backward, and broke her neck against the post."

"Good. Thank God Susan wasn't hurt. So why are you acting like it's something more?"

"Because the crime scene guys are already telling me that to sustain these injuries, this two-hundred-pound lumberjack would have to be travelling at some serious speed. Now, unless your little *chica* has some gorilla tossing skills she's not telling me about, something doesn't add up."

Davis met his gaze, determined not to betray his surprise. He wished he'd gotten a chance to talk to Susan a little more about what had happened before getting ambushed by this nosy detective. "Okay, maybe so. What do you want me to say about it? You're the detective."

"That's right, I am." The statement had a funny ring to it, but trying to read Alvarez to discern the meaning behind it was useless. That calm, unmoving demeanor was frustrating. Davis couldn't even catch the guy *blinking*. "So, just for the record, you know absolutely nothing about what happened here tonight?"

"I drove by as I left the studio and spotted Susan. She's just an old friend."

"What about Tonya Werdner? She an 'old friend'?"

"More like a colleague. We worked on a movie once."

"The infamous *Arterial Slice*, right?"

Davis winced. This guy had done some homework in the last couple of hours. "That was it."

"And would you mind if I asked where you were Friday night when she was killed?"

"With Jared and about thirty other members of my cast and crew for a night shoot out at Hermosa. Ask any of them."

"Interesting." This time, from the way the detective said it, Davis suspected he had a card he wasn't laying on the table. Before Davis could even guess what it might be, Alvarez changed topics. "We also searched Isaac Crosby's hotel room this evening. Seems he had himself a little ashtray bonfire at some point. Looks like he burned up some photographs he didn't want anybody seeing."

Davis thought about the suicide note, which he'd incinerated in a similar fashion. "Yeah, so?"

"So I can't prove it—yet—but my guess is that he was being blackmailed into doing something he didn't want to do. And the way I hear it from his agent, the thing he didn't want to do most in the world is finish acting in your movie. Yet that's exactly what he did today. Correct?"

Davis said nothing. This was no longer quicksand. He felt more like he stood on an ice floe that was quickly breaking up beneath his feet.

"As you can probably guess, I even did a little more research on you and Mr. Mane," Alvarez continued. "See, I remembered about Wickersham right off, probably because of the suicide angle, but I completely forgot that you, he, and Miss Campbell were all involved in that screwy Torsten Gross case a few years back. Along with Tonya Werdner, of course. Imagine my surprise when, ten minutes after learning you all have a history, I get a call to come back out here for a homicide involving Miss Campbell."

"That's not fair," Davis said quickly. "We were victims in that."

"And you might be here also. But see things from my point of view, Lowe. I got three bodies on my hands, all related to Apex Studios or its employees. And, beyond that, they all have ties directly to *you* one way or another. The pieces don't exactly fit, and the circumstances are getting weirder by the minute, but that sort of thing follows you guys around like a cloud of B.O. You can't tell me it's not all connected."

Davis almost laughed. This guy should join Jared and Scott's conspiracy club.

Except if everyone else is saying the same thing, who's the lone conspiracist here, Davis?

"We're innocent," he said. "That's all I can tell you."

"I hope so. Because I'll find the truth, Lowe. Old man Devlin and his golden-gated studio can't protect you forever." He pulled a business card out of his wallet and handed it over. "Just in case you suddenly have the urge to talk."

Alvarez strolled away. Davis slid the card in his pocket and looked down at the form beneath the sheet one more time before hurrying back to Susan.

"What was that about?" she asked.

"He's fishing. They got nothing on Werdner and it's making them antsy."

"Werdner? What does she have to do with this?"

"Nothing at all." He checked to make sure the cops were a safe distance. "So what happened? Did this woman really trip like you told them? Because they don't seem to think so."

Her face screwed up as she rubbed at her forehead. "No. At least, I don't think so. It all happened so fast, but…"

"But what?"

"Well, she went crazy, we fought, and then…" She seemed on the verge of saying something, then withdrew from it. "I don't know. It's just a jumble."

Davis moved closer, wanting to prod her memory but also eager to hold her hand again. "On the bright side, any other nutjob that wants to stalk you will think twice now."

She laughed. It seemed like old times, somehow. He reached for her, and then Killam was there, shoving him aside.

"Susan, baby, are you all right?"

"I'm fine, Dwight. It was nothing. Sorry I called, but…" Her eyes cut hesitantly over to Davis. "I just wanted someone here with me."

"You don't have to apologize! Goddamn the studio, they should post security out here if they're going to have parking overflow! I'll talk to Buddy tomorrow. Now c'mon, you shouldn't have to stay for this, I'll drive you home."

"That's okay, I have my car."

"I insist. You shouldn't be driving after something like this."

"Actually, I don't even know if the police are finished with me yet."

Killam grabbed her arm and pulled her from the ambulance. She hopped down. "Nonsense. They'll find you when they need you. You'll let them know, won't you, Davis?"

He directed his answer to Susan. "Sure. No problem. You really should get some rest."

She nodded but held his gaze. *C'mon*, he willed her, *tell this asshole to get lost and come with me...*

For just a second, he thought she really would, but then Killam tugged and she submitted. Davis watched as the other director led the woman he loved away, one hand too far south around her waist for him to stomach.

TAKE 6

Heady stayed quiet on the way home. Jared stopped and grabbed them take-out and a bottle of Skyy, both of which they consumed while curled up on her couch, still without speaking. Finally, he asked, "Do you want me to stay tonight?"

She looked daggers at him. "You know goddamn well I'm not some frail little female that needs her big strong man to sleep over and protect her."

"If I didn't before, I do now."

"Okay. As long as that's settled, then yes, please stay." She leaned into him. "I just can't believe Isaac is dead. For real dead, not call-the-prop-guy-to-take-away-these-fake-guts dead."

He ran a hand through the baby-soft red hair at her temple. "I'm sorry it happened, and that you had to see it. Crosby made Davis's life a living hell, but the guy didn't deserve that."

"What did that cop say to you?"

"Not much. Like Davis said, he knows I was there when Katherine Wickersham killed herself." Except that was putting it lightly. What the actress had actually done is take a swan dive through her floor-to-ceiling penthouse window, while Jared taped the whole thing.

"That argument you and Davis were having," Heady said, breaking in on his thoughts. "It had something to do with Derek's accident yesterday, didn't it? And then you guys started talking about Torsten Gross."

Jared squirmed beneath her.

"C'mon, Mane. Every time the subject comes up, you dodge. That was fine before, when it was all just some freaky part of your past. But now it's back, and it's affecting me. And if I'm being written into the script, I wanna know my cues."

He still said nothing. He and Davis had vowed to keep this quiet, to let the rumors die. Of course, that had been an easy promise to keep when the only other people in his life were an endless parade of addlebrained one-night stands.

She turned in his lap, shoved him down on the cushions, and mounted his hips. Then she grabbed hold of his ponytail and yanked his head back in that way he loved so much. "Listen dumbass, if this is actually going somewhere between us, you should know that I accept nothing but full disclosure from my men."

"Oh really? And how many men have there been?"

"Enough."

"And is this going somewhere?"

"I don't know. I hope so."

That was all he really needed to hear. Jared scooted back up on the couch, closed his eyes, and began to tell Heady Tillman a story.

TAKE 7

Susan felt better by the time she and Killam reached her house. Her head was much less thick and sore, but the events of the night were still fuzzy. She just wanted to be alone and try to sort through what happened. Unfortunately, Killam insisted on coming in. Then he insisted on staying for a nightcap while he comforted her. Then tucking her into bed. Then getting undressed and into bed with her, and before she knew it, they were engaged in rough, awkward sex. Killam was a machine on top of her, thrusting and jabbing like he was scoring points in a fencing match. In the end, she was only able to get off by fantasizing about Davis, and then her orgasm just about blew her head off.

But the sex was also awkward because Killam refused to remove the chain around his neck. Totally naked, not even any hair on his taut, waxed body, yet he deliberately kept the necklace on throughout. He didn't even comment on it either, but considering he didn't take time for foreplay, conversation seemed pretty much out of the question. And, even though the medallion kept whapping her in the face while he thrashed between her legs, she couldn't get a good look at it.

When it was over, he rolled off and passed out beside her, snoring loudly. Even though she really didn't want to be alone, the idea of having to deal with him in the morning made her want to retch. She'd figured that once she was in bed tonight, trying to fall asleep in the dark, all she would be able to think about was the stalker and…(*that shape, that oily, black shape*)…and whatever happened at the end, but instead, Susan found her mind turning to Davis again.

Which was both comforting and upsetting.

She couldn't help wondering how her life might be different if she hadn't left. But really, she'd had no choice. If things had been progressing slowly in their relationship before she and Davis starting getting known in the industry, they'd come to a grinding halt afterward.

In all fairness, he *had* popped the question—that spur-of-the-moment proposal in a dank warehouse after they'd put an end to Torsten Gross—but the subject had never come up again, she certainly didn't get a ring, and pretty soon the few times they saw one another every month they were actually going out of their way not to mention anything having remotely to do with weddings. It'd been no way to live.

Then take a look at the asshole sharing your bed tonight and tell me if that's any better.

Susan did just that, and caught sight of the medallion again on Killam's chest. She reached out and gently lifted it. Even squinting, it was too dark in here to really see, but her fingertips detected faint lines etched into the metal.

She felt around on its back. She couldn't get the chain over Killam's head without waking him, but perhaps… There. A clasp. She undid the medallion from the chain, slid out of bed and into a pair of shorts and t-shirt from the closet, then padded silently downstairs to her office with the coin clutched in her hand.

This room was just as dark until she turned on a lamp in the corner beside her computer. She pulled her hair up so it wouldn't get it in her eyes and held the medallion under the light. The metal was smooth and clean, no scuffs or nicks, like a freshly minted coin. The design etched onto its otherwise unblemished surface was a simple geometric outline of two isosceles triangles, one slightly above and to the left of the other, so that its lower right corner jutted into the leftmost side of its twin. But beneath them sat another shape even more curious: a long diamond with two curved horns jutting out from either side.

She frowned. Why would Samuel Cordero insist that his old college roommate wear something like this?

Her computer was already booted up. She placed the medallion on the scanner and made a quick PDF copy to her desktop. Then she opened up her email. She would need help with this, *discreet* help, and, even though she didn't know if she could exactly trust him, there was really only one person she could think of that might have the resources. After tracking down the email address, Susan fired off a message with a quick description of the situation and got a reply back almost immediately that requested a breakfast meeting near the studio. She'd have to get rid of Killam first, but she typed back an agreement.

As she hit the send key, she realized the room had gotten darker around her.

Susan spun in her office chair. The solitary bulb in the lamp next to her grew slowly dimmer, like the last embers of a dying fire. Just like in the back hallway of the soundstage, when she'd watched Cordero and Killam's private meeting. The shadows in the room seemed to reach for her as they got thicker.

A memory swam up through the fog in her brain. The creature that had saved her from the stalker tonight. A thing like darkness come to life. She could only recall bits and pieces of it, not enough to know if the blow to her head had made her imagine it. A sense of familiarity came to her this time, and she was clearheaded enough to recall where she'd seen something like it before.

Gross. When he'd melted to black goo at the very end.

A warm breeze whispered against the skin of her bare neck. Every hair there stood up.

She could feel a presence in the room with her. Watching. Waiting.

"*Susaaaan!*"

The shriek came from her bedroom. Killam.

She snatched up the coin from the desk next to her computer. As soon as she touched it, the lamp bulb snapped back to full strength, banishing the shadows. She lurched out of the chair and ran upstairs for the bedroom.

Killam stood naked in the middle of her bed, pressed against the headboard in absolute terror, one hand gripping the empty chain around his neck and the other wielding her bedside table lamp like a weapon. He gripped the glass base in one fist and used the lampshade to concentrate the light on the empty, dark corners of the room.

"What is it, what's wrong?" She did a quick look around herself, scared of what she might find.

"My medallion, where is it?" he demanded frantically, flaccid penis flopping. "*Where is it?*"

"There." She came forward quickly, bent, and pretended to pick up the metal disk from the carpet. "It must've fallen off while you were asleep."

He snatched it from her. Once in his hand, he gave a sigh of relief and sank to his knees on the mattress, then cast one more glance around, as though he expected to be jumped any second. He slowly set the lamp back on the table. "Sorry. I…I have night t-terrors," he stammered.

She pointed at the medallion as he fastened it back to the chain. "What is that thing, anyway?"

"It's nothing," he snapped. "Just…something my mother gave me. The dreams are worse without it."

Even if she hadn't known he was lying, that would still have sounded ridiculous. She studied him in the light from the lamp, watched beads of sweat roll down his lean jaw. This was utterly unlike his usual smarmy demeanor. Without warning, he jumped up and started pulling on clothes.

"I have to go. I can come back to get you in the morning if you want, take you to get your car."

"No, that's all right. I'll call a cab."

She followed him as he hurried through the house toward the front door. Then he stopped and grabbed her hand.

"I like you, Susan," he said.

"I…like you too, Dwight." Great, now *she* was lying.

"I may have to leave on a…a, uh, business trip soon, take a flight. I'd like you to come with me."

"Aren't we supposed to start shooting the movie next week?"

He waved a hand. "Yes, yes, we'll work it into the schedule. Now will you go?"

"I don't know, Dwight. Where is this trip to?"

"I'll explain everything soon." He leaned forward, gave her a sloppy kiss on the cheek, and then hurried out to his car in the driveway, a cherry red Challenger whose throaty V8 growl made her teeth vibrate. She waited in the door as he drove through the massive front gates of the house, suddenly scared to face the darkness of her house alone. That was when she noticed the black sedan parked on the far side of the street.

She couldn't be sure, but she thought there were two men sitting inside, watching through the tinted windows.

SCENE IV

(cut)

TAKE 1

Susan's attack led the news the following morning, beating out even Isaac Crosby's suicide. Her stalker had been identified as 42-year-old Margaret West from Sarasota, Florida, accompanied by a mug shot that must have been taken at a much younger age. But that spark of insanity could still be seen in the large woman's eyes.

A cab honked from the front gate before the story ended, while she was still on a conference call with her agent and publicist deciding how to spin the attack, and Susan punched the button to let the driver in. A few reporters waited out there also, the bloodhound types that had already tracked down where she lived, but she pulled the brim of a ball cap down low over her face as the cab circled her curved driveway and drove back through them. Her breakfast meeting was close to where the attack happened, so she had the driver drop her next to her SUV instead of at the restaurant.

The yellow police tape had been taken down, the body removed. Nothing at all remained to indicate a human being had died here just twelve hours before. Susan felt bad about that fact, even if the human being in question had surely meant to kill her.

But seeing the corner again, even in broad daylight, brought together a few more pieces of her fragmented memory. Margaret West had come from the alley across the street, gotten her on the pavement, and then that black shape—the one that had looked like Torsten Gross after his Wicked Witch of the West impression—had come from under her car to intervene. As she approached the Mercedes, Susan glanced around to make sure the street was empty, then got down on her hands and knees and examined the vehicle's undercarriage. Nothing looked out of place.

Even though it had saved her, Susan still shivered when she thought about the flowing darkness, the way it changed its shape. Was it connected to the presence she'd sensed in her living room last night, as the shadows grew fat and thick around her?

God, she felt completely paranoid, like a child imagining monsters in every closet and corner.

Then she thought about the way Killam had acted last night, standing on her bed with his dick flopping and screaming like a little girl as he searched the shadows.

After checking the seats in her car—and under them—she drove a few blocks away, to a quaint bistro with a fenced-in outdoor patio. At the farthest table to the left, she spotted the man she'd come here to see.

"You understand, this is all completely off the record," Susan said, as she lowered herself into the chair opposite Sidney Spitzen. "I'm coming to you as a friend. We never even had this conversation. Agreed?"

"You got it," he assured her. "I'm just happy to help." She hadn't seen the reporter since the night he'd saved their lives in Gross's old warehouse, by pretending to be one of the director's soulless zombies and then turning his own cameras against him. Based on all the blabbing he'd done since, he wouldn't have been her first choice to help with something like this, but Davis had remained fervent in his belief that Spitzen was a good guy. He looked more disheveled than she remembered, with his bent glasses, filthy jeans, and a stained Foster the People t-shirt with a ripped blazer over it.

The waitress—a teenager no older than seventeen—brought them coffee, recognized Susan even with the hat and sunglasses, made a big deal of asking if she was all right, and then blushingly told her how much she'd loved her last movie. After casually mentioning that she, too, was a struggling actress, she disappeared to leave the two of them alone.

"Why did she ask if you were all right?"

"I was attacked by a stalker last night. It's all over the news, so I'll probably be answering that question all day." She rushed to change the subject, and not just because it made her uncomfortable. Now that she'd been recognized, it was only a matter of time before the media showed up, and the paparazzi would probably be here even quicker. "Davis said you came to see him the other day. About Tonya."

He nodded. "I'm still looking into it, getting what information I can from the police."

"Do they know anything at all?"

"Nada, other than the fact that she was killed quick and brutal."

"You told Davis...that her murder could have something to do with Gross. Do you still believe that?"

Spitzen took off his glasses and cleaned them as the waitress brought their food. "I wanna say yes, but honestly, I don't see how it could. He's been dead four years, and if it's not Lars Krieg..."

"How sure are you about that?"

He squinted at her. "That Gross is dead, or that it's not Lars Krieg?"

"Either. I mean, I understand you know just as little as I do about Gross, but did you actually *see* Krieg?"

"Well, no, I just talked to his doctor. The guy's been a drooling idiot since that night."

"It could still have been someone else though, taking revenge on Gross's behalf." She thought of West as she sipped her steaming coffee, and those deep, bloody slashes on her breasts. "Maybe some insane fan."

The reporter shrugged. "Could be. What's this about, Susan? I thought this had to do with Dwight Killam, the director."

"It does." She gave him a brief rundown of only the relevant events, skimping on the details of how she'd gotten the scan and completely skipping over her newfound fear of shadows. It would be much better to stay focused on the problem at hand. When she got to the part about the medallion, she said, "So anyway, I don't know if I'm making more out of it than I should. It's just that Dwight…he looked terrified at the prospect of losing this thing. I wanna know what it is, and you were the only person I could think of that might have the resources. I could pay you for your time, if you wanted." Susan pulled out the printed copy of her scan and watched as Spitzen's eyes grew huge.

"Jesus Christ." He snatched the paper away and held it under his nose.

"What is it?"

He spoke without looking up. "Davis didn't tell you, did he?"

"Tell me what?"

"The police are keeping one detail about Tonya's murder quiet. I'm presuming it's to help with suspect identification, copycats, that sort of thing. After she was murdered, the killer burned an emblem onto her forehead." He held up the sheet of paper with the copy. "*This* emblem."

Fear chilled the hot coffee in her stomach. "I don't get it."

Spitzen's voice grew excited. "If you're right about where this came from, you just connected Killam and this other guy—what's his name, Cordero?—to Tonya's death! We have to get this to the cops!"

"Wait, no!" She reached out for the paper, but he held it away. "That's not why I came to you, I just wanted to find out what it meant!"

"But this is a solid lead!"

She paused, searching for words. "Spitzen, it's a delicate situtaion. I'm...working with Dwight on a project, and Cordero is VP of Operations for the studio. We can't just start accusing them of murder. Why would they want to kill Tonya Werdner anyway?"

"I'm not saying they would, but they're our best shot right now at finding out who did! And this Killam guy, he's no saint, trust me. I did some digging after you sent me the email last night. Rumor has it he owes a ton of money to various *charitable organizations* around town. The kind that break legs instead of charging late fees."

For the first time, Susan thought about the black sedan parked across the street from her house when the director left. She'd been about to call the police to come check it out, but it drove away soon after Killam did, leaving her to believe it was more of her jumpy imagination.

Spitzen said, "Look, you show this to the cops, tell them what you know, it's probable cause to start investigating these two. What more do you need to think about?"

"I'm sorry." The apology made her feel craven and low. "I just can't until we're sure."

He threw up his hands, then flicked the paper. "Then at least let me take this. I've got a guy already researching the symbol. Maybe this will help."

"All right. If you find something concrete, I'll reconsider."

He threw money on the table for the food he never touched and slid out of his seat so fast it nearly tipped over. She called after him before he could leave the bistro's patio.

"Spitzen…just keep your eyes open, okay?"

He grinned and shoved hair off his brow. "Always do."

TAKE 2

The mood on the *Killing Blow* set Tuesday was grim and dour. They were scheduled to film some intimate scenes between John Harper and his wife, but everyone remained distracted by Sir Isaac Crosby's death. They avoided the dressing room where he'd died as if his ghost could come screaming out at any time. Baxter Devlin made a brief personal appearance to tell everyone the actor's funeral would be in England, but gave an address where they could send flowers. After directing Mahoney and Heady through a few stiff, stilted scenes, Davis called a break.

Scott confronted him before he could even get out of his chair. "Sir, can we talk?"

"Not if it's about yesterday."

"Okay then, it's about tonight."

"What about it?"

"I want us all to meet to talk about yesterday."

Davis scowled and slid past him. "That's not funny, kid."

He tried to walk away, and found Jared penning him in

from the other side. "Would you just for once listen to what someone else has to say, you stubborn bastard?"

"Jared, you and I have way more important matters on our plate right now. I ran into our friendly neighborhood detective again last night."

"Alvarez? Where at?"

"You heard about Susan's attack, right? I got to the scene just after it happened, and he was investigating."

"Whoa, you were there? Is she okay?"

"She's fine. But Alvarez grilled me like a sirloin. He's convinced all of this—Werdner, Crosby, even Susan's stalker—are connected to us somehow. We need to sit down and get our stories straight."

"That's part of what tonight's about."

"We're going to meet at my place around eight, sir," Scott chimed in. "Just to go over all the strange stuff that's been happening. Try to make sense of it."

"And you think having a little support group is the way to do that? What'll we call it, Paranormals Anonymous?"

"Whether you believe it or not, something *is* happening here, Davis," Heady said, as she walked over to join them.

"So now you're involved in this too?"

"She knows everything," Jared said. "I told her the whole story."

"Then maybe we should invite the rest of the crew, huh? They might be *in danger* too. What do you think, Scott, you got room for about fifty people?"

His sarcasm went unanswered until Jared told him, "We're gonna do this with or without you."

"C'mon, admit it Davis," Heady added. "After yesterday, you need answers just as much as we do. You seem as jittery as a cocaine overdose this morning."

"I am not…" He trailed as he looked over her shoulder.

Across the room, in the midst of the Harper household set, a gaunt Hispanic man in overalls crept through the partially-constructed living room where Heady would eventually film the abduction scene. He turned in slow circles, holding a cell phone camera in front of his face.

"HEY!" Davis shouted. The man lowered the camera and looked toward him with obvious fear and guilt. He started to back away.

Davis pushed past Heady and charged him. At the last second, the guy tried to run. Davis tackled him, throwing a shoulder into his back and driving him into the wall of the set. He stumbled, fell to one knee, then Davis threw him to the ground and sat on his stomach.

"*I caught you red-handed, motherfucker!*" he shouted gleefully. "You're outta here, you're done, you're never working in this town again!"

The man beneath him jabbered fearfully in Spanish. Everyone on the soundstage stared.

"What the hell, Davis?" Jared demanded as he caught up.

"It's the spy, Jared, I got him!"

"That's just Paco! He's on the set construction crew!"

"Then why was he taking pictures?"

"No, no peectures," Paco insisted breathlessly. "Only measure, Meester Davis, only measure!"

Jared looked around, retrieved the device Davis had taken for a camera, and held it up. "It's a laser rangefinder, for chrissake."

Behind him, Davis heard Heady snicker. "Cool as a cucumber there, Lowe."

He climbed off Paco and helped the man to his feet. The foreman scurried away.

"That's a lawsuit just waiting to happen," Jared mumbled. "Let me put it this way, douchebag; we can do this at Scott's place tonight, in private, or in front of everyone right here."

Davis looked around at them. "If it will shut you three up once and for all, I'll come."

TAKE 3

The construction crews had finished turning the *Persuasion* set into the Gothic Bath mansion that would serve as Anne Elliot's base of operations for her vampire hunting, a conglomeration of interconnected rooms that didn't follow any sort of logic, one door leading from a lavishly decorated sitting room, the next to a grimy back alley replica where Elliot and Captain Frederick Wentworth—played by a Broadway actor almost young enough to be Susan's son—would share their first kiss after dispatching a bloodsucker.

God, now that she thought about it, this script really was awful.

The set was closed down for now, the last read-through happening tomorrow, followed by light rehearsals until they started shooting next week. Muddy shadows lurked everywhere. She stood at the door for a full two minutes and stared into the gloom, trying to work up the nerve to go in.

Since when are you afraid of the dark?

Since shadows started coming to life, apparently. And that's a pretty damn good reason.

But *should* she be scared? After all, the creature in the alley—assuming it was real—had *rescued* her.

She didn't even know why she'd come here, or what she expected to find, but Spitzen's claims had rattled her. If Killam was somehow involved in Tonya's death, she needed to know. Not just because she was, as of last night, sleeping with the man, but also because she owed it to Werdner to make sure her killer was caught. She just needed to be sure before she screwed herself out of this movie.

Susan wanted to turn on every light before going in, but besides the fact that she needed stealth, she didn't even know where the switches were. Instead, she went back to her car and grabbed the flashlight from her emergency roadside kit and swept the beam back and forth in front of her as she made her way to the director's office at the back of the set. The door was locked, but she bypassed the flimsy lock with a credit card. Only after she'd closed the door did she dare to flip the switch.

Killam's office was mostly bare. He either hadn't moved in yet, or he was one of those directors that didn't use the space the studios provided. She glanced through the window she'd crouched under last time, making sure the dark backstage hall was empty, but kept her distance from the glass. Instead, she rifled through the man's desk. The search turned up a box of condoms, a compact mirror with a vial of coke in it, a baggie of assorted pills of the non-prescription variety...and a loaded revolver. She left them all where they were and exited.

Susan hurried back through the soundstage, feeling disappointed. Some detective she was. Maybe Spitzen had been right, maybe they should go to the police...

A screech echoed off the dark rafters of the warehouse roof.

She froze in the act of crossing a large, tiled ballroom set with a hanging chandelier. Cocked her ears. That noise—a metallic squall like those irritating foley effects they used in the *Elm Street* movies to let the audience know Krueger was around—had sounded very familiar. She shone her flashlight around the large space, looking for the source. Everywhere the beam touched, highly-polished surfaces broke up the light and reflected it in all directions.

Sly footsteps pattered against the slick floor to her left. She spun in that direction. They came again from behind her almost immediately, accompanied by a low chuffing that sounded like a hyena. The feeling of that presence, the one from last night, came roaring back.

And it wasn't her imagination this time.

Susan's blood ran cold. She would focus her attention one place, only to hear noises or see a dark flutter of movement somewhere else. Never anything there except shadows, shadows that were scattered and driven back by her flashlight but surged in again when she swung toward the next disturbance. The darkness thickened, pressed in on her until she couldn't breath, until she could practically feel it caressing her all over.

Then the bulb in her flashlight dimmed, just like the lamp at her house, and the one on the street.

Fear overcame her. She ran before it could lock her up, dropping the useless flashlight and stumbling over set pieces in the dark, barking her shin on a fake Victorian era footstool. Something gave chase as she fled through the rooms, she could hear its footfalls. She headed toward the door out of the soundstage, visible only by the sunlight around its edges. Susan shoved through, and, blinded by the afternoon rays, ran into someone on the other side.

Rough hands grabbed her shoulders. "Susan? What're you doing here, what's wrong?"

She blinked to clear her eyes. Killam stood in front of her, and towering over his shoulder was a larger man with a shaved head, wearing a one-piece track suit unzipped almost to his chest. "I…I don't know, I…was looking for you, and…"

The director released her and backed away, looking from her to the door behind her with wide, fearful eyes. One hand went to his chest and began to massage the area where that medallion would be beneath his shirt. "W-what did you see? What was it?"

He knows, Susan thought, with absolute certainty.

Susan's gaze drifted to the other man. He was a big bruiser, face pitted and scarred, mouth set in a dead line. His open track suit revealed a rack of muscle covered in coarse, wiry black fur. Intimidating, but not nearly as bad as Lars Krieg had been. "Nothing. It was nothing. Just…creeping myself out in the dark."

The bald guy put a meaty hand on Killam's shoulder. Susan saw his fingers dig in. "I am thinking you said this would be a nice, private place to talk, Dwight." His words were tinged with foreign accent. Russian, she thought.

"No, no, not in there!" Killam exclaimed. He still attempted to back away from the door, but was stopped by the large body behind him. "I forgot, we can't go in there, let's just…let's stay out here!"

The Russian seemed on the verge of answering, but instead he looked at Susan and squinted suspiciously. His brow looked like a slab of concrete. "To be holding on one second. You…you are the actress Susan Campbell, correct?"

"Um…yeah," she answered hesitantly.

He held the frown a moment longer, then broke out in a huge grin that completely transformed his menacing face. He bent over and slapped his thighs in excitement. "Incredible! My wife is thinking you are the greatest! Would be okay to ask for autograph?"

"Oh. Yes! Yes, of course!"

She ended up signing a gas station receipt from his back pocket while he jabbered about what big fans he and his wife were. When she handed him back the autograph, he admired it with a huge grin and then clapped Killam on the back hard enough to make him stumble. "Tell you what, Dwight, today your lucky day. We have that talk later, yes?"

"Sure Frankie, absolutely, but really, we're not gonna have to, I'll have it to you before Friday, I promise!"

'Frankie' nodded and walked away, still looking down at Susan's scrawled signature. She would never understand people's fascination with owning another person's name. Killam watched him go, panting for breath.

"Jesus Dwight," she said. "What are you involved in?"

"I'm not *involved*. I just...owe him some money."

"And do you have it?"

He swallowed before answering. For the first time, she realized he still wore the same shirt and pants from last night, now wrinkled and sweat-stained, his hair a mess. "Not exactly."

"Is that what your 'business trip' is about? For god's sake, are you skipping town?"

"Yes," he answered plainly, then gave her a hopeful look. "Will you come with me?"

"How can I? How can *you*? We have a movie to film in just a few days!"

"Oh grow up, Susan! There is no movie!" He gave a hoarse, strangled laugh. "Did you really think I planned on filming that joke of a script?"

She pointed at the soundstage door beside them. "There's a fully constructed set in there that seems to indicate you were."

"I just had that built to buy some time while I drained the accounts the studio funded! But it wasn't enough, and that fucker Devlin wouldn't pony up any more! There's just enough left for me to get the hell out of L.A.!"

Susan squeezed her eyes shut. The conversation she'd overhead with Cordero suddenly made perfect sense. Did that mean the executive—Killam's old college buddy—knew what he'd been up to? He probably wouldn't have told her if he wasn't so obviously terrified of leaving alone. "Christ. What've you done?"

"I don't *knoooow*," Killam moaned. He bunched his hands into fists and flailed them around like a five-year-old. "God, my career is over!"

"Well, mine isn't," she said.

"Fine!" His eyes blazed as he looked at her. "Who needs you? Pussy's cheap, and you certainly weren't a world class lay!"

Killam walked away, but she ran after him. She couldn't let him get away, not before she had answers. "Wait Dwight, tell me what you're so afraid of in there! What are those... those shadows...and what do they have to do with that necklace you wear?"

"You saw them? You actually...*saw* them?" His face went utterly pale, as drained of blood as the vampire victims in the movie they were apparently no longer making. "Oh God, you've drawn their attention. It's my fault. I probably brought them to you. But they'll go away, once they see you're no threat."

"A threat to *what*? Dwight...what are they?"

"Santa's little helpers. Come to decide if you're naughty or nice." Killam gave another high-pitched, manic laugh and then sang, "*They see you when you're sleeping, they know when you're awake...*" She was on the verge of slapping him when he grabbed her arms and squeezed. "I'll explain everything, I swear. Just not yet. I have to tie up some loose ends. I'll come by your place tomorrow, about noon. We'll talk and then, if you wanna go, we'll just leave. All right?"

"All right," she lied. She would meet him, play the supportive love interest a little longer, but as soon as she got the answers she needed, she intended to be on the phone to the cops. "What should I do until then?"

"As long as you go on like nothing's wrong, you should be fine."

"And...if I'm *not* fine?"

Killam paused, eyes roaming past her as if deep in thought. His voice became dreamy as he said, "They come from the shadows, Susan...but they're also *made* of shadows. You see? They need darkness, and the more they have, the stronger they are. And if there isn't any darkness, they'll find a way to make some." Her breath caught as his attention refocused on her. "Just try to stay in the light."

He bent forward and brushed his lips against hers, then released her. This time, she let him walk away.

As she went in the other direction, toward her car, her cell phone rang in her pocket with a number she didn't recognize.

Susan listened to what the person on the other end had to say, and agreed.

TAKE 4

Spitzen timed his arrival to Wollenczak's shop in Lincoln Village for as close to the end of the day as possible, but well before the stubby computer repairman shuttered the place up for the night. Once Wollenczak turned the lock, he didn't let *anyone* in.

Tech Superior festered in a mostly black neighborhood, in the middle of a string of run-down or abandoned shops and a nightclub on the corner that was the most active establishment for blocks after nine P.M. When Spitzen parked across the street, the neon houselights were already up, but the club looked empty. He expected to be gone long before the clientele showed up. The sun had just slipped below the horizon as Spitzen strolled up the empty sidewalk and met Wollenczak at the door.

"Coulda just called, ya know." The man wore a pair of gray mechanic coveralls, stained at the crotch with what Spitzen sincerely hoped wasn't piss. "Wouldn'ta wasted the gas to have me tell ya I ain't got shit."

"Then I wouldn't get to see your pretty face, Wolly."

Spitzen slid by the man, whose balding head barely came up to his chest. The shop was nothing but an indoor computer junkyard, a dim cave of burnt out parts and motherboards, with a few reconditioned models against one wall that probably couldn't do much more than word process.

But you didn't really come to Wollenczak for used PCs or service on your Commodore 64. He'd gained a reputation as a man who could find things in the online world, both tangible and intangible. Spitzen had used him for research on several stories, but he knew the grubby Pollack dabbled in everything from light weapons trafficking to rare eBay auctions.

Wollenczak led the way through the shop to his counter at the back. Spitzen leaned against the filthy register and asked, "So I take it you haven't found anything at all?"

"You mean from your little chicken scratch drawing? No, I ain't found jack." Wollenczak came around behind the counter and climbed onto a stool high enough to make him look normal height. "Could be a flag, could be a family crest, could be a goddamn company logo. Got a guy in D.C. thinks it looks like something they used to stamp on copper bricks back in the 80's. Google don't exactly have a search function for shit like this, and it don't help that you won't say where it came from or what it relates to."

"I told you, it's sensitive."

"Yeah, right. Which means it prob'ly has to do with your goddamn Martians." Wollenczak gave a laugh that sounded like a strangled cat. "Look Spitzen, unless you can gimme somethin else, I'm dead in the water here."

"What about this?" Spitzen pulled out the printed scan Susan had given him this morning and smoothed it out flat against the countertop.

Wollenczak lifted his thick glasses and leaned so close his nose almost touched the paper. "'Zat a coin?"

"Medallion. Worn on a necklace. This should be accurate size."

The other man grunted. "No identifying marks, just the symbol. Not too much more detailed than your drawing. Might help if I had the real thing."

"That's not possible at the moment. But I do have two names for you to cross-reference, as discreetly as possible. Samuel Cordero and Dwight Killam."

"Killam? As in the director?" Wollenczak scratched the back of his neck. "You see that flick he did about the two guys robbin the bank and it turns out one of 'em's the devil? Worst two hours I ever spent in a theater."

"Must've missed that one, Wolly."

"All right, hold on a sec, let me do some checkin. Be right back."

Wollenczak hopped off the stool and went through a door behind the counter. Spitzen had never been into the back room before, but that's where the magic happened. While he waited, he wandered around the store and daydreamed about how this could put him back on top, if he played it right. All he needed was some solid evidence and he could sell this to any one of ten editors before the cops even had Killam booked. Maybe if he broke a real story, people would start listening to him again.

In a way, Spitzen resented Davis and the others for forcing him to be the sole voice of reason about Torsten Gross. They'd gone on about their lives and careers, not concerned for a second over what Gross' mere existence meant in the larger scheme of things, leaving him to be the laughingstock. But that was human beings for you, so intent on ignoring danger until it was in their face.

His inner rant was broken by a shout from the back of the store that abruptly cut off.

"Wolly?" he called. "You fall off your stool again?"

Spitzen went back to the counter and called out again. No answer.

The last thing he wanted was the man mad at him for invading his privacy, so Spitzen eased to the flimsy door and knocked. When he still got no response, he tried the knob and pushed the door open just a crack to peek inside.

Beyond the threshold lay a pit of darkness, lit only by the soft glow of a Mac desktop model nicer than anything in the showroom, sitting on a desk to the left of the door. The folded paper he'd given Wollenczak sat beside the keyboard, and the screen displayed an email in the midst of being composed. Droplets of a dark red fluid dripped down the monitor's glassy surface.

Spitzen raised a suddenly cold hand and pushed the door the rest of the way open.

His own shadow uncurled in front of him, thrown out long by the grimy fluorescents at his back. The far side of the room harbored a dark so complete, his eyes couldn't penetrate it. But he could see Wollenczak's arm on the floor, sprawled out in the shaft of light from the open door, a puddle of blood beneath. The rest of the man was too obscured by darkness for Spitzen to tell what had happened to him.

Then that darkness *moved*.

Something hunched and low peeled away, revealing Wollenczak as it moved aside. He lay on the floor, eyes stretched in terror, a gaping gash in his throat from which scarlet gushed. A thin pall of smoke drifted from his forehead, where the symbol he'd been researching was now burned into the flesh.

Just like Tonya Werdner.

Spitzen tried to watch the dark shape as it flowed and reformed, but it was too hard to pick out until it came to the edge of the light. A four-legged figure about the size of a German Shepherd regarded him. At least, Spitzen thought it regarded him, for it had no eyes, no features at all. Its entire body was made of some dark, almost liquid substance, like crude oil.

A tortured metal noise drifted out of a hole in its smooth head. The sound was obviously meant to menace, but it made no move to come toward him as he stood in the doorway.

"Gross?" he asked, voice no more than a whisper. "Is that you?"

The creature gave a squeaky chitter, like laughter. It tried to edge closer, but he noticed it was careful to stay out of the frame of light around him.

So he was safe as long as he didn't go any further.

Spitzen tore his gaze away and looked back at the desk, just a few yards to his left. The folder paper sat right on the edge closest to the door.

Before he could talk himself out of it, Spitzen launched out of the square of light and leapt for the desk. The shadowy creature bolted around and raced after him. Something whickered by his neck; Spitzen thought the thing had thrown something at him until he glanced over and saw that the monster had extended part of its body, stretching one leg into a sharp point to spear him.

His hand closed around the paper. Spitzen flung himself away from the desk, back toward the light, narrowly escaping another swipe from a sickle-like appendage. He sprawled on the filthy tile and kept crawling. Only when he reached Wollenczak's counter did he turn and look back.

The creature still there, staring at him. Sudden inspiration struck. Spitzen dug in his pocket, going for his cell phone camera. If it really was Gross, the camera would have the power to banish him. If not…well, he still needed a picture of this thing.

Above him, the lights in the store began to flicker.

He forgot about the cell and scrambled to his feet, hopping over the counter instead of going around. All across the store, the fluorescents shattered one at a time in a shower of sparks, leaving minefields of darkness where black, wispy shapes began to fade into existence, like watching smoke dissipate in reverse.

The store would be entirely dark in seconds.

Spitzen ran, avoiding the shadow patches, dodging and ducking as tentacles of pure darkness reached out for him, one managing to caress the bare skin on the back of his right hand. Its touch was feather light, as intangible as the shadows it came from, but enough to utterly disgust him. He fumbled the lock open on the front door and burst out of Tech Superior, back on to the sidewalk.

No help out here. The night had come, and the street was even darker. The closest light, a high streetlamp on the corner, blew out in a miniature explosion. More of the creatures crept out of the resulting shadows, screeching and hooting.

He ran again. Flew down the street away from them, into the neon embrace of the nightclub. The place was open even though it didn't start jumping for another hour, so he shoved his way through the entrance and leaned against the inside of the door to keep it closed.

A line of booths lay ahead with a few customers that looked up at him as he panted in the doorway, and an empty dance floor through an arch to the right. It was dimmer in here than in Wollenczak's shop, but bright enough to make him feel safe. A DJ booth sat in the corner, unoccupied. A slow R&B song that Spitzen didn't recognize pumped through the house speakers.

Now that he was among people, his rational mind tried to tell him he'd imagined the whole thing. He forced his breathing to slow and stumbled further inside, glancing over his shoulder repeatedly to make sure he wasn't followed.

The bar stood on the far side of the dance floor. He collapsed onto a stool.

"Getcha somethin, white boy?" the bartender asked.

"Shot of scotch, whiskey, whatever."

The man poured him a drink and then retreated through a door at the far end of the bar, giving him one last suspicious glance before disappearing. Spitzen downed the drink, felt it burn his throat, steady his nerves.

The cops. He had to call the cops and report Wollenczak's death, or risk being accused of it. But what the hell would he tell them?

A mirror ran the full length of the bar behind the alcohol bottles and in it, Spitzen could see his pale, sweaty reflection. He caught sight of something white in his own hand and realized he still clutched the scan. He unfolded it and studied the photocopied image of the medallion.

He didn't know if it had anything to do with Torsten Gross, but there was no question now that it was connected to Tonya's murder. Those things had killed Wollenczak to keep him from digging. Probably would've done the same to Spitzen, if they'd caught him. And they had *definitely* wanted the scan. He saw now that the one that touched him as he ran from the shop had been grabbing for the paper.

Only one thing didn't make sense: if they were so eager to claim this evidence and silence anyone that knew about it, why then, had they burned the very same symbol on Wollenczak and Tonya's foreheads? It was like advertising the very secret you didn't want anyone to find out. Hell, that was what started him on this trail in the first place. Well, that and...

A sudden, panicked thought occurred to him.

Susan. If she was still looking for answers, she could be in trouble. He had to warn her.

Behind him, the slow song ended, and the DJ returned to the booth long enough to mutter something about 'kicking it up a notch for you early birds.' An up-tempo dance number started. The house lights pulsed in time with the beat, a slow, disorienting strobe effect.

Light, dark. Light, dark. The second-long cycles in between were so dim he could no longer see the paper. He set it on the bar as he reached for his cell phone, glancing up at the mirror at the same time.

And felt his heart drop into his stomach.

When the house lights came up, they lit the room bright enough to see himself on the barstool, and every stark detail of the empty dance floor behind him.

But every time they went down, his silhouette reflection was surrounded by a group of midnight black figures that stood cold and tall around him.

Spitzen leapt backward off the stool, sending it crashing to the floor. He tried to run across the dance floor, but the lights went down, and he rebounded off a shadowy form that suddenly appeared in front of him. Then the lights came back up and the creature *dimmed*, becoming translucent, as if it had no more consistency than steam. Spitzen tried a different direction. He got a few steps further, but this time, when it got dark again, he was shoved backward by something that didn't feel intangible in the least. He spun in a circle, seeking an opening, but they were everywhere, all around him, herding him into the middle of the dance floor and closing in each time the house lights blinked off. The cycles in between just didn't give enough time for him to escape.

"*HELP!*" he screamed. "*TURN ON THE LIGHTS!*"

Something plunged into his stomach. Spitzen looked down to find one of their black appendages impaling him. When the room brightened, it vanished, leaving him with a hole through his torso. He cradled the wound, had time to see a splash of brilliant red before being dropped into the dark again.

This time, they all came for him. Light, dark. A slash, a jab. Light, dark. A slice here, a stab there. They took turns batting at him, like a group of cats with a mouse, waiting through each cycle to continue tearing him apart. Luckily, shock set in, and he didn't feel anything until a sudden searing pain burned across his forehead.

A few seconds later, Sidney Spitzen hit the dance floor in a bloody heap just as the bartender and a few of the other nightclub patrons came running.

TAKE 5

Scott's place was a quaint two-bedroom in Arcadia, located on a street that looked entirely too happy and wholesome to be part of the L.A. basin. If Davis remembered correctly, the city had been named one of the top 10 places in the country to raise children, and, as he drove by a gaggle of kids of all colors playing kickball in the street, he understood why. This was the kind of place he'd always imagined himself and Susan living when they got around to raising a family.

That thought sent a pang of longing through his chest.

He parked at the curb behind a line of cars that included Jared's Range Rover and several other vehicles he didn't recognize, then walked to the house. When he knocked, the door was answered by a bone thin, completely bald man in a robe and slippers. Thin plastic tubing circled his head just under his nose. A huge grin spread across his face as he looked out on the porch.

"My god, wow! I can't believe it, Davis Lowe on *my* doorstep! Please, excuse the robe. I wanted to dress up to meet you, but..." He waved an embarrassed hand at the tubes in his nostrils. "These things kind of clash with all my suits."

"Not a problem," Davis said, instantly charmed. He offered his own hand. "You must be Scott's father."

"Charlie Meyer." The other man pumped enthusiastically, but the grip felt weak. His skin had a pale yellow tint to it except under his eyes, where the hollows were practically purple. Davis couldn't help but wonder how long a man this sick had left in the world. "Scott made me watch that direct-to-video movie you did about the construction foreman and the monster in the woods! Scared the hell outta me!"

"If that's a good thing, then thanks, thanks a lot."

"No, thank *you*, Mr. Lowe! This opportunity to work for you means so much to Scott! That's all I hear anymore, about how he wants to save up and go to film school next year so he can be a director like you!"

"Dad!" Scott's voice scolded from deeper in the house. "Would you let him in and stop bothering everybody?"

Charlie Meyer dropped a wink and shuffled aside to allow Davis past into a quaint living space. Scott leaned out of a set of sliding double doors at the back of the room and beckoned to him. "C'mon sir, everybody's back this way."

Davis walked through the doors and into a secondary den-slash-gameroom, where a couch, loveseat, and a couple of recliners had been arranged around a low coffee table. Behind the couch sat a rolling dry erase board on which had been drawn a grid with the days of the week labeled at the top. Scott perched on one end of the couch, while Jared and Heady cuddled up in the loveseat with two glasses of red wine in front of them. And, in the recliner to the left…

"What is *he* doing here?" Davis demanded.

"Me?" Derek Mahoney asked. "Mr. Mane told me I should come."

"This involves him too, Davis," Jared said evenly.

"No, it doesn't! You're just spreading panic!"

"Panic keeps you on your toes. Denial doesn't."

"I'm real sorry, Mr. Lowe." Mahoney's chiseled face fell. "If you don't want me here, I'll go."

"No, it's not that, Big D. You've been through a lot, and I just don't want you getting distracted or worried about any of this. It's bad enough Heady's bought into this madness, but I can't afford to have both my stars off their game."

"But I'm fine! I really am! And I wanna help if I can!"

"All right. By all means, stay so we can tell ghost stories around the campfire." Davis sank onto the couch next to Scott. "Anybody bring stuff for s'mores?"

As if on cue, Charlie Meyer came into the room with a tray and set it on the table. "Thought everybody could use some snacks!"

"Oh, dude, pizza rolls!" Mahoney leaned forward and began to load food onto a napkin.

Charlie beamed. "I just can't tell you how exciting it is to have all these celebrities under our roof! When Scott told me you wanted to have a meeting about the movie here, I just about died!" He seemed to rethink his choice of words as soon as they were out. Charlie coughed and amended, "Well, Scott's mother really would've flipped."

"Dad, we need privacy, and you have to take your medication." Scott leapt off the couch, led his father back into the living room, and forced him into a recliner in front of the TV. Davis watched as he gave the man pills and water, then turned the television to a local station playing sitcom reruns. He gave his father a gentle kiss on the top of his bald head, then came back into the room and slid the doors shut. "I think we should wait just a little bit longer before we start."

"Why?" Davis asked. "I wanna get this over with. What do I do, stand up and say, 'My name is Davis Lowe, and I'm a Torsten Gross survivor?'"

"Real funny." Jared freed his arm from behind Heady's shoulders so he could lean forward. "You know what, if it makes you feel any better, I say we ban that name from the conversation entirely, and just stick to the facts."

"Suits me."

"And use the board!" Mahoney added with his mouth full of microwave snacks. "I drew the grid!"

"Okay, the facts." Davis reached over the back of the couch and tapped a marker in the Sunday column. "On Sunday morning, Jared and Big D filmed a scene—"

"That's not where it starts," Heady interrupted. "It starts with Tonya Werdner, last week."

"Does it? Does it really? Maybe we're drawing lines between the dots where there shouldn't be any. We don't know for sure if any of these things are connected."

Scott raised a finger politely from his position by the door. "But Detective Alvarez believes so, doesn't he?"

"Only because Jared and I are the common denominators, and we know we didn't have anything to do with any of it."

"Doesn't matter." Jared waved the argument away. "If it's weird, it goes on the list."

"All right. Tonya Werdner gets murdered on the Apex Studio lot Friday night. The police don't know who did it, but they're looking to us because of Gr...because of our past association with a certain German horror director. So now we jump to Sunday—"

"The symbol," Jared reminded him.

"Do you wanna tell this?"

"Yeah, I do." Jared stood up, took the marker from Davis, and crudely redrew the symbol Spitzen had shown them in the Friday column. It was the first time Davis had seen it since the day the reporter came to them. That distant bell of recognition went off again, far back in the corner of his mind. "Werdner's killer burns this symbol onto her forehead. Does it mean anything to anybody?" They all shook their heads. Davis remained silent; the déjà vu was just too vague for him to explain to anyone, even himself. "Then, on Sunday, Davis goes to arbitration with Crosby, so Derek and I film the car chase scene. Derek has an accident that, by all rights, should've killed him—"

"Thanks to your negligence," Davis mumbled.

"—but he's saved by some kind of black tentacles that function as very effective airbags," Jared finished, ignoring him.

"Mr. Mane showed me the footage of the crash," Mahoney said.

"Me too." Heady shivered. "Gave me the creeps."

"Those things...I felt them, like I said at the hospital. It just happened so fast, I didn't really understand it until I saw the tape, but then it made total sense." Mahoney frowned as he relived the memory. "Ugh, I can still remember how nasty those things were. Crawling all over me...wrapping me up..."

Davis held out a hand to the musclebound actor. "But they saved your life, Big D. Maybe you should just be thankful and not question it." Mahoney shrugged and reached for more food.

Jared kept scribbling phrases on the board. "Yesterday, Isaac Crosby commits suicide on the set, after filming all of his scenes. We don't know any more about that either, so we'll move on for the moment."

"That's not exactly true though," Scott said quietly.

"What do you mean?"

Scott gave Davis a pointed look that was mature beyond his years. "This only works if we're all honest, sir."

Now they all looked at him, but Jared's gaze was the heaviest. Davis sighed. "Crosby left a suicide note."

Heady gasped. "What did it say?"

"Oh shit, he didn't do it because of me, did he?" Mahoney asked fearfully.

"No, not because of you." Davis told them about the note's cryptic message.

"Why didn't you give it to the cops?" Jared's voice was even and uninflected, but the question still sounded accusatory.

"How could I? It essentially blames me. That detective already suspects I had something to do with it. And he told me last night he thinks someone was blackmailing Crosby."

"Blackmailing him for what?"

"No idea. But even I have to admit, the limey old fuck did seem awfully eager to come back to work all of a sudden. As if someone put some serious pressure on him to finish filming. When you add in the suicide note, it looks like he believed I was the one doing the blackmailing."

"This is good stuff." Jared snapped his fingers and Davis twisted around to look at him. "We need to get Spitzen working on this, see if he can dig anything up. Shit, we should've had him here for this!"

"Spitzen's already got an assignment," a new voice said.

Davis turned back around to find Susan standing in between the sliding doors.

TAKE 6

For a moment, they all just gaped at her like a zoo exhibit. Then Davis asked, "How did you know...?"

"I called her," Scott said. "I got the number from your cell phone. When you mentioned that her attack might be part of this, I thought she should be here."

From the awestruck grin that spread across his face, Susan didn't think he minded at all.

"Sorry I'm late. Your dad let me in." She gave a little wave. "Hi everybody."

"Jesus, Susan, it's...it's great to see you." Jared came forward, gave her a hug and a peck on the cheek.

"You too, Jared. Sorry I didn't keep in touch."

"No big deal, I know how it is. You guys split up, and ol' dumbass here got me in the separation."

She met Scott next, who was even younger than he'd sounded on the phone this afternoon, and he introduced her to fellow movie stars Heady Tillman and Derek Mahoney. Mahoney was a new experience, not at all as cool and confident—or intelligent—as the action hero he played, but she'd met Heady before, briefly, at a charity auction last year.

Finally, Davis stood and gave her an awkward embrace that, for the barest of heartbeats, she actually wanted to last longer than it did. "You all right? Head better?"

She touched her chin, where all she had left was a tiny bruise on the underside. "A little sore, but not too bad. Did I miss much?"

Jared shook his head. "You have good timing. We were just getting ready to talk about your attack last night."

"What were you saying about Spitzen?" Davis asked.

She sank down into the recliner across from Mahoney, next to Heady Tillman. "I met with him this morning to get him to research something for me. Turns out, he was already looking into it."

"What?"

Susan pointed at the dry erase board behind Davis. "That symbol. The one burned onto Tonya's body."

"You've seen it somewhere else," Heady deduced.

"Oh yeah, you could say I've run across it." Susan began to talk, and didn't stop for nearly a half hour. She told them everything, the entire story of her last few days, without holding anything back: Killam and Cordero's clandestine meeting, her stalker's attack and the black shape that rescued her, getting the medallion from Killam and his reaction, meeting Spitzen with the scan, and lastly, her encounter at the set with the ghostly shadows and Killam's admission about them. When she was finished, she found that she felt better for the first time since she'd inked the contract to star in this ridiculous Jane Austen adaptation.

Even so, she sat and waited for them to tell her she was crazy.

"Whoa," Mahoney said in awe, sounding as though he'd graduated from the same acting school as Keanu Reeves.

"Santa's little helpers." Jared murmured the phrase Killam used, as if tasting the words. "But the one you got a good look at last night, on the street, you said it was some sort of black blob, right? Kind of like...Gross?"

Susan studied him. "How do you know that?"

This time, it was their turn to fill her in about the details of Mahoney's car crash. "It sounds like the same thing to me," she confirmed when they were finished. "I'm just glad I'm not the only one that's seen them."

"What the hell are they?" Mahoney asked.

"I don't know. But everything Killam said about them makes sense, to a degree. When that woman went after me, I remember the streetlight shorting out just before that shape came out from under my car. And if it's the same presence I felt in my place last night and on the set this afternoon, they were trying to do the same thing with my lamp and my flashlight. They need darkness to exist, and if there is none, they *make* some." She shook her head. "I just wish I knew what the medallion had to do with them."

Jared performed a short drum roll on the back of the couch next to Davis' head. "But that's our connection! We may not understand how or why, but this medallion ties Tonya's murder and Derek's accident together! It's all part of the same thing!"

"Not Mr. Crosby's suicide though," Scott pointed out.

"Well, no. At least, not that we've seen. There could still be something we're missing."

"One thing doesn't make sense," Heady said, turning to Susan. "You said you felt threatened by these...these *wraiths* this morning. They killed your stalker, and obviously Killam is terrified of them. So if these things are so bad, then why'd they bother saving you and Derek at all? Or better yet, why did they protect you one day and then terrorize you the next?"

Susan shrugged helplessly. "Who knows, maybe they were never trying to protect me in the first place. I'm hoping Killam will be able to answer that tomorrow."

"Spitzen's right," Jared said. "We have to go to the police. All of us, together."

"And you think that will make any difference?" Heady asked him.

"It will when we show them the tape of the accident."

Mahoney squirmed in his chair. "Um, I don't know. I'd need to talk to my agent first."

"What? Why?"

"Cause that sorta thing could turn out to be, like, *mega* bad publicity. My agent told me I'm always supposed to call him before I do anything, even if I just murdered somebody."

"I thought you wanted to help, Big D!"

"I do, I'm just not convinced that's the way to do it. They're not gonna believe us anyway."

"Oh, for fuck's sake, *Dwight Killam is wearing a symbol that was burned onto a murder victim killed at his place of employment.* What more do you need?"

"He's right, Jared." Susan closed her eyes, but the dark behind the lids wasn't soothing in the least. "Yes, this looks bad, but it doesn't prove he's responsible. He could be as innocent as the rest of us. And even if we did go to the cops, all we have is this story. A story that's every bit as insane as the thing with Gross. And you remember how that turned out."

"We have the tape!"

"Sir," Scott said solemnly, "we're Hollywood movie makers. There's nothing on that tape that couldn't be special effects. Would you believe it, if you were them?"

Jared threw up his hands in defeat and slumped on the loveseat next to Heady. Susan was very surprised when the actress began stroking the back of his neck. He nudged Davis's leg with the toe of his shoe. "I can usually expect you to be the naysayer, but you haven't said a word. Where do you fall on this?"

Davis ignored him and looked at Susan, speaking for the first time since she'd finished her story. "So you got this scan of the medallion while Killam was asleep. Asleep, at your place."

Jared groaned. "Not now, Davis."

Susan felt her cheeks burn. She'd tried to tread lightly over this part of the story, but she should've known Davis would sniff it out. "Yeah. He was worried. Didn't want me to be alone after the attack."

"He spent the night on your couch then?"

"Not exactly."

"So then you fucked him?"

The words—and his tone—were a slap in the face. Everyone else in the room found other places to look. "I don't think that's any of your business, Davis."

"But I think it is." He leaned forward, a vicious smirk on his face. "I think it's *all* of our business. You find out the guy could have something to do with a murder, but then you sleep with him?"

"That was before!" she blurted.

"Maybe it was, but how do we know your motive for telling us not to go to the cops isn't just so you can protect your new boyfriend?"

She said through gritted teeth, "Davis, can I talk to you outside for a minute?"

He stood. They opened the sliding doors, stepped through into the living room, and closed them again. She'd been prepared to drag him outside to have this out, but they didn't have to go that far; Scott's pale, emaciated father had passed out in his recliner with his feet propped up, while an old *Family Guy* episode played on the TV.

"What the hell is up with ambushing me like that?" she demanded in hushed tones.

"I just think we deserve answers."

"No, you think *you* deserve answers! But we are not together anymore, Davis! I find it really sad you can't get that through your head after three years!"

He opened his mouth to argue, then snapped it closed. He turned and stalked away from her, but not before she caught a glimpse of the hurt in his eyes. That made her feel guiltier than anything else he'd said.

"I mean, why *Killam*?" he whined. She remembered that voice all too well. "You can't do any better than him? Even if the guy's not a murderer, he's still a sleaze!"

"I know that now, Trust me, he will not be getting a repeat performance."

"Yeah, but don't you feel disgusting? Ashamed?"

"People make mistakes," she said. She decided that she didn't want to fight, didn't want to make this harder for him than it already was. "All I can say is, I'm sorry."

Her answer seemed to throw off his tirade. "I'm sorry too," he said reluctantly. "It really is none of my business, I'm just...worried about you. I don't understand any of this."

"I know, me neither. But until we know we're actually in danger, we can't panic. I mean, Killam said I didn't have anything to worry about, and these shadow things did save Derek and me, so..." She noticed he was standing stiffly, staring away from her, and followed his gaze.

On the TV, Sidney Spitzen's picture stared out at them.

TAKE 7

All six of them emerged from the den to watch the news story together, being quiet so as not to wake Charlie Meyer.

The reporter on the scene told of violence at an L.A. nightclub; not an uncommon occurrence, but made stranger by the fact that it involved the notorious journalist and that a second, as-yet-unidentified body had been discovered in a store down the street. Details were scarce, witness accounts confusing. In the entire club, not one person had seen the killer, but one woman interviewed claimed she'd seen multiple shadows, so it must have been a gang slaying. When the news moved on, they all retreated back into the den in a cloud of shock.

"Spitzen...Jesus," Davis whispered. He thought of his harsh last words to the man, how they'd left things.

"I'm sorry, sir," Scott said reverently.

"Son of a fucking bitch." Jared clinched his fists. "Whoever did this has gotta pay."

"But don't we know who did it?" Mahoney asked. He looked pale to Davis; all of them did, actually. Before, they'd been treating this as a game, a who-dun-it mystery, but news of the reporter's death had made it much more real. "These shadow whatchamacallits...wraiths? Sounds like they killed him."

"But why?" Heady slid back down onto the sofa and hugged her own torso. "They must have some reason for doing all this. What's their agenda?"

"Revenge," Jared answered. "Because this has something to do with Gross. This just proves it."

"It doesn't prove anything," Davis muttered.

"What are you talking about? This is two down, three to go! The coincidences are getting pretty hard to ignore!"

"Yeah, but Spitzen was only killed when he started poking around Tonya's murder! And not even really until he got his hands on..." Davis trailed, tried to stop himself from looking at Susan, but couldn't.

"Go ahead and say it." Susan stared through him, tears gathering at the corners of her eyes. She murmured, "Killam said I'd 'drawn their attention.' He was afraid that he'd passed these wraiths on to me, like a flu bug or something. Maybe that was true, at the beginning, but they must've kept following me because I was poking around about the medallion. So…what if *I* brought them to Spitzen?"

"You didn't." Davis put a reassuring hand on her neck.

"How do you know? God, I could be putting all of you in danger right now by telling you this."

She sat up suddenly and swung her head around, looking at every corner of the room. It was well lit in here, an overhead light and two lamps, but, even so, Davis found himself searching for shadows also before he said, "Don't get paranoid. These things can't be everywhere at once."

"Maybe not everywhere. But if they follow the people they have a reason to watch…" She wiped at one eye. "Anyway, it doesn't matter. It's still my fault."

"But you're forgetting, you didn't tell Spitzen about the symbol. He knew before any of us. If that's what this is really about, then he made himself a target a long time ago."

"Yeah, but I gave him the scan and told him about Killam. Maybe that was all it took for him to know too much."

"Look," Jared interrupted. "This is pointless. I admit, we don't understand how everything fits, so it may not be Gross. But it sounds like we all agree on *why* Spitzen was killed." He tapped the symbol he'd drawn earlier, on one of those curved horns growing from the side of the central diamond. "Everything seems to come back to this. We find out what this means, why it was on Tonya's forehead and Killam's medallion, and I have a feeling everything else will fall into place."

"I intend to get those answers from the good director himself tomorrow," Susan said.

Davis crossed his arms. "Not alone, you're not."

"I have to. He won't talk if someone else is there. Besides, he's not the danger."

"And it's not him I'm worried about," he said, hoping he wasn't too transparent. Her face clouded over, so he figured he'd failed.

"I'll be fine," she huffed.

"Davis, listen to her," Jared said. "We don't have time to mess up our one lead at figuring this out. You know Alvarez is gonna be after you and me for questioning about Spitzen."

"Shit, you're right. Let's get our alibis straight then."

"We were here all night meeting about the movie." Scott pointed through the sliding doors into the living room. "My dad will back us up."

"In that case, maybe we should head Alvarez off at the pass." Jared scratched his chin thoughtfully. "We've been on the run since this whole thing started. Davis, you should go to him before he can come to us."

"What the hell for?"

"To be preemptive. Show him we don't have anything to hide."

"Yeah, but why *me?*"

"You've talked with him the most, you've got a rapport. Maybe you can see if he knows anything else about Spitzen."

Heady interrupted to say, "This all sounds great fellas, but there's still one element of Susan's story we haven't even touched yet."

"Cordero," Susan said softly.

"That's right. If Killam knows what the shadows are, then Cordero must too. In fact, he might even know more. He's the one that gave Killam the medallion, after all."

"The studio did work pretty hard to keep Tonya's murder quiet," Jared agreed. "Maybe he's the reason for that. We should talk to him."

"Hold on, wait." Davis sliced his hands back and forth. "We've been down this road with Reilly, Jared. These studio execs are running their own little kingdoms right here in Hollywood, completely above the law. He'll have us for breakfast."

"Gimme a break. We're not second unit anymore, Davis. We actually have some clout in this town."

"Not against the studios. Nobody wins against them."

"But if Cordero is helping Killam cover up embezzlement, Baxter Devlin might like to know about it."

"We don't even know for sure that's what happened!"

"All right then, let me follow the guy."

"Huh?"

"You don't need me on the set the next couple days. Let me keep tabs on Cordero and see if I can come up with anything."

"I'll go too," Heady volunteered. "I don't have any scenes to shoot until next week."

"Oh, oh, what about me?" Mahoney bounced in the recliner. "Give me an assignment, I've always wanted to play a spy!"

"No, absolutely not. Everyone stays away from Cordero until we have some idea what we're up against. Understood?" Davis waited for each of their agreements—Jared's the most begrudging of all—then said, "And if anyone sees anything weird, any of these wraiths...do what Killam told Susan. Find some light and then call the others."

The meeting began to break up. They filed out, past the sleeping form of Charlie Meyer. Davis took one last look back at the board they'd drawn all over, and Jared stopped next to him.

"There's a pattern," his partner insisted. "We're just not seeing it yet."

"You still think it has to do with Gross?"

"I don't know. But I hope to God it does."

Davis frowned. "Why?"

Jared glanced at him and smirked. "Because, pal o' mine, if it ain't Gross…then that means we're just a fucking magnet for this supernatural shit."

The statement reminded Davis of Alvarez's assertion that crazy seemed to follow them around like a cloud of B.O. It was true though, wasn't it? Four years ago, they'd all lived perfectly normal—albeit anonymous—lives, but now…

Now it was like some curtain had been drawn away from the world, revealing a dark underbelly that most people had never guessed at.

That sense of impending doom slipped over Davis again, both cold and inescapable.

Outside, he caught up with Susan as she got into her car. "Are you gonna be okay tonight?"

"I think so."

"You sure? Cause I could come over to your place. You know, if it would make you feel safer."

She grinned and rolled her eyes. "I ain't 'fraid of no ghosts. Old boyfriends, on the other hand…"

He chuckled, then got serious. "Please…just promise me you'll be careful."

"Of course. You do the same."

They paused, looked at one another. He wanted to drown in her eyes. But he settled for reaching out and pushing hair away from her face.

"I'll call as soon as I know something." Susan got in her car and drove away. Only after she was out of sight did he pick up the pieces of his heart and walk away.

TAKE 8

Susan left Scott's house, but she didn't go home. She knew when she did, she would only be up all night, jumping at shadows and seeing the deranged face of Margaret West. Part of her actually wished she'd taken Davis up on his offer, but if she'd let him come home with her, there was a more than fair chance they would've had sex, and Marianne Campbell just hadn't raised a daughter who was cool with the idea of screwing two different men on consecutive nights.

Even if one of them was the only man she'd ever really, truly been in love with.

Besides, she had something she needed to do, something she'd been contemplating since her conversation with Spitzen this morning, and she thought it might be easier on her own.

So instead of driving back west, to Beverly Hills, she took the 605 south, and headed into Downey.

Toward Conway Sanitarium.

It was close to nine, long after visiting hours, but after calling ahead and convincing them of her identity, an eager doctor named Viraj encouraged her to come. She pulled up in the parking lot of a modern, two-wing hospital with iron bars on all the windows and guards posted at every door. It looked more like a prison than a mental hospital, but she was just thankful it was nothing like the asylum set for *Arterial Slice*.

She didn't know why she'd come here, or what she expected to find. If these wraiths did have anything to do with Torsten Gross, then Lars Krieg—the brutal sidekick left behind when they'd killed his master—was their only remaining connection. They needed to pursue it, even if the idea of seeing that maniac again terrified her.

Inside, she checked in at an admissions desk, got issued a visitor badge, and was buzzed through a set of two interior cell doors. On the other side, Dr. Viraj waited for her, an Indian psychiatrist with dark coffee skin. He walked at a slow pace with her down the brightly lit hospital corridor. The place was empty and quiet at this time of night, but the silence was punctuated every few minutes by a distant howl or burst of muffled laughter.

"I have been Mr. Krieg's doctor since he was remanded here almost four years ago, and, in that time, he has never had a single visitor." The doctor's words were crisp, with the barest hint of an accent. "As far as I've been able to ascertain, he has no family back in Germany, no estate. I was sure the world had forgotten him until I received a strange call from a reporter on Saturday, wanting to know his condition. Now you show up three days later. Has there been some resurgence of interest in his case?"

"Not exactly," she said, choosing her words carefully. "You're aware of what he...did to me?"

He gave a curt nod. "I am extensively familiar with his file."

"Well, everything that happened...it was traumatic. I still have nightmares." In this, at least, she was being honest. "I thought maybe if I saw him again—faced my fears—it might help."

He grinned and nodded eagerly. "That is excellent. I hoped for as much."

His answer jarred her. "Why is that?"

They turned a corner and came to a stop next to a solid white door. Viraj's forehead creased with concern as he spoke. "Frankly, I am out of options with his treatment. In three years, he hasn't spoken, hasn't eaten anything that wasn't intravenous, hasn't even moved on his own. He displays all the signs of someone with extreme prefrontal cortex damage, but, medically speaking, there's not a scratch on him. That's why I was so pleased when you called. Your history with Mr. Krieg could put you in a unique position to reach him."

"I don't *want* to reach him," Susan said brusquely. "In fact, my goal in coming here was to assure myself that he could never hurt anyone ever again. I think he's a psychopath that should've been put down like a rabid dog."

The doctor shifted uncomfortably on his feet. "I understand. Be that as it may, he's here in this room. Feel free to go in."

Her instinct was to tell him no, that was all right, she would rather walk right back out of here and sit in the dark at home than face Lars Krieg again. But she hadn't come all this way for nothing. She tried to speak, lost her voice, and waved for him to go ahead.

Viraj unlocked the door and opened it wide, then reached inside and flipped a light switch. He moved aside to let her through. Susan took a deep breath, edged to the doorway...

And gasped.

Beyond the threshold was a simple, rectangular room with bare white walls. She had expected Krieg to be lying down somewhere, maybe strapped to the bed against the far wall, but instead, he sat upright in the room's only chair, facing the door, as if waiting for her. His dead, expressionless eyes stared right through her.

"Sorry," Viraj apologized behind her. "We try to keep him moving, since he's not exactly comatose. Usually he's back in bed now, but he's so heavy, we often have trouble getting him from place to place."

Susan understood that; she had forgotten just how huge Lars Krieg was, big enough that he dwarfed the chair he sat in and the plain desk that was the only other furniture in his room besides the bed. He wore a checkered hospital gown, probably the largest available, yet his huge torso still strained the material, and his bare thighs looked like hairy tree trunks where they emerged from the gown's hem. He had been powerful enough to just about tear a man in half, but all of Krieg's thick muscles were slack now, arms dangling at his sides, head slumped to the right on his neck in a way that reminded Susan of a stuffed doll or ventriloquist's dummy. Drool glistened at the corner of his mouth.

Even catatonic though, he was no less intimidating. It was the eyes, set in the middle of his lumpy, deformed face. They had always been completely empty except in the midst of killing, so they really looked no different now. She shivered when she recalled the night he'd busted into her apartment and choked her until she passed out.

"As you can see, he's really not a danger to anyone," Viraj said, stepping past her into the room. "This is how he spends his days now. Please, come in."

She hesitated, still not willing to participate in his experiment. But now that she was here, she found she really did want to face the man. Had, perhaps, been wanting to do so for the past three years.

Susan forced herself to enter the room and approach the slumbering giant, but only with Viraj by her side. She stood in front of Krieg and leaned over until she was hovering just in front of his face. He didn't move, gave no indication he was aware of her presence.

What did it mean? Gross had shot Krieg himself—deciding to kill off his villain in the finale of his last film—and made him into a soulless zombie. But if that was true, why hadn't the man tried to commit suicide like all of Gross's other victims? In any case, it gave her no further clues as to whether the wraiths had anything to do with Krieg or his former master.

"You piece of shit," she whispered, the words making her feel a little better. Krieg's glassy eyes never so much as twitched.

"You can hit him, if you like," Viraj invited.

Susan jerked away from them both, staring in horror at the doctor now. "What?"

"The stimuli might do him some good. And for you, it might be...therapeutic." He gave a pleasant smile, but there was something too eager in it. The doctor suddenly seemed like some stereotypical mad scientist to her, desperate to bring his creation back to life.

"I...I have to go," she told him. "Thanks for your time."

She hurried back out of the hospital.

SCENE V

(take five)

TAKE 1

Wednesday's shooting slate for *Killing Blow 3* consisted of scenes between Harper and some old Iraqi war buddies that died later in the movie. All low-key, testosterone-filled drama stuff, but much easier to shoot than stunts and explosions. For that, Davis was thankful; his head just wasn't clear enough to oversee anything too intricate. He couldn't get his mind off Susan, and the fact that she would be meeting Killam in just a few hours. Sad to admit, but he really didn't know if he worried more that the director might kill her or sleep with her again. He couldn't forget the image of that scumbag between her legs when he'd walked in on them the other day.

And yet, at the same time, her words last night echoed in his ears.

We are not together anymore.

He knew that. He really did. But this morning he'd found himself rummaging in his sock drawer for that little velvety box he'd dropped in there almost three years ago.

Mahoney reported to the set, along with Jared and Scott, but Heady was off today. Davis expected his leading man to slip up and say something about last night, but the younger man surprised him by playing it cool, and Davis coached the actors through the dialogue without incident.

Jared caught him in the office after Davis called the first break. "It was a trip seeing Susan last night, huh?"

"Yep."

"I mean, it's kinda weird. Before she was just plain ol' Susan, the girl whose idiot boyfriend wouldn't marry her. Now she's Susan Campbell, movie star."

"Uh huh."

He lingered in the door. "Hey man…are we cool?"

"I guess. Why do you ask?"

"Well, I know things have been tense, but I just didn't want us to approach this situation like we did last time, at each other's throats. That's…how we lost Otter." Jared looked at the floor. "We all need to stand together, know what I mean?"

Davis sighed. "Yeah, man. I had doubts before, but I'm in this 100 percent now. Spitzen was a real wake-up call." That, and the fact that Susan seemed in deeper trouble than any of them. "We're not losing anybody else."

Jared seemed satisfied. "You call Alvarez yet?"

"Now that, I hadn't planned on."

"Davis…"

"Look, if the guy wanted to question us, he probably would've tracked us down last night. Susan meets with Killam in just a bit. Let's not stir up the hornet nest if we don't have to."

"We got nothing to hide, remember? And we need all the intel we can get. If you won't do it, I will."

"God, you are one pushy SOB. If you wanna call someone, why don't you call your father? We may be needing legal assistance in the near future."

"No, absolutely not," Jared shook his head. His animosity toward Felix Mane, the great L.A. attorney to the stars, was no secret. "If it came to that, I'd rather defend myself."

"Oh, for fuck's sake…" Davis pulled out his cell and fished the business card Alvarez had given him out of his wallet. The phone rang only twice before the detective picked up. "This is Davis Lowe. Do you have a minute to talk?"

"What a coincidence, Lowe. You were my next stop on the Apex studio tour."

"You're here?"

"I'm in your boss's office right now." There was muffled talking away from the phone and then Alvarez told him, "Mr. Devlin says if you have the time, why don't you come on down and we'll have a big pow-wow?"

Davis didn't know quite how to take that. "I'll be right there."

Fifteen minutes later, Devlin's secretary let him into the man's office. The front of the room was apparently still under remodeling, the wall covered in plastic tarps. At a round conference table in the front corner, Alvarez waited for him along with Devlin and Cordero, both dressed in suits. Alvarez wore khakis and a dark blue polo that displayed his biceps.

"Davis, I know you're busy. I'm so sorry to pull you away from the film." Devlin rose to put a hand on his shoulder. "But Detective Alvarez is intent on bothering this studio with every murder that happens in the city."

"Nope. Just the ones that keep leading me back to Lowe here," Alvarez answered.

"Then maybe he shouldn't be talking to you without an attorney present," Cordero said calmly. He sat with his legs crossed, seemingly at ease…but Davis noticed his hands gripped the handles of his chair hard enough to turn his knuckles white. "I can have someone up here from legal in a heartbeat."

"Suit yourself. I just want to ask Mr. Lowe a few questions. But if we're gonna make this official, I can take him downtown."

"It's fine." Davis slid in to the empty chair at the table, trying to keep his eyes focused on Alvarez. "I have nothing to hide. You're here about Sidney Spitzen's death, aren't you?"

"Bingo. He's another 'old friend' of yours, right?"

"Yes, he was."

"Those old friends are dropping like flies lately. You see that, don't you?"

"Detective Alvarez, please show some respect," Devlin chided. "You're talking about a human being who just died."

"Sorry." Alvarez sounded genuinely penitent. "What about Patrick Wollenczak? You have any association with him?"

Davis frowned. "Who?"

"Second victim. Polish guy that runs a computer shop down the street from the nightclub where Spitzen was murdered. There's speculation he was some kind of online scrounger. We think Spitzen went there to see this guy, ran from the killer, and got as far as the club before he was caught."

"I've never heard of the man."

"And I'm gonna go out on a limb here and say you have an alibi for last night."

"I was with Jared Mane, Derek Mahoney, and Heady Tillman, meeting about the movie. Ask any of them."

Alvarez wrote in his trusty pad. "When was the last time you saw Spitzen?"

Davis answered without hesitation, glad that he could start injecting some truth. "Saturday morning, here on the Apex lot."

"The morning after Tonya Werdner was killed?" The answer seemed to surprise the detective into breaking that calm, unflappable façade. "What was he doing here?"

"Just coming to let Jared and me know." Davis couldn't

help glancing at Cordero as he added, "And to tell us about the symbol the killer put on her forehead."

"Son of a bitch!" The VP smashed a fist down on the table, startling them all. "I thought your chief decided to keep that out of the media! Just how the hell did this reporter get wind of it?"

"Now, now, calm down, Buddy," Devlin told him.

"Baxter, if someone is leaking information, we need to goddamn well know about it." Cordero looked at Davis as he said, "I'm getting sick of all the spies around here."

"Frankly, I'd like an answer also, Mr. Lowe," Alvarez said. "How did he know about the symbol?"

"Finding out information no one wants him to know is what Sidney Spitzen does—*did*—best." Davis shrugged. "He said he still had informants in the police department, so talk to your guys."

"Oh, that's fucking great." Cordero sat back in his chair.

Davis looked to Alvarez. "Now, you wanna tell me what the symbol is and why you guys are hiding it?"

The detective paused a moment, then flipped open to another page in his notebook and put it on the table in front of Davis. The familiar triangle and diamond-with-horns was sketched inside. The feeling that Davis had seen it somewhere before was stronger than ever. He searched his memory for anything he might have seen when working with Gross. "We don't know what it is. I was hoping you might be able to shed some light on that. As for the secrecy, we were operating under the assumption it could be a serial calling card. We might need it for positive ID on the killer."

"And we were more than happy to oblige the detective." Devlin wrung his bony hands nervously. "Especially if it avoided publicity for Apex."

"Again, that was the assumption," Alvarez continued. "Now though…I'm not so sure it's that simple."

"Why?"

"Because the same symbol was burned onto Spitzen and Wollenczak's foreheads."

Davis's goal had been to play this meeting as cool as possible, but he couldn't stop his jaw from dropping at this announcement.

"Now, discounting the improbability that someone was able to stab Spitzen to death in an open-for-business night-club and burn this onto his forehead all without anybody seeing a thing…" Alvarez put a finger on the notebook and pulled it back toward him. "Just the fact that the symbol was used on him and Wollenczak gives this more of a conspiracy vibe than a serial killing one."

"Somebody's trying to hide something," Davis translated. He couldn't stop his eyes from flicking over to Cordero once more. The VP's face was a stony mask, his gaze set on the wall of glass across the room.

"Yeah, and they're not doing a very good job." Alvarez pushed away from the table and stood. "Thanks for your time gentlemen, I'll be in touch as soon as I find out more."

When he was gone, Devlin said, "Davis, I'm sure we can trust you to be discreet about this."

"I won't say a word," Davis assured him.

TAKE 2

Alvarez surprised Davis by waiting for him outside the Apex corporate building, cigarette in hand. "Should I get that attorney after all?"

"Relax Lowe, you're off the hook. I don't consider you a viable suspect anymore. Your alibis match up, but, more importantly, it just feels wrong to me." He jabbed the cigarette at Davis, a sudden flash of anger crossing his usually neutral face. "But I do think you know a helluva lot more than you're saying, so I figure I'm better off working with you than against you."

"Why didn't you tell me that upstairs then?"

"Because those corporate suits have their own agendas in this, and it's starting to muddy up my investigation. Cordero, in particular, wants to do my job for me, and he's got a direct hotline to my chief. That's why I wanted to talk to you in private."

"About what?" Davis asked suspiciously.

Alvarez dragged hard on the cigarette, his chest expanding. When he spoke, his words were wrapped in a cloud of smoke. "What I'm about to tell you is only known by me and the few officers that beat me to the scene. I'm keeping it that way because, frankly, I don't know what the hell it means."

Davis waited for him to go on.

"That symbol? It was also burned onto the forehead of your girlfriend's stalker. And forensics confirmed it happened right after death, just like the others."

"What?" Davis thought of the sheet-covered body on the sidewalk two nights ago. "Susan didn't tell me that. What did she say to you about it?"

"Nothing. To be honest, I don't think she even knew it was there herself."

"For Christ's sake, you didn't even ask her about it? Didn't you even consider she's the one who did it?" Davis wanted to smack himself as soon as the question popped out. Was he *trying* to get them all arrested?

Alvarez grinned the same secret smile he had on the street the other night, the one that made Davis think he was hiding something. And he had been; that much was obvious now. "You ever go fishing, Lowe?"

"Fishing?"

"You know, rod and reel? Man against nature? Eat what you catch?"

"I live in L.A. I wouldn't touch anything I caught within a hundred miles of this city."

Alvarez gave a brief snort of laughter. "I head up to Alaska once a year, go out with my father. Beautiful fishing up there."

"Great, thanks for the info. What does that have to do with—?"

"The thing about fishing is," Alvarez continued. "You have to know when to reel in hard, and when to back off, so you don't snap the line. Delicate balance. It works the same way when you're investigating a homicide. Now, of course I considered the possibility that Miss Campbell burned that mark onto her stalker's body herself after their scuffle. I had to. I got her story first, fresh and in her own words, and it seemed pretty truthful to me. Then again…she *is* an actress. She didn't mention the symbol, which meant she was lying or she really didn't know it was there, so asking her about it would've gotten me the same answer in either case. Plus, if she didn't know, I only would've tipped my hand. Then you showed up, and I didn't know what to think. So, like a good fisherman, I decided to back off the line. Instead of reeling you both in, I had unmarked cop cars follow both of you all night, just to see what happened."

"And?"

"You went home alone. She didn't."

Davis grimaced.

"Were you aware she'd been seeing Dwight Killam?"

"It was brought to my attention, yeah." He shifted his weight uncomfortably. "Don't get me wrong Detective, I'm not doubting what Susan said happened at all, but looking at this from your perspective, you must think she's lying."

"Not necessarily."

"Then who burned the mark onto the body, and how'd they do it without her seeing?" Davis thought he knew the answer to these questions, but all that mattered was Alvarez's deductions.

"The 'how' part's easy. Miss Campbell was woozy from the blow to the head, she admits that. She also said she went to the corner of the street to call the police, so she could try and flag down security from the studio lot. While she was away, someone came and did it."

"But why?" This Davis sincerely wanted to know. "Why connect it to Tonya Werdner's murder?"

"That's where I need your help." Alvarez dropped the cigarette to the pavement and ground it under his heel. "If Werdner wasn't a serial murder or a random act of violence, then we have to ask ourselves, why was she killed?"

"You have any theories?"

"No theories, just more puzzle pieces. You see, there was some bad blood between Werdner and the studio. You know that?"

Davis nodded slowly. "Yeah, I'd heard that actually. Hadn't thought about it until just now. Something about a contract renegotiation."

"That's right. But it got to the point where she wasn't even allowed on the premises. She charmed her way through the gate on Friday, in the middle of the night. Why would she do that?"

"Knowing Tonya…revenge."

"My thoughts exactly. We found her fingerprints all over an empty filing cabinet in the director's office. So what was she after? And did whatever it was get her killed?"

Davis's brain burst with a thousand questions. "What about Crosby? There was no symbol on him, was there?"

"Did you see one? And why would there be, anyway? He committed suicide…right?"

"Well, y-yeah. I mean, as far as we know. But you thought his death was part of this, so I figured…"

"There was no mark, Lowe. I don't think he was murdered, but I haven't completely given up the blackmail angle. Maybe it's actually unconnected."

David nodded, but didn't believe it for a second.

The tweet of a cell phone came from Alvarez's pocket. "Excuse me a sec, I gotta grab this."

He stepped a few feet away to speak, leaving Davis to ponder all the information he'd been given in the last half hour. Jesus, what did it all mean? He needed to talk to Jared and Scott, get them to help sort this out.

Alvarez turned back to him. The detective's face was grim. "I have to go. You should come with me."

"What's wrong?"

"It's Miss Campbell."

TAKE 3

Getting through the night was as bad as Susan feared. Every sound in her house caused her to jump, every shadow reached for her. Killam's twisted Christmas jingle played over and over in her head. But the wraiths either didn't visit her during the night, or, if they did, they chose not to make their presence known. She spent the wee hours of the morning awake in bed with all the lights on, pondering what other sort of behavior might 'draw' those creatures to a person. If she could get at least that much out of Killam, she thought she'd be able to rest a bit easier.

Sunrise found her at the table in her kitchen, exhausted and tense. When the last of the night had been chased away, she opened all the drapes in her bedroom to let in the sunlight, then slipped into bed again to try and grab a few hours of sleep, which were plagued with nightmares about Gross and Krieg.

Her cell went off around ten, startling her awake. She flailed and then answered it.

"It's me," Killam said on the other end.

"Are you still coming?" she asked, then almost choked adding, "Darling?"

"I'll be there by noon to pick you up. Be ready."

"You said…we would talk first…right?"

"Yes, I'll explain everything. But first, tell me…" He paused, then asked, in the small, panicked whisper of a ten-year-old, "Have you seen any more of them? Those…those shadows?"

"No. None at all."

He breathed a sigh of relief, then his voice returned to its usual superior tone. "Good. I'll be there as soon as I can. Remember, if you want to come with me, be packed and ready. I won't wait." He hung up.

Susan rose, got dressed in a pair of jeans and a sleeveless white blouse, and made a steaming pot of black coffee. Her weary brain lent the world a blurry edge. But as noon approached, she got so jittery she could only pace through the living room.

Killam rang from the gate. She buzzed him in and walked out to wait on the sundeck connected to the house's front door. The director's car—a brand new, gray BMW M6—rolled onto the grounds and parked on the curved driveway. He got out and started across to meet her.

From the corner of her eye, Susan saw movement on the street beyond the wrought iron fence.

A black van sped toward the house, hugging the curb on the wrong side of the road. As it reached the corner of her rental property, the panel door slid open. Several black gun barrels poked out from the interior.

"*Dwight, look out!*" she screamed from the patio.

Killam spun in slow motion, turning to face the van on the other side of the gate just as it cleared the sight line around his car. The rattle of automatic gunfire split the afternoon.

She threw herself flat to the rolling green lawn, hitting the base of the patio stairs painfully with one shoulder. The shots blurred into one long *purr*. They continued for what felt like an hour. Susan looked up, saw sparks fly as the metal gate took fire. Killam twitched and jerked as bullets riddled his body. He collapsed in a heap on the driveway.

The silence roared in her ears when the gunfire finally stopped. The black van idled in front of the gate for a few seconds and then squealed away. Just before the door slammed shut, she heard a familiar, Russian-accented voice call out, "*Sorry about this, Miss Campbeeeell!*" She had the sudden, giddy urge to wave to Frankie.

Only when the sound of their engine faded did Susan sit up cautiously. Up and down the street, her neighbors crept out of their gated homes. Somewhere in the distance, sirens already warbled through the air. Unlike South Central, gunfire in this neighborhood would garner swift response.

Cold numbness settled into Susan's muscles, but she shook it off as she scrambled across the lawn, on hands and knees until her injured shoulder began to throb, then stumbling to her feet. Killam; she had to see if he was alive, to help him if she could. She reached his prone form in just a few seconds, sank down beside him, and felt her gorge rise.

The director's torso had been shredded from neck to waist, countless holes in his Gucci shirt, all trickling blood. Several rounds had even caught him in the face, caving in one temple and all but tearing off his jaw. Bile flooded her mouth as her stomach tried to empty itself, but she clamped her jaw shut and swallowed until the sensation went away.

She started to turn away from the grisly sight…but a glint of metal on his chest caught her eye. She forced herself to reach out, grabbed an edge of shirt that wasn't bloodsoaked yet, and lifted it aside to reveal the ravaged flesh beneath.

And the medallion, still on its chain around his neck, not a nick or scratch on it. Somehow, the bullets had missed it completely. She thought about when she'd taken if off him while he slept.

A cop car screeched to a stop at the gate behind her, sirens wailing. Authoritative voices shouted at her.

Trying not to think about all that blood, Susan flung herself over Killam's body and sobbed hysterically. She kept this Oscar-worthy performance going while the cops found a way to open the gate and came running up to her.

By the time they lifted her to her feet and led her away, the medallion had been stowed in the pocket of her jeans.

TAKE 4

The ride to Susan's place took an eternity. Davis didn't speak to Alvarez other than to demand updates every time the radio in his car crackled with police chatter. When they reached her house—a sprawling stucco estate on a street lined with equally huge residences behind black wrought-iron fences—Davis saw the crowd of media and onlookers gathered around the entrance to the property. They scattered as Alvarez eased up to the gate. The cops working the barricade recognized the detective and let them past.

The driveway curved up toward the house, where another group of police and crime scene types milled. They seemed to be converged on a body on the ground next to a gray BMW, this one definitely not covered by a sheet. As Alvarez pulled to a stop behind another cop car, Davis spotted Susan sitting on the patio steps with an officer flanking either side, both men full of blank stoicism, like Buckingham palace guards. Dried blood smeared the front of her white blouse. He jumped out and ran to her, panic choking him.

"Oh god! Are you all right?" This time Davis pulled her up and flung his arms around her without reservation, crushing her to him. She buried her face against his neck and hugged him back.

"I'm okay. It's not my blood."

"Goddamn it, I knew I shouldn't have let you do this alone! When I heard there'd been a shooting, I thought..."

She pulled back, smiled, and ran a palm down his cheek. "It's all right, Davis."

By that point, Alvarez joined them and relieved the two

other cops standing over her. "What happened, Miss Campbell? Who did this?"

"Men with really big machine guns in a black van. They opened fire from the street."

"Are you telling me this was a drive-by shooting? In *this* neighborhood?"

"Yeah, but they sure weren't gangbangers." She broke free from Davis's arms so she could speak to them both. "I think they were Russian mobsters that Dwight owed money to. One of them was named Frankie; I could pick him out of a lineup if I had to."

"You get a license plate?"

She shook her head.

"All right, both of you, sit tight for a second." Alvarez moved away from them fast, almost jogging toward the other cops and the body in the driveway.

Davis looked around to make sure no one else was within hearing range. "Did Killam tell you anything?"

"I didn't even get a chance to talk to him before it happened."

"Shit. He was all we had to go on."

"I know. But there's something you should see."

She stepped directly in front of him, using his body as a shield, and her hands moved at her waist. He looked down to see her sliding a thick silver disc halfway out of her pocket. The familiar emblem flashed in the sunlight.

"Where did you get that?"

"I took it off his body before the cops got here."

"You fucking *stole* it?" He shoved the medallion back in her pocket, conscious of the thousand cameras with zoom lenses that were undoubtedly taking pictures of them right this second from beyond the gate. "For Christ's sake, why?"

"I don't know, I panicked! I thought it was better off with

us than anywhere else!"

"Yeah, but now we're the ones that look suspicious if we're caught with it! At least if you'd left it on him, it would've started the cops looking in the right direction!" He didn't say what else was on his mind: that if the wraiths had killed Spitzen just for having a photocopy of the medallion, what would they do to someone who took the real thing?

"Okay, should I give it back?" Susan asked.

"You can't now. The evidence is tampered; there's no proof you got it from him. Plus, Alvarez is starting to see reason about us, and the fact that you took it in the first place might send him right back the other direction."

"I'm sorry." She bit her lower lip in that adorable way he loved. All the anger in him evaporated. "So what do we do now?"

"Let me go talk to him and see what he thinks."

He left her and hurried over to the detective. The body on the ground was a mangled nightmare, no longer even identifiable as Killam. The only way Davis could stand to look at it was to keep his eyes moving and take in the picture as a whole; if he tried to focus any closer, the details—jutting bone and exposed organs—just overwhelmed him. Sure, he'd hated the guy with a fiery passion, had fantasized about killing him in a hundred ways, but Davis never would've wished this reality on anyone.

Alvarez swept a hand through the air above the body like he was displaying it on QVC. "Notice anything missing here, Lowe?"

Holy shit, he already knows! A sinking feeling grew in Davis' chest until he realized the detective *did* mean the symbol, just not the one on the medallion. "Nothing on his forehead."

"Call me crazy, but I don't think that surprises you. Not one bit."

"Did you really expect there to be one? Susan just told you who killed him."

"Yeah, but she also told us how her stalker died. Maybe I should go back to thinking she's the one that burned that mark on the woman herself."

Davis said nothing, just fixed his eyes on a spot between Alvarez and Killam, so he didn't have to look at either one of them. Standing with the detective over yet another corpse was giving him a sense of déjà vu he could've lived without.

"Lowe, I leveled with you earlier, now you gotta do the same with me. I can't help you if I don't know what's going on here."

"Then trust me when I tell you, this doesn't have anything to do with the rest of it."

"That so? Cause it happened on your girlfriend's front lawn, in case you hadn't noticed. This is just one bird in a pack of goddamn vultures that's circling your group. Next time it could be *her* that catches a few stray rounds in a drive-by, or your camera guy that ends up stabbed to death in a nightclub. You want that, Lowe?"

Davis looked over at Susan. The thought of losing her or Jared—or even Scott, Heady and Derek, when it came down to it—was utterly unthinkable. He meant what he'd said to Jared, about no one else getting hurt. But at the same time, where would he even begin trying to explain all this?

"Alvarez, I...I just don't know what to tell you."

The detective nodded while looking down at Killam. "Well, you may be willing to let these people die, but I'm not." He started back toward Susan, leaving Davis to catch up.

"Miss Campbell, you're gonna have to come with me."

Susan looked from Alvarez to Davis and back again. "What for?"

"Questioning, mug shot searches, that sort of thing. And I'm probably gonna want you in protective custody until we see where this goes."

"What for?" Davis demanded.

"Her own safety."

"No, I'll be fine!" Susan insisted.

"Don't you think that's a little extreme?" Davis added.

Alvarez pinched the bridge of his nose in irritation. "I understand you both work in Hollywood, so let me break this down to simplest terms: gangbangers bad; Russian mobsters, far worse. If they think you can identify them, they could be planning to come back and finish the job."

Davis and Susan stared at one another, and he knew exactly what she was thinking: that mobsters were the least of their worries.

When neither of them spoke, Alvarez finally came forward and gently took hold of Susan's upper arm. "C'mon Miss Campbell. I'll take you to the station. Lowe, I trust you can catch a ride back yourself."

He led her away, but they'd only reached the edge of the driveway before she broke free and ran back to Davis. She threw herself against him again and, to his utter surprise, mashed her mouth to his. Their lips parted, tongues finding one another like heat-seeking missiles, and he slipped his fingers through her belt loops to keep her there as long as possible. Davis closed his eyes and enjoyed every second of the kiss, the clean smell of her skin, the swell of her hips beneath his palms, her breasts firm and soft at the same time.

Then he felt her drop the medallion into the front pocket of his slacks, and realized it was all an act to hide the transfer.

Susan retracted her tongue, closed her lips, but stayed up close and tight against him, looking into his eyes from just a few inches away. Neither of them said anything for several long seconds until he whispered, "I'll find out where they're taking you."

She gave her head a small shake. "I'll be fine. Just get this thing somewhere safe and tell the others. Figure out what to do." She gave him another kiss, this one just a small brush across the corner of his mouth that was somehow even more intimate than the tongue bath, and he couldn't help wondering just how fake this whole show had been after all.

He released her, and she left with Alvarez. Davis felt empty watching her go. Sometimes it seemed like that's all he ever did, watch her leave over and over again. It was certainly that way in his dreams.

By the time a cab got there to pick Davis up, Killam's body had been loaded into a coroner's vehicle and the cops were finishing up. But the crowd outside the gate had only continued to grow, despite the fact that the show was obviously over.

In real life, there were never any credits to tell the audience when it was time to go home.

TAKE 5

"So that's it, huh?" Jared wrinkled his nose, then blew air between his lips. "Jesus, I've seen Cracker Jack prizes that don't look as cheap as that thing."

"It's like something you'd throw from a balcony at Mardi Gras," Scott agreed.

Jared snickered. "If we painted it gold, we could probably sell it to Mr. T."

The two of them and Davis stood around the table back in the soundstage office, staring at the medallion on its fine-link chain with every light in the room turned on. The diamond and interlocking triangles were no more than simple outlines, but they were engraved deeply on the smooth, silver face, the etching so slight the edge of a sheet of paper would have trouble slipping between the grooves. It made Davis just as nervous sitting out in the open as a brick of cocaine.

"Well, Killam seemed to think it was valuable," he said. "Unfortunately, it does us no good at all."

"Don't know about that. Looks like you got something out of it." Jared pointed at the small television on Davis's desk, which was playing news footage taken from the crowd in front of Susan's house. The story about the shooting had been on every channel for the last hour, feeding America's obsession for celebrity scandal, and every piece ended with a zoomed angle on that kiss she'd given him. Some of the more enterprising stations had even dug up the fact that they once dated. "Way to go, man. I guess she finally got desperate enough to give you another shot."

"Shut up, pinhead. She was just passing me the medallion."

"Yeah, that and her small intestine."

"Seriously, enough. Susan risked life and imprisonment to get us this thing. We have to figure out what to do with it."

"I'll tell you what we do. We pick up where Spitzen left off. I may not have his contacts, but if I scan this thing and send it out to every chat room in existence, somebody, *somewhere* will know what it is."

Jared reached for the medallion. Davis snatched it away.

"What's up, man? Let me have it."

"Jared, where Spitzen left off is approximately *dead*. He was doing the exact thing you just proposed, and these wraiths killed him for it. Nobody can know we even have this. If it's not too late already."

"Speaking of the wraiths, are we sure this shooting had nothing to do with them?" Scott asked. "Mr. Killam was really killed by the men he was in debt to?"

"It looks that way," Davis confirmed. He lowered the medallion back to the table. It made him feel dirty just touching it, and not because it had been around a dead man's neck just a few hours earlier.

"Then why didn't they try to intervene again, to save Miss Campbell?"

"It happened in broad daylight. There probably weren't enough shadows."

Scott gestured at the TV, now replaying live footage of the cops removing the corpse. "There must have been some inside the van these men shot from, the same way there were inside the car during Mr. Mahoney's accident."

"Maybe the wraiths knew she wasn't the target," Jared offered.

Davis muted the set and turned away before another shot of the kiss could start. "Or maybe we have no idea what their motives are, so we should just stop guessing."

"Okay then, let's add in what we *do* know, from what Alvarez told you this morning." Jared hobbled around the table and turned a chair around to sit backward. He flicked the necklace chain. "It's pretty safe to say that anybody the wraiths kill end up with this symbol on their forehead for some reason. That confirms Tonya, Margaret West, Spitzen, and this Wollenczak guy. It also means Crosby's death really was a suicide."

"But that almost seems like an oxymoron to me," Scott said. "They put the symbol on someone's forehead when they kill them, yet they killed Mr. Spitzen *because* he knew about the symbol. It's almost as if they want to display it and keep it secret at the same time."

"No, they killed Spitzen because he knew who the medallion belonged to and was using that information to dig deeper. Otherwise every cop who'd seen the symbol would be dead, including Alvarez." Davis sank into the seat across from Jared and stared at the silver disc as though a solution might have appeared on it. That niggling familiarity was still in the back of his head, like a submarine whose periscope was the only part visible above the water, and he wished it would either dive or surface the rest of the way. "God, it would be so much simpler if she'd just left this thing on Killam for the cops to find."

Scott shook his head. "Perhaps, but if the police had connected the symbol with Mr. Killam, it still might not have provided any answers. After all, he was only given the necklace. His involvement in whatever is going on was, at most, limited. There's no guarantee an investigation would've gone any further."

Jared nodded. "He's right, Killam's low on the totem-pole. It's just like when the cops are busting up a drug trade. You work your way up the ladder, forcing each guy to turn in the man above him. Except we already know who the next man is."

"Yes, Cordero, I realize that," Davis said, thinking of his meeting with the man earlier in the day. "What do you propose we do?"

"Get him to tell us what the hell is going on."

"And I'm sure he'd be willing to do that if we just ask nicely, huh?"

"We could point your new friend Alvarez in the right direction. Anonymously, if you want."

"They'd have to find proof."

Jared picked up the medallion and let it dangle from his fist. "Suppose Cordero is wearing one of these too?"

"So what if he is? I think we're forgetting that the goal isn't just to get Cordero arrested; the goal is to make sure these wraiths don't come after us. Right now, they seem to be leaving us alone, but if we go running to the cops, who knows what they'll do? So until we figure out your damn pattern, it's just too much risk."

Jared looked thoroughly silenced by this, but Scott—who had picked up the medallion and was frowning at it throughout this exchange—held up a finger like Sherlock Holmes about to deliver a case-solving argument. "Actually...I have a theory on that."

Davis lifted a shoulder. "Lay it on us, kid."

"It just hit me all at once." Scott stood up from the table, taking the medallion with him. "Detective Alvarez told you Tonya Werdner was trespassing on the lot, probably to take some sort of revenge against the studio. She's killed by the wraiths before she can. Then, they save Mr. Mahoney from a fatal accident, an accident that would completely halt shooting on Apex's biggest franchise. Mr. Crosby tries to drop out of the same film, gets blackmailed to finish his part, and then whatever secret he's hiding drives him to commit suicide. And he doesn't know who's blackmailing him, so of course, he logically assumes it's his director; hence, the note."

"I'm really missing that dry erase board right about now," Jared muttered. "I'm more of a visual person."

Scott's words picked up an excited rhythm. "Miss Campbell, another studio actor, is rescued by the wraiths from a homicidal stalker, but when she goes snooping around on her set, they chase her out. And finally, Mr. Spitzen and his researcher are killed while trying to uncover a potentially damaging secret that we know is somehow related to Mr. Cordero, a VP of the studio. These events *are* all connected, just not the way we figured." Scott stopped pacing and looked between the two of them, eyes wide and expectant. "Don't you see the implication?"

When they just continued to stare at him, Scott grabbed the remote from the table and paused the news coverage. They had been showing footage from outside the studio gates, probably for background information, and now a close-up of the iconic black masthead filled the screen. Scott walked over and held the medallion up to the screen, right next to the studio logo of the two stylized, snow-dusted mountain peaks.

Or, put in simpler terms, two offset, interlocking triangles.

"You see?" Scott repeated.

Davis nodded grimly as he resigned himself to the inescapable truth. "All these acts were committed in the best interest of Apex."

TAKE 6

"Santa's little helpers," Jared mumbled, using Killam's phrase. He felt like he used to back in high school, when a difficult algebra equation finally filtered through his dense skull. "Goddamn, it was staring us in the face the whole time. Why haven't the cops figured that out for themselves?"

"Well, it's not exact," Scott said. "The triangles are just a vague outline of the logo, without any of the detail. Pretty easy to overlook, or even see as a coincidence. Plus, the horned diamond is so much more distinct, it tends to draw a lot of the focus."

Davis nodded. "I kept thinking it looked familiar, but not because of this. Something about that other shape…I could swear I've seen it before."

"Has to be something else to do with the Apex," Jared said. "Guess they're not so squeaky clean after all."

Davis reached out and took the medallion back from Scott as he returned to the table. "Just because the wraiths seem to be doing these things for Apex, that doesn't mean the studio is behind them."

"What do you think, they're just some random guardian angels? Sent to make sure stock prices don't fall?"

"I don't know Jared, but do you really think a movie studio would go to these lengths? Murder and blackmail just to keep the cameras rolling and save a little bad press?"

"Why not? You said yourself they're running their own kingdoms, completely above the law."

"Yeah, but that doesn't mean they're maintaining their power with shadow monsters. It just seems a little…bizarre."

"Says the man who helped kill a new-age vampire masquerading as a German horror director."

"Touché."

Jared leaned across the table to make sure he had their full attention, which was, he knew from experience, exactly what you had to with Davis Lowe in situations like this. "Let me draw you a map, boys: we know a) the wraiths are real; b) that they're acting on behalf of Apex; and c) at the very least, Samuel Cordero is aware they exist. Now we just need to know, is he the only one, or does it reach higher?"

"So now you wanna drag sweet old Baxter Devlin into this?" Davis asked, right on cue. Sometimes Jared thought his partner was more predictable than a porn actress's cocaine habit. "The guy's a hundred years old and never said an unkind word in his life."

"I'm just covering bases. I admit, it makes a lot more sense for Cordero to be behind this. He's the one about to take over the presidency after Devlin steps down, right? This could all be about him protecting his investment and making sure the truth stays buried."

"You're jumping to conclusions."

"And you're not jumping at all! C'mon Davis, even you can't believe this started with Tonya. Cordero's been hiding something with these medallions for a while."

"Apex *has* had a pretty amazing winning streak over the last five years," Scott added thoughtfully. "Everyone always attributed it to Mr. Devlin's business savvy, but Mr. Cordero has been with Apex all that time. Just think what he would've been able to accomplish with these wraiths working for him. Perhaps I should do some research."

Jared gave the kid a fist bump across the table. "That's what I'm talking about, man!"

"Are you insane?" Davis asked. "Listen to yourselves! This is the same thing Spitzen was—!"

He slammed his mouth shut as the door to the office opened. All three of them scrambled to hide the medallion, Davis practically throwing himself across the table before they realized the intruder was only Derek Mahoney.

"Mr. Lowe, the crew sent me to ask when we're gonna start again and... Hey, no fair, you guys are having another meeting without me!"

"Shit, we have scenes to shoot today!" Davis rolled off the table, grabbed the medallion, tossed it in his desk drawer, and locked it. "C'mon, let's go. Back to work, everybody."

"Wait, what about all this?" Jared asked. "What're we gonna do about Cordero?"

"Jared, I just…can't afford to think about that right now. We're in the middle of shooting a movie that's falling apart around us."

"Fine, you shoot the movie, Scott can do his research, and I'll hit the streets to snoop around Cordero."

"I'll help!" Mahoney added.

"*No!*" Davis turned back to Jared and Scott. "If the wraiths are only going after people that pose a threat to the studio, we would be pretty goddamn stupid to keep after this, wouldn't we? Think about what Killam told Susan. If we don't bother them, they won't bother us."

Jared stood. His bad leg wobbled, threatening to drop him, but he locked it in place. "Davis…we owe it to Spitzen to see this through."

"And we owe it to ourselves not to get killed. Jared, man… I'm begging you, as your friend and partner…just let this go."

He considered that. Mahoney and Scott seemed to hold their breath as they waited for his answer.

"All right. We'll play it your way."

"Thank you." Davis sighed. "C'mon, let's start rolling, we're already way behind for the day."

He left, followed by Scott and Mahoney. Jared stayed where he was for a long moment, then looked over at the desk where Davis had locked the medallion.

TAKE 7

Susan spent three hours at the police station, exhaustively recounting her story for an official statement—including an embarrassingly thorough examination of her relationship with Killam—and then looking through several large books of mugshots for a face that matched that of Frankie, the Russian with an autograph fetish. She actually saw one that might be him, about a decade younger and without as many scars, but she paused only a second before moving on to the next page. The more she proved she knew about the gangsters that had shot Dwight Killam, the longer she'd be tangled in this mess.

Finally, after giving a vague, intentionally misleading description to a sketch artist, she looked up at Alvarez sitting on the edge of a desk beside her and said, "Sorry. Guess I'm not as much help as I thought."

He gave her a sympathetic frown, no more than the slightest downturn of his thin lips. "It's okay. You're doing great."

"Still, there's probably no need to keep me under protection."

"I wouldn't say that. They could still come after you, just to tie up loose ends. I'll get a couple of officers assigned to watch you. If we let them come to you, it'll make this a lot easier."

She raised her eyebrows. "You wanna use me as *bait*?"

"Well, I'm sure these guys aren't stupid enough to come after a Hollywood actress, but until we can get an ID, we won't know what caliber of criminal we're dealing with." He hesitated. "I don't suppose you'd be any more forthcoming than Lowe about this business with Sidney Spitzen and Tonya Werdner."

Susan spread her palms across the desk. "I can't tell you what I don't know, Detective."

"All right. You guys keep right on claiming ignorance and see what it gets you."

After that, he took her to a private waiting room while he arranged her new bodyguards. A television mounted in the corner played the evening news. She winced when she saw her face appear on screen, a studio still from the film that opened last month, and then the picture jumped to a reporter standing outside the gate of her house for an on-location report. Her agent and publicist were probably going nuts trying to get hold of her, but she hadn't even thought to grab her cell before leaving. Her blouse—stained with Killam's blood—had been taken for evidence, and now she wore a shapeless LAPD t-shirt. She was just about to try changing the channel on the TV when the holding room door opened, and a man she didn't know in a black suit and blue tie came in, followed by Samuel Cordero.

She couldn't help tensing up, but hoped it didn't show.

"Susan, nice to see you again." Cordero's tone was all business, but his eyes gave her a quick devouring, just as when they'd last met. He motioned to the other man. "This is Jeff Walker, head of the Apex legal team. I brought him to represent you as soon as we heard what happened."

"Represent me?" she repeated. "I…I don't think I need representation, do I? I'm not being charged with anything."

"It's not about that, Susan. Although we're at your disposal if the situation goes that direction." He paused, waiting to see what effect his words would have. "But from what little information we've been able to gather, the police are talking nonsense about protective custody. They wouldn't even let us see you until I spoke with the chief of police. Now, I'm sure you don't want to be here any longer than necessary. And just to make sure this is all handled as delicately as possible, you need someone you can trust in your corner."

And that someone is certainly not you, she thought. The fact that he'd been able to waltz in here, bully his way through the police with his connections, was more than a little frightening. But she struggled to find a seemingly innocent response as she said, "Thank you, Mr. Cordero, I really appreciate that, but for now, I think I should just cooperate."

He paused again. Said nothing for a long moment. A single muscle in his cheek twitched, but that was the only indication he hadn't been magically turned into a statute. Even Walker, the silent attorney, seemed apprehensive as he waited for a response.

"Jeff, can you give us a moment?"

Walker nodded and left the waiting room without a word. Susan had to stop herself from asking him not to go. Cordero approached and took a seat on the bench across from her, so close their toes almost touched. He leaned forward casually, resting elbows on his knees, but the position looked forced, engineered to be non-threatening. Everything about him seemed like that, a flawless shell wrapped in an Armani suit, all to hide...what? She thought back to the day she'd spied on him and Killam, how intense and frightening he'd looked, and found herself wishing Alvarez would come back.

"Susan, as you know, Dwight Killam was a friend of mine."

"I know. I'm very sorry. I wish I could've done something to—"

He held up a hand to silence her. "It's not your fault. Dwight got himself into trouble with the wrong kinds of people over the last few years, and what happened today was just his choices catching up to him. Trust me, I met some of these lowlifes..."

Cordero put thumb and forefinger at the corners of both eyes and squeezed, as though pinching off tears. A performance; she was sure of it. A huge, silver ring flashed at her from the pinkie finger on his right hand, bigger even than the wedding band on the opposite side. Over his shoulder, the television continued to display the reporter talking in front of her house.

"You'll have to excuse me, I've just come from the morgue." Cordero gave a theatrical sniff and opened his eyes to watch her again. "I identified the body. Dwight had no family in the city."

"That's terrible," she mumbled. She had an awful idea about where this was going.

"While I was there, I also wanted to retrieve a gift I gave him. A silver medallion necklace. I would love to have it back, to remember him by. He wore it all the time, but... it wasn't on his body. I was wondering if you might know where it is."

His gaze searched her. Susan couldn't meet it. She looked at the floor in front of him—a mistake to be sure, the classic sign of guilt in any movie—but her eyes were again drawn to the ring on his pinkie, a silver band with an ornate, base relief design...

Her jaw dropped. She couldn't be sure, but she thought that, hidden among the beveled surfaces on the ring's face, two triangles and a diamond with horns was visible.

Cordero noticed where her eyes went. "Susan?"

"I...I'm sorry," she said, tearing herself away from the ring. *C'mon, you're an actress, so act already.* "I don't remember seeing it. Maybe one of the morgue workers took it."

"Yes, I'm sure." His brow drew together. "Well...keep an eye out for it and let me know. Perhaps it fell off on your front lawn when Dwight was shot." He rose, paused, and sat again. "Also, if you would...let's keep this between us. No need for anyone else to know what a sentimental fool I am. The police, for instance. Or Mr. Devlin."

"Yes. Of course."

"Good. If you reconsider the legal assistance, just let me know."

He stood and went for the door. The television was now showing the kiss she'd given Davis. Cordero halted beside it, watching the replay.

She saw a small, knowing smirk tug at the corners of his mouth as he left.

Susan waited only two minutes, just long enough to give Cordero and his lackey time to leave, then poked her head through the door and demanded that the officer stationed outside bring Alvarez to her immediately.

"What's so urgent?" the detective asked when he arrived.

"I was just thinking, do I have to go home tonight? My place is gonna be crawling with reporters for the next few days, and I can't see these guys coming after me while there's a circus outside the gate."

"Good point. Sure, I guess we can move you somewhere else, as long as my men are with you. Did you have somewhere in mind?"

She nodded, trying not to grin.

TAKE 8

After Susan called him, Davis ended shooting early—skipping out on two major scenes scheduled for today—and raced home. He panted with excitement by the time he ran through his front door and gave the house a bachelor cleanup, scooping up clothes from the floor and throwing dirty dishes in the sink. His housekeeper only came on the weekends, and he liked to get his money's worth. He went through his kitchen, determined he had the ingredients to make a mean lasagna, and got it in the oven.

She arrived a half-hour later, wearing a baggy LAPD t-shirt and the same jeans she'd had on earlier, and still looked like a goddess. Two uniformed patrolmen were with her. They introduced themselves, gave Davis's house a quick security check, then told them they would be outside in their car all night.

"Thank you," she told Davis, after they left. "For letting me come here. I just…couldn't go home."

"No problem at all. You're welcome any time."

She nodded and took a polite look around. "Nice place. Yours?"

"Yep. Not as swank as that palace you live in, but I'm not making seven-figures."

"Me neither."

"Oh, whatever!" he teased. "Your contract for that Danny Boyle film was reported at what, two-point-five? How does it feel to be an honest-to-god millionaire?"

"I wouldn't know. Whatever the government doesn't eat up in that tax bracket, the rest goes to my accountant, who doles me out an allowance like I'm sixteen." Susan tucked a curl of hair behind her ear, the same maneuver he'd seen her perform in front of the camera to convey embarrassment. "And as for my place, I just rent it. I haven't been in the city enough since my career took off to find something permanent." She started to say something else, but sniffed the air instead. "Oh my god, please tell me I smell your lasagna."

"Sure do. You hungry?"

"Starving."

They had a pleasant dinner: the pasta, salad, and a bottle of wine that was mostly finished by the end of the meal.

Her cell phone went off a few times, all calls from her agent or reporters that had tracked down her personal number, all ignored while they ate. The media was doing their best to draw connections between Dwight Killam and Margaret West—two violent deaths that had happened in immediate proximity to one of the country's most beloved up-and-coming thespians within the last two days—but even their wildest theories were way off base. Davis had been afraid the attention would only serve to stir up the Torsten Gross stories all over again, but his own agent had called him on set earlier to tell him his arrival at the crime scene couldn't have gone better. The news agencies were painting him as the hero, swooping in to comfort an old girlfriend with whom he obviously still had chemistry. He wasn't the type to believe media hype, but that chemistry was never more evident than now. Conversation stayed light and easy as they reminisced about old times and swapped stories about their parallel rise in the industry. As much as Davis wanted to stay in this moment, eventually the topic turned to the matter at hand.

"Did you feel like he was threatening you?" he asked, after she finished telling him about her adventures in the police station and her encounter with Samuel 'Buddy' Cordero.

"Well…not exactly. I mean, I guess not. He just wanted the medallion back. But the look on his face, when he saw us on TV…it was pretty creepy. That's why I convinced Alvarez to let me come here. I wanted to make sure you had a police escort, too."

"Oh. Thanks," Davis mumbled, taking the last bite of his lasagna. And here he was thinking she would just feel safer with him. Reading signals from her was harder than decrypting spy code. He couldn't remember if it'd always been that way, but he didn't think so.

"I'm probably just being overly cautious though." She lifted her shoulders as if to dismiss the whole topic. "At the end of the day, he's still just a VP of the studio, not a psychotic killer."

"The jury is still out on that one." Then it was his turn to catch her up on Jared and Scott's theories.

"Where is the medallion now?" she demanded.

"At the *KB3* soundstage, locked up in my desk."

She slid forward in her chair, bumping the table hard enough to jostle their wine glasses. "Davis, we need to make sure nothing happens to it! Why did you leave it there?"

"Because if Alvarez changes his mind and decides to formally bring me in, I didn't want that thing anywhere near me. Bad enough it's at the set."

"I guess." She tried to rub the end of her nose and succeeded in poking herself in the eye. The wine was giving him a nice buzz, but inebriation had always been fast and sudden for her. "So what do we do with it?"

"Well, we wouldn't need it to implicate Cordero. All we'd have to do is let Alvarez know about the ring he's wearing." He paused to take a deep breath. "But if the wraiths really are working to protect Apex, then I don't even know if we should. Maybe the best thing to do is just give it back to Cordero, so this whole thing will be over."

She gave a derisive snort. The sound would've been obnoxious from most people, but Susan—with her slightly wobbling eyes—made it sound adorable. "I'm sure Jared just looooved that idea."

"Yeah. He's not a big fan of rolling over. But it may be our only choice. Everyone that's gotten involved has ended up dead."

They were both quiet for a moment, picking at the remains on their plates, drinking the last of the wine. Then Susan asked, "If Cordero is in charge of these shadow creatures, then do you think...he might not be...human?" She choked on the last word, then said in a slurred rush, "I mean, just because all this weirdness doesn't have anything to do with Gross, that doesn't mean Cordero might not be something like him. Or even a different kind of monster entirely."

Davis nodded slowly, thinking about that veil that had been lifted from the world. "Once you know the boogieman is real...all bets are off."

"Exactly." Susan shivered. "I...I went to go see Lars Krieg in the loony bin last night."

"Jesus, *why*?"

"I just thought...if this had something to do with Gross... he might be our best lead."

"How was he?"

"As ugly as ever. And completely brain dead. Seeing him... it just gave me this gut feeling that Gross isn't part of this. Which, if you're right about the emblem and Cordero..."

This time, the silence stretched out until she held up her cell phone and waggled it at him. "Do you mind if I excuse myself? I have a lot of calls to make about today. Damage control, and whatnot."

"Sure. Use my room if you want."

She disappeared. He cleared the table, then took helpings of the food to their two chaperones outside. One was asleep, the other playing a game on his phone, but they were grateful for the grub. As Davis washed dishes, he couldn't help marveling at how good it felt to have Susan here, back in his life. God, if he got another chance with her, he would do things right, he would never let her go again.

You don't deserve her, Lowe. The voice belonged to Sir Isaac Crosby, his condescending British accent grating in Davis's head. *You're a talentless hack, and she saw through you the same way everybody else does.*

His cell phone rang as he finished up in the kitchen. Scott's number showed in the display. Davis answered. "This better be good, I'm a little busy."

"I thought you might like to hear an interesting story from the history of Apex, sir."

Davis sighed. "You seemed like such a smart kid when I hired you, so I can only conclude you have a death wish."

"But this is public knowledge. Just information that hasn't been highly publicized. Surely that's not worth killing over."

Davis glanced at his closed bedroom door. "You have about sixty seconds before I hang up on you."

Scott, ever the pragmatist, started talking with no preamble. "Mr. Devlin hired Mr. Cordero as VP of Operations six years ago. No prior association that I could find, and nothing odd about Mr. Cordero's past. He was an executive at an electronics manufacturing company in San Diego before accepting the position at the studio. A month later to the day, Apex acquired the script for what would eventually be the first *Killing Blow*. And, since then, everything has just fallen their way—endorsements, investments, script acquisitions, star power, even all those Oscar nominations. Everything... except the land Mr. Devlin needed to build his studio."

Davis pressed the phone closer to his ear, interested now. "What do you mean?"

"Mr. Devlin wanted realty in Culver City, to compete with the other studios, but they blocked him at every turn. I came across some trade articles about an ongoing feud between Apex and the Big Five, talking about how they kept overbidding him."

"So how'd they get where they are now?"

"A man named James Van Horne owned the property where the studio sits, just about the last tract of undeveloped land left. And even he was getting ready to sell to Universal."

"He change his mind?

"No, he disappeared. Almost five years ago. The police had no leads. His son inherited the property, tried to go through with the Universal deal, then just suddenly sold to Apex for less than market value and moved out of the state."

Davis said nothing. That was one Apex story that didn't get repeated very often.

"That's all I've been able to find so far, sir. I'll keep looking."

"No, Scott, that's fine. Just leave this alone. No more research. I mean it. And for God's sake, don't tell Jared about this." Davis hung up before the kid could argue.

If Jared was right...and Cordero *did* know about the wraiths...where had the creatures come from? What had happened to the VP between the time he'd lived in San Diego and when he'd come here to L.A. to be the enforcer for Apex Studios?

Davis sat on the couch for another hour flipping channels until, about nine o'clock, the door to his bedroom opened and Susan emerged.

She wore an old flannel shirt of his that reached nearly to her bare knees, the sleeves so long she had to roll them up to her elbows, her wavy brown hair pulled over one shoulder with a band. "Sorry, I raided your closet for something to sleep in. Alvarez didn't let me pack a bag."

The year after they'd stopped speaking, she'd starred in a thriller as a prostitute that witnesses a murder, then falls in love with the detective working the case—said detective played by Bradley Cooper. The director had kept her wardrobe minimal throughout the production, but one scene in particular found her character seducing the detective in tight, fish-net lingerie before engaging in a steamy sex scene that had Davis squirming in a jealous rage when he'd finally gotten up the nerve to watch the thing. But he'd never forgotten that outfit, had dreamed about it, had even convinced the one woman with whom he'd been in a pathetically short relationship to wear something pretty close.

This baggy shirt utterly erased it from his mind.

"So, what's the, uh…um…you know…the verdict?" he groped for words. "They want you to hold a press conference about Killam?"

"Nope. My publicist seems to think the more I distance myself from this whole thing, the quicker it'll be over."

He nodded, staring at where her legs disappeared under the hem of his shirt.

"Don't," she said.

"Don't what?"

"Look at me like that. I know what you're thinking."

He realized his jaw was waggling, and his mouth had suddenly gotten very moist. "I can't help it. You look incredible."

She crossed her arms protectively, but not before a smile flashed across her face. "So what's the sleeping arrangement tonight? Do I take the couch, or are you gonna be a gentleman and let me have the bed?"

"Are you sure we couldn't *share* the bed?"

This time, there was no smile. "That's not why I'm here."

He frowned, that jealousy over Killam still smoldering inside him. "I have to say, I'm getting a little confused here, Susan."

"About what?"

"You. This. That kiss earlier. The fact that you're standing here half-dressed in my living room."

Instead of accounting, she just sighed and said, "Damn

it, I knew this was a bad idea. I'll get the cops to take me home." She stomped back into the bedroom.

Davis went after her, entering the room just as she was laying out her clothes to change back. "Susan, please…stop walking away from me. That's how you tried to solve every problem between us and it never worked."

"Just what does *that* mean?"

"It means I wanted to work things out, but it was kind of hard when you wouldn't answer the phone. It means you're the one who left, not me."

She yanked her clothes up from the bed, wadded them into a frustrated ball, then slammed them on the floor. "Davis, what was there to even leave? At the end, we barely saw each other!"

"That's not my fault! You were always gone shooting!"

"Because I'm an *actress*, you fuckhead! What did you think it was gonna be like?"

He had no more answer for her on that subject than he did for himself.

"And it's not like we were going anywhere," she continued. "There was no commitment, it was obvious you weren't ever gonna be ready to take the next step, but I just kept waiting and waiting like an idiot!"

"You want commitment?" He stomped over to his dresser, ripped open the sock drawer, and pulled out the box that had been sitting in there for so long. The diamond inside glittered just as much as he remembered. Davis held it in front of her face, pinched between thumb and forefinger. "Here's how committed I was to you!"

She stared at the ring. "When did you—?"

"Three years ago. I was gonna give it to you after you finished that London shoot. The shoot you never came back from." He laughed roughly, thinking of the ridiculous speech he prepared. "So whattaya say? Wanna get married?"

Her brow drew together again. "Yeah, maybe I do!"

"Then, here!" Davis grabbed her wrist, lifted her hand, and jammed the ring down on her finger. They stared at each other for a heartbeat, faces creased with anger.

And then she was on him, kissing him with that same urgent heat as before. They fell onto the bed, a tangle of grasping limbs. His lips latched on to every inch of skin they could find, sucking and biting. She began to wiggle beneath him, trying to get that flannel shirt off.

Davis stopped her.

"Why don't you leave it on?"

She grinned and wrapped her legs around him.

SCENE VI

(back to one)

TAKE 1

Susan opened her eyes, took a second to remember where she was, and then turned over to find Davis sleeping beside her. One curl of hair lay over his forehead like a comma, and she reached out to brush it back. The diamond on her finger caught the early morning light coming through the shades, reminding her briefly of the cleverly disguised insignia on Cordero's pinkie.

But this ring made her too happy for the comparison to bother her.

"Morning." Davis grinned sleepily.

"Hey." She slid closer to him, laying her head against the pillow to look at him. "Did we…did we really get engaged last night?"

"I think so."

"Are we insane, or are we actually considering this?"

"Probably a little of both." He kissed her, first on the corner of her mouth, then working his way down her neck. "But I'm game if you are."

"You sure? It's not too late to blame it on the alcohol."

From between her breasts, he said, "I'm going to blame it on the fact that I haven't stopped loving you since the day we met."

"You're just saying that so you can have your way with me again."

"Yep. Is it working?"

Rather than answer, she showed him.

When they were finished, they jumped in the shower together. She felt completely refreshed after a good night's sleep, without worrying that every shadow was watching her. They'd been in their own little universe since she arrived here, away from all their problems, but she knew it had to end soon. As they got dressed—him in a fresh pair of slacks and shirt, her in the same clothes from yesterday—he said, "I have to get to the set. I'd ask you to come with me, but I don't think it's a good idea for you to go near the studio again."

"That's okay. I have to go home anyway." She plucked at the collar of the LAPD t-shirt. "I could really use a fresh change of clothes."

"You sure? You can stay here if you want. There's just a few scenes I have to shoot and then I'll wrap early."

Susan slid her arms around his waist. "Don't do that, Davis. We both have careers, and we can't start rearranging them now. You need to finish *Killing Blow*, and if *Persuasion* is really kaput, then I have to start looking over some scripts my agent is sending."

"Already?"

"You know this business as well as I do. It doesn't stop for anything, not even when your director gets gunned down in front of you." She pulled him even closer. "And if I'm gonna be planning a wedding soon, then that's one less thing I'll have to worry about."

"I know." He looked miserable. "I just like having you here."

"I'll see you tonight, I promise. We'll celebrate our impending nuptials." She gave him a quick peck on the lips, then released him. "In the meantime, what do we do about Cordero?"

"I'll get the medallion while I'm at the set and take it to him. Then this will be over."

"Shouldn't I do it?"

"Why?"

"Maybe I can convince him that it fell off when Killam was shot and then I found it. But if you take it to him, it's basically admitting we stole it."

Davis shook his head emphatically. "I don't care. I don't want you anywhere near him. Besides, he should be thanking us for taking it, otherwise the cops would have it right now. Let's just all finish our business with Apex and get away while we still can."

There was a knock at his front door. Alvarez waited on the stoop. Once inside, he looked at Davis, over at Susan, then down at her hand. "I guess I should say 'Congratulations.'"

"Man, you really *are* a good detective."

"Not lately." He nodded his head toward the door. "My officers got nothing last night. We'll go through this routine a few more days and then call it quits. Once these Russians see we're not making any arrests, they'll know you couldn't ID them."

Susan nodded. "Can your men escort me home then?"

"I can take you myself. I was headed that way to check in with the guys I had stationed outside your place last night."

She followed him to the door, where she hugged Davis again. This engagement thing was rash and stupid, but right now, in this moment, it felt so right, so natural, and she was terrified that if she returned to the real world, it would suddenly lose its luster. She wanted this bubble of safety to stay around them for at least a little bit longer.

But it would be much better to face these problems on their own terms than to wait for the bubble to burst, and the walls to come crashing down.

"Don't worry," he said in her ear. "I'll take care of everything."

TAKE 2

The detective's car pulled away. The other two officers left a few seconds later. Davis closed the front door, trying not to think about Susan leaving again for another role. He told himself it didn't matter where either of them went, they would find a way to make it work. Maybe he would take some time off when he finished filming and go with her wherever she went.

At your level of the game, 'taking time off' might as well be retiring, that persistent inner critic told him. *If you wanna sacrifice everything you and Jared have worked for, by all means, take a break, but don't expect the cinematic landscape to reserve your seat when you come crawling back. You have to keep pushing and pushing and brand your name across the sky itself, because Susan was right: this business doesn't stop for anything.*

I just wanna be with her, he pleaded. Crosby's accusations played in his head yet again, that he was no artist, just an incompetent hack, and if he was actually considering walking away from it all so he could follow a woman around from set to set like a puppy, then maybe the man hadn't been too far off the mark. *Is that so much to ask, to have a normal relationship?*

Maybe people like you don't get to have normal relationships, Davis. The price of fame.

Feeling utterly dejected, Davis started away from the door to grab his wallet, keys and phone.

And got only a few steps away before it burst open again behind him.

He spun. Standing in the entryway were two burly men with almost identical crew cuts, both dressed business casual in chinos and short-sleeve Hugo Boss golf shirts in green and blue. They looked like steroid-ridden executives out for a day on the links, but the murderous glare in their eyes suggested otherwise.

His first thought was, *The Russians have landed.*

Davis turned to run; where, he didn't know. He expected to receive a bullet in the back, because that was the only reason for the mobsters to invade his home, a clean sweep of anyone Susan might've told about them, but instead, pounding footsteps followed him through the living room as he sprinted for the bedroom. A hand grabbed the back of his shirt and yanked, ripping the fabric and slinging him around in a circle. Before he could regain his balance, one of the men punched him in the stomach hard enough to expel the air from his lungs. He doubled over and gasped.

"Where is it, Spielberg?" one of the men asked; they looked so much alike, he didn't know if it was the one who hit him or not. His accent wasn't so much Russian as northwestern Jersey. They towered over him on either side like monoliths, keeping his body pressed between their broad chests as he straightened. "Where's the proxy?"

Davis caught his breath and choked out, "P-proxy? What're you talking about?"

The world exploded in white light and pain. He flailed as though he could physically push the agony away, and fell backward over the arm of the couch, sprawling across the cushions. Blood gushed from his nose, raging down the sides of his face in a river he wouldn't have thought a human body capable of.

When he dared to open his eyes again, he saw one of the men still hovered over him; the other had sat down on the furthest couch cushion, so his thigh rested beside the top of Davis's head. He rubbed the palms of his enormous hands together, cracked his knuckles, then looked down. "We can do this all day, Tarantino. Where's the proxy?"

Davis slowly turned on the couch, swinging his legs into the floor so he could sit up, mostly to give himself time to think. Which was hard with his stomach and nose throbbing in tune with his heartbeat. He looked from Blue Shirt beside him to Green Shirt over him as red droplets pattered into his lap at an alarming rate.

"Christ, he bleeds like a fuckin stuck pig," Green rumbled.

"Maybe Aronofsky here is anemic," his partner said.

"Fuck that, I think he's menstruating out his goddamn nose."

"Look, guys…" Davis began cautiously. Blood ran into his mouth every time he opened it. "I…I have no idea what you're talking about…" He winced in anticipation of another blow.

"The proxy, dumb shit," Blue repeated. "You know, the ward, the buffer. *The fuckin medallion.*"

All at once, Davis understood: these guys weren't with the Russians that had shot Killam. The Russians wouldn't be asking questions at all, let alone about the medallion. They had to work for Cordero, which made a surreal sort of sense; only a studio VP would employ such upscale goons.

Blue pulled a handkerchief from his breast pocket and tossed it at Davis. "Look, Hitchcock, here's how it shakes out. Your girlfriend took somethin that didn't belong to her. Silver medallion on a chain. Looks like this." He reached inside the V-neck of his golf shirt and held up a round disk exactly like the one Susan had taken. Davis looked at the other man and saw the same shape outlined beneath his tight shirt. Cordero must be handing the things out like breath mints. "Don't even try to deny it. It ain't at her place, and the only person she could've given it to before the cops took her in was you. So now *you* are gonna give it to *us*."

Davis picked up the handkerchief, wiped as much of the blood off his face as he could, and pressed it gently to his nostrils to staunch the flow. It didn't feel broken, but it hurt like a bastard. His voice came out nasally and wet as he said, "Guys, there's no need to do this. We were gonna give it back anyway, first thing this morning. I planned to call Mr. Cor—"

"*Ut, ut, ut,*" Blue snapped, cutting him off. "No names, De Palma. Names are for friends, and none of us are friends here. Just give us the fuckin thing, we'll walk outta here, and you can get back to makin those shitty B reels you call movies."

"But I can't give it to you," Davis explained patiently, while tilting his head back. Now that he knew who they were and what they wanted, he felt much more in control of the situation. All he had to do was reason with them. "It's not even here."

This time, Green open-palm slapped him across the side of the face, as casually as swatting a fly, but the blow felt like an anvil. Davis let out a startled *ook!* sound and fell against Blue, who pushed him back the other direction. The right side of his face burned, and he could already feel his eye socket swelling.

Blue leaned over him, forcing Davis back into the couch cushions if he didn't want to touch the other man. "Tell you what, Shyama...Shyla...Shya...."

"Told ya not to use that one," Green said.

"Shut up, asshole!" To Davis, he snarled, "If the next words outta your mouth don't tell me exactly where the medallion is, *Coppola*...I'm gonna leave you alone with my partner for about a half hour while I go grab breakfast. Then we'll see if you feel like talking. Course, with the way you bleed, there might not be much left of you *to* talk."

And judging by the eager smile on Green's face, Davis thought that arrangement would suit him just fine.

"It's at the set," he said. "In my desk drawer."

"Good boy. Let's go get it."

There was no more talking as they stood him up and escorted him out his front door, one on either side with hands clamped around his arms, like overbearing bodyguards. Davis looked around for help, but at close to seven in the morning, his neighbors—mostly Wall Street types and investment bankers, all fellow bachelors—were long gone to work. They steered him toward a yellow, two-door, hatchback Mazda CX-7 sitting in the driveway next to his Jeep Cherokee. The sight of the automobile actually made Davis giggle before he could stop himself.

"What's so funny?" Green demanded, shoving him toward the passenger door.

"It's just...you guys are driving *this*?"

"Yeah, so?"

"That color's not exactly inconspicuous, is it? And with the two of you inside, it must look like the clown car at the circus. What, could you not get the boss to spring for something sporty?"

"Hey, it's fuel efficient!"

That made Davis laugh even harder, which resulted in Green growling in his face, "You better feel real lucky your boss's little pets can't touch these proxies, 'cause otherwise... you'd be dealing with a lot worse than us right now."

Davis stopped laughing.

"Shut up with that," Blue told his partner over the vehicle's roof. "Just get Herzog over there in the car."

Green ripped open the passenger door, shoved the seat forward, and then forced Davis inside with a hand on his neck. "And don't get any blood on the interior, fuckwad."

The two of them really did look cramped in the front, but the back seat was even tighter. Davis tucked his knees up and stayed still and quiet as they drove, ignoring the chorus of pain throughout his body and trying to decide if he should attempt an escape or just give them what they wanted. Green's warning kept coming back to him. *His boss's pets.* Had he meant the wraiths? And what was this about them not being able to touch the medallions?

When they reached the gates of the studio, Blue twisted in the driver's seat and lifted a pistol up from the middle console for Davis to see. "Not a word. Just keep your head down and things won't have to get any messier."

Davis nodded, the sight of the gun making him feel cold. He was around prop weapons all the time, but somehow it was different when you knew it was real and in the hands of someone willing to use it. The last time he'd been at gunpoint was the night Torsten Gross showed up on his doorstep.

Blue flashed a studio badge at the guard and pulled in through the gate. He was obviously familiar with the lot, and didn't need directions to get to the *KB3* soundstage. They parked beside the hangar door, and Davis rolled it open just enough for them to squeeze through the crack, all with the gun jammed in his ribcage. The place was dark and quiet, even the earliest of the crewmembers still a half hour from reporting to work.

"All right, Schumacher. Lead the way."

"Hey, now you're getting a little insulting."

"*Move.*"

Davis took them to the office and tried his desk drawer, which wouldn't open. "Shit. I left my keys at home."

"Oh, allow me." Blue pointed the barrel of the pistol down at the lock and pulled the trigger. The explosion was deafening in the enclosed space. A cloud of wood chips peppered them.

Davis pulled open the drawer.

And stared at the great big empty space inside.

TAKE 3

Samuel Cordero's house was a veritable fortress. Not one of the nouveau, cookie-cutter McMansions cropping up across the city that looked like suburbia on steroids either; this was a three-story, castle-like conglomeration of wings and balconies and cupolas set in the middle of at least ten acres of prime L.A. hillside, enclosed by a towering fence and a guarded gate in front with the Cordero name molded into the metal in cursive script. The closest neighbor had to be miles away, but the twisty little mountain road that ran by the front of the property also gave access to a scenic overlook across from the northwest corner, so Jared could blend his Challenger in with the vehicles of the morning sightseers and not look too suspicious. He sat hunched behind the wheel with a pair of binoculars and watched the house that Apex built.

"Jared, sweetheart," Heady said from the passenger seat, around a mouthful of Fritos that had been sitting open in his backseat for at least a week. "I know how bad you wanted to play detective, but I really don't see what we're accomplishing here."

"We're learning about our enemy."

"So far, the only thing we've learned is that the Cordero kids get driven to private school promptly at seven."

"If he makes a move, I wanna know about it."

"From two miles away? Babe, he's not gonna murder someone with the blinds open *Rear-Window*-style."

Jared lowered the binoculars and sighed. She was right; this idea had been ill-conceived, like so many of his others. The only glimpse he'd gotten of their target was when the man came into the vast downstairs kitchen to scream at the cooking staff about his breakfast. Besides, if Cordero really was in charge of the wraiths, he would send *them* to do his dirty work.

And then there was the fact that Jared was breaking his promise to Davis, which, along with making him feel guilty, would earn him a severe bitch session.

"Gimme some of those." He grabbed the chip bag and looked inside. "You ate them all."

"I'm starving! You're the one who wouldn't stop for breakfast!"

He grinned and pulled her close for a kiss. Even this early, with only fifteen minutes in the bathroom at his place to get ready, she smelled like honey and looked like money. "What's with the attitude?" he asked when they broke away.

"I just don't like stakeouts at the crack of dawn that aren't gonna tell us anything. There's gotta be a better way to go about this."

"Okay, all right." He held up his hands in surrender. "I just wanna see the guy leave for the day. Then we can follow him to the studio and I'll feel like I've actually accomplished something."

"How do you even know he's going to the studio?"

"Because yesterday I called his office and pretended to be an investor that wanted to meet with him this morning."

Heady smirked, rolled her eyes, then reached over to lay a hand on his crotch. "Or we can leave now and swing by my place for a quickie before you go to the set."

Jared grinned. He really loved this woman. "You make a compelling argument."

She gave his genitals a friendly squeeze to get the blood pumping, and that's when the knock came at the driver's window. Heady jerked her hand away. Jared turned, expecting to see a cop that would run them in for indecency (which wouldn't be the first time that had happened to him), but instead found Derek Mahoney leering in at him. Jared rolled down the glass.

"You wouldn't be making time with John Harper's old lady, now would ya?" the actor teased, sporting his million-dollar smile.

"Big D, what're you doing here?" God, how could he hope to spy on Cordero when he wasn't even observant enough to see Mahoney drive up in his silver Ferrari? Jared took a look around the parking lot of the overlook now to make sure no one else had noticed the action star, but they were all crowded around the brick wall at the edge of the cliff with their phony maps to the stars, pointing at the house strung out along the wall of the valley below. A beat-up brown van sat idling on the perpendicular row that faced them, but its interior was too dark for Jared to see anything except the driver's hands on the wheel.

"I knew you guys were planning something without me yesterday, so I followed you this morning."

"You mean the whole time we were getting ready to stake-out Cordero's house, you were staking out *Jared's* place?" Heady asked.

"And you got up at like six A.M. to do it?" Jared added.

"*Got up?* Hell no, I haven't even been to bed! A friend of mine screened an indie out in Elmwood and I promised I'd be there for the premiere. Then we partied with these models pretty much all night."

"I remember those days," Jared said wistfully. Heady punched him in the arm hard enough to bruise.

"On my way home, I drove by your house and just happened to see you two leaving. I lost you downtown, but I figured you had to be coming here." He looked across the road and gave a whistle of appreciation. "So that's Cordero's house, huh? Very swank. What's the plan then?"

"The plan is, we keep this between the three of us and get the hell outta here."

"How come?"

"Because unless we wanna catch Cordero brushing his teeth, all this will do is piss Davis off. Now get in your car and follow us back to the studio."

Mahoney gnawed his lip for a second as he bounced a fist against the window frame. "Nope. Not this time, man." He turned and strode away from the vehicles, toward the edge of the overlook parking lot and the street beyond.

Jared jumped out of the car and limped after him. "What are you doing?"

"I'm tired of all the sneaking around stuff. It's boring. And when the audience gets bored, it's time to advance the plot."

"Ummm, what are you talking about?"

"We need to know what's up, so I'm just gonna ask the guy," Mahoney translated.

"Big D, this isn't a goddamn movie, you can't do that!"

"Sure I can. It's cool, he'll talk to me."

They stood at the edge of the road now. A black limo started down the driveway from the massive house, driving toward them. The actor angled toward the front gate of the property as if to meet it, and Jared hobbled ahead to stand in front of him as he started across the street. "And just why, exactly, is Cordero gonna tell you all the details of how he sends out shadow monsters to murder people that get on his bad side?"

The younger man stopped, put his hands on Jared's shoulders, and said, "Dude...I'm Derek Mahoney. I'm a movie star." With that, he walked around Jared and continued down the shoulder of the two-lane road.

"Heady," Jared called out. "You wanna come talk some humility into your fellow actor here?"

She had remained by the passenger door of the Challenger but now she started around the front of the car, jogging to catch up with them. Jared, still in the middle of the street, turned around to watch Mahoney as he waved and called out to the guards at the gate.

An engine gunned behind him. Heady screamed, "*Jared!*"

He spun back in time to see the grill of the beat-up brown van bearing down on him.

TAKE 4

Susan was prepared to duck her head when they reached her house, but the media crews had gone. Alvarez told her a high profile pro-ball player had been arrested for DUI last night and was scheduled to be released from custody this morning, so the attention had probably shifted to him for now. She would have to send the man a thank-you card.

A patrol car sat at the curb though, with two more officers inside, and Alvarez stopped next to them and rolled down his window. "How was it last night, gentlemen?"

"All quiet on the western front," the cop behind the wheel said. "Not a single stray car. Guys around the back said the same thing, but the Chief pulled them for a call about five this morning."

Alvarez nodded and pulled into her driveway after she punched in the gate code. She tried not to look at the chalk outline and bloodstain on the concrete as they passed by. Instead, her eyes went to the diamond ring on her finger once more. The tiny thing was a surprising comfort, an anchor that kept her from giving in to despair and fear. If getting married to Davis Lowe was even half as good, the rest of her life would be a breeze.

The detective caught her inspection. "So you and Lowe? This is for real?"

"I think so," she said.

"Because I got the idea you and Killam were an item."

She shook her head. "Not really. That was just…insanity on my part, I guess. I think I was fighting how I really felt. Maybe I have been for a long time."

Alvarez parked the car in front of her steps. "That's good. You and Lowe…you seem like a good thing. That's why I want to get you out of this trouble you seem to be in."

Susan grinned. "I really don't think you have to worry about us anymore, Detective. But you're invited to the wedding, just so you know."

He smiled also. She got the idea it was a rare facial expression for him. "You're too charming for your own good, Miss Campbell. I hope Lowe knows how lucky he is."

"He does now."

"My officers will be out here the rest of the day. They can either take you wherever you need to go, or follow your car."

"Sounds good. Thank you."

She got out and went up her front steps while Alvarez watched from the driveway. The door was unlocked, just as she'd left it yesterday. Susan pushed it open and halted on the threshold.

Beyond the entryway, she could see the interior was trashed. Furniture overturned, cabinets ransacked. Shattered dishes spilled out onto the tile from her kitchen doorway to the left. It looked like someone had gone through the entire house with a goddamn chainsaw.

"Maybe you're not as far from that trouble as you thought," Alvarez said behind her. She hadn't even heard him come up the steps, which made her wonder how long she'd been standing here gawking at the mess.

He squeezed past her into the house with gun drawn. She waited, feeling numb, while he checked the premises. At one point, she tried to call Davis on her cell, but only got his voicemail. He'd probably turned it off during filming, but it still made her chest feel hot and tight.

When Alvarez came back, he told her, "Looks like they got in through a window at the back, probably after my other guys left."

Susan didn't know much about the wraiths, but she was pretty sure they wouldn't need to smash a window to get inside. Even so, the thought didn't make her feel any better.

"They hit every room," Alvarez continued. "Any idea why?"

"Maybe...they were sending me a message...?"

He shook his head adamantly. "This wasn't revenge, they were searching for something." He studied her with a frown.

"What do you have, Miss Campbell? And why do I get the feeling this doesn't have anything to do with the Russians?"

She leaned against the doorframe as the room began to waver. "Detective Alvarez...I think Davis might be in serious trouble."

TAKE 5

Davis took only a fraction of a second to arrive at an explanation for the medallion's absence.

Jared...you son of a bitch.

Beside him, Blue Shirt looked down into the desk drawer, then blew air through his teeth. "Too bad. I really hoped you'd play ball. Now the world will have to be deprived of the next Uwe Boll."

"Look." Davis showed his palms as he backed away from the desk. He bumped into Green at the door, who stood blocking the exit. "I can get it. I know exactly who took it."

"Sorry. You had your chance. And we got our orders." Blue pointed the gun at his forehead from a foot away. The sensation never got any easier. "Hopefully your girlfriend will be a little more cooperative."

Sudden rage thudded at Davis's temples. He saw the man's finger tighten on the trigger.

From the soundstage, a distance voice called out, "Mr. Lowe, you in here?" Blue's eyes flicked away from his target in surprise.

Davis grabbed the man's arm and shoved the pistol away. Blue pulled the trigger again just as the barrel cleared the side of Davis's head. The shot was close enough this time to make his ears ring, but at least the bullet had missed the mark.

Or rather, missed *a* mark.

Green cried out in pain from the door. Davis and the other goon both looked at him. A dark maroon stain was spreading across the center of his golf shirt. He reached under the garment through the collar and pulled out the twisted remains of his own medallion. The bullet had utterly obliterated the cheap metal and gone right into his chest. "You… *you fucking shot me, moron!*"

"*Oh Jesus, I'm sorry!*"

Davis planted his hands on Blue's chest and pushed. The maneuver wouldn't have worked if the larger man hadn't been so distracted, but as it was, he tumbled backward. Davis fled, narrowly avoiding a feeble grasp by the injured Green just before he collapsed.

Davis barreled onto the *Killing Blow* set and spotted Ralph standing uncertainly in the crack of light from the rolling door. When the hefty studio guard caught sight of Davis's bruised and bloody face, he cringed and took a half step back. "Mr. Lowe, is everything all right? I don't show any filming scheduled for this early, but I thought I heard a—"

"Run, Ralph!" Davis rushed toward him, waving his arms. "Run and get help, they have a gun!"

Ralph hesitated and reached for his nightstick; a valiant but stupid gesture. Davis had almost reached him, would've herded him back out of the soundstage and gone right after him, but another gunshot rang out. Ralph's head jerked to the side, revealing a runny gray and red mess splattered on the metal door behind him. The security guard dropped to the floor like twelve sacks of potatoes.

Davis looked back. Blue was on his feet again and standing outside the door to his office, snarling as he swung the pistol in Davis's direction.

The soundstage exit was past Ralph's body, a good fifteen yards with no cover. But the opening to the deeper parts of the set—the Harper household and Müller's jungle lair—lay just a few steps away to the left. Davis plunged into it as a bullet chewed through the wooden backdrop where his neck had been.

Beyond the entrance, construction hallways led between various set pieces, lined with particleboard and prefabricated sheetrock, all open to the warehouse rafters above and lit only by occasional service lights. Davis knew the layout well enough to navigate, but from the sounds of the shuffling footsteps behind him, Blue wasn't having nearly such an easy time. He ran until he entered a space that was half backdrop for the Harper's bedroom on the right, and a jumble of leftover scaffolding, construction equipment, and set decoration on the left, including a working campfire prop they'd used to shoot some of the outdoor scenes with Harper and his military buddies. Davis slid just to the left of the entry and planted his back against the wall.

He would only be able to run so long. He had to find a way to end this.

When his pursuer came through, he slammed the door. The barrier was no more than cheap, flimsy wood, but the surface still smashed Blue in the face with a sickening crunch that had to be his nose breaking. The man stumbled back, roaring in pain, then tried to charge through again. This time, Davis put a shoulder against the wood and ran all his weight against it.

The other man yelped as the sharp edges of frame and door crushed him. His gun hand jutted into the room; he tried to twist his arm far enough to fire the weapon into Davis's side. Davis grabbed his wrist without thinking and sank his teeth into the meat of the man's thumb.

Blue shrieked and thrashed. His hand popped open, dropping the gun, but then he shoved back against the door until he got it open enough to slip through. Davis pummeled the man's chest with the bottom of his fists, but he might as well be tossing himself against a brick wall. He scrabbled for purchase on the golf shirt, trying to reach high enough to punch the goliath in his injured nose, which streamed blood worse than Davis's had. Blue bashed him in the temple with the heel of his palm, then socked him in the gut so hard he went down backward, sprawling across the fake campfire logs. As he slid into the floor, his shirt caught the handle that operated the device. Hungry, gas-fed flames sprang up from the hidden jets, coating Davis's back with heat.

"You know, this was just business before, Emmerich." The fire danced in Blue's eyes as he bent to retrieve the pistol. "But now...I think I'm gonna enjoy this."

Davis forced himself to uncurl on the floor and held out a shaking hand to plead for his life. Something hung from his fingers, twinkling in the light of the campfire, and it took a moment before his vision cleared enough for him to make out what it was.

Blue's medallion. His 'proxy.' Davis must have torn the chain from the man's neck in their struggle, and now it dangled from his hand.

"Shit!" The goon's eyes bulged in terror as his hand went to his neck to feel for the missing jewelry.

High above them, a screech echoed through the dark rafters.

"No! Stay away!" Blue raised the gun and fired it twice into the air, towards the direction of the noise. "Cordero sent me, I'm on your side! You hear me, you fucking things? *I'm helping the goddamn studio!*"

In response, whatever was up there chittered. It was joined by others. The sound chilled Davis's blood.

Blue panted with panic as he looked back at Davis, still on the ground and holding up the medallion. "*Gimme that!*"

Davis tossed the necklace into the fire beside him.

"*You motherfucker!*" Blue rushed forward, ignoring him, intent only on retrieving the silver disc from the flames.

Davis raised a foot and tripped him.

The large man was moving so fast, he had no hope of staying on his feet. He stumbled past Davis, straight through the fire, and then fell into the metal forest of scaffolding against the wall. The serrated end of a jutting support post impaled his throat and punched out the back of his neck. Blue jerked and twitched like a hooked fish for several seconds as blood splashed to the floor.

The ungodly chorus in the rafters continued, a note of excitement amid the screeches. Davis thought he could see movement up there, in the layer of darkness above the hooded service lights.

He scrambled painfully to his feet. In the fire, the cheap silver medallion was already melting. Davis left it and ran, backtracking through the hallways to the main room of the soundstage, moving so fast this time he rebounded off walls at every turn. The cacophony of the wraiths followed just above. He expected the creatures to appear at any second, for their midnight black tentacles to shoot from the darkness and clutch at him, but he met no resistance. Ralph's body still lay in front of the open hangar door, and Davis leapt over the large blood puddle around it to bolt through the exit. The howls tapered behind him.

Outside, the sunshine was bright. Davis looked around and spotted two other guards further up the row of warehouses. He waved and shouted, "*Help!*" They came running.

"Two men," he told them breathlessly. "They held me captive and shot Ralph, but I think both of them are dead!"

"Radio it in!" one of the guards told the other, before running into the soundstage. His partner followed after telling someone in their dispatch to call the police. Jesus, what was Davis going to tell Alvarez this time?

A minute later, one of the guards emerged. "Mr. Lowe, I didn't see anyone at all. Are you sure they didn't run?"

"No, one is in my office either unconscious or dead, and the other's definitely dead on one of the sets."

"And where did you say they shot Ralph?"

"For Christ's sake, he's right inside the door!" Davis pushed past the man. "You must've just about stepped on him when you…"

He faltered.

Ralph's body—the one he'd jumped over only moments before—was gone, along with every speck of blood from the walls and floor.

TAKE 6

The van sped directly at Jared, aiming to run him down. As the vehicle bounced over the shallow divider between parking lot and street, he forced himself to wait until he was sure the driver was committed to his path. Over the growling engine, Jared could hear Heady screaming his name, but he blocked it out, focused only on the metal grille bearing down on him, and then dove to the right just before the van would've crushed him under its wheels. He landed full out on his side against the pavement, something in his bum leg flaring.

Brakes squealed. Jared rolled over and watched as the driver of the van attempted to turn at high speed to avoid the drainage culvert on the opposite side. The momentum lifted the driver's side wheels off the pavement for a second, but changed the trajectory enough to avoid a head-on crash into the ditch.

But it also lined him up with Mahoney, standing aghast at the shoulder of the road.

On the big screen, the young actor had dodged swords, bullets, and missiles, but he apparently just wasn't as quick without a script and stunt team. He stood frozen as two tons of steel hurtled toward him. At the last second, he seemed to wake up and attempted the same maneuver as Jared, but to less effect. He was in mid-dive when the van's bumper struck his legs with an audible thud and tossed him into the street. The driver floored it, attempting escape, but the loose dirt on the shoulder gave way under the tires. The van slid sideways into the ditch, where it came to a rest at a 45 degree angle on its passenger door.

Heady reached Jared and helped him to his feet. "Oh my god, who was that?"

"Cordero must know what we're up to! Call 911!" Jared limped as fast as he could toward Mahoney.

The kid looked like a bloody side of beef in skinny jeans and a black Versace long sleeve, but at least he appeared to be breathing. The worst damage was below the waist, where his hips looked crooked and his legs were as tangled as two strands of spaghetti. It made Jared sick just to look at him. He pulled off his own windbreaker and draped it over Mahoney's head to prevent pictures by the sightseers gathering across the road.

The wraiths didn't save you this time, Big D.

A revving engine grabbed his attention. The driver of the van hit the gas, trying to rock the vehicle enough to get traction. The back wheels spun, throwing up plumes of dirt.

"You ain't goin nowhere, bastard." Jared marched over to Cordero's would-be assassin, climbed up onto the tilted side of the van, and yanked open the driver's door with a fist pulled back and ready to let fly. It hovered in the air as he took in the driver.

"Mrs. Ottman?"

The last time Jared had seen the obese woman crammed behind the wheel was in court two and half years before, when she'd tried to sue the Lowe-Mane Production Company. Time had not been kind to her. Her clothes, once so conservative and uber-religious, were no more than stained sweat pants and an ill-fitting top that couldn't even hold in her blubber. Snarls of hair stuck out from her head, and her face overflowed with wrinkles and fat pockets so much that she looked bee stung. He might not have recognized her at all, except the insanity in her beady eyes shone just as bright and savage as ever.

"You killed him!" she shrieked, trying to turn her massive girth in the seat. *"You killed my baby boy!"*

Anger pounded through his veins. "How many ways do we have to say it, you crazy bitch? *We didn't fucking kill Otter!"*

She launched up through the nearly horizontal door at him with more agility than he would've dreamed possible. Jared fell off the side of the van. She came down on top of him like a wrecking ball. Her weight forced the air from his lungs, but he didn't have time to worry about that, because her ragged fingernails were headed toward his eyeballs. Jared grabbed her pudgy wrists and struggled.

Hands pulled her off him. He recognized the uniformed

guards from the Cordero gatehouse. In the distance, sirens wailed up the mountain road. Someone must have made the call before even Heady got the chance.

"*This isn't over!*" Otter's mother screamed as they dragged her away. "*You and Lowe are going to pay for what you did! I promise you THAAAAT!*"

Jared had trouble standing this time. He wheezed and his bad leg threatened to buckle, but then Heady slipped an arm around his waist. He leaned on her as two cop cars and an ambulance appeared over a rise in the road.

And, at the massive gate to the Cordero property, that black limo Jared had seen earlier pulled to a stop at the edge of the property. A tinted window in the back slid down.

Even from fifty yards away, Jared recognized Samuel Cordero framed in the door. The unbridled fury on the VP's face was just as spookily intense as Mrs. Ottman's.

But, unlike her, he had the restraint to just roll up his window. The limo turned onto the mountain road and drove away just as the ambulance reached them.

TAKE 7

Davis had an Uber run him home to change and get his car, phone and wallet, then went right back out the busted front door. He called Scott just before he reached Cedars-Sinai, but only had time to give the boy a quick update, ask him to contact the rest of the crew about today's shoot being cancelled, and order him to stay away from the studio. It sounded like his PA wanted to argue, but he agreed. At least that was one person Davis didn't have to worry about.

His new fiancée, on the other hand, was not answering her cell phone.

But he tried not to think about that as he rushed inside and asked the front desk nurse about Derek Mahoney. Heady had given him the barest details on the phone, only that Muriel Ottman was in custody, and that she and Jared were at the hospital yet again. From her tone, Davis didn't think his lead actor would stroll out without a scratch this time.

The nurse directed him to the third floor, where Mahoney had a private hospital suite. Davis waited for the elevator, got too impatient, took the stairs three at a time, hurried down a tiled hallway, and almost ran into Samuel Cordero coming the opposite direction.

"Get out of my way, you m—" The VP's impatient command cut off as he recognized Davis. A look of shock crossed his perfect features, and Davis didn't think it was because his face resembled a deflated punching bag.

So you honestly thought the Executive Twins had taken care of me. Sorry to disappoint you by still being alive. He felt a measure of smug satisfaction at this defiance, followed by cold dread that his life meant so little to the executive.

Cordero recovered from his surprise just as fast, running a hand through his thick hair and skirting around Davis. "Excuse me, Lowe. Derek is just down the hall."

"Wait, Mr. Cordero!" Davis wheeled around and walked after him through the crowded hall. "We need to talk!"

"Not now Lowe, I'm late for a meeting," Cordero said over his shoulder. Ahead, the elevator doors slid open as if waiting for his approach. He muscled his way in amid the other riders and began to jab the buttons rapidly.

"This really can't wait," Davis said, arriving at the elevator as the doors began to shut. "I think we can work everything out if we just—"

"Sounds good," Cordero cut him off, his eyes fixed somewhere over Davis's head. "Why don't you call my secretary and make an appointment?"

The doors closed. Davis stared at his warped reflection in the buffed steel for a moment and then continued on to Mahoney's room.

He found Baxter Devlin and another man sitting in the private adjoining lobby of the actor's room.

"Davis!" Devlin rose from his chair and gawked. "Good Lord, are you all right?"

"Yeah, I just...fell down some stairs." He touched his bruised, swollen cheek and then winced. At least he'd been able to change his bloody shirt and clean up a bit before coming here. "How is Big...uh, Derek?"

"Not good," the other man, lean and stern, said.

"This is Jeff Walker, lead counsel for Apex," Devlin introduced him. Davis recalled the name from Susan's story.

"Mr. Mahoney's injuries are severe," Walker continued. "Spinal trauma and multiple fractures to both legs. The doctors estimate six months of recovery before he'll even be ready to try walking again."

"Oh Jesus." The room started to spin. There was a glass window along one wall of the lobby with drawn privacy curtains on the other side, but through a small part in the fabric, he could see a hospital bed with figures clustered around it. "Can I see him?"

"He's in with family right now," Devlin said. "And I don't know if visitation with you would be, ah, *ideal*, at the moment."

"What? Why not?"

"Davis..." Devlin squirmed, wringing his hands. The palsy seemed to worsen the more flustered he became. Davis found himself looking for jewelry on the old man—another 'proxy' necklace, or a ring like Susan had said Cordero wore—but the studio president seemed to be unadorned. Ditto for Walker. "This week…it's been just an awful time for the Apex family. All this death connected to the studio…Tonya Werdner… Isaac Crosby…Dwight Killam…and now this. It's a PR nightmare, but that could be the least of what it costs us in the long run. Don't get me wrong, I thank God Derek is still alive, but we need to understand how this happened. We were told he was out on some kind of…of location scout with your cinematographer?"

"And that he was run down by a woman who has a vendetta against *you*," Walker added.

"Well, yes, that's sort of true," Davis reluctantly admitted. "This woman is insane, and was probably after Jared. But I don't know anything about any location scout. Who told you that?"

"Mane did. He said they were screen-testing for a scene you wanted to film." Walker's upper lip curled. "Coincidentally, they were just outside Mr. Cordero's home, at an overlook. His security cameras even caught part of the incident."

Davis felt his hands clench at his sides. That explained why Heady had been so vague about the details, and why Jared hadn't called himself. "All I can say is, Derek absolutely was not on any studio-related business authorized by me."

"Are you willing to testify to that if Mahoney decides to sue?"

"Do you really think it'll come to that?"

Walker straightened his tie, somehow managing to make even that simple action look condescending. "A multi-million dollar project is now on indefinite hiatus, Mr. Lowe, and a man's career is destroyed. Between Mahoney and the investors, heads will roll. Legally speaking."

"God," Davis moaned. He'd already considered this on the way to the hospital, before he'd known the extent of Mahoney's injuries, but it had seemed like such a remote, unthinkable possibility. Hearing someone else say it forced the truth to blossom in his head.

Killing Blow 3—Davis's entrance to big-budget, blockbuster status—was over. The world had thrown everything it could in his path to keep him from finishing, and now it had succeeded. This must be how Terry Gilliam felt about the *La Mancha* ordeal. Davis slumped against the wall and looked at his feet.

Devlin said to the attorney, "Jeff, give us a minute, would you? I'll meet you downstairs." Walker nodded and left the room. The studio president stood in front of Davis and put gaunt hands on his shoulders. "Davis, listen to me. Don't let this get you down. You're part of the Apex family, and we take care of our own."

Tell that to your VP. "Yeah, well, I think the Apex family has every reason to disown me if I get them into a costly lawsuit and lose their most profitable franchise."

The old man let go of one shoulder to flap a hand at that—almost angrily, Davis thought. "The movie will get made eventually, even if we have to replace Derek. We were thinking about doing it after his contract expired anyway. Not to sound harsh, but he's just not essential to Apex, not in the long term, so let him sue. You, on the other hand...I said I expect great things from you, and I meant it. You are on your way up, my boy, and I want you on my team no matter what."

Pride swelled Davis's chest. He had to blink away sudden tears. Nobody had ever given him praise like that, voiced confidence in him to that degree. Certainly not in this town, which would just as soon eat its young as compliment them. "Okay. Thank you. I want that too."

"Good man." He patted Davis's cheek, his palm dry. "You just stay on the back burner for now while this all blows over. And start distancing yourself from this cinematographer of yours, in case things get bad. I'll be in touch when the time is right."

Davis followed the president back out to the hallway, shaking his hand warmly before he left. He watched Devlin get on the elevator before someone behind him said, "How's Big D? The old man's Gestapo force wouldn't let us anywhere near him."

He turned around, saw Jared, and lunged.

TAKE 8

His partner barely had time to look surprised before Davis had him slammed against the closest wall.

"Davis, what the hell is wrong with…*Chrrrist*, what happened to you?"

"I got the ever-loving shit kicked out of me and was almost shot in the face because of you!"

"What are you talking about?"

People up and down the hallway stared. Davis grabbed the front of Jared's shirt and slung him back inside the private lobby of Mahoney's room. "You promised me," he spat. "You promised you were gonna leave this alone, but instead you went skulking around Cordero's home."

"I know, I'm sorry." Jared backed away with hands held out as though to ward him off. "I can't say it enough. Heady and I just went to check the place out, that's all. Derek showed up on his own, and then Otter's goddamn mom came outta nowhere. It all happened so fast, I couldn't do anything."

"And you told Devlin you were on a location scout?"

"I had to. Cordero…he saw us outside his house, Davis. I was just trying to come up with a cover story to make it look innocent."

"Perfect. That's just great. I'm trying like hell to get us outta trouble and you drag us even deeper." Davis bared his teeth as he thumped his index finger against his partner's forehead. "Did you stop to think that if Derek is hurt while working on the movie, the studio is liable?"

"Who gives a shit about that? They've got him insured. Hell, they'll probably turn a profit off this!"

Davis snorted. "You're a real piece of work, Jared. It wasn't enough you almost killed him last time. You had to give it another shot, and let Cordero know we're on to him at the same time. What about the medallion?"

His partner squinted. "What about it?"

"You fucking stole it, you asshole! What did you do with it?"

"Davis, man, slow down. I didn't take jack shit."

"I put it in my desk drawer right in front of you, and now it's gone! Who else would've taken it?"

"Maybe the wraiths got to it."

"No, they didn't."

"How do you know?"

"I just do. Trust me."

"Then maybe the set spy! Maybe the janitor, how should I know? Would you just tell me what happened?"

"Some guys showed up this morning after Susan left—"

"Left where?"

"My place."

"Why was Susan leaving your place?"

Davis waved his fists in silent fury and then performed a frustrated, foot-stomping jig. "She stayed over last night and we got engaged, okay?"

Jared looked around in feigned confusion. "Did…did I step into an alternate dimension at some point?"

"Do you wanna hear this or not?"

"By all means. You slipped her a rufie, right?"

Davis forced himself to calm down before he said, "Jared… three more people are dead. Including Ralph."

This had the desired effect of sobering his partner up. "Ralph? As in, security guard Ralph?"

"Yes. No. I mean, I don't know, I think so." Davis rubbed at his eyes and sank into a chair. He'd been running high on adrenaline since his front door had been kicked in and now he was beginning to crash. "Two guys that work for Cordero came to my house this morning. They wanted the medallion, slapped me around until I told them where it was, then drove me to the studio to get it. When I opened the desk drawer and it wasn't there, they were gonna kill me, but Ralph walked in on the middle of it. One of these idiots accidentally shot the other, then he shot Ralph, then he came for me and…I killed the guy on the set."

"Jeeeesus," Jared backed away and leaned against the wall, eyes wide. "What did the cops say? Wait, what did *Alvarez* say?"

"They don't know about it."

Jared stood for a second, glanced behind him at the windows into Mahoney's hospital room, then went to the door and stood in front of it. He lowered his voice and whispered, "Are you telling me there are three corpses on the set right now, as we speak?"

"That's the thing. I left the soundstage for maybe thirty seconds, long enough to get security, and when they went in…everyone was gone."

"I don't get it."

"The bodies…they disappeared. No corpses, not even any blood. Like I dreamed it all." Davis had gone with the guards to search the entire building. The fake campfire had still been burning, but the medallion he'd thrown into it was nothing but a charred blob of melted metal. Only the goons' bright yellow car remained, parked illegally in front of the soundstage, but that had been no proof, and, though they couldn't reach Ralph by radio, by that point they had become far more suspicious of Davis. He remembered the way the guards looked at him while they cancelled the police dispatch, like he was another drugged-up Hollywood scumbag on a bender. He'd played into it, pretended to be even more disoriented than he already was, and begged them to keep the whole incident to themselves.

"Are you sure they were dead?" Jared asked.

"Considering Ralph's brains were painted on the wall and one of Cordero's guys had a pipe sticking out the back of his neck, yeah, I'm pretty sure." Davis sighed. "I think… the wraiths took them all. They showed up right before I killed the last guy."

"You saw them?"

"I heard them. These two guys were wearing medallions too. I pulled one of them off in the struggle."

"Damn things are multiplying like rabbits," Jared murmured. "What'd you do with it?"

"Burned it to keep the guy from getting it back. But as soon as it was off his neck, the wraiths started shrieking from the shadows, just like Susan said. It was creepy. Like a bunch of pissed-off monkeys. And the goon, he was terrified of them, just like Killam. Started screaming Cordero had sent him."

"See? I told you that corporate shill was the one holding their leash!"

"Yeah, these guys all but confirmed it. And that's not all." Davis leaned his head back against the chair. "They called the medallions 'proxies.' As in 'to act on behalf of.' I think they're some sort of talisman, to keep away the wraiths. Cordero wears one, and he must give them out to people who do his dirty work. That's why he had to send these idiots to get Killam's from me: because the wraiths can't touch them."

From the other side of the curtained windows, a muffled sob drifted out that caused another ripple of anger in Davis. "Why couldn't you have saved him, Jared?" he asked through clenched teeth.

"I tried, all right? But a better question would be, why didn't the wraiths?"

"What do you mean?"

Jared's brow wrinkled as he tucked hair distractedly behind one ear. "When I saw that van coming at me, my first instinct was that Cordero had sent someone to kill us. It wasn't until after I found out it was Otter's mother that I realized it wouldn't have made sense anyway, because if Cordero wanted us dead, he could've just sent the wraiths in the first place, right? So if this wasn't some sort of assassination attempt, then why didn't the wraiths save Mahoney instead, like they did in the accident? Surely they could've done *something*. Appeared in the shadows of the van like they did in the stunt car, and cause it to miss him. Isn't he just as valuable to the studio now as he was then?"

Davis was about to say he didn't know, when he realized Devlin might've given him the answer.

Not essential to Apex. That was the phrase the old man had used to describe Mahoney. The wraiths had protected the actor before, when the movie was in the midst of being filmed, but perhaps his essentiality had only extended so far. If the studio considered him replaceable, then maybe his protection had been revoked as soon as he'd begun helping them snoop. Not dangerous enough to eliminate, but not important enough to rescue.

If so, that made Susan expendable as well, since her film was kaput.

From across the room, Jared told him, "I say we go to Alvarez right now and tell him the truth."

Davis shook his head wearily. "Susan and I were going to just give the medallion to Cordero to get us out of this. Before it disappeared, that is."

"Cordero. The same guy that just tried to have you killed."

"He was protecting himself. And I'm gonna do the same thing by telling him we don't have the medallion, to make him see we're not a threat."

"And who says you get to decide that for the rest of us?"

"I do. You wanna see the results of what happens when you make a decision, go look in that hospital bed."

Jared slammed a fist against the wall hard enough to rattle the framed flower painting hanging beside him. "Oh, go to hell, Davis! Maybe if you weren't so concerned with making sure you didn't slip down a few rungs on the Hollywood elite ladder, none of this would've happened!"

"That's complete bullshit!"

"Whatever! I'm so sick of your holier-than-thou routine!"

"And I'm so sick of having you drag me down!"

Whatever insult Jared had planned next died on his lips. Davis pushed on before he could recover.

"I've been doing all the work since we teamed up, while you sit back and fuck anything in a skirt! *I'm* the drive in this relationship, *I'm* the talent, and now that this movie is finished...*so are we!*"

He felt ashamed saying it, but cleansed somehow also.

Because, once again, Baxter Devlin—that wise old media tycoon with a heart of gold—had put it best: Davis was on his way up, and the sky was the limit.

Best to jettison all this extra baggage to make the flight as smooth as possible.

Jared's mouth opened and closed a few times before he murmured, "So much for us going into this as a team."

The door to the private lobby opened, and Jared was forced to move out of the way to allow Alvarez inside. He looked between them, "This a bad time?"

"I was just leaving." Jared squeezed past the detective and disappeared into the hall.

"Where the hell is Susan?" Davis demanded, jumping up from his seat. "I've been calling her for the past two hours!"

"Her cell phone was confiscated."

"*Why?*"

"I've put her into mandatory protective custody in a safe house. Her house had been ransacked when we got there this morning. And since she won't tell me what they were looking for, I have no choice but to keep her isolated."

"She can stay with me!" Davis said. Even he heard the desperation in his voice.

"You taken a look in the mirror, Lowe? I don't think she's gonna be any safer with you."

"Please," Davis pleaded, denying the urge to drop to his knees and literally beg. "I just need to talk to her. Just for a few minutes."

"Then talk to me first. Tell me what you're mixed up in, and who did the number on your face. Unless you're willing to do that, I'm not budging any more for you."

For just a second, Davis considered. He wanted to let someone else handle this.

It wasn't fear of Cordero and the wraiths that stopped him this time, but rather Devlin's last instructions to keep his head down and let this blow over. Would the old man still be as eager to *have him on the team* if he got Apex's VP arrested?

He didn't need the police or Alvarez. He could find a way to get them out of this himself.

"We're not mixed up in anything," he said evenly. "It's just...bad luck."

"Now that I can believe." Alvarez turned without another word and started out of the room. He pointed at the windows on his way out. "This Ottman woman really has it out for you, from what I hear. If I were you, I'd add her to my growing list of enemies."

TAKE 9

Jared saw that Heady had been crying when he got into the car in the hospital parking lot. As upset as she was about her co-star, she refused to stay inside and face Davis with him. Which was, he now saw, probably a good idea.

"What happened?" she asked. "What did he say?"

"Cordero's really behind it all. He tried to have Davis killed."

"*What? How?*"

"Doesn't matter. The asshole's got his nose so far up Apex's ass, he actually wants to roll over and offer them his throat. And it sounds like Susan agrees with him."

She sniffled and ran a finger under both eyes, smearing mascara. "Then maybe…we should, too."

"NO!" Jared roared suddenly, causing her to flinch away from him. The outburst—and flood of anger behind it—surprised him as much as it did her. "He doesn't get away with this! No matter what happens, Cordero has to pay!"

Heady took a deep breath and composed herself as she did when stepping into a role. "Okay then. What do we do?"

"*You* don't do anything, except leave town immediately and don't come back until this is over."

He couldn't imagine the look on her face being any different if he'd slapped her. "You think I'm gonna run away and leave you to face this alone?"

"Heady, look how many people have already died. And that's just a worst-case scenario. I'm talking about taking on a major studio. Being involved could destroy you professionally. I'm not gonna let you get hurt."

"If you want me to leave, then you better start packing to come with me, because that's the only way I'm going."

He couldn't keep from grinning. "You're such a stubborn bitch. God, I love you."

"Love you too, fucko. So like I said before, what do we do?"

This much, at least, he had an answer to. "We find a way to take down Samuel Cordero."

TAKE 10

The 'safe house,' as Alvarez called it, was a grimy, two-bedroom stucco house somewhere in Van Nuys. Susan wouldn't be surprised if it had been used as a porno set at some point. It reeked of stale beer and copper, had stains on the furniture and carpet that would probably glow under a black light, and felt like a prison with all the blinds pulled shut.

She'd pleaded with Alvarez not to do this, then tried to bully him with every ounce of uppity Hollywood bitch she could muster, then even insisted that he let her speak to an attorney. But she finally agreed when he told her it was either go into voluntary hiding, or he could detain her for 24 hours for questioning that would not, he implied, be as pleasant. Either way, she was checking out of the world for at least the next day without so much as watering her plants.

"Believe it or not, this really is to protect you," Alvarez told her sternly, before leaving her with two armed undercover officers in the safe house. These two men, Stoffer and Bartlett, spent most of the day playing poker in the living room on a couch that looked rat-chewed while she watched television on a 16-inch, black-and-white television. Alvarez told her that besides himself, the two cops, and his chief, no one else on the planet knew where she was.

When evening came, Stoffer went to get them fast food. Susan declined a greasy burger and went into the bedroom she'd been assigned, where she flopped down on the creaky bed and stared at the diamond on her finger.

"Davis...where are you?" she whispered.

TAKE 11

By the time Davis could get back home, the media was in a frenzy over Mahoney's accident. They talked about the hit-and-run and Crosby's suicide on what they called 'the troubled *Killing Blow 3* production,' and, because of Davis and Susan's televised make-out session yesterday, they'd even connected the dots to the rest of her woes this past week. All this wouldn't have been so bad by itself, but some brilliant news jockey had finally brought up Davis's involvement in the Torsten Gross case, and now they were dredging up every fact they could find, including that the homicidal German director's whereabouts were officially listed as unknown.

It was a huge tornado of shit, and the media had placed Davis right in the eye of the storm through the same guilt-by-association deductions that Alvarez had made. The more tactful news sources began implying that he had some kind of curse himself.

And the less tactful were just coming out and saying it.

His agent's advice dovetailed with Baxter Devlin's: keep his head down and let some of this blow over. Which would drive him insane. He practically itched with the need to take action, make a declaration of his innocence, but all he could do is put his faith in Devlin, and hope the old man had been sincere about getting him through this.

Leo also called while he was in the car on his way out of the hospital lot, first to moan that they were ruined, then to tell him they should sue immediately, that it would solve everything, but he couldn't say exactly who this magical lawsuit was to be brought against. Davis got him calmed down by reminding him that Mahoney might be crippled for life.

"Ah Davis, you're right, you're right, of course you're right. This is such a terrible, terrible thing. I'm just so rattled!"

"I know, Leo. We'll just have to wait and see."

"*Gevalt geshreeyeh*, such a dark day for Apex. And I thought all that Oscar business last year was bad."

Davis narrowly avoided hitting a parked car. "What Oscar business?"

"You don't know? Ah, well, probably not. PricewaterhouseCoopers did their best to keep it mum. They were none too pleased with the accusations."

It took Davis a half second to realize he was talking about the accounting firm that managed the Academy Award votes, which were treated with more secrecy than nuclear launch codes. "Leo, *what Oscar business?*"

"Well, you didn't hear it from me." The old Jew lowered his voice over the line. "Last year, when *French Calling* won for Best Picture, some of the other studios claimed there was ballot tampering. They said they'd done their own polling of Academy members, and the numbers just weren't there to support a win. They even started questioning some of the other nominations and insisted PWC do a recount. They refused, and assured everyone there was absolutely no way any person could've gotten to those votes."

Davis agreed with that part. There likely hadn't been any *person* that tampered with the ballots. "Why haven't I heard about this before?"

"I only know because a friend of mine over at MGM told me. Some of the studio heads wanted to push it further, maybe even bring legal action, much to Baxter Devlin's embarrassment. But he pulled out a victory, just like he always does. Sometimes I think that *shmendrik* must *kakn* out *gelt*, if you catch my meaning."

"Just tell me what he did, Leo."

"He set Samuel Cordero loose on them, of course! I got the idea Cordero bullied the other studios a bit, convinced them it would be bad for everyone if this sort of thing got out to the public, so they all hushed up. People barely want to watch the Oscars anymore as it is. I'll tell you, that Cordero is not someone I would want to cross. Woe to us if he should take over." Leo sighed heavily. "Keep me informed about Derek."

"Will do." Davis hung up, feeling sick.

He was only moderately surprised to see that his house had also been searched and wrecked since he dropped by earlier. Cordero must've sent more goons after finding out Davis had escaped the other two. Or hell, maybe Alvarez had done it. Did the cops even need a search warrant when the front door was busted open?

He couldn't stay here. Besides the fact that he would be too jumpy to sleep, he expected the media to have a vigil set up on his front lawn by nightfall. Davis hastily packed a bag and went to the first cheap roadside motel he could find. He hid his swollen face behind wide sunglasses, paid in cash, and grabbed a bucketful of ice before locking himself in his room and turning on all the lights.

After trying—and failing—to get through to Cordero at the studio, he called Susan's cell again and left her a message about where he was. He fashioned an ice pack for himself and held it to his throbbing nose and eye socket while he flipped through channels. Most news outlets were playing four-year-old footage of himself being released from custody. He'd almost dozed off when his cell phone rang with a number he didn't recognize. He answered in case it was Cordero returning his call.

"Doesn't seem like they've connected Werdner or Spitzen's deaths to you yet, but with all this renewed interest in Torsten Gross, I'm sure they'll get there eventually."

It took Davis a long moment to place the nasally grunting on the other end of the line.

"Brown," he growled.

"It *is* all connected though, isn't it? Surely no one's naïve enough to think that two people involved in the Gross case just happened to end up dead within a week of each other, and people all around the other three are dropping left and right."

"What do you want, Brown? I doubt you'll be getting any more mementos from your little spy. It's gonna be hard to keep filming when the star is having his legs rebuilt."

"I know. And it's for that very reason I find myself with a copy of the script that has skyrocketed in value. I've had offers to buy it for ten times what I paid."

"Congratulations, your suckling at the underbelly of Hollywood has paid off."

"Indeed." Brown chortled. "But I would sooner burn my VHS copy of *Seven Samurai* signed by Kurosawa himself than sell that script, you understand. The whole world should be able to enjoy this wonderful piece of writing, and absolutely for free."

"Spare me your Wikileaks, we-are-the-digital-world propaganda. You just wanna be in the limelight for five minutes because your daddy didn't hug you enough."

There was a moment of befuddled silence from the other end of the line. "Wow, that hurts. I thought we were building a rapport here."

"Do I sound like a case of jelly donuts to you, Brown? No? Then trust me, we don't have any rapport."

"Fine," Brown huffed. "Since I'm a man of my word, I'll still say what I called to say. My offer stands. If you want to meet with me and answer my questions about Gross, I'll hand over the script. If not, I post it tomorrow morning."

Davis was about to tell him to roll that script into a tight little tube and insert it where the blog doesn't libel, when a sudden thought occurred to him. Just because *Killing Blow 3* was on indefinite hiatus didn't mean the script was a total loss. Three months from now, he might be making the same movie with a different actor in the lead, or there might be a rewrite from which entire chunks of the original were lifted.

In any case, now that he'd lost the medallion, what better way was there to show Devlin—and of course, Cordero—that he was on the studio's team than to get their property back from Marion Brown and his online tabloid?

"I'll be there at nine AM," he said.

SCENE VII

(print it)

TAKE 1

Davis awoke in the motel room Friday morning, one week after Tonya's murder, and tried Susan's cell again. Her voicemail was full, so he didn't even get to hear her recorded voice this time. He considered calling Jared, to apologize about yesterday, but instead got up, showered, and dressed in jeans and a collared green shirt to go to the *Naked Hollywood* offices. The swelling on his face had gone down quite a bit, but the bruising was still visible.

Naked Hollywood was located in a non-descript office tower in the heart of downtown, a sheer, trapezoidal structure with strips of dark, plate glass running around it. Davis was only sure he was in the right place when he found the online publication listed in the lobby directory for the fifteenth floor.

As much as he disliked Brown and everything the man stood for, Davis still expected one of the biggest Hollywood rag websites in the world to have a professional office. In this, he was sorely mistaken; the place made their old studio at Lowe-Mane look like Trump Tower. The sign on the entrance door was hand-lettered in blue Sharpie, and when Davis walked inside, he found a beaten-up schoolteacher desk in the reception area, separated from the rest of the suite by a velvety purple curtain that made him feel like he was at a high school theater production.

The front desk was unmanned, with no sign of the girl who had answered his call earlier in the week. A bellhop ringer sat on the corner, in front of another homemade sign that read, 'Ring for Service!' Davis did so.

A few seconds later, the curtain behind the desk was thrown dramatically open, and a trollish little man straight out of Billy Goats Gruff emerged.

"Davis Lowe! I can't even begin to tell you what an honor it is to have you visit my humble journalistic endeavor! You're the first famous—well, *semi*-famous—person who ever has!"

Marion Brown stood on the other side of the desk, back slightly bowed by the rotund weight he carried around his middle, hands held fingertip-to-fingertip on top of the greasy, copper-colored nest of beard that spilled from his piggish face down between his considerable breasts. He wore a baggy gray tunic and matching pants with intricate gold piping, both of which looked like something from the Tolkien Spring Collection, and the remaining ring of curly red hair that grew on his bulbous head was braided in twin rolls that hung over one shoulder. His nose was big and squashed to the left, his eyes buggy and wide, and he had a general air of unkemptness about him. Otter had been just as big and ill-proportioned, but at least he'd been clean. As Davis watched, the other man gave a humble bow over his steepled hands, like a druid priest.

"Save it," Davis told him. "I'm not here to LARP with you, I just came to meet your extortion demands and take what belongs to me."

Brown's face fell. He snorted once, a sound like a snuffling warthog, then held aside the curtain and mumbled, "Right this way. We can talk in my office."

Davis went in first. The large space on the other side of the curtain was unimpressive, to say the least. More yard-sale quality desks were gathered in the middle of the open floor, adorned with battered computer equipment and surrounded by coils of electrical wire and overflowing trash cans. Most of the overhead lights were out, and those that remained flickered and buzzed. The place was a dump, more of a run-down clubhouse than a bullpen, but Davis figured that was the advantage of having your entire business exist in the false reality of the internet. Still, he did find it odd that the office was deserted; no way did this hobbit run the entire website himself.

"My staff is gone for the day," Brown said, as if reading his thoughts.

"Are Woodward and Bernstein out trying to crack an important case your readers will really care about? Like the color of Scarlet Johansson's panties?"

"I wanted you to feel like we had complete privacy for our chat, so I closed the office."

"Oh my, what a sacrifice. How *will* the world wide web survive?"

To his credit, Brown took all the sarcasm without a peep of protest. He led the way through another door that opened onto a long hallway against the outside of the building, the left wall made of those dark, floor-to-ceiling windows Davis had seen from the street. The sun was high enough now that it created steeply slanting shafts of light that fell across the dirty carpet in glowing rectangles. At the end of the hall was another door, and Brown's office beyond.

This room, on the other hand, was everything Davis envisioned from a pop culture junkie. Movie posters covered every wall along with shelves of new, in-the-box action figures, and, in the far corner behind his desk, where men like Baxter Devlin and Phillip Reilly usually kept a stocked wet bar, was a small credenza stacked with comic book longboxes, and a plate of Oreos and what appeared to be a pitcher of Kool-Aid set out, like diabetic Santa was on his way. The only light came from the last plate glass window in the row that had started out in the hallway; it made the rest of the room seem darker by comparison. Brown offered him the refreshments, then settled himself in a black leather recliner behind the desk while Davis slumped into one of the plastic chairs in front of it. The arrangement left him in the stingingly bright sunlight streaming through the window, and Brown in the cool shadows just beyond.

"First of all, let me assure you once more," Brown began, keeping his hands in that awkward, steepled position on his Buddha belly, "that anything you say goes no further than this room. I'll never tell a soul that you were even here."

"I don't trust psychiatrists or priests when they say that, so I'm certainly not gonna trust you. Where's this non-disclosure agreement you promised me?"

"Oh yes, of course." Brown retrieved a bundle of papers from his desk and slid them over to Davis. "That's your copy, all signed and notarized. Basically says I'm liable to you for pretty much everything I own if I breathe a word."

"Great. I'll be able to open a Toys 'R Us." Davis gave the documents a cursory glance—a sin for which his agent would've killed him—and said, "I still don't get why this is worth so much to you, if you don't wanna do anything with it."

Brown pushed back in his recliner and popped up the footrest. Davis wouldn't have thought it possible for the little dwarf to make himself look any more ridiculous, but, lo and behold. "Have you ever had one of your favorite TV shows cancelled? A storyline you were really intrigued by, characters you really loved? One week you're immersed in their world and the next, ripped out of it forever because some network fat cat claims it wasn't making enough money. No ending, no closure, just…unanswered questions."

"Yeah, I was pretty disappointed about *Firefly* too, but Jesus, let it go."

Brown didn't seem amused. "I loathe unanswered questions. That's why I've dedicated my professional career to exposing all of Hollywood's scandals to the light of day. I can't stand to have secrets kept from me. I *need* to know these things."

"They have medication for that," Davis said. But, after meeting the man face-to-face and seeing what he surrounded himself with, Davis thought he understood; this information was just another collection for Marion Brown, no different than his comic books or action figures. The idea actually made Davis feel a little safer talking to him.

"And nothing…" Brown continued, "…*nothing*…has fascinated me more over the past decade than the rumors about what happened between you and Torsten Gross."

Davis sighed. He had the non-disclosure and a personal promise; he was as armed as he could get for this. "All right. Ask away."

"I just want to hear the whole story from you, from beginning to end. But first, just tell me if what Sidney Spitzen claimed was true." Brown licked his lips and shifted around in the recliner until he was leaning forward. "Was Gross really…*not human*?"

"No. I don't think he ever was." With that admission, Davis launched into the unabridged version of their encounter with the great Torsten Gross, a story he'd revealed bits of to the police, but never told in its entirety to another person. At first he had to struggle to explain events, especially his own actions, but once he got rolling, the words came fast and easy all on their own. He distanced himself from the material, tried to view it objectively, until he almost felt like he was listening to someone else talk as he neared the end. It was only when he reached the portion of the tale dealing with Spitzen's involvement that he began to feel some grief and guilt, in equal measures. The reporter had tried to get people to believe the truth, had begged Davis and Jared and Susan to back him up, and all they had done is shun and ignore the man, all the way to the end. Brown listened intently, never interrupting, never even nodding his head, but when Davis reached their final encounter in the warehouse, he began to practically jitter with excitement.

"The thing about Torsten Gross," Davis concluded, "Is that, yes, he was a monster that could steal souls through a camera, but he was also some kind of…of interdimensional refugee. I know that sounds like a line from a sci-fi pulp magazine, but it's true. He came from some other world or plane of existence or whatever, and he escaped from something, some dark, evil…*presence*…that took over his home and scoured it of art and hope and life."

He stopped. His throat had suddenly gone dry. The vague, anxious terror that had started to work on him when Spitzen first showed up at the *KB3* set a week ago was back with a vengeance. That veil between him and the other world had never felt thinner.

Brown spoke for the first time, which startled Davis because he'd all but forgotten the man was there. His tone was grave. "Before Spitzen was laughed completely out of legitimate journalism, he implied that this thing—this presence—

could be coming here next, to our world. He said that we needed to be ready. Do you believe that?"

Davis suppressed the mother of all shivers. "Yeah. I do. And I'm pretty sure Gross thought so, too. In fact, he was terrified of it. And that begs the question: what could be worse than him? What scares the Boogeyman?"

Brown used his stubby legs to force down the footstool on the recliner and leaned to the edge of the desk, where the edge of that bright bar of sunlight began. Dust motes spun across the air in front of his snout-like nose. "What if I could get you that answer?"

This was the last thing Davis expected to hear from the other man. "How?"

"Through my position here, I've made contacts in a lot of unusual places around the world," Brown said gravely. "There's a group right here in L.A. that needs to hear your story—"

"No, no, absolutely not." Davis cut the man off with his hands. "I'm not gonna be passed around like a party favor to every whack job and conspiracy nut in the city. And if I find out you went around telling them, I'll have my lawyer after you."

Brown's demeanor darkened. "If you honestly believe the world is in that much danger, how can you just sit by and do nothing?"

"The world can take care of itself. It always does. And I have far more immediate problems anyway. Now give me the damn script."

"But that's not the end of the story! What about all the deaths this week? How do they fit in with Gross?"

Davis uttered a harsh bark of laughter. "Sorry, but they really *aren't* connected, Brown. That's a whole other story, and we didn't negotiate for that. Give me the script or you're in breach of contract."

The threat sounded weak to him, but it was good enough for Brown's inflated sense of honor. Looking like a sulky child, the fat man struggled up out the recliner, yanked open another drawer, and removed a sheaf of bound pages. He tossed the script on the lighted desktop in front of Davis, who rolled it up in a tube along with the non-disclosure.

"Do I have to ask if there are any copies?"

Brown stood rigid on the other side of the desk. "I'm a man of my word."

Davis swung up out of his chair and headed toward the door, then stopped. "Oh, and I want the name, too. Who the hell gave you this and the pictures?" It would just be an added bonus when he presented the script to Cordero.

"Some kid named Meyer," Brown groused. "Scott Meyer."

Davis would never have been able to convey the shock that rippled over him at the name. He opened his mouth, wanting to ask if there was any way the man could be mistaken.

But he never even got the chance, because the shadows surrounding Marion Brown picked that moment to reach out and slice his head off.

TAKE 2

Davis watched it happen, saw the darkness on the far side of the room come together, to...*coalesce*, thickening and spreading like an inkblot that hung in the air behind Brown as he spoke. It had no specific form, just a gelatinous, quivering mass of purest black. And, just as the scandal-monger finished accusing Davis's production assistant of betrayal (except, when Davis had time to replay events in his head later, he would realize it was actually as if the wraith had been *waiting* for Brown to say the name), a single tentacle like those that had saved Mahoney flicked out like a sickle.

One second, Brown's bulging, greasy head sat upon his lump of a body. The next, it was rolling across the floor toward Davis, the ridiculous hair braids leaving a snail's trail of blood behind it. It came to a stop face up just in front of him, with an expression of mild surprise more befitting gastrointestinal pain than a beheading.

On his forehead, a horned diamond and two interlocking triangles smoldered, the emblem seared into the flesh.

Guess I didn't need that non-disclosure after all, Davis thought distantly. It almost seemed a shame that the one person he'd told the story to was now dead.

A screech brought his head back up, a metallic scream like the ones he'd heard yesterday. Brown's body collapsed on the other side of the desk, taking the plate of Oreos with it. The wraith continued to hang in the air for a moment, a pillar of liquid smoke, and then one of those tentacles extended through the air toward Davis.

Raw terror made his guts clench, his muscles freeze. As the appendage entered the light from the window, it became insubstantial. It continued to stretch toward him, but the farther it got from the shadows, the lighter it became until, by the time it reached Davis, it was almost invisible. All the same, he backed away, and the tentacle withdrew.

The wraith began to move around the desk with the eerie, floating motion of a tornado. It gave the rectangle of light from the window a wide berth this time.

Davis ran from the office, still gripping the paper tube of the script, but stopped long enough to pull the door closed behind him. He continued to back down the sunny hallway slowly, so he could keep an eye on the door.

Black tar bubbled through the crack at the bottom, forming a puddle on the carpet, then oozed up the wall. Now it reminded him of a jet-black version of that classic movie monster, the Blob, a creature that had terrified him as a boy because of its inescapability; no crack had been too small for that beast to squeeze through. Once the protoplasmic mass got high enough to reach the small, triangular wedge of shadow above the windows, it began to creep along the ceiling quickly, coming for Davis.

He turned and fled. The cackling shriek of the creature followed him as he entered the deserted bullpen of *Naked Hollywood*. It was only then, when he saw the newsroom drenched in gloom, that he realized he should've stayed in the hallway, cowered in one of the squares of sunlight where it wouldn't be able to touch him, but it was too late to turn back now. The wraith had reached the end of the hallway just a few feet behind him and was reforming into the canine shape that Susan had described.

Davis plunged into the tight congregation of desks, weaving through them toward the curtain at the front of the office suite. He didn't know how far he would have to run to escape Cordero's pets, but he didn't intend to stop until he was back out on the street.

But now those screeches came from everywhere, every black corner and desk kneehole, anywhere that darkness had opportunity to gather. They were like schoolyard taunts, forcing him to change directions every time one sounded. Just as Susan said, he could feel them all around him, hostile forces that didn't belong here, whose very existence in this world was an abomination of nature and light. Soon he'd been driven into the corner farthest from the exit.

The dog wraith popped out from between two desks and bounded toward him on all fours. The goddamn thing was the same size and sleek shape as a greyhound.

Davis's feet tangled in a computer cord. He fell backward, dropping the tube of paper and taking an entire monitor down with him. The glass screen shattered on the carpet. Davis landed on his backside and scooted away as the wraith stalked toward him. Within seconds, his back was against the wall.

The wraith lowered its head as it approached. A hole opened in its black snout, less a mouth than it was a tunnel, and loosed a high-pitched garble.

Laughter. Davis was sure of it. This thing was intelligent, and enjoying every second of his fear.

It moved closer, walking up his body until it crouched on his chest. He could feel its consistency through his shirt, like a sponge soaked in oil. The blob that must be its head lowered until it was just inches from Davis's nose. This close, he should've been able to see details, but there was nothing, no features, just the rippling, liquid sheen that formed its body. The midnight black color held him transfixed even as he tried to turn his face away from it.

The creature tilted its head from side to side as though studying him, but, since it had no visible eyes or nose, Davis wasn't sure exactly how it could do so. The moment stretched out as he waited for it to kill him.

Then it turned and loped away.

The move was so unexpected, Davis thought it surely must be wishful thinking on his part. The wraith trotted toward the darkest corner of the room just a few yards away without even a look back. When it reached the well of shadows in the corner, it leapt into them, blended with the rest of the darkness like two drops of water meeting, and disappeared, along with that alien presence he'd sensed from the others.

He was alone. The monsters had left.

And he had an awful feeling he knew where they were going in such a hurry.

Davis sat up, dug out his cell phone, and frantically began to dial.

TAKE 3

Scott awoke to his father's screams.

He sat up, blinking at the bright light streaming through his window, unsure of what he'd heard. At first, when he glanced at the clock beside his bed, he had a panicked moment where he thought he was late to the set, but then he remembered Davis's phone call last night, and that Derek Mahoney was in the hospital.

Another frightened shout came from elsewhere in the house.

Heart pounding, he threw back the covers and hurried out to the living room. The shades were all drawn out here, leaving the entire room in a muddy yellow glow. Charlie Meyer reclined in his favorite chair in front of the television, where he'd fallen asleep once again. Since his diagnosis five months ago, he only made it to his own bed maybe once or twice a week, as though refusal to adhere to his normal schedule would somehow slow the progress of the disease chewing through his body like a hungry caterpillar through a leaf. He was still awake ahead of Scott every morning though, preparing breakfast before his son left for work. But right now he thrashed beneath the blanket as if fighting off an invisible enemy, and gave a terrified moan every few seconds.

Scott sighed in relief. The doctor had warned them that the latest round of meds might cause intense bad dreams as a side effect. He leaned over and gently shook the man until he woke.

"C'mon Dad. Let's get you into bed."

"Dee Dee?" his father asked, looking around with doped, confused eyes.

"No Dad, it's Scott." He didn't bother to remind the man that his wife—Scott's mother—would be in the grave four years this coming July, from an auto collision with a drunken asshole. But then again, he really didn't have to. His father's eyes focused, and heartbreak flooded his sallow face as reality caught up with him.

"Oh. Scotty. Lord, what time is it? You're late, I gotta make you breakfast!"

He jerked in his chair and tried to get up, but Scott forced him to stay seated; a feat which was dismayingly easy to accomplish. Charlie Meyer—once a man that had seemed big enough to move mountains—had the strength of a kitten these days. "We're not filming today, remember? Why don't you just come to bed and sleep a little longer? I'll make you breakfast today."

His father allowed himself to be led to his bedroom, making feeble protests all the way. Without his cane, he had to lean heavily on his son's shoulder. Scott got him tucked in, but the man grabbed his hand as he tried to turn away.

"You're a good son, Scotty. Your mother and I...we're so proud of you."

Scott didn't know if he meant the woman in heaven, or if he'd slipped into delusion again. So all he said was, "Yeah, I know."

"And when…after I…"

"Don't talk like that," Scott cut him off quickly. "Please, Dad."

"No, it needs to be said. The two of us can't go on avoiding it like it's never gonna happen." He coughed against his other wrist. The flesh there was so tight, it outlined every curve and jut of the bone. It looked delicate enough that you could take it between two fingers and snap it cleanly in half. Scott got angry every time he noticed something like that; angry at God, angry at the doctors, angry at himself. "After it happens…you just have to go on, you understand? Get back in school and become a director, if that's what you want. And stick with Mr. Lowe and that Mane fellow. They won't steer you wrong."

Scott grimaced and nodded. That last part may not be possible, as much as he wanted it to be. In fact, he'd be lucky to ever work in this business again. He crept out of the bedroom. Uneasy snoring drifted from the bed before he could even get the door closed.

On the way back to his room, he passed the den where the six members of the 'Gross-busters' (as he secretly called them in his head) had met a few days ago. The dry erase board still held their scribblings; Scott had told his father they were notes for the movie. Looking at it now, a pang of loss hit him. The movie was over, and so was their tiny fellowship.

He went back to his room to pick out some clothes before he hopped in the shower. As he removed a clean shirt, the object buried at the bottom of the drawer reflected a spark of light, grabbing his attention. He reached in and lifted out the medallion he'd taken from Davis's desk before leaving the set on Wednesday.

Not taken; *stolen*.

He winced as a guilty eel squirmed around in his stomach. It'd been bad enough when he'd taken the photos of the filming with his phone and sold them to Marion Brown, and even worse when he'd photocopied the script. But what choice did he have? His father's treatments had burned through the man's savings, swallowed up every one of Scott's paltry studio checks and the two grand he'd gotten for the script. Creditors called all day now; the electricity had been turned off twice. By Scott's calculations, in another two weeks they would be refused services by the hospital. That would spell the end for his father, without a doubt.

And Scott would be left alone.

The idea was too horrible to contemplate. It just wasn't fair. Life had already taken his mother; he wasn't ready to lose his father also. So in desperation, he'd turned to the one alternative cash source he could think of—selling movie secrets like a Hollywood Benedict Arnold—while he waited for a miracle that he knew, deep in his heart, would never come.

But that guilt had been nothing compared to the sheer nausea induced by the thought that he'd not only betrayed Davis this time, but all of the Gross-busters, and in something much more important than just spying on the movie. He'd tried to rationalize the act, to tell himself that Susan Campbell had stolen the medallion even before he had, but it did nothing to assuage this horrible regret, especially when he started to believe that he was, in some small way, responsible for what had happened to Derek Mahoney. That was the only reason he hadn't already tried to unload the necklace on Brown, or someone equally sleazy.

Well, that, and the fact that he was terrified the wraiths might come for him. He often wondered why they hadn't already.

The tweet of his cell phone from the bedside table pulled him from these thoughts. He dropped the medallion with its strange symbol back into the drawer and went to answer it. The screen told him it was Davis.

Maybe this was exactly the opportunity he needed to come clean, and throw himself on the man's mercy.

"Hello sir, I'm—"

"*Scott, where are you?*" the director demanded.

"I-I'm at home. Why?"

"*Get out of the house, right now! Go outside, in the light!*"

"What? I don't understand, sir."

On the other end of the line, Davis screamed, "*The wraiths, Scott! They know you're the spy! I think they're coming for you!*"

As Scott struggled to comprehend this, the shadows beneath his bed came to life.

TAKE 4

Something thrashed under his low mattress, hard enough to buck the bed a few inches off the floor. Scott looked down in time to see a thicket of black tentacles as big around as his pinkie finger come whipping out from beneath the hem of the comforter and wrap around his ankle. They yanked his leg out from under him.

Scott hit the ground hard on his side, crying out as his head bounced off the hardwood floor. The cell phone clattered beside his ear, and from the tiny speaker he could hear Davis yelling distantly, "*Scott? Scott, are you okay?*"

Then he was in motion as the thing that had hold of his foot reeled him into the darkness under the bed, the only place in his otherwise bright room where shadows could form.

He grabbed hold of the door frame with both hands just

as his calf disappeared beneath the edge of the mattress. When he glanced down the length of his body, trying to get a look at his attacker, there appeared to be only a black cave under the bed, an unnatural darkness that squirmed and pulsated. But he could feel a disgusting, sticky warmth spread up his leg as the wraith moved beneath his pajamas. Its grip strengthened. Scott thrashed, attempting to pull his foot back into the light from his window. The pressure increased, the bones of his ankle grinding while his knee and hip joint separated. He screamed in pain.

"Scotty? What's going on?" His father appeared in the doorway and looked down at him in bewilderment. Then he glanced at the bed and cried out, "*Good God, what is that?*"

"*Dad, help me!*" Scott shouted. His fingers slipped, allowing him to slide another few inches into those living shadows.

His father didn't hesitate, just grabbed hold of his hands and pulled. For a moment, he and the creature under the bed played tug-of-war with Scott, but the older man's stick-thin body and waning strength were no match. A metallic chortle drifted out of the blackness as Scott's lower body disappeared all the way up to his thighs.

"*Run, Dad! Leave me and get out!*"

Charlie Meyer looked down into his son's eyes, set his jaw, then released the boy's hands and dove across him. He landed on his belly next to Scott, and wiggled his upper half into the narrow space beneath the bed frame. "*LET GO OF HIM!*" the man commanded, his voice muffled by the mattress but still stronger than he'd sounded in weeks. Scott heard the dull thud of striking fists.

The pressure on his leg disappeared. He pulled it out from under the bed and crawled away with a sob, into the brighter parts of the room.

His father screamed as his lower half flailed and jittered, feet kicking a staccato rhythm against the floor. The thing was killing him. Scott pushed his fear aside and moved forward to help on hands and knees. He made it halfway there before a geyser of blood sprayed out from under the bed, hitting him in the face and chest.

Dripping with scarlet, he fell back against the bottom of the dresser in shock. The entire structure rocked back and then forward, spilling drawers and clothing on top of him and across the floor. Scott wiped blood and tears out of his eyes. His father had stopped moving. Under the bed, that darkness writhed and jittered, as if frustrated that Scott was out of reach.

Before he could even try to figure out what to do next, he realized the room was getting darker. The sunlight streaming through the window was being cut off as the drapes slid shut, seemingly on their own. Then he caught sight of the tiny black threads creeping out from the sliver of shadow high up in the corner of the room, tentacles as fine as filament that worked to seal out the light.

Shadows grew and lengthened. A viscous black blob emerged from under the bed, as if the mattress were blowing a giant spit bubble. It screeched at him.

Scott scooped up handfuls of the spilled clothes around him and threw them at the wraith, anything to keep it back. His fingers brushed metal amidst the socks and underwear. He looked down.

The medallion gleamed.

He picked it up.

As soon as his fingers made contact with the metal, the wraith paused, looking somehow confused. It stayed where it was a moment longer, a sludgy ball with tentacles sprouting from it, then began to retreat, shrinking back into the cave beneath the bed.

The room fell silent. The shadows were once more only shadows.

Scott couldn't say how long he sat there in the dark with his father's corpse, clutching the medallion and trying to breath, but when there was a resounding crash from his living room followed by shouts and the sound of booted feet, he finally let the silver disk slip from his numb fingers and then shoved it into one of the piles of clothing beside him.

A few seconds later, cops piled into his room with guns drawn. They took one look at his Charlie Meyer jutting out from the bed, and the blood on Scott's face, and then leveled their weapons at him.

TAKE 5

The cops whisked Davis away to a small interrogation room painted in faded mustard yellow upon his arrival at the police station. He'd only just sat down in one of the chairs at the table when Alvarez flew into the room with a thin manila folder, today wearing khakis and a white dress shirt with the sleeves rolled up. He pulled out the chair opposite Davis, eased into it, crossed his arms, and sat like a stone without speaking for what felt like an hour. Davis remembered some bit of advice from a journalism class he'd taken in film school about never being the first one to speak in an interview. Or had that been from some *Law and Order* episode about interrogations? Either way, he was hesitant to commit himself to anything until he found out what the other man knew, so he kept his mouth closed and stared right back.

"You knew something was going to happen," Alvarez finally broke the standoff. The statement had that unnatural calm to it like so much about the detective, but Davis still thought it carried a dangerous, razor-sharp edge. Fishing season was over, apparently.

"I didn't *know*," Davis answered awkwardly from the opposite side of the table, then added quickly, "What *did* happen, anyway? No one will tell me anything."

Alvarez ignored his question. "You called me screaming. Begged me to send every officer I could to that young man's house."

"I had a hunch."

"It didn't sound like a goddamn hunch."

Davis swallowed and looked at his hands, unsure what to say. He'd paced in the sunlit lobby of the *Naked Hollywood* building while waiting for Alvarez to call him back, feeling even more helpless than when Gross had kidnapped Susan to force her to finish his film. With the way Scott had screamed over the phone, Davis was sure the kid would be dead by the time the cops could get to him. But when the detective finally called, he would only say that Scott was alive and had been brought in; for his own safety, Davis presumed. He'd also asked Davis to come in as well, in the same somber, coiled-spring tones he used now. Davis had been so relieved the boy was all right, he didn't even puzzle over it.

But now, he wondered. The police must have seen the wraiths, or at least seen *something* to make Alvarez act this way. If they had—if Davis wouldn't have to lift that veil and convince the man of the supernatural element at work here—then he could come clean and tell everything he knew.

And what would that accomplish, except ensuring Cordero sends his pets after you next, and probably Alvarez, too.

"I'm waiting," Alvarez prompted. He was all business again, stony and hard-edged, just as he had been on their first couple of encounters. Whatever relationship they'd developed was now thoroughly destroyed.

"I just...thought he might be in trouble."

"He's in trouble all right." Alvarez scooted violently away from the table, the legs of his chair squalling against the bare concrete floor. Davis was genuinely surprised at the outburst; it was the most emotion he'd seen from the man. He paced to the far wall and stood in front of the room's only window. "You just better hope whatever attorney he gets can make an insanity plea stick, because I'm sure his scrawny white ass will be dead in prison long before the state can put him in the chamber."

"*What?*" Davis asked in horror. "What do you mean, what the hell happened?"

"Why don't you use your newfound psychic abilities?"

"Alvarez, please...talk to me."

The detective answered without turning around. "The kid's father is dead."

"Oh, Jesus." Davis slumped in his chair.

"His head was just about torn off. The responding officers found him shoved under the kid's bed like dirty laundry."

"Where is Scott? Is he okay?"

"He's fine. Locked up where he can't hurt anyone else."

All at once, Davis understood why he was in this room, being questioned. "For Christ's sake, you can't honestly believe *he* did this!"

The detective finally turned back around and looked down his nose at Davis. "The kid was covered in his father's blood, right next to the body, and he refuses to say jack shit to defend himself. You do the math."

Davis thought about Charlie Meyer from the one time they'd met, his frail form, kind eyes, and cheery demeanor when he'd clearly been at death's doorstep. Even though his life had probably only been cut short by a few months, it still seemed like more of a tragedy than any one else who had died since this all started.

And you know what Jared would say: it's all your fault, for letting it get this far. For not doing something when you had the chance.

Maybe it was, at that.

"Scott did *not* kill his father," Davis said adamantly.

"If only it were that simple." Alvarez stalked back toward him and opened the manila folder he'd put on the table to reveal its contents: a sole, black-and-white, crime scene photograph of Charlie Meyer's death-slackened features, and the ragged ruins of his throat.

"Christ!" Davis exclaimed. He looked away, but not before he caught what Alvarez had intended him to see: the familiar scorch marks on the man's forehead.

"Yeah, not pretty, is it? But I'm guessing you recognize the symbol, since it's the same one on nearly every body in the morgue right now."

"You think Scott is behind all the killings?" But of course he did; wasn't this the exact scenario Davis had been afraid of all along, that whoever got caught with the hot potato would be blamed for the entire thing? Still, he had to try to make the man see reason. "That doesn't even make sense."

"Doesn't matter. It's outta my hands now. My chief likes him for our prime suspect, and so does the D.A. With the heat on this, they'll have a case built by Monday."

"They'll never make it stick. Hell, I'm an alibi for him myself on the nights that Werdner and Spitzen were killed!"

"All that means is they're gonna tear your life apart, too. Between the fact that you and the kid are so tight, and your little precognizant phone call today, it doesn't look good for you either." Alvarez slammed a fist down on the table and loomed over him menacingly. "No more bullshit, Lowe. Scott Meyer is gonna rot in a cell unless we get some solid evidence to clear his name. If they scrape together even a shred of proof that you or your new fiancée or your camera guy were involved, you're all gonna join him. This is your last chance to get out of this mess."

"But I don't have *solid evidence*!" he shouted. "All I have is...a bunch of insane stories that would get me slapped in the cell right beside him. Or in an asylum."

"Then tell them to me and we'll go from there."

Davis clenched his fists so hard, he felt the nails bite into his palms. "I can't," he whispered.

"Of course not." Alvarez gave him a disgusted frown. "That boy's facing prison, but what do you care, right? Everyone's disposal to you Hollywood-types."

"Can I...can I talk to him?"

"Ordinarily, I'd tell you to go fuck yourself. But the kid says he won't give us anything until he talks to you. So I want you to tell him to his face that you're not gonna do a goddamn thing to help him. Let him see what a waste his loyalty is. Then maybe he'll wise up and try to save himself."

Alvarez led him out of the interrogation room and down the hallways of the precinct to the holding cells. Both sides of the corridor were lined with floor to ceiling metal bars that marked off two long, open prison blocks, with men on the left and women on the right, separated by a privacy wall. A guard was handing out trays of food on the male side, so Alvarez and Davis went toward the narrow aisle on the other side of the privacy wall. Scowling female faces watched them from the bunks.

"What about Susan?" Davis asked as they walked. "Is she okay? Where is she?"

"She's fine. Just as close-lipped as you about whatever you're hiding. I'm going to the safe house right after I finish here, so I'll tell her you said hello."

As they continued on, a hand shot out from the cell to Davis's right, grabbed his shirt sleeve, and yanked him over to the bars hard enough to knock his already sore face against them.

Davis found himself staring at Muriel Ottman.

"*You'll pay, Davis Lowe!*" she screamed at him. She held him in a death grip with one hand, while the other clamped around his throat hard enough to cut off his air. "*Divine retribution is coming for you even as we speak! You can't escape your sins forever!*"

Alvarez came to his rescue, prying her pudgy hands off and shoving her away through the bars. Davis stepped out of reach, gasping and rubbing his throat.

"Sorry," the detective told him. "I forgot she was in here."

Otter's mother continued to shout insane gibberish at him as they left, but Davis suddenly felt like her threats were a harbinger of even more awful things to come.

Although how things could get much worse, he couldn't imagine.

Past these open cells was a block of private rooms behind solid iron doors with tiny windows. They headed toward the first on the row, but the duty guard stopped them and hiked a thumb at the door.

"Detective, he's been acting kinda…weird."

"How so?"

"Yelling all the time, asking not to be left alone." The guard frowned. "And he keeps begging us not to turn the lights off."

A sub-zero chill kissed Davis along the nape of his neck.

Alvarez glanced at him, then back at the guard. "Probably working on his insanity defense. Let Mr. Lowe inside for no more than five minutes, then make sure he's escorted out."

The guard nodded, opened the door lock, and let Davis walk inside.

TAKE 6

Past the door was a traditional wall of metal bars like the ones outside, forming a square cell twenty feet long. Bright yellow bulbs overhead gave the white walls a dirty tinge. The cell was empty except for one steel bunk anchored to the right wall, but Scott sat on the floor across from it, pressed back into the corner and watching the thin shadows beneath it warily. When he saw Davis walk in, he ran to the front of the cell and grabbed the bars.

"Mr. Lowe!" Tears of relief slid down his pimpled face as he looked out. He was shaking hard enough to rattle the bars. The orange jumpsuit he wore was big enough to just about swallow him.

Davis came forward and grabbed the boy's hand. "Are you okay?"

"No! They, t-hey said they have to turn off the lights tonight! Please, *please* tell them they can't do that! There can't be any shadows!" He twisted his head around to take in the rest of the cell, as if something might be sneaking up on him.

"Okay, all right, I'll tell them. But you have to relax, Scott. We need to talk, and I don't know how much time they're gonna give us."

The kid gulped at the air, squeezing Davis's hand until his fingers hurt, but he finally stopped shaking enough to say, "I'm sorry, sir. I'm so, so sorry, it was me, I sold the script to *Naked Hollywood*, and I stole the medallion out of your desk so I could do the same thing with it. I never would have, but we needed the money, my father…" He trailed and broke into fresh tears, his face screwing up and shoulders rising and falling in short jerks. In that moment, he looked both eternally younger and infinitely older than his eighteen years.

"I know, Scott. I'm not mad at you. It doesn't matter."

"But it does! I…oh god, this is all my fault! *I killed my father!*"

The sight of the teenager crying made Davis's heart ache. But before comforting the boy, he gave a nervous glance around the room himself, but his was to search for recording devices or cameras. "No, it isn't. It's my fault. And you can't let them hear you talking like that or we'll never get you outta here. Tell me what happened."

It took another half minute for him to calm down enough to speak. "The wraiths…they came for me, just like you said. One of them came out of the shadows under my bed and grabbed me. My father tried to stop it. After it…finished with him…it came for me again."

"So how'd you escape?"

"The medallion. As soon as I touched it, the wraiths went away."

Davis nodded. "Where is it now, Scott?" he asked urgently. "Did the police find it?"

"I don't think so. I hid it in a pile of clothes on my bedroom floor. As far as I know, it's still there." He leaned his forehead against the bars, hard enough to make the metal ring. "I just don't understand why they went after me now. Why not stop me before I even sold the script?"

"Because they didn't know, and neither did Cordero." Davis gave him a quick run down of events at the *Naked Hollywood* office, lowering his voice so much when he got to the part about Brown's death that Scott had to put one ear between the bars to hear him.

"Marion Brown is *dead*?" Scott whispered. "Do the police know?"

"Not exactly." Davis had left the *Naked Hollywood* offices in a hurry after calling Alvarez and Scott, but not before he'd worked up the nerve to have one last peek in Brown's office. Unlike with Ralph and Cordero's executive goons, the wraiths hadn't done him the service of disposing of the remains. Brown's head still stared up from the floor, the symbol on his forehead charred into the skin like griddle marks. Davis had no choice but to leave the man where he'd fallen, wipe every surface he could remember touching, and retrieve the script. He could only hope that Brown had told him the truth about their meeting being a secret; otherwise, Alvarez's chief would have that last scrap of evidence needed to arrest Davis, too.

Scott was almost frantic on the other side of the bars. "Then we have to tell them! I couldn't have killed both of them at the same time! That could clear my name!"

"I wouldn't count on it. The way things are now, I would probably just wind up in here with you. And I might anyway, if we don't figure a way out of this. Anyway, the point is, the wraiths never came after you before because I don't think they had any idea who the spy was until Brown told me. They were right there listening, ready to pounce as soon as he talked. After they got rid of him, they came after you."

"Then I'm a loose end." Scott suddenly looked like he might cry again as he moaned, "They're gonna come for me! I have to get outta here before it gets dark!"

"Scott, just stay calm. All they wanted is you out of the way, and they've got that."

"*You don't know that!*" he shrieked, the words echoing off the cold, concrete walls. "*You don't know anything about them! Goddamn it, I can't stay in here!*" He launched into a frustrated fit, beating his fists against the bars and finally sliding down onto the floor, where he curled up into a miserable, sobbing ball.

Davis thought about his vow to Jared, that they wouldn't lose anyone else, but they had. Mahoney and Scott may not be dead, but watching them go through this was a thousand times worse.

The guard pulled open the door and asked, "Everything all right in here?"

"It's fine, just give us a few more minutes."

"You got one left."

Davis waited until the door was closed again before dropping to his knees next to the bars. "Scott, listen to me. Do you trust me?"

The boy continued to cry, but nodded his head.

"Then please believe that I will get you out of this. I have a plan that will fix everything. You just have to give me some time."

"Okay," Scott muttered miserably.

"In the meantime, don't say *anything* to the police, all right? Just keep telling them you're innocent."

This time, there was no reply from the huddled orange mass on the other side of the bars. Davis sat on the hard floor with his production assistant, neither of them speaking, until the guard finally came to get him.

TAKE 7

Davis left the precinct and drove hard for Arcadia, never doing less than thirty miles over the speed limit on the freeway. He lucked out; traffic was light, and he encountered no cops. Still, it took him almost an hour to reach Scott's house.

The place was covered in yellow police tape, but the crime scene was abandoned for now. The front door was unlocked. He studied the neighboring houses until he was sure he wasn't being watched and then crept inside, turning on lights as he went.

He passed the small den where they'd held their supernatural summit earlier in the week. The six of them had been so optimistic then, so naïve and foolish. For the first time since this morning, Davis let himself think about Susan. Missing her was a constant, fierce ache in the middle of his chest, but it was probably best that Alvarez had taken her away. As long as she stayed out of this—away from Apex—she should be fine. Rather than dwell, he moved on, deeper into the house.

In the short hallway beyond, he found the room that must be Scott's, the walls covered in movie posters. The bed had been flipped onto its side and leaned against the wall, and evidence flags had been planted across the floor. A large puddle of blood had dried on the hardwood. Davis got a mental flash of the picture Alvarez had shown him and squeezed his eyes shut until it went away.

The rest of the room was strewn with laundry and dresser drawers. The crime scene analysts had probably taken pictures but not gone through it all. Davis used his foot to sift through the wreckage, sure the silver disk would be gone, but a few minutes later he uncovered the medallion. Davis picked it up by the chain and started to shove it into his pocket, the way Susan had on her front lawn while she kissed him, but then slipped the necklace over his head instead, dropping the medallion down the front of his shirt.

Relief instantly flooded through him.

After that, it was straight back to Apex. This time, he hit the first tricklings of rush hour traffic, so it took him even longer to get back. By the time he passed under the Apex arch, he was exhausted, emotionally wrung-out...but he felt determined too, an absolute resolution so fiery and all-encompassing it made the bruises on his face start throbbing all over again. The gate guard informed him that Ralph had been reported missing and that they were asking everyone if they had seen anything. Davis feigned ignorance and told the man he would keep an eye out. It would only be a matter of time until that mess found its way back to him, but one problem at a time.

At the main building, he parked, marched inside, and went straight to Cordero's office. It was at the opposite end of the hallway from Devlin's. The receptionist at first told him the Vice-President of Operations wasn't in, then changed her story to him being in a meeting when Davis insisted it was an emergency, and only after she saw he wasn't taking no for an answer did she admit she would have to check if he was available. Davis pushed past her, ignored her outraged shouts, and began throwing his shoulder against the locked door beyond her desk.

It opened after his third attempt to bust through. Cordero's face appeared in the opening. "What do you want, Lowe?"

"To give you back your goddamned proxy," Davis told him. The gloves were off now; all the secrets and subtext had to be ripped away if this was ever going to be over.

Cordero squinted in suspicion...but Davis thought he saw surprise on the man's face as well. "I have no idea what you're talking about."

"That's not what you told Susan. But that's okay, if you don't want it, I'm sure the cops will take it off my hands, since it goes so well with all those bodies they've been collecting. Maybe I'll even tell them about that lovely matching pinkie ring you wear."

"Brittney, go home," Cordero told his secretary without taking his eyes from Davis. They continued to glare at one another silently while the office girl scurried away, then the VP stood aside and held open the door. "Come in."

"I think I'd be more comfortable talking out here."

The other man clenched his jaw, but stepped outside. Davis led him into the neutral ground in the middle of the hallway. "All right, Lowe, what the hell's going on?" he demanded quietly. "What happened to my men?"

"They're dead."

This time, the surprise in Cordero's flinty eyes was unmistakable. "*You* killed them?"

"One of them accidentally shot the other one, then killed Ralph from security, then tripped and impaled himself. You don't employ the most competent goons."

"Oh, for Christ's sake..." He squeezed a fist in front of his mouth until the knuckles turned white. "What about their medallions? What happened to them?"

"Both destroyed."

This seemed to calm him. He glanced both directions down the empty hall, ran a hand through his gelled hair, straightened his suit jacket, and said, "So Killam's is the only one unaccounted for. Where is it?"

"Close. But I'm more than willing to give it to you."

"Excellent. I'm glad you've seen reason."

"Yeah, now it's up to you to do the same. Before I hand it over, I need some assurances from you."

"Such as?"

"For starters, that you'll call off your dogs."

"The lawyers won't be a problem. Jeff Walker wants to hold you responsible for Mahoney's accident, but Devlin keeps standing up for you, for reasons I can't begin to understand."

"That's great, but I'm not talking about the lawyers," Davis said. "I'm talking about your *dogs*. You know, the ones that look like they went swimming in crude oil and have an aversion to your crappy silver jewelry."

Cordero stared at him, his mouth working soundlessly for a few more seconds before he finally got out, "How do you know so much, Lowe?"

"It wasn't hard to figure out. But there's more, I need—"

He was cut off by a burst of talking and noise from the far end of the hall. They looked up to see Baxter Devlin stepping off the elevator with a group of men in suits, all of them talking and laughing. Cordero grabbed Davis's arm and yanked him around the corner, into his receptionist's area, then slammed him against the wall. His big hands fell on Davis's shoulders. The silver pinkie ring was just visible in his periphery.

"*Not here*," Cordero hissed. "Meet me at your sound-stage alone in ten minutes and we can...negotiate."

TAKE 8

The *Killing Blow* set was dark, so Davis turned on all the lights. Even though he had the medallion now, he still felt better when the shadows were banished. Not that it seemed to help; as Killam had told Susan, the wraiths always found a way of making more darkness when they needed it.

The soundstage looked the same as yesterday, when he'd been brought here at gunpoint. Despite all the awfulness that had happened here, it was sad to think he would probably never see the place again. His first shot at the big leagues. He wanted to walk through the various set pieces, but was too afraid of what might be lurking.

As he moved toward his office, there was a creak from the film room. Davis grabbed a boom mic pole and held it over his head with one hand while he gripped the medallion through his shirt with the other. *They can't hurt me, they can't hurt me*, he thought. He eased to the door, took a deep breath, then jumped through.

Jared was across the room, with a metal cart full of electronic equipment.

"Hey," his partner (*former* partner, he reminded himself) said awkwardly. He eyed the boom mic pole and asked, "Did you finally pull that outta your ass?"

"What are you doing here?" Davis demanded, setting the metal rod on a table as he hurried toward Jared.

"Relax, I'm not here to rob the place, I just wanted to get some of my own personal equipment. I'll be outta your way in a few minutes and then you never have to see me again, I swear."

"You gotta get out! Right now!"

Jared sighed. "Let's not do this, man. You know this stuff is mine, so don't make me take you to court for it."

"I don't give a shit about that, you just have to come back later! I need the set!"

"How come?"

"None of your business! Now go before I call security!"

He took Jared by the arm to lead him toward the door, but the man planted his heels. Davis dragged at him, tried to throw a shoulder into his stomach to lift him off his feet, and within seconds the two of them were almost wrestling. After a minute or so, Jared gave a grunt of pain that quickly turned to laughter. "Ow, ow, watch the leg, asshole!"

Davis let go and stepped away. "Damn it, I'm serious! You can't be here right now!"

"Why, you gonna whack off in here?"

Telling him the truth was probably a mistake, but hiding it would be like admitting guilt. "Cordero is meeting me here in a few minutes."

Jared gaped. "Are you fucking nuts? The guy already tried to kill you once. Now you're gonna make it easy for him to finish the job?"

"I'm not an idiot, Jared. He wants the medallion, but I'm not gonna give it to him until he agrees to call off the wraiths."

"And you really think you can trust him?"

"That's what I'm here to find out."

Jared rolled his eyes. "What does it matter anyway, Davis? If all you want is to run for the hills with your tail between your legs, then do it. If our theory is right, the wraiths will leave you alone if you're not messing with the studio. You don't have to suck up to this motherfucker."

"There's more." Davis wet his lips with a tongue that

was too dry for the job. "I'm in trouble, Jared. So is Scott. Cordero might be the only one that can save us from going to prison."

Jared frowned at him, waiting.

"Scott was the spy. He's the one that stole the medallion from my desk and sold the script to Marion Brown. The wraiths tried to kill him for it, but ended up getting his father instead. Alvarez arrested Scott, and now they wanna pin everything on him."

"Why am I just now hearing about this?"

"It hasn't hit the news yet. I imagine they're still trying to figure out if they have a real case before they charge him and make the official announcement."

"No, I mean, why am I just now hearing about it from *you*? I don't care if you have a problem with me, I should've been told the kid was in trouble."

"Jared...there's so much more that I can't even get into right now. All I can tell you is that reasoning with Cordero is the only shot Scott has. Maybe the only shot all of us have."

"Then I'm staying."

"No, you're not!"

From the soundstage floor, someone shouted, "Lowe? Where are you?"

"Stay here, and be quiet," Davis hissed, leaving before Jared could argue.

TAKE 9

Cordero stood in the narrow wedge of late afternoon sunlight streaming through the open hangar door, looking like an eel in a grey tailored suit as he cast a long, gunslinger-esque shadow before him. He looked in control once more, the momentary slip in his condescending façade shored up, just as impeccable and perfect as usual.

For a moment, he thought about Susan asking if the man was even human. It seemed like such a farfetched notion; or *would* have, before they'd met Torsten Gross.

Cordero kept his hands in his pockets while Davis came forward to face him. "We need to talk, Lowe."

"I tried to get you to talk yesterday, but you wouldn't listen." Davis pulled out a tightly rolled tube of paper from his back pocket and tossed it at the other man. Cordero managed to yank his hands from his pants and catch it.

"What's this?"

"The copy of the *Killing Blow 3* script that Marion Brown had. Consider it a peace offering."

"A little late. In case you haven't heard, your movie's DOA." Cordero thumbed through the pages. "How'd you get the fat fuck not to post it?"

"I convinced him. With words. Had the situation entirely under control, until he was murdered in front of me."

The VP looked up sharply. Davis decided he would never get tired of shocking the man, if only to see his superior grin vanish.

"Your wraiths showed up and cut his head off. They could probably use some lessons in subtlety."

"*Wraiths?* Is that what you call them? Well, I suppose it's as good a name as any." Cordero sneered. "They can be a bit…overzealous."

"Like a nuclear response to long lines at the post office. Then again, they say pets and owners eventually begin to resemble one another."

Cordero slammed the script shut. "You really have no idea what you've stumbled into here, Lowe. There are forces at work in this world, supernatural factors you couldn't possibly—"

"Yeah, yeah, save it. Trust me, I've had firsthand lessons about the *supernatural factors* of the world from people a lot scarier than you."

The other man didn't answer, but he studied Davis with a look of renewed interest as he walked across the soundstage with the script clutched in both hands at the small of his back. He approached one of the digital cameras, a big Panavision mounted on a hooded tripod. "That's right. All those stories about Torsten Gross. So would it make you a little nervous if I were to do...*this?*" Cordero grabbed the handles and spun the front of the camera to face Davis. The move itself was so abrupt and unexpected, Davis actually did flinch away, which caused the VP to boom laughter across the silent warehouse. "Lowe, c'mon...don't tell me there's actually any truth to those old claims from the late Mr. Spitzen."

Davis snorted and shook his head. The irony—that not even this man, with his army of shadow dogs, would believe him—was just too much.

"Let me clue you in on a little secret, Lowe: you were a laughingstock. An oddity, a sideshow. That's the only reason you got even those minor directing jobs. Once the novelty wore off, you would've faded into obscurity."

"Didn't stop Apex from hiring me."

"That was all Devlin. The old goat insisted we bring you on for this project. You're nothing but another goodwill case for him."

"And you're nothing but a coat hanger holding up an expensive suit." Davis took a deep breath. This conversation was beginning to remind him of the failed arbitration with Crosby. He had to control himself, for Scott's sake, if not his own. "Look, I'm sorry. That was out of line. I came here to see if we could call a truce, so we can both get what we want."

Cordero continued to stare at him for a long moment, and then, to Davis's astonishment, he actually seemed to relent. Something in him gave as he stepped out in front of the camera he'd just turned, something that left him looking tired and used up…and completely human. Davis didn't believe any otherworldly creature masquerading as a person would be able to pull off haggard so convincingly. "I agree. This situation has gotten completely out of control. The police are unraveling this thing fast, and there are too many arrows that lead right back to me. I'm willing to work with you Lowe, but before I can, I need to ascertain my liabilities. So tell me what you know, and how you know it."

Davis nodded. "I know you've been using these wraiths to better the studio for a long time. That they might, in fact, be the whole reason for Apex's success. I don't know what they are, but Killam told Susan they needed shadows. Along with the fact that he'd embezzled their entire budget."

"*Dwight.*" Cordero spat out the word with the disgust people usually reserved for names like 'Hitler.' "I should've let him burn in the bed he made, but instead, I took pity for old time's sake. Now he's dead, and I'm left trying to figure out a way to cover his theft." He waved a hand. "Go on."

"I know that they killed Tonya Werdner because she was going to take some sort of revenge on the studio, that they helped you blackmail Isaac Crosby, that they killed Susan's stalker and saved Derek from that car accident, all to protect studio investments, and that they killed Spitzen because he was searching for a way to connect it all to you. I also know the proxies keep the wraiths away, which must be why you gave one to Killam in the first place."

"But where did you hear that word?"

"Picked it up from your men. They were pretty chatty."

"That was money well spent." Cordero sighed and rolled his eyes. "You say those two are dead, and that their proxies were destroyed. I'm assuming the wraiths took the bodies."

"Yeah, they did." Davis grimaced. "You really have no idea about what they do? Don't they…I mean, I figured they would've…" He trailed, realizing that he had no idea what he figured. An image popped into his head, of Cordero sitting at a board room table to receive updates from those pillars of amorphous darkness, but it was almost like something from an old Gary Larson strip.

Cordero must've understood his confusion. "It doesn't work like that. Think of the wraiths as…independent contractors. For the most part, they go about their business, doing what they feel is best for the studio. But obviously, their particular skills have a limited range of usefulness. Sometimes I need manpower for studio business, and if that business might be questionable to the wraiths, I supply the men with proxies to keep them away. Just so there are no… misunderstandings."

"'Misunderstandings' meaning 'cut their fucking heads off.'"

"Precisely. In this case, once the proxies were destroyed and the men were dead, the wraiths spirited them away to God knows where, all to save Apex from another bloodbath on studio property."

"But why take them and not the others? Why leave them with a big tattoo on their forehead for the police to find?"

The VP sighed in exasperation. "If you can't figure that one out for yourself, you're not half as smart as even I gave you credit for. Now, *where is the goddamn proxy?* Once I've secured this last one, most of my problems are over."

It wasn't even close to answering every question Davis had, but it looked like all he was going to get. He reached into his shirt and lifted the medallion chain over his head. Cordero's eyes grew huge when he saw it. He raised an eager hand, like a child reaching for a cookie, but Davis stepped away. "Not yet. I need some assurances."

"Of course. I'll make sure you're not bothered by the wraiths any further."

"I'm beginning to wonder if you can even make that promise without me wearing one of these things for the rest of my life. But no, I need something different." He told the other man about Scott's predicament.

Cordero's laughter this time had a mean-natured ring to it that made Davis want to hit him. "Isn't that a nice, tidy end to all this? I'll have to call my good friend the chief to congratulate him on catching his man."

"Not so fast. I want you to help me get him free."

"And why would I do that? Sounds to me like the little thief got what he deserved."

"He's a kid, he made a mistake. And I'm not gonna let him pay for your sins."

"What do you expect me to do, Lowe? Organize a prison break?"

"Just give me something I can use to clear him. Point the cops in a different direction. Get Apex to pay his legal fees. I don't care, just help him. It shouldn't be too hard for the man that rigged the Oscars."

The VP considered this for a long moment. "If I do...is

this over? You give me the proxy, and we forget about this?"

"Yes. I swear."

"And what about the rest of your group? Are they willing to keep quiet?"

"They don't even really know anything."

"What about Mane? I'm not going to find him skulking around outside my house again?"

"Don't worry, I can keep him under control," Davis said.

"Then we have a deal."

Cordero held out a hand, palm up. Davis hesitated. There was no reason for the man to keep his word after he had the medallion, but what alternative was there but to trust him? He would send the wraiths, or more hired goons, and they couldn't fend him off forever. That was the way of the world. Rich, powerful men like Cordero got what they wanted, and all you could do is stay out from under their feet.

Davis moved to give him the medallion.

A polite cough came from the hallway leading to the offices. Jared stepped out, holding a large silver pistol pointed at the ceiling.

"I have a better idea," he said. "We keep the medallion, and you go directly to prison."

SCENE VIII

(that's a wrap)

TAKE 1

Jared watched Cordero and Davis freeze in mid-handoff. The two of them had such guilty expressions, you would've thought he'd just caught them in the act of initiating sex. Then Cordero looked from him back to Davis and snarled, "Lowe, you son of a bitch."

"No, it wasn't…I didn't…" Davis stammered, unable to word the truth in a way that wouldn't sound like a lie. Jared had been disgusted listening to him bargain and pule from the other room. He'd wanted to leave, had almost snuck out through a back door and left Davis to get chummy with this monster, but stopped with his hand on the knob as a better idea occurred to him.

"Don't be so modest, man. Everything worked just like we planned." Jared limped forward, keeping the pistol trained on the ceiling but ready to lower it at a moment's notice if any of the shadows in this room so much as twitched. "I recorded the whole conversation with the soundstage mics. And, thanks to dipshit over there turning the camera, I even got the whole thing on film." Both men's heads jerked toward the camera, where they noticed the glowing red film light behind the hood for the first time. Jared was thrilled to see the color drain from Cordero's face. "Yeah, that's right, fuckhead. The cops might not believe us about the wraiths, but I don't think even your good friend the chief will be able to ignore a taped confession that you had a hand in the murders."

"Jared, for Christ's sake, what are you doing?" Davis hissed. He was still holding the medallion out. "He said he was gonna help us. This can be over."

"It'll be over when he's behind bars. We'll see how much his wraiths can help him then." Jared reached out and plucked the necklace from the executive's hand. "I'll be taking this as evidence now."

"You insignificant little shit," Cordero growled. "This won't make any difference. I'm a *god* in this fucking town. You think you can touch me? You think anything you do will—"

Jared reared back and smashed the pistol across his face. He knew it was a mistake as soon as he did it, but he just couldn't stop himself. Cordero stumbled back into the camera. A gash across his cheek trickled blood, a single imperfection on that pretty-boy face.

"Seems like I touched you just fine," Jared said.

Cordero's expression turned as dark as a thunderhead, like the look on his face when he'd rolled down the window of the limo in front of his house. A smile touched his lips that was so murderous, it made Jared take a step back. He backed toward the door, keeping the VP covered with the gun. "Davis, come on, let's go."

"No, I'm not part of this!" Davis said to Cordero.

Jared halted at the hangar door. "Davis...*snap the fuck out of it*. Somewhere inside that corporate-apologist, studio-grubbing shell is my best friend, and he's better than this. I know you have an allegiance to Apex, but this asshole is not the one you owe it to; he said so himself. And if you think he's gonna let you go on your merry way with everything you know, you're a moron. So do what's right, and help me put this scumbag away where he can't hurt anyone."

"Don't listen to him, Lowe," Cordero said. Jared thought he detected a hint of desperation. "We can still make a deal here. You and me. But if you leave here, that's all over. We are enemies."

Davis shifted his weight from foot to foot, looking uncertainly from Jared back to Cordero. Jared was sure he would stay, and, if he did, it really would be the end for them, an irreparable rift that would divide them for good. Just as he was about to turn away, Davis started moving toward the door.

"You're dead," Cordero called after them. "All of you. Once it gets dark, there won't be anywhere for you to hide."

Jared dangled the medallion. "We won't have to, as long as we have this."

"You can't all use it at the same time, genius! And if the wraiths don't kill you, *I* will!"

Cordero's last threat echoed in the soundstage as they ran out through the door.

TAKE 2

"You better have a great plan!" Davis shouted, as they emerged onto the studio lot. Why, why had he done this, why had he listened to *Jared*, of all people, when this was so close to being over?

Because you know you couldn't trust Cordero. And if you'd given in to him, you'd be no better than the sellout Crosby said you were.

Whatever the reason, he was committed now, and they had no choice but to move fast. Overhead, the sun was starting its late afternoon descent from the blue L.A. sky. They had an hour of daylight, at best.

"I do. We call Alvarez, get him to meet us, and tell him everything. The medallion and the tape should help convince him."

"So you really did record that whole thing?"

"Yep. The only thing is, I had to upload it to my home server. We need to go by Heady's place to grab the hard drive. She'll have it ready."

"We don't have time for that!"

"Then we better make time. You heard Cordero; he's coming after all of us. I'm not leaving her alone."

Jared's car was closer, parked around the corner from the soundstage entrance, so they sprinted for it. Or rather, Davis sprinted, and Jared performed a hobbled lurch. When they reached the Charger, he collapsed against the trunk, then dug in his pocket and tossed the keys to Davis. "You drive."

"How come? What's wrong with you?"

"My leg. I was already having a bad day, and our wrestling match didn't help. Just get us outta here."

Davis got behind the wheel as Jared limped around and climbed in the passenger side. He gunned the engine and peeled out of the alley, startling some actors nearby wearing dolphin costumes.

"What made you come with me?" Jared asked.

"You didn't give me much of a choice after you busted in. Where did you get a gun, anyway?"

Jared pointed the pistol he'd used to whip Cordero at Davis and pulled the trigger. He flinched before realizing it produced nothing but a tiny click. "It's a prop, stupid. We're making an action movie, remember?"

"That's not funny."

"It was a little bit."

Davis turned onto the main boulevard of the studio lot. "Besides…you're probably right. Once he had the medallion, there would've been no reason for him to… Wait, what's this?"

Ahead of them, the gate guard who had told him about Ralph came running out of the shack, a walkie-talkie pressed to his ear. When he saw Jared's car, he waved frantically, signaling for them to stop as he planted himself in the middle of the exit. Davis braked.

"What are you doing, don't stop!" Jared commanded.

"I have to!"

"You stop, and we'll be bound and gagged in Cordero's car trunk in fifteen minutes!" Jared stuck a leg over the middle console and stomped Davis's foot into the gas pedal, grunting in pain. The Challenger's engine growled as the vehicle surged forward.

The gate guard dove out of their way as they sped toward him. The car crashed through the lowered wooden barrier, and Davis jerked the steering wheel as hard as he could, taking the turn onto the street beyond at better than forty miles per hour. Only once they were down the street did Jared let up, sliding back into his own seat. "Cordero's not being subtle anymore if he's sending studio employees after us."

"I guess that means we've got him scared."

Jared gave directions to Heady's place. They had just reached the onramp that would take them there when he asked, "You saw the wraiths again this morning?"

"Yeah." Davis gave the quickest version possible of his morning at *Naked Hollywood* as they raced down the freeway, which was just beginning to slow with afternoon traffic.

"You didn't have the medallion yet?"

"No. I didn't even know Scott had taken it by then."

"Then why did the wraiths not kill you?"

"Because the studio needs me. I think that's what it all comes down to, how essential you are to Apex. Devlin said he still wants me to direct for them, so maybe that was good enough for them to leave me alone."

"What about me? Or even Heady? You think it extends that far?"

"I don't know," Davis said quietly. But secretly, he was thinking about how the elderly studio president had told Davis to distance himself from the guy in the seat beside him. And, even worse, he had been prepared to do it. "Anyway, I don't think it matters if Cordero orders them to kill us."

"Then let's end this." Jared held up his phone. "Call Alvarez and tell him we're ready to talk."

"Okay," Davis agreed. "I'll get him to bring Susan."

"Good idea. The more of us there are telling the same story, the more credible it'll be. We'll have Scott out of the slammer in time for dinner."

When they reached Heady Tillman's place—a high-rise condo downtown that Jared said reminded him of Katherine Wickersham's luxurious skybox home—the sun was just sinking below the horizon, casting all of the skyscrapers in an amber glow. Alvarez agreed to meet them at the station after he collected Susan from protective custody. The detective sounded very eager to hear what they had to say.

They parked in the adjoining garage structure and hurried inside the lobby, Jared limping even worse than before. Heady had left word with the doorman to let them up, and minutes later they rode the elevator to the sixth floor and walked in the front door of her condo.

"I'm almost ready!" she shouted from the bedroom. The

place was very swank, all post-modern décor and pricey furniture. Davis noticed that every light was on. That would probably be a habit for all them for a long time to come.

"Please hurry," he told her. "If Cordero is really sending the wraiths for us, they're gonna have plenty of shadows to use in about ten minutes."

"But we have the medallion," Jared reminded him.

"Which, as far as we know, only protects whoever's wearing it."

Jared nodded slowly, then raised his voice to ask, "Hon, where's the drive?"

"Over by my purse!"

He went to a nook in the corner, still favoring each step with his left leg. Sweat beaded on his forehead from the effort.

"You sure you're okay?" Davis asked.

"I'm fine. I just need to pop a pill and sit for a while till it eases up."

"I had no idea it'd gotten this bad."

Jared slipped into the desk chair while he hooked the portable drive to a laptop and opened a file. Davis watched a few seconds of raw footage from the conversation between him and Cordero before Jared shut it back down and pulled the drive.

"I really wish I'd known that was being recorded."

Jared gave him a tired smile. "Don't worry, there's nothing on here that incriminates you too much, especially when we tell them it was all part of the sting."

They sat looking at one another for a long moment until Davis said, "Jared...about yesterday...what I said..."

"Forget it, man. You're here now, and that's all that matters." One corner of his mouth lifted in his most obnoxious grin. "And anyway, I'm used to you making an ass of yourself."

Davis swallowed hard against the lump in his throat. "Ditto."

Heady emerged from the bedroom, carrying a small duffel bag that she set on her leather couch.

"What is that?" Jared asked, getting up from the table.

"Just some things we might need." She threw her arms around Jared's neck, a sight that made Davis miss Susan all over again. If he could just hang on a little longer, she would be back at his side.

And this time, he would make sure they were never apart again.

"Hey guys," he interrupted, "not to break up the lovefest, but we really should go. I'll feel a lot better when we're at the police station. Cordero wouldn't dare try anything there."

"Oh, I'm sure he would send his little pets if he got desperate enough. Something tells me we'll only be safe once we've blown this thing wide open, and killing us would only implicate him further." Jared pulled the proxy out of his pocket and held it by the chain in front of Heady. "I want you to put this on." He cut her off before she could argue. "Just do it for me, all right?"

She pouted for a moment, then dipped her head so he could slip the chain over her red locks. The silver medallion lay between her breasts. "It's not the greatest fashion accessory."

"No, but it'll keep you safe. And that's all I care about."

She held the silver coin and turned it back and forth, catching the light from a nearby lamp. "So we're actually doing this? We're gonna tell Alvarez the truth, the whole truth, and nothing but?"

"That's the plan."

"So let's not keep him waiting," Davis urged.

Heady picked up her duffel bag. Something inside clacked.

They all turned to the door just as every light in the condo flickered in unison and went out, plunging them into darkness.

TAKE 3

The last feeble rays of sunlight streamed in low through the condo's wide windows, but the shadows were too long and deep for Davis to even see his way back to the front door. He froze beside what he thought was Heady's designer coffee table and asked hopefully, "Power outage?"

There was the sound of shuffling footsteps, and then Heady's silhouette appeared at the window. "The rest of the building is lit up like Christmas."

As if to punctuate this, a familiar screech drifted through the condo, seeming to come from every direction at once. The darkness around them suddenly felt alive.

And dangerous.

"Shit," Jared cursed softly.

"I don't think they like our plan too much," Davis added. He was afraid to make any sudden moves, like a man facing a wild animal that might be provoked to attack at any moment.

"Then they can deal with this," Heady said. A blue-tinged light blazed on, so bright Davis had to look away until his eyes adjusted. The darkness receded. When he looked back, he saw the actress now held a huge halogen flashlight big enough to use as a premiere spotlight. The bulb was so bright, the backwash created a diffuse glow for several yards in all directions.

"My emergency earthquake stash. Here, I have more." She pulled two more out of her bag and handed one to Davis.

He switched his on, brightening the apartment even further. He could definitely see now, but the flashlights created an intricate web of shadows that streamed away from them in all directions. "If they found a way to turn off the lights in the apartment, they'll find a way to get past these. We need to move fast."

"I can't," Jared said. Sweat drenched his face. In the bluish glow of the halogen bulbs, it looked like aquamarine diamonds glued all over his skin. "My leg is killing me, I can barely walk."

"Don't say it, you dickhead," Heady warned him.

"I'm only gonna slow you two down. Just go and leave me with a flashlight. Maybe I can draw them away until you at least get out of the building."

"You think I'm letting you be a hero? Christ, I'll never hear the end of it." Davis went to his left side and put an arm around his waist. After a second, Jared reciprocated, leaning heavily on his shoulders, but balked and flailed when Heady approached, pulling the medallion back over her head.

"Please." Her voice was barely audible as she laid a hand on his stubbled cheek. "You need this more than I do right now. I can't live without you."

Davis had seen Jared drunk, stoned, depressed, horny, and combinations of all four, but he had never seen his partner speechless. He let go of Davis long enough to grab a handful of red hair and bring the woman's lips to his again. This time, Davis let them finish. When they finally broke apart, Jared allowed her to slip the proxy's chain over his head. "Stay close to me then. We can't both wear it, but maybe it will protect you if you grab hold."

They went to the door, which Heady opened. The power had gone out in the hallway too; the corridor yawned in front of them like a mineshaft. Soundproof walls kept the occupants of the building from hearing one another's loud music and orgasmic moans, but they also left this corridor as oppressively silent as the moon.

Davis used the hand not supporting Jared to point his flashlight at the sealed elevator doors just a few steps from the entrance to Heady's condo. "I don't think we should chance getting caught in the elevator."

"They'd probably keep it from coming anyway," Jared muttered.

"Where are the stairs?"

Heady's eyes were huge and moist as she answered. "Other end of the hall."

"Terrific." Davis shined his light down the passage. The halogen beam should've been bright enough to illuminate the far side of a football field, but the shadows in the hallway stubbornly refused to part. His flashlight beam barely stretched three yards before encountering a wall of gathered darkness, like midnight fog. Killam had told Susan the wraiths became more powerful the more shadows they had, but Davis never expected they would be able to bend the laws of physics.

"I don't wanna go out there," Heady whispered.

"One step at a time," Davis told her. "Stay in the light."

They went out, Davis and Jared holding on to one another like contestants in a three-legged race, Heady right behind them, only pausing long enough to close her door. "Just keep going straight," she said. "There's a branch off midway, but the door to the stairs is just past it on the left."

They walked, easing past a neighbor's door to the right. Davis considered knocking, but whoever was inside couldn't help them.

It took only a few steps before the exertion of having Jared use him as a crutch caught up with Davis, but he kept on.

Their flashlights created a somber, cerulean bubble around them, at first reflecting off the art deco wallpaper and textured plaster overhead, but it seemed to continually shrink as they walked, until the ceiling and walls to either side disappeared into the murk. Davis wondered if they only had that much breathing room because of the medallion. Their whole world was reduced to the stretch of carpeted hallway around their feet. He concentrated on putting his left foot forward, then helping Jared hop along with his right.

From the edge of his vision, he saw a flutter of movement.

Heady did too. She gave an involuntary squeal and grabbed at their backs. Jared swung his flashlight toward the disturbance, but it was no use; the beam stopped short, reaching no more than a foot or so beyond their bubble. Almost immediately, another shadowy flit came from the opposite side, bursting into their circle of light and back out again, as quick as a fish darting at the surface of calm waters. That garbled, chuffing laughter came from all around, as if to let them know they were surrounded.

"Keep going," Davis said. He tried to pick up the pace, but the faster he went, the less useful Jared's leg became. He was practically dragging his partner now. The flutters of activity resolved into semi-solid shapes, four-legged creatures that prowled the periphery of the light as they searched for a way to breach their protection. Behind them, Heady's flashlight beam swung wildly, but when she cried out again, it sounded further away than before.

"*Stay with us!*" Davis yelled over his shoulder. Even their voices sounded muffled out here.

"*I'm trying to keep them back! Just get Jared out!*"

"*But he's the only one of us they can't touch!*"

"Give her...the medallion," Jared wheezed in his ear.

"There's no time for that!" Davis kept moving, but the hallway seemed to have no end as it rolled past beneath his feet.

TAKE 4

Heady pretended the flashlight was some futuristic ray gun as she swept it back and forth, shifting the sphere of light around her and driving back their attackers wherever she spotted them. She couldn't help it; she'd always been a method actress that immersed herself in the worlds of the characters she played. Plus, looking at the situation as just another role helped to assuage some of the fear burning through her veins.

For a while, she'd been right up against Davis and Jared, but then the screeches had come from behind her, and she began backing down the hallway to make sure their rear was covered. She was creeped out to find a pack of the wraiths right on her tail, hiding at the boundary of the unnatural darkness that smothered the hallway. Now, Heady glanced over her shoulder and was surprised to see Davis and Jared were a full five yards further up the corridor, so far that their bubble of light had completely separated from hers, leaving her on her own tiny island. It didn't matter though; all she cared about was giving Davis enough time to help Jared escape. She meant what she'd said, about not being able to live without him.

"*How long is this fucking hallway?*" Davis shouted.

"*I don't know!*" Heady answered miserably. The darkness had become claustrophobically oppressive. One of the wraiths feinted forward as if to leap at her. She pointed the flashlight at it. Visually, the beam didn't appear to do much, but it was enough to get the creature to back off.

If she had to guess though, she would say these things were toying with her.

"*I see the branch off!*" Jared's voice sounded exhausted but jubilant. "*We're almost there!*"

In her hand, Heady's flashlight began to flicker.

"Oh no, you don't." She jammed a hand into the duffel slung over her shoulder and pulled out yet another electric lamp. The whole bag was full of every flashlight she could find in her condo, and even a few that she'd had the doorman bring up from the little boutique store on her building's ground floor. After hearing Susan's story, Heady had been prepared. The new flashlight blazed on just as the old one guttered out, and she dropped it to the floor. The line of wraiths gave an angry screech. She grinned in triumph.

Behind her, there was a rattle as Davis and Jared reached the stairwell door. "*Heady, get your ass over here!*" Jared thundered.

"*On the way!*" she called back. She turned away from the line of shadow creatures, meaning to sprint up the last stretch of hallway between her and the boys, but was stopped cold as a much more solid figure swung around the corner of the other hallway branch, blocking her path. It stepped directly into her island of light.

Samuel Cordero's face swam into view a split second before she registered the pistol he jammed between her breasts.

But she was too slow to move before he pulled the trigger.

TAKE 5

Jared saw the figure step out in front Heady, the square-shouldered frame recognizable even with its back to them. He bellowed her name, trying to warn her, but could see it was too late.

A gunshot sounded—unnaturally muffled, as though the shadows had become acoustical padding that absorbed all sound—and then Heady Tillman fell backward with blood pouring down her chest, blood darker than even the deepest shadow in this hallway. For Jared, it seemed to take a thousand years for her to hit the ground. She landed awkwardly on top of the duffel bag still slung on her shoulders, then rolled into the floor on her side. The big halogen flashlight bounced across the corridor and came to rest facing her.

After that, nothing else in the world mattered except reaching her. Jared flew down the corridor, his heart feeling like a dead, shriveled lump in his chest. He was only distantly aware that Cordero said something, and paid no attention to the screaming of the nerve in his leg or the explosion of another gunshot followed by the grunts of a struggle. His vision tunneled down until all he could see was the woman he loved lying in a puddle of black blood and blue light.

She was alive—eyes open, chest heaving in short, shallow breaths—but with the way the blood gushed out of her, she wouldn't be for much longer. Most of her body lay in darkness beyond the flashlight's glow, where the shadows seemed to roil and pulse like a boiling cauldron. His own light was gone, lost somewhere in his heedless flight down the hall.

His damned leg finally gave out just before he got to her. Jared fell to his knees, then crawled toward her. Her eyes seemed to focus on him briefly as he reached out, meaning to pull her into the light, but her eyelids fluttered shut.

Black, oily tentacles unfurled behind her, no more than stringy silhouettes, dark on top of dark. They wrapped around Heady's waist and limbs and, just as his fingertips brushed hers, she was yanked backward away from him, into the darkness.

"Heady?" he asked, his voice a rough whisper.

The darkness in the hallway lifted, the overhead bulbs buzzing back to full strength and bringing the real world with them. Jared found himself on the floor, looking at the spot on the carpet where she'd been, a spot that was no longer even bloodstained.

Heady Tillman had vanished.

TAKE 6

After shooting the actress, Cordero spun around, but his face was too dark for Davis to see anything but the white of his bared teeth.

Jared ran past him, going for Heady. Cordero tracked him with the gun. As he pulled the trigger, Davis threw his flashlight. The VP grunted as it struck him in the side of the head, and the bullet shot into the darkness somewhere over Jared's head.

The chaotic motion of the halogen bulb and the sudden burst of muzzle fire threw the dark hallway into an army of dueling shadows. Davis caught a brief flash of the wraiths all around them, doglike shapes that shied away from the light like cockroaches. Cordero tried to bring the pistol back around, but by then, Davis had seized his wrist. They grappled in the darkness, straining and grunting in each other's faces.

"I knew you'd come here, Lowe. You're just as predicable as your movies," Cordero snarled. His voice sounded different, hoarse and raspy. "It's actually better this way, if I kill you myself. Then all they have to do is clean up the mess."

Davis didn't answer, just concentrated on the pistol. Cordero outweighed him by a good twenty or thirty pounds, but he wasn't nearly as strong as his hired muscle. Davis was able to force the gun down to their side and hold it there as he rammed the other man against the wall with his shoulder.

From the corner of his eye, he saw Jared on the ground, outlined in the backwash of Heady's flashlight as he tried to reach her. Then Davis blinked, and the actress seemed to disappear. A split second later, the lights in the hall came back on.

The wraiths had left just as abruptly as in Marion Brown's office.

"*Where are you going?*" Cordero screamed. Davis could see him clearly now, the cut on his cheek where Jared had hit him, the bruise from the flashlight at his temple, a sheen of crazed sweat across his forehead. His eyes looked like two loose marbles as they rolled around in his skull. "*Get back here and kill these two RIGHT NOW!*"

And suddenly, Davis understood the truth. "You don't control them at all. You never did."

The petulant anger that swept over the other man's face was all the confirmation he needed.

Cordero fought back with renewed energy. He ripped his hands away from Davis, freeing the pistol.

But then Jared was there, shoving Davis aside. He punched Cordero over and over again, first in the stomach and then in the face, the blows landing with such savage fury that the VP dropped the gun and sank into the floor. He covered his head with his arms, so Jared kicked him in the side. Up the hall, one of Heady's oblivious neighbors finally poked their head out and shouted something about calling the police.

"*Where is she?*" Jared demanded. He stopped beating on Cordero and stood with chest heaving. "*What did they do with her?*"

Cordero lowered his arms. There was no trace of the good-looking, high-powered executive any more; his face was nothing but a raw, bloody mess. One of his eyes was swelling shut, and it looked like he was missing a tooth in the front, but he sounded positively gleeful as he said, "Don't you get it, you idiots? If the wraiths took her, then the bitch was already dead! When *they* kill someone, they have to leave their goddamn calling card!"

Davis drew in a sharp breath. There was the answer to his earlier question, what separated deaths like Tonya's and Spitzen's from those of Ralph or the goons. As Cordero had said, the wraiths were a convenient disposal service, getting rid of corpses that could be traced back to the studio or, in this case, its Vice President of Operations. But when *they* were the ones that actually committed the deed, the bodies were left with that symbol on their forehead. It still didn't make any sense, but at least he understood the rule.

The rage went out of Jared in a rush. His shoulders fell. With jerky, robotic movements, he turned and picked up the gun that Cordero had dropped, the one that was not a movie prop this time. Davis wanted to stop him, but then thought of Jared and Heady's kiss earlier, of how happy the man had been since he found her, and how he himself would feel if he'd just watched Susan die and had the person responsible in his grasp. So Davis stood by and said nothing as Jared put the barrel of the gun against the VP's forehead. Cordero hissed in pain as the hot metal scalded him.

"If she's dead…then so are you."

Cordero didn't look frightened in the least. He looked up…but his eyes went to Davis instead of the man who was about to kill him. "Go ahead. But the reservation in hell will be for three. Because Campbell will be joining us."

At the mention of Susan's name, Davis took a step forward. "What do you mean?"

"I always hedge my bets." Cordero's red-rimmed grin sent a shiver up Davis' back. "Just in case I couldn't finish this myself, I set another fuse burning with some of Campbell's old friends. One that should be going off right about now."

TAKE 7

Bartlett had just lost his seventeenth straight game of Chinese checkers to Susan when the knock came at the grimy door of the safe house. He looked at Stoffer, stretched out on the couch with a five-year-old issue of *Esquire*.

"Your turn," Stoffer said with a shrug.

"You ordered the pizza," Bartlett argued.

"And you owe me for the last one."

"God, *I'll* go," Susan groaned. The two of them had been bickering in the close quarters all day. She rose from the footstool where they'd been playing and crossed the room.

"Thanks, ma'am," Stoffer said from the couch. "You know, you're real down-to-earth for an actress."

"Yeah," Bartlett echoed the sentiment. "I usually hate dealing with Hollywood folk. Back when I was on traffic, I pulled over Catherine Zeta-Jones for running a red, and she threatened to tie my testicles to my tongue if I wrote her. And when I pulled out my pad, she reached through the window and had the zipper of my uniform pants torn out before I could jump back. True story. Oh, but you've been really great about all this."

"Thanks. You guys are too sweet. I guess." Susan checked the peephole first and exclaimed, "It's Detective Alvarez!"

She reached for the knob and yanked the door open just as one of the officers made a squawking sound of protest.

Alvarez wore a jacket for the first time since she'd met him, a dark turquoise blazer that covered the pistol slung under his right arm. Beyond him, night had fallen on this quiet, inner-city block.

The detective raised an eyebrow, then looked around her at the cops, who had jumped to their feet and rushed to her side. "Is this a new protocol I'm unaware of? Letting the protectee answer the door?"

"Sorry," Stoffer mumbled, as Susan stood aside to let Alvarez inside. "Why didn't you call?"

"Maybe because I didn't want anyone tracking your location through your cell. Or maybe because I wanted to see how fast two of L.A.'s finest could be busted back down to patrol."

"It's just been really quiet. I don't think we're gonna see any action on this."

"I'm sure Miss Campbell would say that's a good thing."

"Of course," she said, then asked hurriedly, "What's going on? Has anything else happened?"

A flicker of something dark swam through his eyes. "We can discuss that later. I'm taking you back."

Panic twisted her guts. "Just tell me, is Davis all right?"

"He's fine." Alvarez turned to the other officers. "Move your asses, gentlemen. Right now. I want this place closed up and all of us ready to roll in five minutes."

Stoffer and Bartlett set to work, and Susan hurried to the bedroom she'd been assigned to pack up the small suitcase she'd brought from home. While she was tossing clothes in the bag, Alvarez entered the room.

"What's really going on? You swear Davis is okay?"

"As far as I know. He and Mane have agreed to talk. They

have some sort of evidence they want to show me, but not unless I bring you. We're meeting them at the station in an hour."

"Then why are we in such a hurry?"

Alvarez frowned. "Because this afternoon, my chief was ready to close this case and have me release you from custody. Then he gets a phone call from who I believe was that Vice-President over at Apex. The pushy one."

"Cordero?" Susan offered, her legs suddenly shaky.

"That's him. Then, suddenly, the chief wants me to leave you here for another night. Even when I told him I needed to trade you for hard evidence about a suspect, he forbid me from coming anywhere near the safe house until in the morning. No reason given."

"Meaning he doesn't want you to have the evidence?"

Alvarez hesitated, that glimmer in his eyes once more. "That, or he wants you isolated and alone here. And I'm even beginning to think he pulled my detail off your house on purpose just before it got ransacked."

Susan stopped midway through zipping up her suitcase as she grasped his implication. "You don't really think the chief of police would help the studio get to me, do you?"

"Let me put it this way: I think if his tongue was any further up the collective asshole of Hollywood's power players, they could all share one breath mint. I watch him play golf with these men, eat dinner with their families. If someone high enough up at Apex had a hand in these murders—which I'm beginning to see as a distinct possibility—I have no doubt he would be willing to assist in cleaning up the mess."

That was enough to convince Susan. She grabbed her belongings and followed him back out to the living room, where Stoffer and Bartlett had their own bags slung over their shoulders.

"Checklist completed. The house is secure and reset for

the next visitor," Stoffer reported dutifully. Then he turned to her and said, "It's been a privilege."

"I'll see all your movies from now on," Bartlett added. "Even the romances."

There was another knock at the door. Alvarez gave the officers a sharp look. Susan saw his hand drift toward the pistol holstered under his blazer. "Check it."

Bartlett crept to the door, pulling his own weapon. He stood beside the jamb and eased over to check the peephole. "Shit," he sighed in relief. "It's our pizza." He pulled open the door.

There was a roar loud enough to temporarily deafen Susan. Bartlett flailed a half step back and then crumpled to the floor, screaming in pain and clutching his midsection. Susan saw a waterfall of blood seeping between his fingers. For just a moment, her mind's eye saw Killam superimposed over the officer, his torso thoroughly shredded by gunfire.

"*Back! Get back!*" Alvarez shouted over the injured man's wails, drawing his pistol as he pushed her toward the bedroom. Susan tried to move with him, but her legs wouldn't obey. Time melted like candle wax around her, flowing with a dragging, hazy quality, all scored by Bartlett's shrieks.

A man came through the front door of the safe house, dark hair and complexion to match, wearing a Tony's Pizza cap and carrying a shotgun at his hip. He stood over Bartlett and aimed the shotgun down at his writhing form. Susan looked away before the blast. Bartlett's cries ceased, but the sound of trickling blood in the new silence made her stomach curdle.

The shooter pulled off the pizza cap and tossed it aside. His eyes scanned the room for targets. Alvarez squeezed off two rounds at him as he herded Susan out of the room, but they both missed. The man with the shotgun ignored them and turned his attention to the other cop.

Stoffer was caught on the far side of the room. Susan saw him hustle through the kitchen door just as a load of shotgun fire peppered the walls. The officer leaned back out with his gun and traded fire. His aim was better than Alvarez's. Blood blossomed on the shooter's chest. He slumped to the floor, shotgun still in hand.

But he wasn't alone. Two other men rushed inside, spraying bullets from huge submachine guns. Susan heard Stoffer cry out just before Alvarez shoved her into the bedroom and followed close behind.

"The window," he told her brusquely. He covered the door while Susan tore the blinds out of the way, undid the latch, and hauled at the frame. It wouldn't budge, the bottom of the metal window rusted to the sill. Alvarez joined her, but they were still trying to slide the glass up when there was a knock from the bedroom entrance. One of the gunmen leaned casually against the doorframe, his weapon pointed at Alvarez.

"Drop the piece," he commanded. Susan caught a familiar accent to the words.

Alvarez glared, then bent and placed the gun on the floor. "Who are you? What do you want?"

Instead of answering, he lowered his own weapon to allow another man into the room, someone bigger and taller, with a scarred face that Susan instantly knew.

"Frankie," she whispered.

The Russian loan shark put a hand over his heart. "I can't believe it, famous actress remember my name! Is very flattering!"

"Yeah, well...you're not easy to forget."

"I hear that often." He grinned shyly. "I am being very sorry to bust in on you so rudely." His tone suggested that he might've interrupted dinner to borrow a cup of sugar.

Susan glanced at Alvarez. "Frankie, listen...there's no need to do this. I didn't tell the police anything about Killam, I didn't even see anything—"

He waved the words away like gnats. "No, no, I am not worried about that! Is water under bridge between two friends like us, eh?" Frankie lumbered forward and sat on the corner of the bed, reminding her of a trained circus bear. "I would never have bothered you again, but I get a call from man who say he good friend of Dwight. He say he willing to pay off debt—plus 20 percent!—if I bring you to him. Even had address where you would be!"

"Oh fuck," she groaned.

"Do not worry!" he assured her boisterously. He grabbed her wrist and pulled her toward him, away from Alvarez. She could feel the strength in his massive arms. "I ask man why he want you, and he assure me, no harm to you will come. He say your boyfriend have something that belong to him, and he just want it back. Not everyday someone offers to pay off another man's debt, so, of course I could not refuse! I am hoping you understand."

"You won't get away with this," Alvarez said calmly. "If I don't report an all-clear in about five minutes, every cop in the city will be looking for her." Susan knew it had to be a bluff, but he looked completely serious as he gave it.

Frankie looked from her to Alvarez, his face darkening. When he spoke, the cheerful tone he used with her was gone. "Unfortunately...no one pay me to bring back spic pig."

The man at the door opened fire. Alvarez was thrown back against the window by the force of the bullets as they ripped through him, his head cracking the glass. He slid into the floor, leaving a trail of blood down the wall before he fell forward on his face. Susan slapped a hand over her mouth and let out a broken sob.

"Again, very sorry to be inconvenience." Frankie sounded like sunshine and rainbows again. "I hope there are being no hard feelings."

Susan refused to let herself cry as Frankie guided her to the door with a hand on her elbow. She wouldn't be scared, not this time. After all, she'd played the damsel-in-distress before; she was practically getting typecast.

"Come, boys," Frankie told the other men waiting in the safe house living room. "We are all going to Hollywood!"

TAKE 8

"This is your last chance," Davis told Cordero. "We're not setting foot in there until we get some proof that you really have Susan."

They were back at Apex, sitting in Jared's car in front of the soundstage that would've been the *Persuasion* set, if its director hadn't been a self-destructive moron. In front of them, the hangar door stood open just a sliver, revealing cold darkness. They hadn't seen a single soul besides the guard that had admitted them through the broken gate. At first, he'd tried to detain them, until Davis pointed out that Cordero was in the car also, and then the guard just tried hard not to stare at the VP's wrecked face as he let them pass. The rest of the studio grounds were dark and quiet, as foreboding as a cemetery at midnight. Comparisons to their final standoff with Gross kept trying to sneak into Davis's head, but he pushed them away. Gross was dead, he wasn't coming back, and Davis refused to be haunted by him any longer.

In the passenger seat, Cordero said nothing, just as he

had for the entire trip. Davis drove and continued questioning him about the wraiths, but he'd refused to speak since promising them that Susan would die if they didn't give him the medallion and let him return to the studio. Rather than let him go, they'd kept him hostage and brought him here, narrowly escaping a platoon of cops that had raided Heady's condominium.

Jared rode in the back seat, also silent. He'd kept the pistol trained on the back of Cordero's head and glared at him through the rearview mirror during the drive. Now he leaned forward, shoved the barrel into the other man's neck, and said through clenched teeth, "Answer him, goddamn it."

Cordero's hand slid up inside his jacket. Davis and Jared both tensed, but the man only pulled out his cell phone. He dialed a number, waited while it was answered, and then said, "Are you inside? Good. Put the girl on." He stared ahead through the windshield as he handed the phone to Davis.

"Hello?"

"Davis?" Susan's voice. "Just go, don't come after—!"

That was all. The line went dead. Davis's fingers curled around the phone until cracks raced across the glass screen. "They have her?" Jared asked. His voice was mechanical, but when Davis met his eyes in the mirror, they were sharp and aware.

"Yeah," he answered.

"What do you wanna do then?"

It was Cordero that answered, still without looking away from the front of the car. His puffy face and missing teeth made him sound like he was talking through a mouthful of marshmallows. "Give me the proxy and the recording, Lowe. I will walk inside, and send Susan out."

"And then you'll just let us all go, huh? This will all be over?"

"Oh no, you had your chance for that, and you pissed it away. All I'm granting you now is a short reprieve, so we can lick our respective wounds." A hint of that smug grin touched his split lips. "Besides, even if I was still willing to let bygones be bygones, I think you only have to look at your cinematographer to know this will never be over until one of us is dead."

Behind him, Jared said nothing. The proxy still dangled from the chain around his neck, but the emblem was invisible in the dark car.

Davis said, "Can I talk to you outside?" They got out of the car, leaving Cordero in the passenger seat, and stepped far enough away to be out of earshot. "What do you think?"

Jared held the pistol sideways in both hands, staring down at the weapon that had murdered his girlfriend like he suddenly couldn't understand what it was. "I think it would be a mistake to trust him."

"I agree. Why don't you stay out here with the medallion, and I'll take him in to—"

"No." Jared's voice was deadly quiet. His hands shook as they tilted the gun back and forth. "You can be the one to stay out here if you want, but he doesn't leave my sight. Not for a second."

Davis could see the pain in his eyes. While most men—himself included—would've succumbed to despair after witnessing what Jared had an hour ago, he seemed to be converting all that grief into the anger he needed to keep moving. "Jared...are you okay?"

"I'm fine. Car ride gave my leg a little time to rest, but I'm still not gonna be very fast when we get in there."

"That's not what I'm talking about. Heady...Jesus, I'm so sorry, I—"

Jared threw up a hand and turned back to the car. "I don't wanna talk about this, Davis. The only reason I haven't executed that piece of shit already is because Susan's in trouble. I will help you get her back, but all I want from you is a promise that Cordero will pay."

"I promise," Davis whispered. *For whatever my word is worth these days.*

Jared limped back to the car, threw open the passenger door, and yanked Cordero out. The VP fell to one knee before getting drunkenly to his feet. The eye that wasn't swollen shut roamed over them. "So we're all going in then?" he asked.

Jared shook him. "Yes. And I will be right behind you with the gun. So just give me an excuse to put you out of my misery."

"I won't need to." He pointed at the shadows waiting for them in the soundstage, a darkness that made the night around them seem bright in contrast. "Once we get in there, the wraiths will have all the opportunity they need to finish you."

"Except I don't think they will." Davis stepped in front of him. "Jared has the proxy, and they've had a chance to kill me twice, and they didn't. Even back there in that hallway, they could've taken me if they'd wanted—hell, it's dark out here, they could probably kill me right now!—and yet they don't. It's because the studio still needs me. When Devlin told me he still wanted me to work for Apex, it gave me some kind of immunity. Am I right?"

Cordero didn't answer him. He seemed to be sulking.

"Then maybe, to be on the safe side, I'll just take that ring off your finger and wear it myself."

This got a reaction. Cordero clutched his own hand and snarled, "You'll have to shoot me before you take this, Lowe."

"That's what I thought. You really don't control the wraiths. You wanted me to think you did, maybe you wanted everybody to think you did, but you're just as scared of them as Killam was. So then what are they, and why are they protecting Apex? Do you even know?"

Cordero shook his head in dismay. Bloody drool leaked from one corner of his mouth. "You're a blind fool, Lowe."

They started across the cobblestones toward the soundstage. Jared clamped one hand on Cordero's forearm and jammed the pistol in the small of his back with the other. Davis fell into step on their prisoner's other side and tried to keep a lookout. He'd brought one of Heady's big halogen flashlights with them, and turned it on as they slipped through the hangar door.

The *Persuasion* set was a maze of Victorian-style rooms. They used the flashlight to navigate, Cordero giving them directions where to turn. After their experience in Heady's building and the executive's warning, the dark was claustrophobic, thick as soup, but they saw no sign of the shadow creatures. Ten minutes later, they came through a doorway into a large space that stretched away into darkness on all sides. A single bright light burned in the middle from a chandelier, casting a circle of illumination down on the intricate tile floor. Based on what little Davis could make out of the décor and walls, it looked like this place had been designed as a grand ballroom for the film.

Ahead, a group of men waited on the far edge of the light, spread out around the perimeter. Davis tried to count them as he turned off the flashlight, but lost track somewhere close to twenty, all of them armed with shotguns, assault rifles, and submachine guns. A serious arsenal; his bowels tightened as he realized these men were infinitely more dangerous than Cordero's previous goons. He saw no sign of Susan, but as they reached the edge of the light, the man at the center of the formation stepped forward to meet them, a musclebound guy with a scarred face, wearing a gray tracksuit.

"That's far enough!" Jared told him, raising the pistol to the side of Cordero's head to make sure he saw it.

"Wait, wait. I am being confused." A thick Russian accent coated every word. These were Killam's murderers, Davis realized. The big man's brow wrinkled. "You have hostage also? I was not being told about person exchange. We will need to be waiting until man who hired me shows up to sort out."

"I *am* the man who hired you," Cordero said.

"Oh. Well…it is being wonderful to meet you. I am guessing we will discuss payment arrangements when you are not quite so…eh…restricted?"

"Enough." Davis stepped forward. "Where is Susan?"

The big man shot him a grin filled with teeth. "Miss Campbell is fine, just fine! Are you boyfriend? She is great girl, I wish you two big love and much success!"

"Um. Okay. Thanks." Davis rubbed the back of his neck. This wasn't going at all like he expected. "Can you please bring her out here?"

"Afraid I cannot do that yet, *comrade*. I am being instructed not to release until Mr. Cordero has the necklace he wants."

Jared shoved Cordero forward again, pushing the pistol barrel against his temple so hard, the man's whole head was forced sideways. "Tell him to do it."

Cordero cleared his throat. "Mr. Borovsky?"

The Russian held up his hands. "Please. Friends call me Frankie."

"Frankie…kill these men."

The words were so calm and reserved—not to mention unexpected—Davis wasn't even sure he heard correctly. The Russians seemed to feel the same. There was a moment of silence during which no one moved. Then Frankie asked, "What is that now?"

"*Kill them, kill them right now!*" Cordero shrieked, all composure abandoned.

Jared wrapped an arm around him his throat and pulled him close. "*Any of you moves and he's dead!*"

"*You shoot me and they kill you anyway, you dumb sh—!*" Jared's forearm choked off the end of Cordero's threat.

A murmur of discomfort rippled through the armed men. Davis raised his voice above it and said, "Let's not get crazy. All we want is Susan."

The Russians looked around at one another in confusion as Frankie said, "I am being in awkward position. I would rather not be having man who is paying me dead. So, here is solution: you give me necklace as show of good faith. That keeps everyone reasonable. Then, we put down our guns, you do same, release Mr. Cordero, and I give you Miss Campbell. Easy!"

Davis hesitated. "You swear?"

Frankie put one gigantic hand over his heart. "On mother's ashes."

Davis didn't know this man in the least, but he already trusted him far more than Cordero. He looked to Jared, who took off the proxy and handed it to him. Davis tossed it through the air to Frankie. The mobster caught the chain and held it up for inspection. "So much trouble for *this*? *Comrade*, I get you much better deal on higher quality merchandise."

"Your turn," Davis said.

Frankie shoved the medallion in his pocket. "Okay boys, guns on floor." The other men complied, setting their arms on the tile.

Davis looked at Jared. "Let him go."

A brief war took place on Jared's face, during which it looked like he might scream or sob. Then he removed his arm from Cordero's throat and shoved the man forward as he put his pistol down.

Cordero walked quickly past Davis to the other side of the circle of light. When he reached Frankie's side, he demanded, "I said I want them dead! *Kill them!*"

"Hey, no, we had a deal!" Davis shouted.

"So did we," Frankie told Cordero coldly. "And killing was not part of agreed upon price."

"Fine! An extra fifty grand if one of your men just picks up a gun and shoots these two right now!"

The Russians looked to their leader, who raised a considering eyebrow.

"Your mother's ashes!" Davis reminded him.

Frankie shrugged sheepishly. "Ashes are ashes, *comrade*, but business is business. If you have no counter offer, then... Sergei?"

The man to Frankie's right dove for his gun. Jared did the same, but Sergei turned out to be faster. He snatched up a submachine gun, pointed it at Davis and opened fire.

At the same time, the darkness beyond the circle of light gobbled the shooter up.

TAKE 9

Susan had to admit, the last time she played the damsel, it had been much more interesting than this.

After leaving the safe house, Frankie had driven her back to the studio with a platoon of his men. They'd been able to get right through the gate, so she figured Cordero must've cleared them ahead of time. Once inside the Apex lot, they drove around lost for fifteen minutes before she took mercy and guided them back to the *Persuasion* soundstage, where she'd first met the Russian boss days ago.

She was taken to Killam's old office. Frankie waited with her until his cell phone rang, then put her on with Davis for a precious few seconds before ending the call. Then he took the bulk of his men and left her with two guards that bickered just as much as Stoffer and Bartlett. They played some Russian card game at the table while she sat in the corner, not even tied up.

It hurt to think about the two officers, and even more so Alvarez, since he'd been murdered in cold blood, disarmed yet still trying to defend her. He wouldn't be dead if he'd just listened to his crooked chief and stayed away. Instead, he came to help her, the same way Davis was now. All these people, throwing their lives away for her. The thought of being used as bait disgusted her.

Susan would give anything to be with Davis right now, somewhere far away from here. She spread her fingers out against her leg and looked at the diamond. They were going to get married. All they had to do was get out of this. The problem was, she didn't believe Cordero would let them go anymore, even if they gave him the medallion. She and Davis had been dreaming if they ever thought he would.

From beyond the door of the office came the distant rattle of automatic gunfire. She sat bolt upright, spine made rigid by fear. They'd killed Davis, and soon they would be coming for her.

But if this was part of the plan, the two guards didn't seem to know it. They looked questioningly at one another, said something in guttural Russian, then got up from the table and went to the door. One of them stepped out and started down the hall, while the other one stood just inside the door and watched.

Susan got up and walked toward Killam's desk, trying to appear nonchalant. The guard at the door ordered, "Stop! What are you doing?"

"Just getting some gum. Jesus."

He waved for her to go on and went back to looking down the hall. Susan moved to the desk and pulled out the drawer, digging past Killam's cocaine and condoms until she found what she wanted.

"Freeze," she told the guard, turning the little six-chamber revolver on him.

Not only did he not freeze, he went for the machine gun slung over his shoulders.

She pulled the trigger without aiming.

The revolver kicked in her hands. The guard jerked halfway around and fell back through the door into the hall. Susan rushed forward and found him on his back with his eyes open, staring at nothing. She didn't feel bad about killing him in the least.

No sign of the other guard. Susan carried the revolver and eased into the hallway. Somewhere ahead, she could hear lots more gunfire, and, beneath it, the sound of terrified screams.

She rushed toward the commotion. This time…she would be the one to do the rescuing.

TAKE 10

To Jared, the darkness beyond the chandelier looked like it had grown a gigantic pair of lips. Sergei had been standing at the border of light and dark when he was enveloped by oily, black waves that encircled his body in the blink of an eye. The Russian gunman got off a quick burst from his weapon before being lifted off his feet and pulled away. They heard him screaming from somewhere out in the darkness.

"What in fucking fuck was that?" Frankie asked, more wonder in his voice than fear. Everyone froze, staring at the place where the man had disappeared. Even Jared stopped with his hand inches away from Cordero's pistol.

An object came sailing into their midst and smashed into the tile in the middle of the ring of light, making them all jump away. Sergei's dismembered torso lay in a smear of startlingly red blood, like an insect with all its limbs pulled off. The twisted stumps of his arms showed the gleam of bone. On his forehead, the familiar seared emblem still leaked smoke.

"*NO! WHAT ARE YOU DOING?*" Cordero demanded in a voice so shrill, it cracked on the last word. "*GO AWAY, GET OUT!*" He sounded like a man trying to shoo away a stray dog as he screamed into the pitch dark.

Even though it was the last place his mind wanted to go, Jared recalled the hallway outside Heady's condo, when the executive had been ordering the wraiths to come back and finish them off. *It's like they're going out of their way NOT to listen to him.*

Before anyone could react, another of Frankie's men on the opposite side cried out as a smaller shape snatched him into the shadows. Jared caught a glimpse of it, a tall, narrow ghost with sickle-like claws. A gleeful screech echoed back to them.

"*Kill them!*" Frankie commanded his men.

The room erupted in utter chaos as the Russians picked up their weapons and opened fire into the darkness. Bullets flew at random as they targeted anything that moved, and, between the whispering motion of the wraiths and the flicker of their own muzzle fire, there was plenty for them to choose from. Jared hit the ground, and dragged Davis down beside him. The mobsters seemed to have forgotten all about them.

"*What's going on?*" he asked Davis. Even though he'd shouted the question, he couldn't hear himself over the constant roar of gunfire. Davis shook his head in response, indicated the collection of thugs with a sweep of his hand, then curled it into a fist and hit the tile between them. Jared thought he understood the message: something about these men had pissed off the wraiths in a big way.

In the midst of the Russians, Jared spotted Cordero on his knees, covering his ears and shouting something at the men around him. Jared's hatred for him was the only thing keeping him from sinking into despair. The pistol that had killed Heady still lay on the floor; it would be poetic to end Cordero's life with it. Jared reached over, picked it back up, and fired two quick shots. In all the chaos, he couldn't tell if he hit the bastard, but one of the Russians went down with blood spurting from the back of his leg.

Out of sheer instinct, the crowd of mobsters moved further into the light, crowding in the middle, but it did no good. The chandelier overhead swung violently back and forth as something up there shook the chain anchoring it to the ceiling. Every time Frankie's men found themselves beyond the safety of the light, one of the wraiths swirled out of the shadows like dense fog and snatched them away. After losing three or four more soldiers, the entire group broke into panicked flight, scattering in all directions. They were visible only in quick bursts of light as they continued to fire at their intangible attackers.

Cordero went with them, scurrying behind two other

men toward the closest exit. Jared got up and took aim, but the VP disappeared through a door across from them before he could squeeze off another shot.

Davis grabbed his arm. "C'mon, we have to get out of here while the wraiths are distracted! I still don't think they'll hurt me, but without the proxy, *you're* fair game!"

"I don't care! I'm not letting Cordero get away! You promised he'd pay!"

"And he will, but you can't do anything if you're dead!" To Jared's surprise, Davis grabbed his ears and forced their eyes to meet. "Just help me find Susan. Then I'll let you kill yourself going after him, if that's what you want."

Jared let out a shuddering breath. Davis was right, in more ways than one. He did intend to die after taking care of Cordero—by his own hand, if the wraiths didn't do the job—but that would have to wait until Susan and Davis were both safe. Bitter, frustrated tears flooded the back of his throat. He nodded.

Together, they headed back through the door they'd entered, Jared having to lean on Davis once more. The flashlight they'd used on the way in had been lost, so they quickly got turned around in the labyrinthine soundstage. Within minutes they fled through random set pieces in the dark. They could still hear distant, booming gunshots through the thin walls, and the shrieks of the wraiths as they claimed more victims. If Jared had understood Cordero's explanation about the creatures, this place would be full of mutilated corpses with burned foreheads by the time it was all over.

They had just entered a dimly lit stage decorated to look like a 17th century brothel when they spotted a glowing EXIT sign ahead.

"We can't leave yet, we have to find Susan!" Davis insisted. He started to turn away, but Frankie jumped out from a stack of crates and hit him in the stomach with the butt of a shotgun. He gave a single, explosive cough and stumbled back into Jared.

"*You brought these fucking monsters!*" The Russian looked like a snorting bull as he pointed the weapon at them. "*They are killing my men! Make them stop!*"

Davis held his stomach as he sucked enough air to say, "They don't have anything to do with us!"

"*You lie! I find out if your death make them stop!*"

He raised the shotgun just as another figure glided out of a doorway behind him. A revolver eased over his shoulder and pressed against his scarred temple. He froze.

"So sorry about this, Frankie," Susan said.

TAKE 11

After the Russian dropped his shotgun and kicked it away, Davis leapt to his feet and wrapped his arms around Susan, then pressed his lips to hers. She kissed him back while keeping Frankie covered over his shoulder.

"I missed you," she told him.

"Missed you, too. Let's get outta here."

She wagged the gun at Frankie. "What about him?"

Without a word, Jared raised his pistol and shot the big man through the kneecap. He screamed and collapsed to the floor. Jared bent, reached in the pocket of the other man's tracksuit, and pulled out the proxy.

"Let the wraiths have him," he said, and handed the necklace to Susan. "Put this on. Davis doesn't need it, and I don't want it."

She did, giving him an odd look. Davis figured he would spare her the details about Heady for at least a little longer. The three of them made it to the exit and emerged into the night. They were on the opposite side of the building now, in one of the narrow alleys between soundstages. A few feet away, one of the security carts sat charging at a docking station. Davis moved toward it, anticipating how good it would feel to sit.

"We need to get to lights and people," he said. "The wraiths will probably be back after us, and—"

Another door opened farther down the warehouse, and Cordero staggered through. The VP looked like absolute hell—suit torn and bloody, face so swollen it resembled a ghoulish jack o'lantern—but he carried one of the Russian submachine guns. When he saw them through his one good eye, he snarled like an animal.

"Go!" Davis pulled Susan into the golf cart.

Cordero opened fire. Bullets spanged off the cart's front bumper, but the chattering recoil of the weapon threw his aim wide.

Jared stood his ground as shots ricocheted off the concrete around him. He raised the pistol and took careful aim. Davis saw several fingers on Cordero's left hand explode as he tried to get back into firing position. The VP let out a string of curses and fell back on his ass. He scrambled for cover behind a nearby dumpster, clutching the wounded hand to his chest.

"*Jared, come on!*" Susan cried. She grabbed his arm and hauled him into the tiny backseat of the cart. Davis floored the gas pedal, and they hummed off toward the end of the alleyway at a brisk twenty miles per hour. In the rearview mirror, Davis saw Cordero emerge from the dumpster and jog after them, stopping to fire wildly every few steps. Jared shot back at him until his pistol was empty. Davis took the first turn he could, cutting the man off from view as they wove deeper into the warehouse alleyways.

"We can't keep running forever." Jared leaned over the seat and plucked the revolver from Susan's hand. He cracked open the cylinder to check the remaining shells. "We have to finish this."

"Not with Susan here." Davis wondered how long he could come up with excuses to keep his best friend alive before Jared stopped listening. "Besides, I don't think killing Cordero will stop the wraiths."

"Look!" Susan pointed ahead of them. The main corporate building was visible over the roof of the next sound-stage, its glass front blazing with warm light. If anyone was there this late, it would be studio guards. Not the best option, but if they could get inside, the building might provide some sanctuary.

Davis drove toward it. He stopped the cart next to the entrance doors and pushed on the handle. They were un-locked. The fact registered as strange somewhere far back in his mind, but he was too rushed to question it as they stepped inside.

An angry howl drifted up the avenue as Cordero caught sight of them. He looked like a crazed soldier charging the Normandy beachhead as he ran in their direction with the gun against his chest. All secrecy and hidden agendas had been laid aside; he meant to kill them even if the entire city was watching.

In the lobby, Davis and Jared dragged a bench in front of the glass doors. It would only hang Cordero up for a sec-ond if he shot out the glass, but at least it was something. He spun and looked around, trying to figure out where to go, when Baxter Devlin's voice boomed over the PA system, "Davis my boy, is that you?"

Davis looked around in confusion before spotting the camera pointed at them from above the main reception desk. He waved a hand and yelled, "Yes, it's me, sir!"

"Is everything all right?"

He glanced over his shoulder, at the vice-president of the studio running toward them with a submachine gun. "Not really, sir!"

"Come on up to my office then and we can talk about whatever's wrong." Before Davis could say anything more, the PA system shut off with audible click.

"Both of you, get going." Jared hefted the revolver he'd taken from Susan. "When Cordero comes through the door, I'm shooting him."

"He's got a machine gun, and you have six bullets, Jared."

"Five," Susan corrected.

"Let's just go to Devlin." Davis started for the stairs.

Behind him, Jared asked, "No offense, man, I know the old coot's your hero, but what's he gonna do for us in this situation?"

The answer came to him in a lightning stroke. "I don't know, but I do know Cordero didn't want him finding out about any of this."

"That's right," Susan added. "Back at the police station, he specifically asked me not to say anything."

Davis nodded. "And Devlin's blessing is what granted me an immunity to the wraiths. He might be the only hope we have against both them *and* Cordero."

That seemed enough to convince Jared. They mounted the stairs, helping Jared hobble, and Davis grabbed hold of Susan's hand, which, he was thrilled to see, still wore the ring he'd given her. She smiled wearily as they reached the hallway that gave access to the executive offices. For the first time all day, Davis found a kernel of real hope blossoming in him.

A second later, they flew into Baxter Devlin's cavernous office. The lights of the city twinkled in the panoramic view through the left wall. The old man sat at the far end of the huge room, behind his obsidian desk. He waved them in warmly, but his smile fell when he got a good look at their sweaty, disheveled faces. He stood. "Good lord, what on earth is wrong?"

"Cordero is trying to kill us!" Davis babbled. Probably best to keep this simple so he didn't blow the old man's mind with stories of monsters and medallions. "We found out he's behind all the murders, and that he and Dwight Killam were embezzling from the company!"

"It's true!" Susan assured him.

Devlin put one bony hand to his cheek. The appendage shook so much, his whole face seemed to vibrate. "Oh dear. Oh dear me. These are serious accusations, Davis."

"We have proof." Jared pulled the hard drive from his pocket and held it up.

The door burst open behind them. Cordero hurtled through, still looking like shit, but at least he'd ditched the weapon somewhere along the way. He hurried around them, moving into the middle of the long span between them and Devlin. His mangled hand was tucked into his dress shirt, which was now stained a deep crimson. "They're lying, Baxter! Don't listen to a goddamn word they say!"

Susan jabbed an accusatory finger at him from where she hid behind Davis. "*He's* the liar!"

"You're fucking dead, Cordero!" Jared declared. He moved forward, but Davis threw out an arm to hold him back. "You hear me? You're gonna pay for everything you've done! Prison is too goddamned good for you!"

"*Prison?*" Devlin held out his hands like a father quelling his feuding children. The fingers were a trembling blur. "All right everybody, hold on, just calm down now, we can sort this out. Buddy, good lord, look at yourself, you're a mess!"

"Baxter, you have to listen to me," Cordero pleaded, approaching the desk. "I didn't do it! It was Killam, that egotistical prick, he robbed the studio and—"

"Buddy, Buddy." Devlin shook his head sadly. "With as long as you've worked for me, did you really think I wouldn't find out about those cheap, tinpot, proxy knockoffs you've been using to deputize all your two-bit thugs?"

A steely cold slipped over Davis. Something in the pit of his stomach lurched.

Apparently, it did for Cordero as well. The VP's eyes bulged from their sockets as he stammered, "B-Baxter...I was only t-trying to...I never told any of them more than they needed to know...I was protecting both you and the studio, I swear!"

"By helping your old college roommate steal from me. I could've overlooked a lot from you, Buddy—I have, in fact—but that was the last straw."

And with that, the President of Apex Studios lifted a huge pistol out of a drawer in his desk and shot his Vice-President of Operations through the forehead.

TAKE 12

The single moment of violence was like an electric jolt, an exclamation point at the end of an otherwise calm sentence. Jared took an involuntary step back, his mouth dropping open. Susan uttered a short scream and jumped against Davis, who was too stunned to move at all. The top half of

Cordero's head sheared away in a red mist. He stiffened as he fell backward on the floor beside Baxter Devlin's desk, the hole in his skull leaking a slippery, gray mess on the carpet.

"I apologize for that unpleasantness," Devlin said, as cheerfully repentant as a waiter who's just brought the wrong order. His smile remained as grandfatherly as ever. "But it was time for Buddy to pay his dues. I've let him play at being the boss around here for so long, I think he was actually beginning to believe he was in charge. Maybe I only have myself to blame."

"You're behind this." Susan clung to Davis. "Cordero was just a front man. *You* control the wraiths."

Devlin gave a noncommittal shrug. "As much as anybody can control those magnificent beasts."

"We couldn't have known," Jared murmured. He stood rigid on Davis' opposite side, with one hand slightly behind his back. Davis realized he was still holding the revolver. "The tacky jewelry was a dead giveaway for everybody else, but I guess you don't need a proxy."

Devlin nodded as he set the pistol he'd just used to kill Cordero back on the glass desktop. "You're absolutely right. I don't need a proxy. In a way, I *am* a proxy." One hand rose to the collar of his dress shirt, a hand from which the rough palsy had entirely vanished. His skeletal fingers slipped the buttons from their holes with as much dexterity as a teenage video game addict.

"The emblem." Davis said this aloud but really to himself, while Devlin continued his decrepit striptease. "I know why it was so familiar now. God, I'm such an idiot, I've seen it right here, in this office." He turned to look at the front wall, where all of Devlin's awards and trophies had been taken down and replaced by a tarp for his 'remodeling.'

"It's your *family crest*."

Devlin had finished unbuttoning his shirt. He shrugged out of the garment and let it drop to the floor behind his desk, revealing his elderly chest. Pale, papery skin was stretched taut over the stack of his ribcage, but the eye could only linger on these details for a moment.

Emblazoned in the middle of his narrow torso in vivid black tattoo ink was a detailed depiction of a creature that had always looked to Davis, when he'd seen it on the burnished silver plaque hanging up in this office, like a cross between a buffalo and a demon. A shaggy, horned beast with snorting nostrils and fierce eyes. The artistry of the skin design was so good, it almost appeared three-dimensional.

But the outline of this drawing would've been no more than a rough diamond with horns.

"It was most unfortunate," Devlin lamented. He used a finger to trace one of the tattoo's glaring eyes, just to the right of his hairless, shriveled nipple. "When the police began investigating, I made hasty arrangements to hide all signs of my family insignia. I'm quite good friends with both the chief of police and the mayor, so the connection could probably have been hidden, but since they're not privy to my little secret, I didn't want to take any chances." He sighed. "Your reporter friend was the one weak link, catching wind of the mark on Tonya Werdner's body and spreading it around."

"So you had the wraiths kill him." Tears glistened at the corners of Susan's eyes as she made the accusation. "Or was that because I told him about Cordero and the medallion?"

"No, no, my dear, I was only recently made aware of Buddy's treachery. With him and Dwight Killam wearing proxies, the wraiths couldn't report back to me about their shenanigans. You see…well, it might be easier to show you."

He reached over to a panel built into his desk behind his computer monitor and twisted a knob. The lights in the room dimmed. Through the bank of windows along the wall, the lights of downtown L.A. burned, but they weren't enough to keep the darkness in this room at bay. Shadows shot out of every crevice like they were on springs. They painted the room black until the shirtless Devlin was nothing but a silhouette.

To the left of his desk, just past Cordero's body, the floor of the office began to fade.

Davis thought at first he must be hallucinating. The lush carpeting collapsed in on itself, to be replaced by a swirling vortex, a hole at least ten feet wide whose edges blended with the darkness. From this angle, Davis couldn't see what was down there, but a ruddy light pulsed through, illuminating the office in harsh tones and dancing against the ceiling like a nightlight he'd had as a kid that spun a galaxy of stars over his bed. Except this display wasn't anywhere near as comforting as that one had been. This light—the color of blood and fire—made him feel unclean. A litany of distant, anguished screams drifted out of that tear in reality, so forlorn and horrible they set Davis's hair on end. He, Susan, and Jared backed toward the door as wraiths climbed out of this strange portal in droves. The dog-like shapes gathered around the perimeter of the pit, watching them silently.

Devlin flicked another switch on his control panel. The door lock clicked behind them. "Don't worry about them. They won't attack unless provoked. Or unless I command them to, of course."

"And did you *command* them to come after us earlier tonight?" Jared demanded. "Did you tell them to kill Heady?"

"Heady's *dead*?" Susan asked. Davis held her closer.

"No. I actually tried to keep them back," Devlin answered. The red light from the hole flickered across his face, turning it into grotesquerie. "All this time, I tried to make them leave you all alone, in the hopes you would stop this foolish crusade. But once you decided to go to the police, you made yourselves an untenable threat. Even though he betrayed me, I couldn't allow Buddy to be implicated. So I finally released my pets to come after you. It just so happened that Buddy reached you first."

"Then you're as much to blame as he was." Without warning, Jared brought the revolver out from behind his back and opened fire.

The old man never flinched, never lost his beaming, friendly smile. The wraiths were the only thing that moved, surging across the room in a flicker of motion. Two of them leapt in front of the desk and expanded, morphing into a solid wall. All five shots were absorbed into their black bodies. The wraiths shrank back to their canine forms, but remained in position in front of their master like hideous gargoyles.

Devlin made a *tsk-tsk* noise as he started around the desk. The drawing on his chest seemed to ripple and breathe with his movements.

"What are they?" Davis nodded at the wraiths. "Where did they come from?"

"He's a monster just like Gross," Jared said. "What more do you need to know?"

Devlin shook his head emphatically. "I'm afraid I'm just as much a regular person as you are. And as to where the wraiths came from…that's a story worthy of a movie all its own, Davis my boy." He stopped just in front of Cordero's body and patted the head of one of the wraiths beside the portal. Davis recalled their greasy, spongy texture and almost gagged. "Seven years ago, I was on the verge of losing this company.

It's just too hard for an upstart studio to compete with the big names in this town. Those bastards have ways of keeping you down, and I had all but given up." He chuckled. "Then I met a man that changed all of that. Met him in a bar about two blocks from here, if you can believe it. His name isn't important; I'm pretty sure that he, on the other hand, was anything *but* human. What is important is that we struck a bargain: my soul, in exchange for a thriving movie studio. I was skeptical, but, as you can see…he delivered."

"Hold on," Jared interrupted. "You mean to tell us you made a *deal with the devil*? I got news for you pal, that movie *has* been made. Too many times."

This time, Devlin threw back his head and roared with laughter. "The devil? Oh my, my no! I don't even think there is such a thing! And you three, of all people, should know there are far worse beings in the world interested in our souls." None of them had a response to that, so Devlin continued. "And it wasn't just a deal. This is Hollywood, after all. I signed a contract, inked in blood and stamped with the sigil that's been handed down through my family for generations."

"We've met people without souls," Susan said. "And they sure don't act like you."

"I haven't surrendered mine quite yet, my dear. I've still got a few years before payment is due."

"I hope you still think it was worth it."

"I'm sure I will. For my recompense, you see, was these creatures, who would fulfill the other end of the contract and ensure that Apex grew. And grow it did. The wraiths—as you call them—took care of what needed to be done without me even asking."

To demonstrate this, he knelt by Cordero's body and pulled the silver ring off his pinkie. The wraiths went to work, wrapping the VP in tentacles that grew from their formless, liquid bodies. They dragged him toward the vortex. Davis, Susan, and Jared watched as the corpse was tossed into that horrid light. The last Davis saw of him was the soles of his designer shoes. One of the wraiths even crouched over the bloodstains left behind and wiped them away as easily as Billy Mays used to clean up spills with his amazing shammy cloth.

"That's what happened to Ralph and Heady," Davis said. He glanced at Jared, whose mouth had drawn up into a furious, crumpled line in the middle of his face as he came to the same realization. "You have them killed, and the wraiths make them disappear into…into…"

"To tell the truth, I'm not sure what's on the other side. The wraiths' home is surely some awful place where we wouldn't be welcome. But it makes matters easier here when there's no pesky body. The police tend to ask less questions that way."

"But it still doesn't make any sense. Why can't the wraiths do the same thing with the people *they* kill?"

"As with any contract, there was fine print," Devlin said. "Fine print that I was unaware of before this week. The wraiths have done plenty in order to get Apex where it is today, but they have never been forced to kill. Last week, when they found Tonya Werdner getting ready to embarrass one of our directors, they did what they believed was best to preserve the integrity of the studio."

"Oh yes, it's so noble of them," Davis said, sarcasm dripping from each word. "Let me tell you, I've seen those things kill, and they don't seem too hesitant about doing it."

Devlin considered this while drawing a rattling breath. "I believe you're right. I think they quite enjoy it. Might have even been *waiting* for such an opportunity. But once they did, it opened up a Pandora's box I'm still trying to close." He held up a crooked finger. "Because the taking of a human life is a powerful sort of magic all its own. We slaughter each other in scores, but for certain other beings outside of our realm, there has to be a…a sort of *cosmic balance*. An accounting, if you will. I could kill as many people as I wanted, and the wraiths would spirit them all away. But when the wraiths themselves commit the deed, there is a ritualizing that must occur. The body becomes taboo, off limits, and they mark it with the sign of the one whose name they did it in. With Tonya, it was my family crest, and the logo of the studio. The two components I used to seal the contract."

"Too bad you didn't just sign your name on the damn thing," Jared told him. "Then this would've been over by now."

Devlin gave another of his boisterous laughs, the bull-demon jiggling between his saggy breasts.

"All right, we get it," Davis said. "We've had it figured out for a while now, even if we didn't know the specifics. All of this—all the deaths and blackmailing and even saving Susan and Mahoney—has been about protecting the studio, and keeping your secret."

Devlin smiled at him and gave a gentle head shake. "Yes, some of it was exactly that, cleaning up the mess Buddy made of things when he gave Dwight Killam that proxy. But mostly…this has all been about protecting *you*, Davis."

TAKE 13

Susan felt Davis stiffen in her arms when the words left the old man's mouth.

"What do you mean?" he asked slowly. There was a strange waver to his voice.

"Did you think the wraiths were nothing more than cheap, lowbrow bodyguards? Saving the studio from disgruntled employees and workers' compensation claims?" Devlin shook his head again. "If that was all I wanted, I could've paid for some of those underlings Buddy loved to employ. This business—this *city*—moves too fast for the wraiths to aid me merely by reacting to situations. In order to build a successful studio, they must be able to stack the deck in my favor. By *forseeing* possible outcomes."

"They…they predict the future?" Davis muttered, so quietly that even Susan barely heard him.

"Not just *the* future. *All* futures. And then they take the steps necessary to marry Apex to the one in which it will be most profitable, most successful. For instance, at this year's Academy Awards, Ronald Nealy's *Island Breeze* will win the Oscar for Sound Editing, due to some tampering from the wraiths. That may not seem like much of a victory, but four months later, because of that win, a young man named Michael Havert is going to begin working for Apex straight out college. He will, in turn, design a revolutionary new form of digital audio technology that will replace the current systems in every theater and television in the world. And Apex will have proprietary rights."

"That can't be right," Davis said. "What about Scott, my production assistant? They didn't even know he was the set spy until after they heard it from Marion Brown."

"You misunderstand. The wraiths aren't omniscient. They foresee events in broad strokes, from a larger perspective."

"It still sounds like bullshit to me," Jared challenged. "How come your little pets didn't *foresee* how much trouble killing Tonya Werdner was going to cause you?"

Devlin gave him a sharp look. "Perhaps they did. Perhaps everything they've done was meant to bring us right here, to this moment. After all, they only take action based on how much potential that action has to help the studio. And in you, Davis my boy, they have seen *great* potential!" He came forward, lifting his bare, flabby arms and raising his voice in excitement, reminding Susan of a half-naked mad scientist. The awful red light from the hole in the floor looked like the reflection of twin flames in his eyes. "They were the ones that encouraged me to seek you out, to hire you! *Killing Blow 3* was to be your introduction to the world! After that, all possible futures foretold that you would be one of the *greatest directors of all time!* Welles, Spielberg, Kubrick...all would pale before your work! With you by my side, Apex would be unstoppable!"

Susan leaned away from Davis, to look up at his face. On the other side of him, she could see Jared doing the same. Her fiancée stared straight forward at Devlin, not moving, not swallowing, not even blinking.

"It's not too late." Devlin's voice had calmed. "The wraiths did all they could to protect the film—keeping Isaac Crosby working, saving Derek Mahoney—until they saw those around you had become dangers to the studio. Then they tried to keep you personally safe, but there was only so much they could do with Buddy and all of his thugs wearing proxies. I only became aware of the situation myself when poor Ralph was killed, and I tried to warn you away when I saw you at the hospital just afterward." Devlin came all the way to the front of his desk now and took up a position with the two guardian wraiths on either side. "But now, we have the chance to set this right, once and for all. But that's up to you. The wraiths may've led you here, but they can't force you to fulfill your destiny. If you only agree to follow me, we can march into that glorious future together."

She saw Davis's throat work as he swallowed. "And what happens to Jared and Susan?"

"Why…they must die, of course. Along with Mahoney, and your young production assistant. They all know far, far too much, Davis. It's either that, or all of you must be eliminated, right here and now. And anything you were to become is lost forever." His bushy brow fell into a deep furrow. "All you have to do is bring me that proxy from around Miss Campbell's neck, and I'll take care of the rest."

Davis turned to her. His eyes roamed her face. She wanted to smother him with kisses. If she had to die, she felt like she would be able to face it with him at her side.

And then his hands were at her neck, gently lifting the necklace chain over her head.

"I'm sorry," he told her. "I'll always love you."

TAKE 14

Davis took the proxy from Susan and wrapped the chain around his fist, so that the medallion lay across his knuckles. The pain in her eyes was too much for him to bear, so he looked away.

"Davis…you can't be serious." Jared said behind him. "You didn't take Cordero's deal, so don't take his."

"The difference being that Cordero only offered to let us live. Baxter is offering—"

"Everything you ever wanted," Susan finished for him.

"And this is how you wanna make it?" Jared asked. "With our deaths on your conscience?"

"It's been nice working with you, Jared," Davis said mechanically, as he started across the room. Jared tried to go after him, but one of the wraiths gave a screech and stepped up to block his path.

As Davis approached the vortex in the floor, he could look deeper down inside, into the place the wraiths called home. That ugly, red light was too bright to see whatever was down there, but the tormented screams sounded closer.

Devlin might not know what was on the other side, but Davis did.

It was hell. If not the fabled, Biblical one, then someplace close enough that it really didn't matter.

The old man waited for him just ahead, a wraith still sitting on either side, like stone cats outside the entrance to an Egyptian tomb. His hand was outstretched the same way Cordero's had been earlier today. All Davis had to do was put the proxy in it, and he could take his rightful place in history.

He had no trouble believing what the man had told him, because he'd felt that same sort of destiny in his bones since the day he figured out he wanted to be a director. And Susan was right: this was everything he'd ever wanted.

"Good boy," Devlin told him. "You won't need one of those after today, I promise you."

Davis gave the silver medallion wrapped around his hand one last look. "Cordero said these things keep the wraiths away from you. Like bug spray, or something."

"That's a simple way to explain it. More accurately, they make you invisible, by creating a gap in the wraith's awareness. Both on a physical and temporal level."

An hour ago, Davis wouldn't have thought the old guy even knew a word like 'temporal.' "Meaning they can't touch you, or predict what you're going to do?"

Devlin nodded with a fatherly excitement. "Absolutely!"

"Then you probably shouldn't let someone get close to you with one after you threaten to murder everyone they care about."

Understanding dawned on the old man's face just as Davis swung the chain at it.

The proxy may've been cheap, but it was still sharp-edged. The disc flew through the air and sliced across Devlin's left eye. The old man cried out and clutched at his face. From the other side of the office, Jared gave a whoop.

Davis tightened the necklace chain around his palm, then grabbed Devlin by his wrinkled throat and said, "Thanks for the offer, but I'll fulfill my own potential."

The wraiths had stood by dumbly, making no move to intercede, but now Devlin twisted his head toward them and commanded, "Kill the other two!"

"Davis!" Susan shouted his name. He looked over his shoulder. The wraiths had left the perimeter of the portal and were closing in on her and Jared like a pack of wolves, backing them into the corner where Devlin's family crest had once hung. One of them rose on hind legs to swipe at Jared almost playfully, drawing blood across his chest.

Devlin used Davis's distraction to break free. He turned and dove for the desk, going for the gun, but Davis grabbed hold of his belt and yanked him backward.

"*Let go of me!*" Devlin howled. He tried to hold on to the desktop, but Davis pulled his stick thin arms away, spun him back around, and punched him right in the middle of that leering tattoo etched on his frail stomach. He doubled over, wheezing and gagging.

Davis reached over to his desk and spun the dial to bring the lights back up. The wraiths faded away into wisps of smoke.

But that would only hold them at bay for so long. He had to find a way to end this.

"Call them off!"

The cut across the old man's eye leaked a thin thread of scarlet all the way down the loose skin of his neck. "*Never!*"

Davis looked over at the unearthly vortex the wraiths had come through. Turning on the lights hadn't been enough to close the strange portal.

He told Devlin, "Then let's see what the fine print on your contract says when you go through that thing."

"No! *NOOO!*" Devlin screeched. Davis slung an arm around his neck, got behind him, and forced him toward the portal. When they got close, he let go and gave the old man a shove.

Devlin teetered at the edge and screamed, the bloody light from below bathing his face as he tried to keep his balance. Davis stepped forward to give him one last push.

The other man's hand latched on to his wrist.

Devlin fell forward, his weight pulling Davis with him.

TAKE 15

On the other side of the room, Susan saw Devlin and Davis go tumbling into the portal.

She ran forward, Jared limping after her. When she got close, she sank to her hands and knees and crawled to the edge of the weird, glowing hole in the floor.

Davis was there, his hands scrabbling at the carpet where it gave way to the black ring marking the edge of the vortex. The rest of him dangled with Devlin clinging to his legs. Beyond them, she could see nothing but a pulsing red void. It was how she imagined looking into an active, steaming volcano must be.

But those screams…god, there were other *people* in there, and they had to be under horrible torture to produce a noise like that.

"*Davis!*" She grabbed hold of his wrist just as one of his hands slipped. The sudden weight of two grown men would've pulled her in with them if she hadn't been lying down. As it was, she felt her shoulder socket give as tendons and ligaments were slowly pulled apart.

"*Get back!*" he yelled at her. His other hand found purchase again, granting her a tiny measure of relief.

"*I won't leave you!*"

Jared reached her side. He leaned through the portal and grabbed Davis's other hand. They hauled, but the load was too heavy for even both of them. "*Davis, you gotta get him off you!*"

Hearing them, Devlin grabbed tighter, his bony arms squeezing Davis like a child with a teddy bear. The old man stared down into that awful red nothing below them and shrieked.

Davis looked up at them. His face was dead set. "*Let us go!*"

"*No, goddamn it!*" Jared shouted.

Above them, the lights in the office blew out in a magnificent explosion, raining down glass.

TAKE 16

Davis wouldn't let himself look down, but it didn't matter; that red light was everywhere, caressing his skin, seeping in through his eyelids. He could actually *feel* it, like some loathsome sheen of oil. He concentrated only on Susan and Jared as they tried to haul him back over the edge. Then the lights went out, and he could only see their faces by the glow of the portal.

But beyond them, unnatural shadows gathered along the ceiling of the office.

The wraiths would be back any second, to finish off Jared and Susan.

Unless, perhaps, their boss was dead.

Davis realized—with startling clarity—that there actually was one thing he wanted more than to have his directing talents recognized by the world, and that was to be with the woman holding his hand.

Too bad he wouldn't get that, either.

But at least he could make sure that she, Jared, and Scott were safe.

Davis opened his hands and let go.

TAKE 17

Susan felt his grip loosen.

"*Don't you fucking do it!*" Jared screamed.

"*It's the only way!*" Davis shouted up at them again, over the screams of the damned.

Without the extra tension, his hands slipped through theirs. Susan lurched forward, whimpering under the strain, but he slid through her fingers an inch at a time, past the diamond ring there.

"*Davis,*" she cried, as the shadows gathered around them, reaching for her with black, fluid appendages.

He smiled at her.

And then he was falling.

She watched as that terrible red light swallowed Davis Lowe up, and, just when she'd worked up the nerve to fling herself after him, the entire portal closed with a sucking sound like a sink drain, leaving behind only carpet. The encroaching darkness fell away, turning back into plain old shadows again.

A sudden, unbearable anguish ran through her like electricity, so brilliant and piercing that the rest of her world was consumed by it.

Susan Campbell fell against Jared Mane, and sobbed.

Like this novel?

YOUR REVIEWS HELP!

In the modern world, customer reviews are essential for any product. The artists who create the work you enjoy need your help growing their audience. Please visit Goodreads or the website of the company that sold you this novel to leave a review, or even just a star rating. Posting about the book on social media is also appreciated.

About the Author

Russell C. Connor started writing horror at the age of five, and is the author of two short story collections, five eNovellas, and twelve novels. His work has won two Independent Publisher Awards and a Readers' Favorite Award. He has been a member of the DFW Writers' Workshop since 2006, and served as president for two years. He lives in Fort Worth, Texas with his rabid dog, demented film collection, mistress of the dark, and demonspawn daughter.

Final Reel, the third novel of the "Box Office of Terror Trilogy," will be available soon.

www.ingramcontent.com/pod-product-compliance
Lightning Source LLC
Chambersburg PA
CBHW030358200726
48286CB00015B/1566